Dear Eva and

Thank you for allowing me
to be your teacher. I always
feel your contributions to the class
are the best!

Warmest regards,

September 21, 2013

The Ezra Scroll

The Ezra Scroll

MARK LESLIE SHOOK

ISBN: 978-1-4834-0019-8 (sc)
ISBN: 978-1-4834-0021-1 (hc)
ISBN: 978-1-4834-0020-4 (e)

Library of Congress Control Number: 2013912127

Lulu Publishing Services rev. date: 08/22/2013

For

Carol Strauss Shook

Jeremy Shook and Elizabeth Kodner Shook

Amy Shook Lowery and David Lowery

Max and Sam Lowery

Henry and Zoe Shook

Table of Contents

BOOK TWO

BOOK THREE

Glossary

Abba—Hebrew—Father

Alte kocker—Yiddish Lit. old Fart

Amah—Hebrew—Unit of length equal to two hand spans

Bavliim—the Babylonians. Singular—*Bavli*

Beit—Hebrew—Lit. House. Also, ancestral house, i.e., dynasty as in *Beit David*, the House of David.

Bubbe meises, Yiddish—As used, Grandmother's fables

Cherem—Hebrew. Under the ban of excommunication.

Chevre—Hebrew—idiom—[My] friends

Chotein—Hebrew—Father-in-law

Cohein—Hebrew—(Cohanim)—Priest (s)

Cohein Hagadol—Hebrew—Title: The great or high priest.

Dati. Hebrew-Orthodox

Emah—Hebrew—Mommy or mother.

Ephod—Hebrew—A rectangular cloth with a hole cut in the center, worn as an over garment.

Eretz Yisrael. Hebrew—Lit. The Land of Israel. A traditional Jewish way to describe the territory without reference to the modern State of Israel.

Galil—Hebrew for Galilee. Area of Northern Israel from Haifa in the west to the Sea of Galilee in the east.

Genizah—A space set aside in a synagogue for the storage of texts no longer in regular use, which bear the sacred name of God.

Giveret—Hebrew—Form of Address to women roughly equivalent to Miss, Ms or Madam.

Habibi—Arabic—My Friend.

Hava Nagilah—Israeli Folk song "Let us rejoice!"

Kibbutzniks—Members of a Kibbutz, an Israeli collective farm.

Kippa—Hebrew—curved dome. Common usage is skull cap.

Kaddish—Hebrew, Aramaic Lit. Sanctification. A prayer recited in memory of the departed

Mamzer—Hebrew. Person born of a prohibited relationship. May only marry a person of identical *Mamzer* status.

Mazel—Hebrew—Lit. Planet. Idiom-Luck

Melekh Shomron—Hebrew—Lit. King of Samaria.

Mezuzzah—Hebrew—Lit. Doorpost. Idiom—A box or container or small carved niche affixed to the doorpost containing scriptural passages.

Migbahat—Hebrew- conical headdress of the Aaronide priesthood.

Mishegas—Yiddish meaning craziness.

Mishkan—Hebrew Lit. Dwelling. The Biblical Tabernacle of the Israelites in the wilderness described in the Book of Exodus

Mishna—Hebrew—Lit. Second teaching. A text of Rabbinic legal discussions from as late as the second century CE.

Mossad—Hebrew Lit. The Institute. The Israeli equivalent of the CIA.

N'shama—Hebrew—Spirit, soul.

Parasang—Hebrew, Aramaic Unit of distance measure equal to 8,000 Amot.

Parsa—Persian Unit of measure equal to four Roman miles.

Pehcha—Aramaic/Babylonian title of government official

Sabra—Hebrew—Idiom Lit. a prickly pear cactus, used to denote native born Israelis.

S'gan—Hebrew—Lit. assistant. The full term is sgan l'cohein hagadol—the assistant to the High Priest.

S'gan Aluf—Hebrew. Military rank equivalent to Lt. Colonel.

Sefer Torat Moshe—Hebrew—Scroll of the Teaching, or revelation of Moses.

Shammes—Hebrew Lit. The server. Person designated by synagogue leadership to attend to the maintenance of the synagogue and its contents.

Sharav—Hebrew—The name of a strong wind that comes out of the Arabian desert.

Sheol—Hebrew—Place name for the dwelling place of the dead.

Shin Bet—An acronym from two Hebrew letters standing for the words *Shirutei Bitachon*—security service. This is an arm of the Israeli Ministry of Defense charged with the prevention of terrorist attacks on Israeli soil.

Shomronim—Hebrew—Samaritans

Sofer—Hebrew—Scribe.

Taggim—Hebrew. Decorative crowns on certain Hebrew Letters in a Torah text.

Tallit—Hebrew—Fringed garment. Sometimes referred to as a prayer shawl, it is worn outside the clothing for worship. For traditional males a smaller one is worn as an undergarment with the fringes outside the clothing.

Tuches—ass—Yiddish from the Hebrew Tachat, lit. below or bottom.

Yasher koach- Hebrew—Lit. "Straight is [your] strength." Idiom—Well done.

Yeshiva Bochers—Yiddish/Hebrew phrase for rabbinical students.

"It is…clearer than the sun at noon that the Pentateuch was not written by Moses, but by someone who lived long after Moses."
Benedictus Spinoza, *Tractatus Theologico-Politicus, 1670 CE*

BOOK ONE

The Ezra Scroll Timeline

CHAPTER FOUR	CHAPTER TWENTY	CHAPTER TWENTY-FOUR	CHAPTER TWENTY-SIX
Seventh day of the Fifth Month, in the Nineteenth Year of The Reign of King Nebuchadnezzer of Babylon	Fourth day of the Fourth Month, In the Tenth Year since the destruction of Jerusalem.	Second Day of the First Month in the Thirteenth Year since the destruction of Jerusalem	Second day of the Twelfth month, in the Forty-Sixth year since the destruction of Jerusalem

586 BCE 576 BCE 573 BCE 540 BCE

The Sacred House is destroyed by the Babylonians. The remainder of Judean leadership is taken captive and marched to Babylon.	The Judeans in exile in Babylon begin to develop a spiritual life for themselves. Maintaining hope for a return from exile and a restored Sacred House are the central features of this period.	The *Mishkan* is completed. The Judeans in exile maintain their allegiance to the God of their ancestors	Pumbedita is devastated by a massive spring flood. The *Mishkan* is washed away. The Persian Empire defeats Babylon. The Judeans are informed their exile is at an end.

CHAPTER TWENTY-EIGHT	CHAPTER FORTY	EPILOGUE
Second day of the Twelfth month, in the Sixty-Eighth year since the destruction of Jerusalem	In the Twentieth year of King Artaxerxes of Persia/ The One Hundred Forty-First year since the destruction of Jerusalem. In the month of Nisan, on the twentieth day of the month.	On the first day of the seventh month, Tishri In the Twenty-second year of King Artaxerxes of Persia/The One Hundred Forty-Third year since the destruction of Jerusalem.

518 BCE   445 BCE   443 BCE

| The Judeans in Samaria are forced to return to Judah. The Second Temple is being rebuilt by the returnees from Babylon. *Sefer Torat Moshe* is hidden by Yeshai son of Gilad son of Eliezer the scribe. | Nehemiah returns to Jerusalem to rebuild the walls of Jerusalem and the Temple, desecrated by the Samaritans, the Edomites, the Moabites, the Ammonites and the Phoenicians. | And all the people gathered as one man at the square which was in front of the Water Gate, and they asked Ezra the scribe to bring *sefer torat moshe* which YHWH had given to Israel. Then Ezra the priest brought the torah before the assembly of men, women and all who could listen with understanding, on the first day of the seventh month. |

The Battle of Fallujah—May 1941

On 3 May, German Foreign Minister Joachim von Ribbentrop persuaded German dictator Adolf Hitler to secretly return Dr. Fritz Grobba to Iraq to head up a diplomatic mission to channel support to the Rashid Ali regime.

On 6 May, in accordance with the Paris Protocols, Germany concluded a deal with the Vichy French government to release war materials, including aircraft, from sealed stockpiles in Syria and transport them to the Iraqis. Before the end of May, one hundred German and about twenty Italian aircraft landed on Syrian airfields.

On May 17—During the night of the 17-18 May, elements of the Gurkha battalion, a company of RAF Assyrian Levies, RAF Armoured Cars and some captured Iraqi Howitzers crossed the Euphrates using improvised cable ferries, They crossed the river at Sin el Dhibban and approached Fallujah from the village of Saqlawiya.

On 19 May, 57 aircraft began bombing Iraqi positions within and around Fallujah. The RAF dropped ten tons of bombs on Fallujah in 134 sorties.

(source: History of the Royal Air Force)

Chapter One

DATE: May 19, 1941

TIME: 6:30 A.M. Local Time

PLACE: Al Jolan District, Fallujah, Iraq—the basement of the house occupied by Avraham ben Yoshuah

The curved, razor sharp blade jumped dangerously in Avraham's hand. It was not designed to cut through a solid wall. Time was running out and he did not know where to look for the proper tools. If he had to claw his way through the wall with his bare hands, he would do so. His sacred duty was to open the *genizah*.

This is what happens when you elect a sandal maker as the Shamash of the Beit Ezra Synagogue he thought. Then he pressed the knife deeper into the slash in the wall.

Back in his stall in the central market, the blade in his hand would cut through thick leather hides. In ordinary times, the knife traced against the lines of a template passed down through the generations. But Avraham knew that these were not ordinary times.

Avraham worked in the basement of the small house assigned to him as Shamash. Eight years ago his father had shown him this very location. "When I am gone, you will be the Shamash, you will be the caretaker of the *genizah*.

Our sacred treasures are here. These books and scrolls represent the heritage of our community. If our community is in danger, you must gather the sacred books you can't carry into exile and place them behind this wall."

"How will I know that the community is in such danger?"

"You will know. I'm certain of that."

Avraham cut deeply the shape of a square at the precise spot his father had shown him. He wondered if now was such a time of trouble. Rumors of impending annihilation for the Jewish community had been making the rounds of the local coffee shops for more than two weeks. The rebels and their Nazi "advisors" had been battling the overmatched British garrison for control of Iraq. The British needed air bases to maintain their lines of supply and communication with Egypt and India. The real war began in Europe, but Britain's life or death depended on putting down this rebellion and securing Iraqi oil.

Late the previous afternoon, a vanguard of rebels and Nazis marched into the center of Fallujah and declared Marshal Law. At the regular evening service that same day, the leadership of the synagogue held a meeting of the synagogue council. Their ultimate decision was to abandon Fallujah to the Nazis and the rebels and escape down river. They would only take with them what they could carry on their own backs. They were convinced that the crisis would pass and, as had been their lot for generations, they would be able to return to their homes.

They read the papers and listened to the BBC. They knew that the Nazis would desecrate their synagogue and its contents. To prevent this, each Torah scroll would be carried out by a council member At the same time, there was no way they could carry with them the precious contents of the community *genizah*. They decided to remove all of the remaining sacred books from the synagogue and place them in the *genizahh* and seal it up once again. As soon as Avraham had created an opening in the wall, the twelve members of the council hastily assembled the books and descended into the Sexton's basement.

The British pilots flying the Lancaster Bombers over Iraq that day bore the members of the synagogue council no personal animus. Their primary target was a rebel-manned garrison in Fallujah. They had no idea that a burial of precious Jewish texts was underway in the house next to the rebel stronghold. The bombardiers were ordered to release their full loads.

All of the synagogue council members were crushed to death by the weight of the falling rubble. It certainly was not what they had planned, but the ancient *genizah* was now sealed once again.

As the Iraqi Army, Fallujah Police and U.S. military work to secure Fallujah, the war in the shadows continues. Insurgents rarely fight in the open. Their tactics consist of intimidation, drive by shootings, roadside bombs, indirect mortar fire and the increasingly dangerous sniper attacks. The units currently here in Fallujah have yet to encounter a coordinated attack where the enemy maintained contact. (Bill Roggio, *The Long War Journal*)

Chapter Two

DATE: March 12, 2009

TIME: 0600 Hours, Local Time

PLACE: Al Jolan District, Fallujah, Iraq

Beneath the cloudless blue sky the cool, crisp air smelled of spring flowers. Iraqi Police officers on patrol in al Jolan hoped they would not get shot. Each one began making promises to Allah, should he be so fortunate as to survive this gunfight. Today's exercise in Fallujah brought the Iraqi squad to Al Jolan. The neighborhood was desolate. For the past two years, Sunni insurgents had camped here and launched attacks on any and all American and Iraqi government targets. Then, two months ago, an enormous amount of American and Coalition firepower was concentrated on this one square kilometer of Fallujah. Forty-one bodies were hauled from the rubble. Some were insurgents and some were collateral damage.

This particular morning, the routine monotony of training police cadets in urban search tactics was broken by heavy machine gun fire. The patrol dove for cover behind a two-meter high mud brick garden wall. The wall had a window opening in its center. High caliber rounds chipped away at the bricks around the window ledge. Kevlar vests and helmets might not stop bullets, but they were pretty good at stopping mud brick fragments.

Marine Gunnery Sergeant Ron Keller was not in charge of this patrol. Lieutenant Abdel Wahab of the Iraqi National Police was giving the orders. Keller came along as an advisor and instructor, doing his part in the "Iraqification" of the Iraq war. The sooner the Iraqi Army and police were trained and capable of controlling insurgencies, the sooner Keller and his fellow Marines could go home.

Keller was pleased that the cadets did not turn and run. Their training had begun to kick-in. Lt. Wahab barked orders in Arabic. Keller's Arabic was not good enough for him to follow Wahab's commands. Whatever he said, the cadets responded immediately by taking cover behind the wall, loading their assault rifles, and chambering the first rounds.

Across the street, a muzzle flash sparked from a low roof-top. The cadets now had a target, but still held their fire. They were waiting for Lt. Wahab to give the word. With exaggerated hand signals he sent three men away from the wall and back down the street in an attempt to encircle the shooter. He motioned for one of his men, Maheir-the fast one, to dash across the street and place himself directly below the shooter. Maheir jumped a few feet away from the house and lobbed a grenade hook-shot onto the roof. The concussion slammed him against the wall, but not before he caught sight of body parts from the machine gunner falling from the roof. And then there was silence.

Sgt. Keller followed the patrol into the house and observed their search techniques. He wanted to make sure that the Iraqi policemen were not letting down their guard. He made his way into the main room of the dwelling, took two more steps and crashed through the floor.

"I'm all right," he shouted in Arabic. "I didn't break anything—at least I don't think so. Drop a rope or something down here and get me out of here. It really stinks in this hole!"

"No problem," Officer Ibrahim said. It was his all-purpose, handy dandy, line of English. Ibrahim drove Keller nuts with his gap-toothed smile and his "no problem." In the middle of a combat zone, everything was a problem. Survival was a problem. Getting stateside in one piece was a problem.

Down in the hole, Keller located his LED flashlight and turned its brilliant beam on his surroundings. In trying to break his fall, he had kicked out with his boots against a nearby mud plaster wall, trying to get a foothold. As the LED beam was passing over this four-inch wide toe-hold depression, Keller saw something shiny reflecting back into his eyes.

"Someone get me a shovel, a pick, something to dig with," he shouted up.

Lt. Wahab yelled down to Keller, "Sergeant, we have no time to play in the sand. This is not our day at the beach. Get out of there, now! We have to keep moving or we become a very inviting target for the *jihadists*"

"Just give me one more minute, I think I found something interesting."

"Your life and the lives of my men are the only things that interest me, at this time. Get your ass out of there!" There was a very urgent strain in Wahab's voice.

Since a shovel was not forthcoming, Keller inserted his K-Bar knife into the busted wall opening and enlarged it by wedging it into the space and moving it from side to side. He reached into the hole with his right arm and grabbed what felt like a piece of dried out leather. It was exactly that, a piece of worn leather, rolled up into a tube and tied with a leather thong. The tube was nearly eight inches long and an inch and a half in diameter. Keller trained the light back into the hole and was able to make out the shapes of books. With his knife, he enlarged the hole even more, and then extracted one of the books for a closer look. Again, cracked leather formed the cover. It was a dark chocolate in color, about twelve inches tall by seven inches wide. It was a slim volume, only a half inch in thickness. The edges of the pages were neatly trimmed. The cover was decorated with intricate geometric patterns embossed in the leather.

Carefully, he opened the book. It was an Arabic manuscript. Since Keller was only able to read a few street signs in Arabic, he had no idea of the contents of the book. He stashed it in his day-pack so he could show it to Wahab.

A heavy rope dropped on Keller's head.

"Owwww! Watch it. That hurt.

"Yallah, yahllah—come on get a move on. Grab the rope. The patrol is moving on and if you do not get up out of there I am going to abandon you to Al Qaeda. When they behead you, it will be a very popular item on U-tube." Wahab was nothing if not imaginative.

Keller was about to grab for the rope, when he remembered the leather tube. "Just a second, I'm almost done," he shouted.

The leather thong was so dry and the knot so tight, he could not simply untie it. Frustrated, he cut the thong and began to unroll the tube. A roll of greyish parchment was revealed. As soon as he exposed the writing on the parchment he gasped. It was Paleo-Hebrew.

Keller knew this because fifteen years earlier his rabbi, Rabbi Mann of Congregation Beth Elohim in Charleston, South Carolina, made him research and write a report on the Dead Sea Scrolls as make-up work before his Bar Mitzvah. The letters on the parchment in his hands were relatively well defined and appeared to be very much like the writing he had seen in pictures of the Scroll of Isaiah at The Shrine of the Book in Jerusalem. This meant that the scroll could be at least two thousand years old.

Gunnery Sergeant Aaron (Ron) Keller had a big problem. He had to get the scroll out of that hole without Lt. Wahab and the Iraqi Police patrol knowing about it. There was no way he could explain to them how he knew the writing was Hebrew—Paleo or any other kind of Hebrew. They didn't know he was Jewish. He intended to keep it that way.

Keller re-rolled the scroll with the leather cover in place. The leather thong was unusable so he simply placed the scroll deep into the long cargo pocket of his pants. He returned the book manuscript to its hiding place in the wall. There was no sense in drawing more attention to this discovery than necessary. He was not exactly sure what his next step would be, but he did know that the Iraqis would not be overjoyed at any discovery that would remind them of the two thousand five hundred year long presence of Jews in Iraq.

"Wahab, I'm coming up—don't shoot."

"Just give me a reason, Habibi."

"It is…clearer than the sun at noon that the Pentateuch was not written by Moses, but by someone who lived long after Moses." (Benedictus Spinoza, *Tractatus Theologico-Politicus, 1670*

Chapter Three

DATE: October 26, 2008

TIME: 11:00 A.M. Local Time

PLACE: The Dan David Classroom Building Seminar Room 4B,
Tel Aviv University

The course was officially known by its catalogue title, *Graf-Wellhausen and Hypotheses of Sacred Text Authorship.* The department of Biblical Studies routinely referred to the course internally as *Who Wrote the Bible—520.* This particular seminar appealed to the next generation of Israeli-trained Bible scholars and archeologists. Not all of them would become famous for Indiana Jones discoveries. Most would end up as high school history teachers or tour guides.

"Graduate Student Bible Seminar 520" was hand printed in royal blue marker on the white, dry erase board opposite the doorway. A silent ceiling fan rotated slowly over the center of the fifteen-foot by fifteen-foot square room. A single white, eight-foot by eight-foot laminate topped table occupied the center of the room. Twelve charcoal grey molded plastic stack chairs with polished chrome legs were set out around the table. Fluorescent lamp squares recessed into the ceiling gave off more light than the room needed. Above the dry erase board was a round wall clock. The only sound in the

room was provided by the minute hand moving forward one space at a time. Nervous anticipation filled the small room.

Ten of the chairs were occupied. No one sat on the side of the table closest to the door. With each click of the minute hand, all eyes looked at the clock. Their seminar instructor was now eight minutes late. The calculations being made at that moment were part of academic folklore. How long must one wait in a classroom for a full professor who is a no-show? Is it less for an assistant professor or an associate professor?

They would sit as long as it took. The ten around the table were here because of internet-based due diligence. Shlomo Malik was someone special, someone who could teach what they needed to know. At fourteen and a half minutes past eleven o'clock in the morning, Shlomo Malik arrived.

"I'm deeply honored that you have allotted to me the fifteen minutes grace time usually reserved for full professors. I was summoned by my friends at the ministry for an unscheduled meeting. Hopefully, this will not happen again, but I can't make promises. But enough about me and my *mishegas*. Tell me who you are and then something that will help this old man remember you, long after this seminar is over."

For the next fifteen minutes, one by one, the students introduced themselves to Malik and the rest of the seminar participants. Some chose to highlight their military service, a few chose to describe the summer digs on which they served as volunteers, others spoke of special talents or interests in music or the arts. Since the first student to speak concluded with a comment about why she was taking the seminar, each in turn found a way to include the same information. Six men and four women made up the class. Four were *kibbutzniks,* two were from small towns in the *Galil,* two were from Jerusalem and two were from settlements on the West Bank, or as the government prefers, from the territories of Judea and Samaria.

"Thank you for revealing something about yourselves. I know I'll find it helpful. I'm assuming you have consulted with your cousins in the *Shin Bet* and know everything our government knows about me, so I will just leave it at that. Now, shall we begin?

"Let me, as the Yiddish saying would have it, put my *tuches aufem tisch*—put my ass on the table."

The seminar students were visibly surprised by Malik's use of Yiddish.

"Don't look so shocked. When I arrived in Israel in 1948, I was placed in an Orthodox Yeshiva run by Lithuanian rabbis. My Iraqi family was *dati*. Not to worry. I'm not religious. I am not your rabbi, nor do I, God forbid, want to be. I have spent my entire life dealing with facts, not myths.

"Here are the facts, my friends. God did not write the Torah. God did not dictate it to Moses who, for forty days and forty nights, sat calmly on a rock in Sinai and took it all down with quill pen, ink, and parchment scroll. The sacred text we reverently call Torah today was invented by Ezra the scribe sometime between 445 and 443 BCE."

"Professor Malik, how can you say that with such conviction? Where is your evidence?" The inquisitor was a woman from the West Bank. Judging by the length of her dress and the tautness of her headscarf, she was Orthodox. Since she was a student at TAU and not one of the religiously affiliated universities, it was probably a good bet she was Modern Orthodox—probably an Orthodox feminist.

"*Giveret,* have you ever watched old episodes of the American series *Perry Mason* on TV? I suppose not. Anyway, what I'm doing now is laying out the broad outlines of the case for the defense. Today, I will tell you what I believe I can prove. Starting on Tuesday and for most of the rest of the course, I shall place what evidence I have before you, the jury. You are free to conclude whatever you wish. Your grade shall be based—not on your willingness to agree with everything I say—but upon your ability to state your own case convincingly, using available archeological discoveries and historical accounts.

"As I was saying: Torah was invented by Ezra. Would one of you please name an invention of the modern world? Go ahead, I won't mark you down if you get it wrong."

"How about cell phones?" This, from a lanky strawberry blonde male, slouched low in his chair.

"Why not?" Said Malik, rising to meet the challenge.

"What needed to exist before the invention of the first cell phone?"

"An understanding of electricity."

"Voice communication via a telephone."

"Rechargeable batteries."

"Wireless radio."

"A two year contract."

The answers came in rapid succession. The last one broke them up with laughter.

"Precisely so! The genius of those who actually invented the cell phone was in organizing a host of individual technological components in a certain way that would produce something very new.

"I'm going to make the case that Ezra took large quantities of Hebrew literary material in a dozen different writing styles from a span of nearly a thousand years and brought them together in a single document. I will show that Ezra had motive to do so. I will show that Ezra had the means to do so, and I will show that Ezra had the opportunity to do so."

"Is there a smoking gun?" A female with short black hair and flashing dark brown eyes asked.

"If, by 'smoking gun' you mean: Is there a DVD of Ezra arranging the texts in his workshop in Babylonia? I'm afraid not. In this field there is no such thing as incontrovertible proof. Let me be clear. This class is going to touch some very sensitive religious nerves."

"Going to touch those nerves with a cattle prod, most likely. Spinoza got placed in *Cherem* for saying just about the same thing." To Malik, these comments confirmed his opinion that she was not just another pretty face.

"Precisely! In fact, Spinoza, arguing this hypothesis three hundred and fifty-five years ago, had even less evidence to work with than we do now."

"Does it bother you, Professor, that your hypothesis has the potential to do such grievous harm to human faith?"

"There are times in my life when I feel very connected with Spinoza's *n'shama*—his spirit. Although his writings are enjoying a bit of a surge in popularity these days, not many of his new fans recall why he wrote those words that would get him banished from Jewish life.

"We tend to think of the Netherlands in the 17th century as safe haven for Jews and Protestants fleeing the Inquisition. In fact, there was religious violence taking place in the streets around Spinoza's neighborhood almost on a daily basis. In so-called liberal Holland, people were still dying because of their religious beliefs. Spinoza believed that he could show humanity a way to understand and worship God without resorting to death and destruction. It would be a path illuminated by human reason and not subject to the mistranslations and distortions of alleged divine revelation.

"So, in direct answer to your question: No, *chevre,* a thousand times no!

Nearly four hundred years later, we came to understand that it was human faith that did grievous harm to Spinoza. Please—have no illusions. We have seen with our own eyes what human beings can do to each other because of their faith.

"I see our purpose in this class from an idealistic and humanistic perspective. Our task is to bring Ezra's work out into the open. Let all people come to admire his skill, his hope, his confidence in the future of the Household of Israel.

"My goal is to help you realize that, while routine sacrificing of animals as the central act of Jewish worship has gone by the wayside, the ethics and morality championed by Ezra in the pages of his *Sefer Torat Moshe*—scroll of the book of Moses—continues on. If that is not work worthy of being recognized as divine inspiration, I do not know what is."

Silence entered the seminar room. A few heads were nodding in agreement. A couple of tight grimaces appeared on faces already tense.

"What's next, Professor Malik?"

"I think we will begin our seminar in the place where I was born. You cannot go there, today, but I can take you back there on the strength of your imagination. We begin our study of Ezra and his *Sefer Torat Moshe*, on the banks of the great Euphrates river…"

At that time, the troops of King Nebuchadnezzar of Babylon marched against Jerusalem, and the city came under siege. King Nebuchadnezzar advanced against the city while his troops were besieging it. Thereupon King Yehoiachin of Judah, along with his mother, and his courtiers, commanders, and officers, surrendered to the King of Babylon. The King of Babylon took him captive in the eighth year of his reign. He carried off from Jerusalem all the treasures of the House of the Lord and the treasures of the royal palace; he stripped off all the golden decorations of the Temple of the Lord—which King Solomon of Israel had made—as the Lord had warned. He exiled all of Jerusalem: all the commanders and all the warriors—ten thousand exiles—as well as all the craftsmen and smiths; only the poorest people of the land were left. (II Kings 24:10-14)

Chapter Four

DATE: Seventh Day of the Fifth Month in the Nineteenth Year of the reign of King Nebuchadnezzar of Babylon

TIME: The Third Hour of the Third Watch

PLACE: The Sacred House, Jerusalem, Kingdom of Judah

The twins were terrified of fire. They just did not know why. Sometimes, in nightmares, they remembered the screaming—but nothing else. Abba decided it was time to tell them the whole story when they had reached the tenth year since their birth.

The awful fire occurred during their first "going-up," their first pilgrimage to Jerusalem. Zadok and Eliezer "Eli" were almost three years old. In accordance with family tradition, after the festival was over, their hair would be cut for the first time. They would be spoiled with sweet treats and hugs from relatives and friends. It was supposed to be their joyous introduction to their father's large clan in the holy city.

On that "going up," Achituv—Abba, had two duties to perform. His first task was not a task, but rather a great honor. As an honored and respected scribe in Hebron, he had been invited to prepare a ceremonial scroll of the Song of the Sea. It was to be presented to the Levitical musicians in the Sacred House. The Levites would raise the scroll up in the presence of the festival crowd and then, accompanied by a choir of stringed instruments, cymbals and drums, would chant its ancient melody.

Achituv's second task was to honor the memory of his father, Chanan. He would do so by offering a special sacrifice in the Sacred House. Nearly a full year had passed since the twins' grandfather had descended to Sheol in peace. Achituv planned to purchase a yearling goat in the market and present it to the cohanim/priests in the courtyard of the Sacred House. He and his sons would lay their hands on the goat and follow the priest to a place where they could witness the slaughter of the animal and its placement as an offering on the stone altar. The twins had no idea what a memorial or sacrifice meant. It was the excuse that brought them to Jerusalem.

For shelter, a single, musty attic room was all they could manage. Even when the uncles and cousins pooled their funds, the cramped room was the best they could find, considering the crowded conditions brought on by the festival. The landlord enjoyed the laughter and noise of the twins, so he let Achituv and his sons make use of the small rooftop for sleeping. The sweltering heat, was almost bearable on the roof. While the rest of the uncles and cousins were stuck in the hot attic room, Zadok and Eli could see the festival full moon and the entire host of heaven while lying on their backs.

A wind blown spark from a pilgrim's campfire landed on a blanket in the attic room. The fire spread with incredible speed through the straw on the floor and into the dried hay in the corners. Draughts of air from the small windows at the top of the wall fanned the fire like an ironsmith's forge. The hatch to the rooftop was in the corner above the burning hay. The only door out of the room was jammed shut, having expanded in the heat.

It seemed like an eternity, but the shouts and then screams of the uncles and cousins lasted only for a few moments. Achituv wrapped the twins in his traveling cloak, commanded them to grab a hold of his neck, and leapt off the now burning rooftop to the roof of the building next door. By the time they had managed to awaken the neighbors and reach the street, black smoke was billowing from all of the windows of the house. Achituv, Zadok, and Eli were the only survivors. The rest of the men in their clan were dead.

A year after hearing the whole fire story from Abba, Zadok and Eli were granted the privilege of becoming students of the Sacred House School for Scribes in Jerusalem. Their joy at being admitted into the school was overwhelmed by the sadness of war.

The Babylonian siege of the city began almost from the moment they first arrived to begin their studies. After months of little or no military action against the city, the enemy decided to burn it down to the ground. Fires were now everywhere. Jerusalem was in flames. These fires were not the twins' imaginations running wild. They, of all people, should not have been chosen to rescue the scrolls. They should not have been ordered to return to their burning school in the Sacred House. Nevertheless, they were chosen for their quick feet. In happier times they were the fastest runners in the school. But now, in the debris-clogged corridors of the Sacred House, speed was no help at all.

Zadok and Eli stumbled and scrambled along the smoke filled passageway. The heat burned and the smoke choked. The siege was almost over. The School for Scribes of the Sacred House, guardian of the words of the Covenant, their home for the past three years, was no more immune to the barrage of flaming arrows launched by the *Bavliim* than the rest of the city. The Most High had abandoned the Sacred House. A curved vault of thick smoke hung a few hundred cubits above the city. The reddish-orange reflection of active fires shimmered against the bottom of the smoke canopy, casting dancing shadows of death.

The twins' teacher, Akkub, son of Shallum, Scribe to the High Priest, made them swear an oath to The Most High. He had given them two care-worn sacks made from sheepskin and the iron key to the scroll cabinet in the writing room.

"Swear to me that you will get to the writing room and gather as many of the covenant scrolls as you can fit in these two sacks. Don't bother with any scrolls on the south wall shelves. The only ones that matter are the old scrolls—the ones in the cabinet next to the Scribe Master's desk. When you have collected the scrolls, meet me by the Southern Gate. You must move quickly, the babblers are nearly finished in their efforts to burn the entire city, including the Sacred House, to the ground."

The Bavliim were the latest in a long line of conquerors tromping through the Land of Israel on their way to glory or death in Egypt. In more recent days, the Kingdom of Judah made a monstrous diplomatic mistake in forming an alliance with Pharaoh Hophra of Egypt. The Bavliim were determined to make an example of Judah. The city would be laid waste as a warning to any petty kingdoms that might contemplate joining other alliances against the Bavliim.

The twins made their way along the southern corridor, nearly overcome by the thick plumes of smoke rising from the western parts of the city. Street by miserable street, the Bavliim were setting fires.

Small rectangular windows, spaced about six cubits apart at the top of the wall, provided what meager light there was in the corridor. By now, the smoke had grown so thick it was impossible to determine the time of day. Zadok and Eli put their backs against the wall and slid cautiously along its length. Finally, they located the opening to the stairway that would take them up to the Scroll Room. Before the siege, these stairs were filled with the noise of sandals scraping and polishing each stone. Now, black flakes of ash hung in the air as first Eli and then Zadok mounted the steps and entered the Scroll Room.

Six rows of six stand-up desks were evenly spaced and faced the North wall. A squat clay pot, the size of a closed human hand, sat on each desk. The black stain beneath each pot revealed its purpose. Each day, after the morning prayer, the twins would fill everyone's ink pots for the day's work.

"If we can find the Scribe Master's desk, we will be close to the scroll cabinet. Can you make it out?" Eli asked.

"Just barely. Grab my tunic Eli and hang on. We're almost there."

"Give me the key, Zadok. I know just how to turn it."

"Here. Just don't drop it. We will never find it in all this smoke."

"It won't turn!"

"Give it back to me. If I have to I'll force it." Zadok slammed his fist on the top of the cabinet while pulling on he door. On the third attempt the door gave way. The cabinet was filled with scrolls of equal length, but varying degrees of thickness.

"Zadok, stop trying to read the scrolls and just put them in the bag."

"Shouldn't we look to see that we get the important ones?"

"First, you read so slowly, we will be cooked before you get beyond two lines. Second, our master said to get as many as we can carry. It doesn't matter what's on the scrolls. Hurry, start stuffing them in here."

Zadok gathered up an armful and placed them in the first leather sack.

Eli attempted to count the scrolls as they went in. The first sack was filled with twelve scrolls of varying lengths. An additional twelve scrolls went into the second sack. The twins tied up the sacks with ropes they wore as belts around their waists. Each threw a bag over his shoulder.

"It should be easier going down the stairs than going up with this load," said Eli.

"Let's......get........going. I can barely breathe.......and it is getting very hot in here. Have you found the stairway?" said Zadok, coughing and gasping.

"I am at the top step, Zadok. Come to the sound of my voice. I see your form," Eli said.

In the menacing shadows of fire and war, the twins made their way out of the Sacred House compound and down the narrow street to the Southern Gate. But there was no gate. A pile of rubble was strewn on both sides of the street where once the gate had been. The Bavliim had battered it open. The actual wooden gate was probably smashed up for firewood and carted away by the cave dwellers, the poor wretches who abandoned the city months ago for hiding places among the surrounding hills. An encounter with the cave dwellers at this time would almost be as dangerous as one with Nebuchadnezzar's soldiers.

The city walls beside the Southern Gate had been toppled. Only the heavy stone lintel and post remained standing. Rubble in and around the gateway made the twins' progress frustratingly slow. Thin sandals were not made for walking on sharp broken stone. Eli tripped over something in his path.

"Eli, watch your step! We don't have time for a broken leg or arm. Where is our teacher? Do you see him?"

"Zadok, I just tripped over his body. I think—no—I know he's dead."

Chapter Five

DATE: March 12, 2009

TIME: 1030 Hours, US Military Time

PLACE: Fallujah, Iraq

On the Humvee ride back to the Central Police Station in Fallujah, Keller was so preoccupied with the meaning of his discovery, that he was not clutching the door handle ready to bail out in anticipation of an attack with an improvised explosive device.

He considered his options. The leatherbound scroll in his pocket was probably nothing important—perhaps a two thousand year old shopping list or a nursery rhyme. On the other hand, it was an ancient Hebrew text buried behind a wall, in the middle of Muslim Iraq. It had to be worth something. Whatever he did, he had to preserve his undisclosed religious identity. His Marine superiors understood his need not to broadcast the fact that he was Jewish. His effectiveness as a training advisor would be compromised. He could also get himself killed by one of his own trainees.

In the entire Marine Corps, there was only one place where a soldier could go for advice and not have it come back to him in a negative fitness report. Conversations with chaplains carried the "seal of the confessional." Generals could not pry information out of a chaplain. It was the most secure line of communication in the Corps. It also helped that the Corps did not have its own chaplains. Navy chaplains served the Marine Corps as well as their own sailors. Navy chaplains were even less likely to bow to pressure from a Marine officer than one of their own.

Now that he knew he was going to seek advice from a chaplain, the next question was which chaplain? The last Navy-Rabbi-chaplain he encountered in this part of the world was shopping for his wife in a Sharper Image store in Dubai. Keller recognized the Rabbi from his training days as a "maggot"-Marine recruit at Parris Island.

Keller had two problems. First, how was he supposed to get time off in a war zone? His work with the Iraqis was considered essential. Even supposing he did manage to get the time off, how was he going to get out of Iraq to meet with a Navy rabbi, since there was no way the U.S. Military would station a rabbi in-country? The key to dealing with both issues was in the Chaplain's Office on his own base. As soon as he could get cleaned up, he would go and see the base chaplain. This action would raise more than a few eyebrows in his unit. Asking for help was totally out of character for Keller. What he needed was a plausible personal life crisis that would make his urgent request to speak with a rabbi reasonable.

An ordinary life crisis would not do the trick. In all likelihood, the base chaplain would set up a video conference call with some rabbi six thousand miles away. Keller needed to be able to sit down and have a one on one-face to face. He had to be able to show the scroll to a rabbi in person.

He came back to the idea of a meeting with his base chaplain. What did Clint Eastwood say in *Heartbreak Ridge*? "Marines improvise, adapt, overcome…"

Fallujah was home to two military bases occupied by the United States Marines. The larger of the two bases was a training base for Iraqi recruits. It was known locally as Mujahideen-e-Khalk or MEK Compound. The Corps shortened it to simply Camp Fallujah. At the beginning of the year Camp Fallujah was turned over to the Iraqi government to serve as the home of the Iraqi Army's First Division. The smaller base used to be a Baathist resort for politically connected mid-level government officials. The Baathists referred to it as Dreamland. The Marines called it Camp Bahariah.

The chapel at Camp Bahariah was completely devoid of anything resembling religious architecture. There were just two boxes attached to each other, one high, the other low. The total length of the structure was fifty feet. The width was twenty-five feet. The high building rose to a commanding twelve feet in height, while the low building was eight feet high. Laminated sheets of medium density fiberboard were bolted together. Some sections had seams that were tighter than others, and that must have been interesting during the frequent Iraqi sandstorms.

The low building served as the Chaplain's office. A small reception area contained two folding tables as desks, some beat up metal folding chairs, and a couple of wooden packing crates used as shelving. One of the crates was crammed with an ecumenical assortment of religious books. Keller knew this because they had fake cordovan leather bindings and gold leaf lettering. He could not tell to which denominations these books belonged, and he also did not care. A door on the east wall led into the chapel. A door on the opposite wall led into the Chaplain's office.

A rather stocky young girl in Navy-issued desert camo, looked up from her laptop.

"Can I help you, Sergeant?"

"I would like an appointment to speak with the base chaplain, if you would be so kind, Seaman Billingsly. "

"May I tell Commander Weber what this is all about?"

Keller was not happy to hear the chaplain referred to by his rank. His brief experience with Navy chaplains already taught him to beware of clergy who went by their military rank rather than their clerical title. It usually meant he was dealing with a "lifer", a career chaplain whose priorities were the Navy and God, in just that order.

"Actually, I would prefer to share that information with Commander Weber. I hope you can understand?"

"No problem. He just likes to know if he is going to need a lot of time or a little time to handle your issue. That way he can block out the time on his schedule."

"I can tell you this. I need just five minutes."

"If you keep to that five minutes, you may go in and see him now. But remember—just five minutes. He's having lunch with the C.O. We wouldn't want Commander Weber to be late now, would we?"

In proper Marine fashion, Keller rapped with authority on the chaplain's door.

"Come in," came the even baritone reply.

"Gunnery Sergeant Keller requests permission to speak with the chaplain—sir!"

"Forget the Parris Island crap, Sergeant. Here, of all places you can relax the gung-ho routine. What's on your mind?"

Commander Weber sat behind a folding table serving as his desk. He appeared to be about forty years old, and just over six feet in height. He looked trim in his pressed camos. The sharp creases were a sign he did not leave the base much. His salt and pepper hair was high and tight. His eyes were hazel. His face was burned from the sun. He came around the desk and offered his hand. His grip was solid.

"I need to speak with a rabbi, sir."

"How do you know that I'm not a rabbi?"

"The cross on your lapel is a dead giveaway, sir."

His laugh was genuine and hearty, from the gut.

"Brilliant piece of detective work, Gunny. Care to tell this Jersey priest why you need to speak with a rabbi?"

"It's very personal: I am having a crisis of faith. If you check my personnel jacket you will see that I'm listed as an MOT-uh, that is, I'm Jewish, a member of the tribe. Here in Iraq, I have not revealed my religion to anyone I work with, and I train Iraqi police officers. As you might imagine, letting them know I'm Jewish would not be a good idea. But everyday I'm feeling more and more Jewish. The thing is I was never uh, umm, clipped, if you get my drift."

"You aren't circumcised?"

"That's it in a nut shell sir, pardon the pun."

"So you want to speak with a rabbi about getting circumcised, is that it?

"Actually sir. I am kinda hoping that I will be able to speak with the rabbi and get clipped on the same pass, so I don't take too much time away from my duties. It would take a big load off my mind. Every day I face death. I'm not afraid to die. It's just that I do not want to die as an incomplete MOT. I want to be totally authentic, Jewishly speaking, sir. This would mean everything to me."

Weber rubbed his face and ran his hand through his hair. After a very long moment of silence, he leaned forward. "OK, Gunny, but I can only get you three days. To keep this matter between us, and so as not to compromise your situation with the Iraqi police, you will have to be ready to go back to your duties immediately upon your return. There can be no sick-bay for you. Is that completely clear?"

"Absolutely, sir! Shapiro and I will be ready for action."

"Shapiro?"

"Uh, that's the name I conferred upon my——"

"Your schmuck?"

"Sir, I did not know that you spoke Yiddish."

"There are a lot of things you do not know about me, Gunny. I grew up in North Jersey. I am a bit of a linguist. I also know the slang for essential body parts in Italian, Polish and German."

Weber got up and walked over to a packing crate that had six narrow shelves. Each shelf was filled with what Keller presumed to be forms. The chaplain picked the pen from his shirt pocket and began writing. When he finished, he extended the form to Keller.

"Give this to my clerk so she can type this out in proper form. I will sign it then and you can be on your way. The nearest rabbi is with the Sixth Fleet in the Mediterranean. I think they are somewhere in the Eastern Med. Lieutenant. J. G. Rabbi Stone is on the Roosevelt. With some luck, you will make the Roosevelt in under 24 hours. Just make sure you're back here in three days-72 hours. Have Rabbi Stone sign this form indicating that you two actually met. You would be amazed at some of the stories I hear in this office."

"Really, sir?"

"Just do not mess with the Navy or the Corps."

"Of course, sir! Aye, Aye!" Keller braced to attention and snapped off a smart salute, which Weber returned in kind. He did an about-face and made his exit.

When the door to his office closed, Weber allowed himself a big grin.

"I would love to be a fly on the wall in the chaplain's office when Keller explains himself to Rabbi Abby Stone."

Chapter Six

DATE: **Seventh Day of the Fifth Month in the Nineteenth Year of the reign of King Nebuchadnezzar of Babylon**

TIME: **The Fifth Hour after Noon**

PLACE: **Valley of Kidron, Jerusalem, Kingdom of Judah**

The twins carried the body of their master, Akkub ben Shallum, across the narrow valley between the Mount of the Sacred House and the Mount of Olives. They knew enough about the customs of burial to know that they were supposed to cleanse the body and wrap it in a linen shroud. They also knew that in time of war many customs were ignored. After setting the surprisingly heavy body of the Scribe Master on the ground, Eli reached behind his master's neck and untied the leather cord and cylinder seal with which their master sealed official documents. The seal was a thumb-sized piece of fired clay on which Akkub ben Shallum's name had been impressed, along with the image of a feather. When rolled in ink and then on parchment, the seal would reveal his special sign and name.

They looked around for anything likely to be of some use in digging, then settled on gnarled branches from an olive grove that gave the mount its name. The twins each carried a small flint knife, a tool of their trade. The knives were used to prepare quill pens for their master. Scribal knives were not very efficient in shaping olive wood spear points.

They struggled with the sharpened sticks to break through the rocky soil and scoop out a shallow grave so that their teacher would not become food for the jackals and wild dogs. With great care they lowered their master into the shallow grave and then pushed the rocks and soil back in over the body. Zadok rolled a heavy stone over the center of the grave. He wasn't sure if he did so as a way to mark its location or as a way of making sure it would go undisturbed. For several moments the twins stood in silence, not quite knowing what to do. Then Eli spoke softly:

"May the God of our ancestor, Abraham, grant peace to our master, Akkub ben Shallum. May he go down to *Sheol* untroubled, there to meet his ancestors. And may Akkub ben Shallum know that we have carried out his bidding exactly as he instructed us."

"Amen," Zadok said, trying to hide his emotion in a strong voice. "We cannot stay here. We must join up with the exile column and hide among them."

"Zadok, are you forgetting what we carry? Our master had us gather these scrolls for a reason. You saw for yourself, these scrolls are very old. They must be very valuable. Do you think he wanted the scrolls to go into exile with our people? Why should the scrolls be banished to Babylon? We must hide them somewhere safe."

"Safe? Safe? Where is safe, Eli? If we hide them in a cave, then what? Suppose we are killed. Who will know about the scrolls? The best thing for us to do now is not call attention to the scrolls. Yesterday, you saw for yourself the Bavliim brought a dozen ox carts to the gates of the Sacred House and forced the Levites to load them with all of the sacred utensils. They were stealing everything but the stones of the compound. The ox carts, priests, and Levites are being herded right now to Babylon. These scrolls belong with them. The priests will know what to do with them, how to protect them. We must join them on the road without drawing the attention of the Bavli soldiers. The longer we wait to slip in among the exiles, the greater is the danger of our getting caught."

"I guess you are right, Zadok. One thing is certain, we cannot stay here."

With the scroll satchels slung over their shoulders, the twins turned toward the desert road and started walking.

At sunset, a powerful *Sharav* blew in from the Judean desert. The sandstorm added an eerie quality to the tableau of defeat. All creation was joining in the humiliation of Judah. Nebuchadnezzar's prisoners, the once mighty elite of Judah, shuffled along in silence. Throughout the night the Bavliim herded their charges down the twists and turns of the road to Jericho. At dawn there was no brilliant sunlight. The hills east of the Sacred City had disappeared in clouds of flying sand.

With improvised bundles of their most precious possessions slung over their shoulders and baskets balanced on their heads, here were the once powerful leaders of Judah. The captives wrapped headscarves across their noses and mouths to keep out the sand. From a distance, the slowly moving column of the defeated must have looked like a file of termites or soldier ants departing their colony. At this pace, the Judeans would not reach the Oasis of Jericho until late the next day, if then.

Slipping into the line at night was not very difficult. The Bavli escort was too busy trying to keep the sand out of their own eyes to notice two small shapes running and disappearing into the column. The march came to a halt an hour after sunrise.

After a brief fitful sleep, Eli and Zadok set out to locate the *Cohanim*-the priests. Zadok's plan was to look for the largest concentration of Bavli soldiers. He figured that the *Cohanim* would be closely guarded—along with the treasure from the Sacred House. They found them sooner than they imagined. The twins were able to spot the *Cohanim* by their distinctive conical headdress, the *migbahat*. Eli recognized the *S'gan*—the assistant to the High Priest, perched on a boulder, engaged in conversation with a group of four, much younger looking priests.

The *S'gan* was four cubits tall and very thin. He wore the starvation of siege on his gaunt and pale face. His once pure white vestments were covered in dust and ash, as was his *migbahat*. The gold threaded decorative bands at his collar and the end of his sleeves were gone—stripped away by the Bavliim before the march began.

Two very large and very fearsome looking Levite guards were standing with their backs to the *S'gan* and other priests, facing outward and shifting their gaze constantly back and forth across the mass of exiles milling about the makeshift camp. The guards were there to protect the *S'gan*—to keep riff raff like Eli and Zadok as far away as possible.

Eli approached the closest Levite. In an instant, Eli was lifted off his feet and held by his throat in a vise like grip.

"What do you want?" the Levite growled.

As much as Eli wanted to respond, he was choking and gasping for air, all the while kicking his feet in mid-air. Zadok commenced to kick the guard in the shins and yell at the top of his lungs.

"You're killing him! Put him down! We are here on a mission from the Scribe Master of the Sacred House. We must speak with the *S'gan*—now!"

The last and vehement "now" seemed to have penetrated the Levite's state of consciousness. He turned to Zadok and slowly lowered Eli to the ground.

"How do I know that you are who you say you are? Everyone wants to speak with the *S'gan*. He is too busy to speak to specks of dust like you."

"Here is our master's cord and seal. Please show them to the *S'gan*. He will recognize them," Zadok pleaded.

"Stay here. If either of you move from this spot, you will die!"

The Levite turned and approached the *S'gan*, tapping him softly on his shoulder and handing him the cord and seal for his inspection. Rolling the cord and seal around in his hand, the *S'gan* turned and faced the twins, looking them over carefully. With his right hand he waved them forward.

"What is your name?" The *S'gan* directed his question to Zadok. Both boys answered in unison like a choir in the Sacred House.

"We are the sons of Achituv the Scribe of the House of Chanan of Gezer. We are students in the School for Scribes of the Sacred House. Our master is Akkub ben Shallum, the Scribe Master."

"How is my old teacher?"

"The Bavliim killed him. We found his body yesterday, outside the Southern Gate. We buried him on the Mt. of Olives last night."

"Blessed be the True Judge," the *S'gan* murmered. Then he looked up at them.

"You say Akkub sent you on a mission. What is your mission?"

The twins brought their satchels forward, untied them and revealed the scrolls to the *S'gan*.

"Our master sent us with these scrolls to present them to the *Cohein Hagadol* for safe keeping." Eli explained.

"The *Cohein Hagadol* is not here. The Bavliim took him away in chains along with the royal household. Wait here a few moments. I must take counsel with the other *Cohanim*. When did you last eat?"

"Two days ago," Eli said.

"Go with Yalon," the *S'gan* indicated the guard. He will find you some bread and cheese. It is all we have. Then come back here and await my answer. Now, give me the scrolls."

After engaging in a heated debate as indicated by the violent gestures of the participating priests, the *S'gan* returned to the twins.

"You are very brave boys. You have risked your lives and have redeemed the heritage of our people. One day you may be remembered as the twins who rescued the house of Israel from despair. I realize that we have no right to ask you to do this, but we must make absolutely sure that these scrolls remain with our people, no matter where we may go.

"My fellow priests and I have decided that the scrolls must be divided. We will make sure, as much as possible, that identical scrolls are sent to two different locations. This way, the likelihood is that one set will survive. I know this is going to be very difficult for you, but you have shown us how resourceful you are. You must separate and journey with the scrolls in two different directions. One of you must escape to the land of the Samaritans. A number of our people are established in that community. They will care for you and the scrolls. The other will join us in Babylon or wherever. We shall have need of as many scribes as we can find. These scrolls must have copies made from them, so we do not lose track of who we are."

"I will go to the Judeans in Samaria," Eli said. "Who shall I say has given me this mission?"

"Tell them Ezekiel the son of Buzi, the assistant to the High Priest has sent you to them. You will take with you this letter I have prepared."

Chapter Seven

DATE: March 14, 2009

TIME: 0930 Hours, Local Time

PLACE: U.S.S. Roosevelt, The Eastern Mediterranean

The U.S.S. Roosevelt and her crew of more than five thousand sailors and marines, was making its way to Haifa for a brief but well deserved weekend of shore leave. Arab-Israeli politics precluded the possibility of a direct flight from Baghdad to Haifa. Keller was flown directly to the carrier on a non-stop overnight transport flight from Qatar. The pre-dawn landing reminded Keller why he had no ambitions of being a Marine pilot: two hundred miles per hour one second, and then a dead stop the next. His precious cargo was doing better than he was.

The leather bound scroll was wrapped in a Marine issue towel, tucked away in a cheap camel skin pouch. The pouch was about fifteen inches in length and eight inches from the zipper to the seam at the bottom. It wasn't COACH but it would do. He purchased it in the *souk* in Qatar. He paid half of what the stall owner asked for it and ten times what it was actually worth. The pouch fit tightly into his daypack, which he wore on his shoulders. The pouch never left his sight.

The carrier crew had no idea who he was or what he was doing on board. They welcomed him as a brother-in-arms. The ample decorations on his "B" uniform chest spoke for him, announcing that here was a grunt Marine with lots of combat experience in Iraq and Afghanistan. Each sailor or Marine he encountered was upbeat and friendly.

His first stop was the enlisted man's head for a civilized dump and a hot shower. That was the only time he felt the scroll to be out of his control. The best he could do was to hide it beneath his clothes. Uncharacteristic for him, he borrowed a steam iron and gave his uniform a quick going over. It was, after all, Saturday morning—the Sabbath. The khakis did not do well jammed into the bottom of a duffle for seven months. He wanted to make a good impression on the rabbi. Keller had already resigned himself to the fact that he was going to have to join in the Jewish worship service.

After sprucing up, Keller dined with a few hundred Marines at breakfast. The food was hot and as fresh as can be, six thousand miles from home. One hour later, having presented his orders to the officer of the watch, he was guided through the labyrinth of the Roosevelt's nineteen decks, to the Gallery Deck, which was just below the Flight Deck. Here the Chaplain's Office and multi-faith chapel were located. The office was used by all three of the carrier's chaplains. At least that is what Keller deduced from the slots on the door plaque. Only one slot had a name. The others were empty. The nameplate informed him that Chaplain Stone was in. He made sure he was ship shape, all squared away, and then rapped on the door jam.

"Come in," said a mellow female voice with just a hint of the mid-west in its tone.

Keller entered, expecting to meet a female Bossun's Mate or other such support personnel. Instead he was staring at a Lieutenant, Junior Grade— and a rather good-looking one at that. She was about five feet six inches tall. In her khaki uniform she looked trim and fit and definitely female. Her eyes were big and very dark brown. Her hair was shiny black and cut short in such a way as to look like it was no big deal to manage on board a carrier. But on her it looked like the head of a Greek goddess.

"Can I help you, Gunny?"

"Ahhhh, yes ma'am. I need to see the rabbi."

"You're looking at her, Gunny. I am the rabbi."

"Oh shit! I mean excuse me ma'am. I was just…"

"You were expecting someone taller?"

"You are not going to make this any easier for me, are you? You must get this a lot."

"Yes, Gunny, I do get this a lot. What's on your mind?"

"First, may I wish you a Shabbat Shalom?"

"Why, thank you! And now that we have established that you are a member of the tribe, who are you and what are you doing here on Shabbat? If this is an emergency, let's get to it. If not, you are going to have to wait until 2100. I don't follow the times of sunset strictly—I am a Reform Rabbi, after all—but I do observe Shabbat in my way. It is the closest thing I get to a day off and I am looking forward to shore leave in Haifa."

" Yes ma'am. I understand, ma'am. Commander Weber gave me this three day pass so I could…"

"You're the guy with the sudden need to get circumcised? At your age, you need to speak with a urologist. We don't have one on board. Do me favor and cut the crap. Why are you really here? Father Weber e-mailed me about your lame excuse for a pass. What's really going on?"

"Nothing gets by you, does it, ma'am?" With that, he opened the daypack and withdrew the camel skin pouch, took out the towel-wrapped bundle and exposed the leather-covered scroll.

"Permission to sit, ma'am?"

Silently, she nodded.

Keller walked across her cramped office and sat at the small desk against the wall in the corner. He turned on the desk lamp and a harsh fluorescent brightness glared down on the desk surface. Slowly, he untied the leather string and pealed the cover away from the scroll. He very carefully unrolled the leading edge until the first column of writing appeared.

"It's Paleo-Hebrew, ma'am."

"I'm familiar with this kind of ancient writing. Where did you get this?"

"How much time do we have before services? It's a complicated story. I need your advice."

"You're in luck. Because we start shore leave in Haifa at 1300, I have to shorten the service, at least the sermon part of it. My departure for shore is with the fourth boat, about 1430 hours. I can give you from 1400 to 1430. Then I am off to see my relatives on the Carmel. How about joining us for services?

"My Bar Mitzvah was a few years ago. My Hebrew is a bit rusty."

"Oh, and you think I am the rabbi of a congregation of *yeshiva bochers*?" The way she tossed out the Yiddish phrase for orthodox rabbinical students made it clear that she was familiar with the language in more than an academic way.

"Come on, Sergeant Keller—it will do you some good. I don't care about your Hebrew. Can you sing? I need a good voice to lead the music. Mine is not it."

"I can't carry a tune in a duffle bag."

"Perfect! You will fit right in."

The chapel was actually a simple rectangular room with some bookshelves for prayer books and hymnals, a wooden lectern and some all purpose non-denominational religious posters placed around the room. Twenty-two sailors and Marines attended the Sabbath morning service. Seven were female. In another time and place, someone would remark that many of them did not "look" Jewish. Rabbi Stone would later confirm that about half were not Jewish in the traditional sense. Many were exploring their religious identity.

Keller observed the rabbi with more than casual interest. He was intrigued. With a strong but pleasant voice she led the service, assigning parts to the attendees as they went. Not all accepted the honor, but most did. Rabbi Stone had a very colorful *tallit* draped across her shoulders. She wore a *kippa* that was a match to the *tallit*. No one sang very well, except for a Seaman Second Class with an opera quality baritone voice. His only problem was that he did not actually know the music. He would hum along until he caught on to the tune and then he would let loose. When he did, it sent chills down Keller's spine. The service concluded with a hymn Keller remembered from his childhood. He got so caught up in singing with gusto, he did not realize that the rest of the congregation was staring at him.

"*Yasher koach*, well done, Gunny!" the Rabbi laughed. "You are welcome to join us any time. Meanwhile, how about some wine and cake?"

The offer of food was greeted with mild enthusiasm by the congregation. But they all stayed for the after-service social hour. Rabbi Stone introduced Keller to the worshipers. They were a true cross section of America, not just the Jewish community. Twelve different states were represented, including

Hawaii. Keller wondered about the Hawaiian. He went about three hundred and twenty pounds packed into a six foot three inch frame. Not too much of it spilled over.

"Hi, Gunny. I'm Robert Bernstein. Nice to meet 'cha!" Bernstein saw the puzzled look on his face and anticipated Keller's question.

"My dad is Jewish, from the mainland. My mom is Hawaiian. They met at the Naval Hospital at Pearl. He was an internist in the Navy. She was a Navy nurse. What's your story? You don't look too Jewish yourself."

"Oh, I'm Jewish—South Carolina Jewish to be exact: Sixth generation Jewish. Mah great, great, great granddaddy fought in the War of Northern Aggression on the Confederate side." Keller's southern drawl got thicker with each word. The only thing missing was a well placed "Y'all" or two.

Rabbi Stone interrupted. "I hate to break up old home week, but all of us have preparations to make before we enjoy our shore leave. Speaking of which, on the table over there is a sheet with some interesting things to do in Haifa. I put in the names of some good restaurants and hotels that are not too pricey. Most Israelis speak English, and this is especially true in Haifa. The Israelis will assume you are sailors, even without your uniforms. They are very adept at identifying nationality by facial type. For them, it's a matter of national security. I know you have heard all of this from the Captain, but for us MOT's, this shore leave is special. This is our homeland. Enjoy, but don't be stupid."

Keller sat at the small desk in the chaplain's office and stared at the scroll. Rabbi Stone entered two minutes behind him. She motioned for Keller to move aside and opened the top desk drawer. From the back of the drawer she pulled out a magnifying glass. Unlike most, this one was rectangular, about two inches by three inches.

"Gunny, see if you can unroll it so that about four inches of the text are visible. Be careful! We don't want it to tear before we know what it is."

Keller slowly unrolled the scroll and exposed more writing than he had seen the first couple of times he opened it. The rabbi brought the magnifier close to the parchment, then backed off a bit, setting the focus.

"Can you read it?"

"If I had a sample alphabet in Paleo-Hebrew it would be no problem. All I can do is make out a couple of words. See these four letters. They are *yod, hey, vav, and hey.* They spell the name of God. I can only guess the rest and we need to know much more about this scroll. Are you up for a road trip?" Stone said this with emphatic determination. She was telling more than asking.

"That depends. I can't go AWOL. I'm due back in Iraq by midnight tomorrow."

"I think that will be enough time. You are going to rent a car and we are going to drive to Jerusalem. With a little *mazel* we'll arrive just an hour or so before Shabbat ends. Since almost nothing else is open in Jerusalem, we need to pay a quick visit to the Shrine of the Book. In the gift shop at the museum they have just the book we need. It is filled with sample ancient alphabets.

"That's my backup plan. Plan A is, we drop by Professor Carlson's home and he invites us in for an end of Shabbat dinner. I don't even know if he's home and I can't call in advance because it would be rude to do so on Shabbat."

"Who is Professor Carlson?"

"Daniel Carlson is the director of the Nelson Glueck/Hebrew Union College School of Biblical Archeology. If he cannot read the text himself, he can put us on to someone who can. Ten years ago, before I began my first year as a rabbinical student, I worked on a dig outside of Ashkelon. He was the archeologist in charge. Besides, he is a great guy."

"Lieutenant, there are two problems with Plan A and Plan B. My pass will not get me off of this ship. If we solve the first problem, my second issue is I have no civies to wear ashore."

"You forget, Gunny, I am a chaplain. I get to issue weekend passes. You're going on a spiritual quest this weekend. As for the clothes, I'm going to ask a friend who is about your size to lend you his. You won't need much—a pair of jeans a t-shirt and maybe a jacket for Jerusalem in the evening. As for underwear, you're on your own."

Stone instantly regretted the crack about Keller's underwear. Where did that come from? After four years at the University of Michigan and five years at Hebrew Union College, she had a promising career. She needed to maintain the distance between commissioned and non-commissioned officers. She had worked too hard and endured too many little sexist insults to throw it away on some allegedly Jewish Marine man-candy. He was ruggedly good looking. She would give him that. Why is she even having this dialogue with herself? It must be the effects of a sea duty tour in its fourth month.

Keller, on his part, was suffering from bifurcation of a Marine grunt's brain. One side of his brain was looking at Rabbi Stone as a Naval Chaplain, an officer and a Lt. J.G. On that side she was all Navy. The other side of his brain was focusing on her mellifluous voice, her beautiful lips and her sparkling eyes. This was definitely not good. No part of his brain was able to tell him why it was not good. He resolved to follow the rabbi's orders. How much harm could there be in that?

Chapter Eight

DATE: Ninth Day of the Fifth Month, in the Nineteenth Year of the Reign of King Nebuchadnezzar of Babylon

TIME: One Hour After Sunset

PLACE: Three Parsa on the Road from Jerusalem to Jericho

The secret to escaping from Judah under siege was rather simple. Despite their superior numbers, the Bavliim could not be everywhere. The trick was to make your appearance look as miserable and pathetic as possible. Eli had no problem with his disguise. His ragged clothing was in shreds. Zadok and a few younger priests assigned to assist in Eli's preparation, heaped dust and dirt upon him with enthusiasm. A few dabs of dung carefully applied would manage to keep most people from paying too close attention to this disgusting refugee from the Sacred City.

Ezekiel ben Buzi put a great deal of effort into preparing Eli for the long walk to Samaria. He wrote letters to Judeans already taking refuge on the slopes of Mt. Gerzim in Samaria, introducing Eli and explaining his mission and the origin of the sacred scrolls.

"These letters should protect you, my son. Guard them well. But remember not to reveal your true purpose to anyone whose name is not on the list that I have sewn into the hem of your garment. As soon as you are alone—truly alone—memorize the list and then destroy it."

A loaf of coarse bread in a pouch and a gourd of water on a string suspended across his body were the only provisions the captives could give Eli for his journey.

"You have demonstrated great resourcefulness in getting to us here. Now we ask God's protection over you. Do what you must to find our fellow priests in Samaria. May the One who preserved our ancestor Jacob on the road to Haran, preserve and sustain you on your mission."

Ezekiel kissed Eli, first on the right and then on the left cheek. Zadok fell upon Eli, sobbing uncontrollably. It was as if all the tension and worry of the last two days had been held back until the boys had a sense of what their immediate future would be. When Zadok finally took a breath, Eli sought to console him.

"Don't worry, Zadok. I can take care of myself. You be careful."

Eli took a brief survey of his own retched appearance. Then he sniffed the air and wrinkled his nose.

"I know you would not be able to tolerate the stench of the dung anyway. It reminds me of our home—well, at least the stables at home. Remember that I will forever be your loving brother. Now let me get started so I shall have the entire night to hide my escape. I am going to have to move quickly to get as far away from here as possible. The Bavliim do not know I am here and I want to keep it that way."

Stars beyond counting were finally visible in the night sky. As part of the preparations for Eli's departure, Levana ben Kochav, a wizened old astronomer from the Sacred House, now himself a captive, prepared to give Eli a basic understanding of the night sky. Eli did not know if he had any sense of direction at all. He thought he would know the East when the sun rose and the West when it set. What more did he need?

"You must travel at night. The stars will guide your way. I will point out to you a number of basic guideposts in the sky. You will then be tested to see if you remember where they are."

After almost an hour of instruction, Levana suddenly grabbed Eli by the shoulders and spun him around several times in an effort to make him dizzy and disoriented.

"Now, show me the constellation K'sil, the one that looks like a belt."

"I think I am going to be sick. Give me a moment."

"The Bavliim, if they find you, will not give you a moment. Show me!"

Eli staggered first to his right, then his left. Finally he looked to the sky. He turned a half turn to his right and pointed to the sky.

"Exactly so, my boy! Not bad. It is not foolproof, especially if the sky is filled with clouds. But it will at least get you going in the right direction."

It was time for Eli to leave. A sackcloth bag had been sewn into the inside of his walking cloak. The cloak was worn over his shoulders and served as an outer garment over his rags. The bag held the precious scrolls. If he was very careful, most people would not pay attention to the extra weight he was carrying. Fortunately, he would be walking at night so there would be no one to notice precisely how he walked. Zadok, Ezekiel and Levana escorted Eli to the edge of the camp, careful to make as little noise as possible. Levana pointed him in the direction of Samaria and Eli's journey began. After walking over the extremely rocky terrain for sixty *parsa*, Eli looked back toward the camp of the exiles. His escorts had vanished.

The night sky was blacker than the concentrated ink at the bottom of a scribe's jar. The stars, the armies-of-the-heavens, were brilliant. Just before dawn, Eli located a likely sleeping spot at the upper side of a *wadi*. He made sure that during the daylight he would not be visible to ordinary passers-by. As quickly as he could, he hollowed out a shallow hole in the ground and tried to remove as many of the rocks as he could. He used the scroll cloak as a pillow and tried to make himself as compact as possible.

Half a day later, the heat of the sun beating down upon his shoulders caused him to awaken. He was on his back. Slowly he stretched his arms and legs, careful to not raise them above the edge of his sleeping space. In the distance he could hear barking dogs. The dogs sounded fierce and angry. Eli raised his head above the edge of the depression when, suddenly, the sun disappeared and a crushing weight fell upon him.

"So this is how my life ends," he thought. "I am going to be buried in a rock slide." Except for the fact that the rock slide grunted when it hit him.

"Hey! Get off of me! I can't breathe. Who are you?"

"Shut up! You will get us both killed. The Bavliim are only a half parsa away. They will hear us."

"Who are you?" Eli whispered. An angry edge took over his voice.

"I am Shoshana bat Talmon."

"A girl?"

"You know, you are pretty smart—for a Judean."

Chapter Nine

DATE: March 14, 2009

TIME: 2:30 P.M. Local Time

PLACE: Haifa, Israel

The motor launch to shore was an adventure. The Mediterranean was running heavy and the small vessel was crossing the troughs and swells with an exaggerated up and down motion. Keller remembered that riding in small boats on rough seas and carrier landings were the two reasons he did not join the Navy. He was a Marine recruit at Parris Island for two days before he realized that the Navy was bound to the Corps like a mother to her child.

"I must have been out of my mind," he thought.

After clearing shore security and making their way to a cab stand near the pier entrance, Rabbi Stone engaged in a quick conversation in Hebrew with the driver of the next cab, a compact Subaru, and signaled for Keller to get in. Almost immediately, an argument broke out between Stone and the driver.

"What's the problem?" asked Keller.

"Typical for Israel. He didn't turn the meter on, hoping we would not notice. At the end of the ride, he'd attempt to negotiate his fare based on what he thought the ride was worth, or the phase of the moon, or whether he won or lost in the football pool last week. I set him straight."

"How'd you do that?"

"I told him that I worked for the Department of the Navy and that I would see to it that he and his cab would never be allowed to wait at the pier again."

"You are nasty. He will hate American sailors for the rest of his life."

"Only the ones who speak Hebrew."

Keller used his own credit card to rent the sub-compact Subaru sedan. Getting to the Hertz location and taking care of all the paperwork had taken only an hour. Stone remarked that this was close to a record for Israeli bureaucracy. It was 4:00 P.M.

The day was clear, the air smelling of salt and seaweed, the waters of the Mediterranean, easily visible on their right as they headed south. Cream colored high and low rise apartment buildings nestled into the slope of Mount Carmel looked like a set up for a Ministry of Tourism photo shoot.

Keller drove and Stone navigated. They joined the Number Four Highway just south of Haifa. They rolled by Mount Carmel and the Cave of Elijah. They passed Zichron Yaakov, a town named in memory of a Rothschild for his generosity. The highway took them past Ceasarea, once the capitol of Roman interests in the Holy Land, now a very well-developed archeological park and even trendier neighborhood.

To the east, more agricultural lands were visible, brilliant green fields separated by fire-scorched fields. On land that was not under cultivation there was just a scruffy light brown cast to the bare ground. At several points there were wrecked cars or abandoned farm implements.

On a low hill overlooking the highway, Keller saw six Israeli flags on six white poles fluttering in a steady breeze above a compound of sorts. His instincts told him that this was some kind of military installation. This was soon confirmed by a pair of olive green Humvees with long spring-mounted antennas attached to their rear bumpers. Keller stared as the Humvees passed through a guarded opening in the chain link fence.

"Hey, Gunny! Watch the road!"

He was drifting in thought but quickly brought the Subaru back on course.

"Sorry about that—just my training kicking in. I started to wonder if they were friend or foe. Where I work, we can't always be sure."

"Relax Gunny. We're in Israel, not Iraq."

"I am just beginning to process that information. I thought I would feel, you know, different about being here. My parents came on a tour about fifteen years ago. My father, who is not a guy who wears his feelings on his sleeve, said that he burst into tears when he saw his first road sign in Hebrew. My mother described her emotions as overwhelming. I'm not sure I feel any of that. Is there something wrong with me?"

"There is nothing wrong with you. In all likelihood, your parents arrived on a jumbo jet filled with American Jews overflowing with the excitement of having made it to the Promised Land. The whole arrival thing is one giant, calculated, emotional manipulation, complete with a perfectly timed arrangement of *Hava Nagilah* performed by the Israel Philharmonic.

"You, on the other hand, arrived in a Naval launch with a couple of dozen horny sailors singing 'Louie Louie'. My advice is to stop worrying about how you think you are supposed to feel. Just take it all as it is."

"You're probably right," Keller sighed.

"Tell me about yourself, Gunny. We still have quite a ways to go on this highway before we head inland to Jerusalem."

"What would you like to know?"

"How about starting with why, in God's name did you become one of Uncle Sam's Motherless Children."

"That's connected to my love life and my love life is personal."

"But I'm your rabbi, your spiritual advisor—at least for the time being. Anything you say will have, as the Catholics say it, the seal of the confessional. I am duty and honor bound to keep this conversation between us. Not even Admiral Mullen can pry it out of me."

"I was dumped by my high school sweetheart. After graduation me and a couple of friends went on a road trip out west in a used Toyota Four Runner—you know, Texas, New Mexico, Arizona, and California. This is sort of a tradition with guys from South Carolina. After bumming around for a couple of months, my plan was to attend a Junior College in one of those states, if I felt good about the area. My parents were really pissed about my lack of direction, but they resigned themselves to the fact that it was better for me to do this with their permission than without it. We ran out of money in Albuquerque. I had to take a job as a shoe salesman at a Timberland store. The manager said I looked the part so that I would have an easy time waiting on women. Anyway, that's when I got the 'dear Aaron letter' from my girl."

Chapter Ten

DATE: Tenth Day of the Fifth Month in the Nineteenth Year of the reign of King Nebuchadnezzar of Babylon

TIME: Four Hours After Sunset

PLACE: One Day's Journey North of Jericho On the Western Bank of the Jordan River

The clear night sky that guided Eli on his way to Samaria was also providing a curved vault of astonishingly brilliant stars that seemed to mock Zadok, as he slowly walked alongside the fallen leadership of Judah. The journey from Jerusalem to Jericho was forty-two *Amah* over very difficult ground. The ragged line of Judean exiles could only travel at a pace of two Amahs per hour. Fortunately, this part of the trip was mostly down hill. Otherwise, many of the elderly would not have been able to keep up even this slow pace. When the exiles reached the marshes of the river east of the walls of Jericho, the Bavliim pushed them northward toward Damascus, following the path of the Jordan.

Ezekiel and the other Judean leaders were placed in line under heavy guard following close behind the ranks of Bavli chariots. Zadok was instructed to stay close to the *cohanim* and continue to carry the sacred scrolls hidden in his cloak.

"If we are being taken to Bavel, why are we on this route? There are very few wells and almost no shade. The night air chills the bones of our old ones and our infants will surely die in the heat of day," said Levana the sky-watcher.

"It gives me strength to hear you not include yourself among the old ones, my friend. But that is clearly their intention. They want most of us to die. They will kill off the collective memory and wisdom of our elders and destroy the hope that the little ones represent. Our losses will keep us docile. By the time this journey is over, those who survive will do anything they command us, in order to survive," Ezekiel said.

"Where are we going? How many days' journey?" Zadok asked every Bavli soldier he passed. Only one soldier bothered to respond.

"We are going home. We have no idea where you Judeans are going."

Each day on the move felt like the one before it. The exiles were beginning to lose all sense of time and distance. Eating and sleeping and caring for the sick and the injured took all of their energy and what remained of their rations. In the hour before the march began, the priests would gather together and make a symbolic meal offering on a crude stone altar. Stones were the only things that were never in short supply on the journey. The meal offering was, in reality, more dust than flour, but the prayers of the priests on behalf of the people were heartfelt and sincere.

The offerings were actually intended to lull the Bavliim into a sense of security. As the march of exile began, they would watch the proceedings with interest, convincing themselves that the Judeans had given up hope of rebellion or escape. At the same time, a small group of priests of the first order were meeting in an area that looked like a pile of baggage. A small space had been left at the center of the baggage pile that would remain hidden from view of the Bavliim. These meetings were presided over by Ezekiel ben Buzi. On the second day after Eli had begun his journey to the north, Zadok was summoned to the hidden meeting space

"Zadok, do you remember enough of your training to make notes for me? Most of my brother priests cannot read or write. You are the closest thing we have to an actual *sofer.*"

"Yes, your Excellency, but I have nothing to write with."

"This pouch contains a couple of sharpened burnt wood sticks and some scraps of parchment. See how small you can write, there is no telling when we shall be able to get more treated skins."

"How will I know what to write?"

"Keep your eyes on me. If I nod to you, that means I want you to make note of what was just said in our discussion. If I shake my head, do not write. Sit over there with your back against that wooden box. Say nothing. Do you understand? Say nothing at all."

"I understand."

"When the meeting is over, give me all of your notes, every scrap. You are to speak to no one about what takes place during the meeting. Is that clear?"

"Yes, Excellency."

As the meeting progressed, it seemed as though a dozen priests were speaking all at once. Zadok wrote as quickly as he could. By the time it was over he had used up the writing sticks and most of the parchment. He approached the *S'gan* with the notes in his outstretched hand. Ezekiel took the notes, began reading for a moment then stopped.

"Is there anything wrong, Excellency?"

"I am trying to understand how one as young as you can be so gifted in your craft. Not only did you manage to capture most of what we said, but the letters themselves are unlike any I have ever seen before."

"I am sorry if you can't read them, Excellency."

"No, no. I can read them. I just didn't expect to be seeing such beautiful shapes in the letters. They're extraordinary! I need you to stay close by. I may have to call upon your skills at anytime."

"Are you sure?"

"Start looking around for more parchment and writing sticks. I will ask my brother *cohanim* for their help in getting you all the materials you'll need. In the hard days ahead, we shall be discussing the future of our people. Making and securing a careful record of those discussions will be very important."

The daily meetings started with the same conflict. Ezekiel knew how to stir things up.

"What will the future bring for us? The God of Abraham and Jacob has determined our fate. In truth, we have determined our fate. Did not Isaiah son of Amotz warn us that exile and death would be our companions unless we rid our land of the idol worshipers and child killers?"

"Ben Buzi, how are you so certain? How do you know that we are not supposed to escape and return?" said Amari son of Yerocham, the oldest of the exiled priests and the teacher of Ezekiel.

"We must resist the Bavliim. They are the idolators! They are the ones who have brought death and suffering to our people."

"Calm yourself, my teacher. I know that you will not believe this, but each day as we sleep, I am seeing visions. I am hearing a voice. It speaks to me in these visions. I know it is the voice of our God."

"Stop! You speak words of blasphemy. Say no more!" Amari was frightened.

"I cannot stop! I'm being forced to say these things. My words are no longer my own."

"Master, may I speak?" said Zadok. He emerged out of the shadows.

"Zadok, you are here to make a record, not to participate in these discussions."

"It isn't about the discussions but about the your visions that I request to speak."

"Very well, what is it?"

"I have written down your visions."

"What do you mean?"

"Each time, at the beginning of your vision, you would shout out something, I don't know what. The shouting caused me to awaken. Since you told me to write down your words, I believed it to be my duty to start writing down what you were saying. Here is the record of those visions."

Zadok handed Ezekiel a parchment scroll that the priest read slowly and deliberately. Then, without a word, he handed the scroll to Amari. When the old priest had finished reading, he let out a long sigh.

"It is as Ezekiel has described. Since the *S'gan* was unaware that Zadok *hasofer* was taking all of this down, it must be that the visions came from God."

A deep silence fell over the priests in the baggage circle. A smile slowly crept its way onto Zadok's face. This was the first time in his life that anyone had addressed him with the title: *Hasofer*-The Scribe.

Chapter Eleven

DATE: March 14, 2009

TIME: 5:30 P.M. Local Time

PLACE: Highway Four between Haifa and Tel Aviv

Keller wished that Chaplain Stone were driving. This would allow him the freedom to sightsee doing seventy kilometers per hour. At the moment, the only contact he had with The Holy Land was its expressway system. Passing exits off the Number Four Highway for Givatayim and Qiryat Ono, Stone confirmed their position on the road map and instructed Keller to be on the lookout for the interchange, which would put them on Highway One to Jerusalem.

"Watch your speed, Gunny. Israel has a very serious problem with traffic fatalities. I got stopped for excessive speed around here a couple of years ago. We do not need that kind of delay."

"Ma'am, I'm familiar with the concept of a speed trap. After all, I'm from South Carolina. I think we invented the damned thing."

"The interchange is the next right, in one and a half kilometers."

"Got it."

Highway One took them southeast around Lod and Ben Gurion Airport. Traffic was light. It was Shabbat and there would not be much airport activity before sunset. The place would be jammed around midnight. Many flights back to the States took off around midnight or one a.m. in order to arrive in New York early in the morning.

"In a few minutes we will be at Latrun and the highway will bend eastward toward Jerusalem," Stone observed.

"I know that name. Wasn't there a major battle at Latrun during the '48 war?"

"The Jordanian-Arab Legion controlled this approach to Jerusalem. They were well-trained and well-equipped. The Hagganah was bringing new arrivals from the boat docks almost directly to the battlefield. They were untrained, underequipped, and unintelligible."

"What do you mean, 'unintelligible?'"

"Nine or ten European languages were spoken by the new Hagganah recruits. They showed no hesitation to join in the battle. I am sure they were all trying to make up for the powerlessness they experienced in the camps and forests of Eastern Europe. But they couldn't comprehend their orders or process information about the locations of the Jordanians. In short, it was a fiasco. For years afterward, the Israelis studied the battle and made sure that the mistakes made at Latrun would not be repeated."

"Isn't this where a parallel road was built, bypassing Latrun?'

"Very good Sergeant! You've done your homework."

"I've been known to read history from time to time. Actually, I caught an old movie about Colonel Mickey Marcus, on cable before I left the States for Iraq. "Cast A Giant Shadow" I think it was called. It was not Kirk Douglas' finest performance, but it was mildly entertaining."

"Marcus died only a few miles from here, shot by one of his own sentries because he could not remember the password. What a waste!"

"All war is a waste."

As the highway began the climb into the Judean hills, the air was cool but Keller kept his window open. He wanted to experience Jerusalem with all of his senses.

"I wonder which tree is the one I donated in memory of my grandpa," Keller said. He smiled at the thought. Single trees planted fifty years ago have become forests. At least this part of the Zionist dream has come true.

Below the groves of trees was the rock, just kilometers of endless rock, limestone, piled in layers like a cake, but of uneven thickness. Most of the limestone was the color of sand, but a few veins carried traces of red and brown.

"Rabbi, when was your first trip to Israel, if you don't mind my asking?"

"I don't mind. I was a junior in High School, as a matter of fact."

"Did you speak Hebrew back then?"

"Only a few words, just enough to get by on my Bat Mitzvah. I was in a group of kids from all over the U.S. It was a very insulated experience. Every moment was programmed for maximum emotional effect."

"Did you decide to become a rabbi then?"

"It probably had something to do with it, yes. A few years later I came back for my junior year of college. But now this road brings back memories of my third visit to Israel. Ten years ago I came as a rabbinical student. I was on an inter-city bus loaded with a motley assortment of Israelis. Each one had a bunch of bags and carry-ons. They got on at the airport. I remember them jabbering away in Hebrew and feeling very much a part of them and apart from them."

"What the hell is that supposed to mean?"

"The bus was going to Jerusalem. Years of Sunday school had managed to connect me to the glorious and sad history of this place. I believed in my heart that this was my country, the land of my ancestors. As I looked around the bus, I got depressed. Back then the only thing I had in common with them was a religious identity. Culturally, I was a total stranger. At the same time I was beginning to have doubts about my ability to be a rabbi."

"You must have done something right. You're doing OK for yourself now. The Navy seems to think so, any way. Only the special ones serve as chaplains on the big carriers."

"I have done OK, haven't I?" Abby nodded slowly. She glanced down at the road map in her lap.

"Listen up, Sergeant. As the expressway ends it becomes Ben Gurion Avenue. Then it will become Weizman Avenue. We need to turn right off of Weizman onto Herzel and then go left at Wolfson then right again at Hemuzeonim. It will take us directly to the Israel Museum. Got that?"

"Whoa, slow down, Lieutenant. One street at a time please!"

"Gunny, I would appreciate it if while we are on this mission you would address me as 'Rabbi' or 'Rabbi Stone', not 'Lieutenant'."

"Rabbi works for me. How about you do likewise and call me Aaron?"

"I can do that—at least until we are back on board the Roosevelt."

"Rabbi, I have to tell you, these street names sound like a synagogue *Kaddish* list. Now I know that I am in the Jewish State. Except for "Hamuzeonim", they all sound like relatives of mine."

"They are, Aaron. They are."

They arrived in the main parking lot of the Israel Museum. The Museum wasn't particularly interesting as architecture goes, but the adjacent Shrine of the Book with its pure white dome, shaped to resemble the clay lid on a Dead Sea Scroll jar, was unique. The lot was about three quarters full with dozens of taxis spilling beyond the boundaries of the official cabstand. There were no tour buses visible—another effect of the Sabbath in Jerusalem.

"Aaron, we have to leave the scroll in the trunk. If we have it on us, they are liable to think that we stole it from the museum."

"Good point, Rabbi."

Keller encountered his first security check in an Israeli public place. Having no knapsack or other bags they went through quickly, purchased tickets, and entered the museum gift shop. Stone made a bee-line for the book shelves and in less than twenty seconds had a book in hand and was walking it over to the cashier at the check-out counter. While they waited in line, Abby opened the book to a page filled with what must have been examples of Hebrew alphabets. She pointed to one near the top of the page.

"Does this look like the lettering on the scroll?"

"Pretty much. I'm not sure. There seems to be something missing from the letters. I would need to compare the scroll with this page to make sure."

"We will do exactly that when we get to Professor Carlson's home."

Stone paid for the purchase and, in rapid fire Hebrew, must have made a request for a local phone book, because that is what the store clerk produced and handed over to her.

"What are you looking for?" Keller inquired.

"I don't have Professor Carlson's current home phone number. He won't be at the college on Shabbat."

From a black fabric fanny pack which Stone wore around her waist, she withdrew a pen and a note card. Once she had located Carlson's phone number she wrote it down on the card and returned the phonebook to the clerk.

"Got it, let's go."

"No time to see bit of the museum?"

"I'll tell you what. Follow me. You can take a look at the Jerusalem model while I make a call to Carlson and tell him that we're coming."

They went outside the Museum entrance and gift shop and beyond an impressive sculpture garden, to an open-air plaza enclosed by an aluminum railing. The plaza was several hundred feet across and almost as wide. In the center was a fascinating re-creation of the city of Jerusalem in the days of the Second Temple. Like a three-dimensional stone mosaic, the model had been painstakingly built one small stone at a time. The model seemed to blend seamlessly with the surrounding hills and the overall effect was—wondrous. Stone put a brochure in Keller's hand that explained the layout of the model.

"I will be back as soon as I have made contact. Don't leave this place."

"You sound like my mother on a trip to the Atlanta Zoo."

"Just like your mother, I don't want to spend the rest of the day searching for you. Be here when I return. That's an order!"

"Aye, Aye, ma'am!" Keller began to raise his arm in a sharp salute. Stone blocked his arm with her left forearm before he could raise it above his shoulders.

"Ouch! You are rock solid. That hurt."

"I can't believe that you are that dumb. We don't need to draw unnecessary attention to ourselves."

Keller grabbed her arm and pulled her into a very close embrace. They were nose to nose, looking directly into each other's eyes.

"This ought to confuse them—whoever "them" is."

Taking a quick look around and deciding that no one was paying them any attention, Stone shoved Keller back, hard.

"Don't you ever do that again," she said.

At that moment, she was not the only one that felt confused.

Chapter Twelve

DATE: **Tenth Day of the Fifth Month, in the Nineteenth Year of the Reign of King Nebuchadnezzar of Babylon**

TIME: **Three Hours Before Sunset**

PLACE: **One Days Journey North of Jericho On the Western Bank of the Jordan River**

Shoshana daughter of Talmon the Samaritan smelled worse than Eli. Her rags were not a costume. The dirt on her face was not a cosmetic to give her the appearance of being desperate. She was desperate.

"You address me with contempt as a Judean. What does that make you?"

"Silly boy! I am a Samaritan."

"You say that with such pride, like you are some kind of princess, yet you are as filthy as I am. You wear rags, as I do."

"Keep your voice down," she said.

"The Bavliim are in pursuit of me. I will be killed if they find me."

"Why should they be concerned with the afterbirth of a sick dog?"

The force of the slap that struck his face nearly lifted him out of the shelter hole. It made a sharp, quick sound like a tree snapped in half. His cheek burned as if it was on fire.

"Owww! What did you do that for?"

"I'm not Bavli. You will speak to me with proper words. My father is a tribal chief among the Samaritans."

"The Samaritans daily lick the feet of the Bavliim."

Shoshana raised her hand but Eli blocked it and held it tight.

"Perhaps you might want to reflect on your situation." Shoshana stated in a flat matter-of-fact tone.

"What do you mean?"

"Your people are in chains. Jerusalem and the Sacred House are a charred ruin. The Bavliim are on their way to conquer Egypt. My people are secure in their homes and in their fields. And you—you are crawling out of a hole in the ground like a pathetic rabbit. Now might not be the best time to imagine that you Judeans are better than anyone."

"You still have not answered my question. What do the Bavliim want with you?"

"I can't tell you."

"Then get out of my hole and dig one of your own."

"I'm a messenger. I carry messages from Judeans in Samaria to their families in the train of exiles," she said.

"Judeans would never trust a Samaritan—especially one like you- to carry messages. You're lying!"

"Are all Judeans as stupid as you are? It is precisely because the Bavliim are well aware of the hatred between our peoples that they cannot imagine we would ever cooperate with each other. They see me wandering the hills and think I am some poor lost Samaritan shepherd who will be kidnapped by Judeans and sold as a slave to the Egyptians for a few shekels. They don't pay attention to me. That's the point."

"If it is such a marvelous plan, who are you running from? I mean, of course it is the Bavliim, but why?"

"A Bavli patrol saw me leave the exile camp just before dawn. In the dim light they could not tell if I were Judean or whatever. All they knew was that I was escaping from the exile camp."

"If you continue to remain free, where will you go now?"

"My mission is done. I am returning home to Mt Gerizim."

I do not know this girl at all, he thought. *She could be a spy for the Bavliim or the Samaritans.*

"I have family in the hills of Samaria," he said. "I would rather die than face exile in Babylonia. So, I escaped, but without any real plan. All I know is that I face Northwest and keep walking until I reach Samaria. Take me with you?" he asked.

"You have a lot of nerve for a stupid Judean, I'll give you that. I have no intention of carrying you through the wilderness like an empty water bag. I can move faster, farther, and safer on my own."

"But you will not be paid for this journey if you are alone," Eli said.

"Paid—paid by whom?"

"By my relatives for my safe passage to them."

"How do I know I can trust you?"

"I'm a fugitive. Where am I going? Who will assist me in capturing you? Who would want to capture you? What have you got to lose?"

"How much?" Shoshana asked.

"Whatever the going redemption rate is at the time. The last I heard it was fifteen shekels of silver."

"That was for a Judean man. What's the redemption rate for an impudent child?"

"My family will pay you the fifteen shekels. Do we have a deal?"

"You have a deal, Judean."

"My name is Eli-Hasofer ben Achituv Hasofer."

"Oh ho! *Hasofer,* indeed! And when did you attain this lofty position in life?" Shoshana said.

"Two days ago, when the Bavli killed my master. I think I'm the only scribe left alive from the school of scribes in the Sacred House."

"You probably can't even write your name."

He picked up a stick from the ground and began to write in the red soil. The letters were uniform, clear and distinct. He wrote them from memory. It was the first poem his father had taught to him and to Zadok.

Az yashir moshe uvnai yehudah et hashir hazot....Then Moses and the Judeans sang this song...

"You are a scribe, indeed. Your writing is beautiful. What are those words?" she asked.

"It is a song that Moses sang on the other side of the Reed Sea, after God had rescued the Judeans from the Egyptians."

"Can you sing it?"

Eli began to sing the words as his father had sung for him. Tears streamed down his cheeks as he thought of all that he and his family had lost in the siege of Jerusalem and Judea. His tears were followed by sobs. His singing was cut short. He bowed his head and continued to sway, sobbing all the while.

Shoshana reached out to Eli, wrapped her arms around him, at first to console him and then to join him in his grief. After several moments she straightened Eli up, looked him in the eye, kissed him on the lips, then whispered in his ear:

"We shall journey to Samaria together. My father will be pleased to employ a great scribe like you."

Eli kissed her with all the strength he could muster. His heart sang, even while he questioned whether it was possible for one to be so happy in such a sad and tragic time.

"Who is like you, Adonai, among the gods that are worshipped?"

"What's that?" she asked.

"It is just another part of the song my father taught me. He told me it would always serve as a reminder that the God of our ancestors would see to my people's redemption—eventually."

"And Samaritans are not worthy of God's redemption?"

"Maybe a few of them are."

Chapter Thirteen

DATE: March 14, 2009

TIME: 8:30 P.M. Local Time

PLACE: **The Northern Talpiot Neighborhood, Jerusalem, Israel**

All was prim and proper. To say that the atmosphere in the Volvo was frosty on an unusually warm spring evening would be an understatement. Stone spoke only to give Keller directions to Professor Carlson's home.

Before the Six Day War of June 1967, Talpiot was a virtual no-man's land. It was constantly in the sights of snipers of the Arab Legion, posted on the Southern walls of the Old City. Only the very poor would even think of trying to live under those conditions. Abandoned in 1948 by the Arab inhabitants fleeing toward the safety of the walled city, Talpiot became, in the 1950's, the de-facto home of new Jewish immigrants from North Africa. Stolid, uninspired blocks of apartment houses were hastily constructed with only the barest minimum façade of Jerusalem stone tolerated by local law.

Scattered throughout the Talpiot area were small stone houses built by a Jerusalem based Arab middle class in the 1920's and 30's, with family ties to Beirut and Damascus. For nineteen years, the Arab homeowners were not anxious to press claims for reparations. When the dust settled on June

13, 1967, Talpiot suddenly became a hot neighborhood—at least in the mind of enterprising real estate agents. The original owners of the stone houses attempted to press their claims in courts of law, but their ability to prove ownership and nationality was severely compromised by the state of diplomacy and the muddle of Middle Eastern politics. These leftover problems of sixty-plus years of war and terror would not go away quietly. Professor Carlson owned one of these stone houses.

The haphazard quality of Jerusalem municipal lighting revealed the outlines of Carlson's house. Built entirely out of thick blocks of stone, it had a massive quality, even for so small a home. In all probability, the builders made liberal use of the easily found dressed stones left lying around from previous cultures and civilizations. A low wall of stones capped by a mangled wrought iron fence, defined the property. A rust-pitted gate hung open on one of its hinges, offering a sort of Addams Family welcome. Even in the dim light provided by street lamps you could see that the house was completely surrounded by a grove of mature cypress and eucalyptus trees. Some squat, palm-like bushes marked the path in from the street. Only a visit in daylight would reveal the other features of the property.

Stone and Keller walked down the path toward what they presumed to be the front door. In the light of a single bare bulb over the doorway, they could make out a solitary figure sitting at a wooden picnic table, pipe smoke curling lazily into the night air.

Daniel Carlson unfolded his six foot three lanky frame and extended a hand and warm smile in greeting. He was wearing what some catalogues described as a "bush shirt," an open collared cream colored cotton shirt with the sleeves rolled up and held in place by tabs and buttons. Epaulets continued the adventurer look. Roomy and serviceable khaki cargo slacks that had probably never felt the heat of an iron, judging by the proliferation of wrinkles, emphasized his long legs. Tan work boots finished off the image of the casual archeologist home from the dig. His face was oval-shaped, sun wrinkled and ruddy. His skin looked like it would burn easily in the harsh Israeli sunlight. His hair was thick and wavy with a salt and pepper color that many women found irresistible. Beneath his round steel framed glasses with Coke bottle thick lenses, his eyes were a dark blue and penetrating in their effect. If Harrison Ford was unavailable, this was central casting's nearsighted version of the American archeologist.

"Margie, my bride of thirty-two years, wants me to quit pipe smoking. Won't allow it in the house anymore. I'm almost finished with this bowl full. I started almost immediately after I got your call from the museum. Smoking helps me to concentrate—at least that's my story and I'm sticking to it." Carlson said, as he tapped out the spent tobacco from his pipe against a leg of the picnic table.

"Shalom and welcome to *Beit* Carlson!" The professor pronounced those last words with a heavy Israeli Hebrew accent, as if the name Carlson was found originally in the book of Joshua or Judges. He stood up and extended his hand to Keller, offering a powerful grip on the shake. His skin felt very coarse and calloused. Three decades of digging could do that. He wrapped his arms around Stone and gave her a bear hug.

"Abby, it is so good to see you again! She was my best assistant ever, don'tcha know!" He explained to Keller in a mid-western twang that sounded a bit Minnesotan.

"At our excavations, she always found amazing stuff the volunteers missed. You should know—it is Rabbi Stone now? I use you for an example of how a digger needs to be vigilant. The volunteers still don't get it. How are you? Where did you find this hunk? When are you getting married?"

"Whoah there, professor. Take it easy. Let's start at the beginning. In my present life I'm Lieutenant J.G. Abby Stone, United States Navy, currently serving as a chaplain on the carrier, U.S.S. Roosevelt. Allow me to introduce Gunnery Sergeant Aaron Keller, United States Marine Corps, Military Transition Team 2, embedded with the 2nd Brigade, 1st Iraqi Division, currently serving in Fallujah, Iraq. He is not my fiancé, boyfriend, significant other, or date. He is one of my military flock with a story you need to hear."

"I always knew the draft board would come looking for me when I failed to extend my divinity student deferment in 1969. We better go into the house. Ever since you called, I have been dying to get a look at the scroll. Let me see it first; then you can tell me the entire story."

They entered a room, roughly twenty feet by twenty feet. The walls were just the other side of the massive blocks that formed the exterior of the house. A bright white plaster was thinly painted over the stone. A large window with an interesting handmade wrought iron screen was centered on the wall that faced the street. In the middle of the wall to the left of the front door was a huge stone fireplace with undressed stones for a mantel. By the blackened floor of the hearth, it was clear this fireplace was put to frequent use during the damp and cold Jerusalem winters. Colorful wool rugs were scattered about the grey/green terrazzo floor. Others of a more delicate appearance were suspended on the walls, adding brilliant color to the room. The furniture was mostly dark, heavy, and from the looks of it, handmade but serviceable. Artifacts, presumably from Carlson's excavations, lined the top shelves of two bookcases, which flanked the fireplace. The rest of the shelves were crammed with books and periodicals. What looked to be a very comfortable, Danish modern reading chair and ottoman stood in the far right corner of the room. Three goose-necked floor lamps that could have been purchased at the Israeli equivalent of Walmart, were strategically placed around the room. Two were pointed at the ceiling, giving indirect light. One lamp was at the side of the reading chair, poised over the shoulder of an attractive woman in her early fifties, reading the Friday edition of the Jerusalem Post.

"Shalom! Hi there; I'm Margie." Introductions were made all around.

"Would any of you care for some coffee or tea? Have you had dinner?" Margie asked.

"Coffee would be great!" Keller said.

"If it's not too much trouble, tea would be wonderful. Might I use your bathroom to freshen up?" Stone asked.

"Of course, go through the kitchen. It's the door on the right." Margie said.

In what seemed like only five minutes of elapsed time, Margie Carlson had managed to lay out an astonishing array of foods on the kitchen table, along with plates and utensils: Fruits, nuts, hummus, techina, tabuli, pita, some unidentifiable but delicious crackers loaded with sesame seeds. Tubs of butter—salted and unsalted, and three jars of preserves completed the meal no one had requested. They all helped themselves to the food, coffee and tea, and made small talk. When most of the goodies were consumed, they all pitched in to clean up. Margie wiped down the kitchen table and then put a bright red tablecloth on top. It was clear that Margie had been briefed by her husband about Keller's discovery and knew they were about to actually see it.

From his daypack, Keller produced a camel skin sack containing the towel-wrapped scroll package and set it down in the middle of the table. He removed the towel from the sack. Delicately, he unrolled the towel until the leather-covered scroll was revealed. For a moment, no one said a word. Professor Carlson retrieved a lamp from the living room and plugged it in. A brilliant flash of light exploded over the table and everyone except Margie Carlson jumped and gasped with surprise.

"What was that?" Stone exclaimed.

"Just Margie doing what Margie does best. She has been my official dig photographer since the day I met her," Carlson explained.

Margie held in her hand a very expensive NIKON digital single lens reflex camera. The lens was rather short but very large in circumference. Attached to the camera was a professional quality grip for a flash that was the source of the light explosion. She slowly moved around the table and photographed the scroll from a number of angles.

"OK, let's open it up," Carlson said.

Gently, using long surgical tweezers, Professor Carlson untied the leather knot that held the scroll cover over the scroll.

"Uh, Professor, you needn't be so gentle with that knot. I retied it myself each time I opened the thing to look at it," Keller explained.

"Well, that may be the case, but even doing that you may have damaged the scroll with the pressure of your knot tying. I do not want to do any more damage than necessary."

Keller was hurt by the implication of his ineptness and his face showed it.

"Don't feel bad, Gunny. You are not an archeologist. You were not trained in the delicate art of excavation and examination," Stone said.

Keller mumbled something incomprehensible in reply. The scroll was now free of its leather wrapping and all eyes were on the scroll. Carlson brought a lighted magnifying glass down close to the scroll surface. He began a running commentary.

"It is sheepskin parchment. While I believe it to be very old, I'm amazed at how supple it is. It's not as fragile as it should be. Sergeant, can you recall if the place you found it in was dry or damp?"

"Sorry, Professor, but I wasn't exactly in a position to take a humidity reading."

"Well, never mind, the skin tells all. It must have been in a near perfect environment for preservation. You say that other books and scrolls were in the same space?"

"That's right."

"You may have come upon a *Genizah*."

"What's that?"

Stone explained. "A *Genizah* is a Jewish storeroom or hiding space for sacred documents that are no longer in service. It may be because the ink has faded or they have been torn beyond repair. According to Jewish tradition, such documents must be either buried in a consecrated cemetery or stored in a consecrated space designated for the purpose."

"What makes a document sacred?" Keller asked.

"More often than not, if the document contains God's name, *yud, hei, vav, hei,* it can't be simply discarded but must be respectfully stored or buried," Margie said.

"It's time to have a look at the text itself." Carlson said, as he began to peel the scroll open with the surgical tweezers.

"Wow, wow, and double wow!"

"What is it?" The rest of them exclaimed in unison.

"The writing on the scroll is in near perfect condition. Each letter is beautifully formed. This is the work of a very talented scribe. Most of the time when we discover an ancient text, which is not very often, by the way, we get faded or damaged parchment and letters that are barely legible. This scroll looks like it was written yesterday."

"How do you know that's not the case?" Stone asked.

"I will not know for sure until I examine it in my lab at the college. But for the time being, I'm hoping that the condition of the text is a result of being stored in the right place under perfect humidity. I can tell you that the style of the letters makes me believe that this scroll is the real deal. Paleo-Hebrew is very difficult to fake with style. All of the fakes I have seen look like they have been painstakingly copied one letter at a time, each letter taking a great deal of effort. In this scroll these letters have a flow to them, as if the scribe was very comfortable in shaping the letters because this is what he did for a living."

"Any idea what it says?" Keller asked.

"Oh, of course, let me read it to you."

Carlson read in Hebrew and Stone began to translate in his wake.

"*Al naharot bavel sham yashavnu…*"By the rivers of Babylon…Wait a minute, I know this very well. It is the beginning of Psalm 137!" Stone exclaimed with great excitement.

Carlson continued reading for a bit and then looked up.

"Rabbi Stone is exactly right. It is indeed Psalm 137. The famous, 'Psalm of the Exiles.' "

"Why is it famous?" Keller asked.

Stone closed her eyes and recited the Psalm from memory.

"By the rivers of Babylon,
there we sat,
sat and wept,
as we thought of Zion.
There on the poplars
We hung up our lyres,
For our captors asked us there for songs
Our tormentors for amusement,
"Sing us one of the songs of Zion."
How can we sing a song of the Lord
On alien soil?

If I forget you, O Jerusalem,
Let my right hand wither,
Let my tongue stick to my palate
If I cease to think of you,
If I do not keep Jerusalem in memory
even at my happiest hour.
Remember, O Adonai, against the Samaritans
The day of Jerusalem's fall;
How they cried, "Strip her, strip her
To her very foundations!"
Fair Babylon, you predator,
A blessing on him who repays you in kind
What you have inflicted on us;
A blessing on him who seizes your babies
And dashes them against them against the rocks.

"Except for that last nasty bit of revenge seeking, it is a lovely Psalm. So what?" Keller asked.

"Well, for starters, you may have come upon the oldest Hebrew text from the canon of the Hebrew Scriptures...you know, the Bible."

"How can you tell its age without testing the scroll?" Stone asked.

"The orthography, the writing, is in the style of the oldest form of Hebrew we know of from the Dead Sea Scrolls. It is actually the location of your discovery that gets my blood pumping. There are no other examples of Paleo-Hebrew discovered outside of ancient Israel. The rabbis of the *Mishna*, on several occasions, describe the writing style of the Jews living in Babylonia as being in the form of Aramaic, which makes a certain kind of sense. The Babylonians and subsequently the Persians used Aramaic as their diplomatic language. The Aramaic letter style supplanted that of Paleo-Hebrew shortly after the Romans put down the Jewish revolt in the year 70. In fact, the Aramaic style is the style we use when printing Hebrew today."

"And this means what, exactly?" Keller asked.

"It means that a Paleo-Hebrew document cannot be newer than the year 70."

"OK, that gets us into the Dead Sea Scroll ballpark," Margie said.

"We cannot prove this yet, because there are no Jewish documents to back it up, but local Babylonian texts are already written in the Aramaic style around the time of Cyrus the Great—say sixth century BCE. My point is this text is in the wrong place. The style is wrong. It should be in Aramaic letters not Paleo-Hebrew. As crazy as this sounds, this could mean the scroll was written by the exiles from Judah, between 586 and 440 BCE. That would make it more than four hundred years older than the oldest of the dead Sea Scrolls!" Carlson was so excited he did not realize that he was shouting.

"Take it easy, Daniel. You'll give yourself a stroke." Her words were wasted. Not even Margie could settle him down when he was enjoying the thrill of discovery.

Chapter Fourteen

DATE: Fourteenth Day of the Fifth Month, in the Nineteenth
           Year of the Reign of King Nebuchadnezzar of Babylon

TIME: One and a Half Hours before Sunrise

PLACE: Four Days Journey North of Jericho Along the Western
           Bank of the Jordan River

Two more nights of painful and awkward walking north along the
West Bank of the Jordan and then Shoshana suddenly, and without
warning, turned westward.

"What are you doing?" Eli asked.

"I'm turning toward my home. Where did you think I was going?"

"What did you see that I didn't see? How do you know this is the right
place to turn west?

"This is my home. I know these hills, this wasteland."

Wasteland indeed. They were, in fact, walking through a desert. It was
a desert without sand. It was a desert before sand. It was endless rocks and
boulders. Fortunately, the moon was nearing its full face. In the growing
moonlight, the large rocks could be avoided. The small ones were surprisingly
sharp and cut through the thin leather of their sandals and into their feet. Eli
just assumed that his feet were bleeding constantly. He refused to look down

and check their condition. He marveled at Shoshana's agility and strength. For most of their nights of travel, she hummed some melody to herself. On their third night of walking he realized that she was humming the Song of Moses at the Reed Sea. She had memorized it from the one time that Eli sang it. Shoshana never complained about the pain but Eli knew that she was getting as cut to pieces on the rocks as he was.

During their dawn to dusk rest, each stood guard while the other slept. Eli spent a great deal of his time on guard looking at Shoshana's form curled up against the side of the latest pile of rocks that provided shade. He wondered if she was pretty. He really couldn't tell beneath the rags and dirt. He didn't even know the color or the texture of her hair, or even if she had any hair. Whatever was on her head was wrapped in the same kind of rags she wore on her body.

Shoshana did not spend much time gazing at Eli. On guard duty, she spent her time worrying about everything. What was her father going to do to her when she arrived on Mt Gerizim in the company of this foolish Judean boy? Her tribe did not tolerate boys and girls spending any time alone together. The old women and the old men of the tribe would assume that after four nights and four days, Shoshana and Eli had lain with each other. This could be very bad. According to local custom, if sons and daughters over the age of twelve were alone together for too great a period of time, their clans were forced to contract marriage for them. She did not want to be the wife of this Judean whelp. She did not want to be any man's wife, not now and not ever. She cherished her freedom, a freedom she discovered in these very rocks running messages between Judea and Samaria.

For the past two nights they had not encountered any Bavliim. Several times they skirted camps of nomadic shepherds, taking care not to make any sounds that would alert the camp watchdogs. The cooking fires looked inviting and the aromas of hot food drove them crazy with pangs of hunger. Their own rations, a few pieces of stale bread and careful sips of warm water graced with a distinct goatskin flavor, would have to get them through their journey.

"Wake up, lazy Judean dog! If it is God's will, this should be our last night in this wilderness." Shoshana struck Eli on his back with a branch from a large and very dry bush.

"Enough with your insults," Eli said. His throat was as dry as the ground he had slept on.

"Where is the water skin?"

"On my shoulder, but it is empty. We will have to finish this journey without water."

"But why?" Eli asked.

"Because around here drinking someone else's water without their permission can get you killed. They guard their streams and watering holes, especially at night. We are in the territory of a clan of Jebusites. There is great hatred between them and my people. Come on, let's get moving." Shoshana turned to the west and took only a moment to reach full stride and a brisk pace, as if the conversation was pushing her along. Eli struggled to talk and catch up at the same time.

"Why do they hate you? Are you not the mighty Samaritans?" Eli said with more than a hint of sarcasm and a bit out of breath.

"The Jebusites hate my people because we took over as the masters of this land. They imagined that once the Israelites were gone, they would be in charge. For the son of a Judean scribe, you sure must not read much of what you write. Do you ever copy the records of the King? Did your father ever copy the records of the Kings of Israel?"

"How do you know of these writings?"

"My father and the elders of our tribe read from these king stories all the time as a warning to our people. Just as your people are being marched into exile, so my ancestors were exiled to Samaria from beyond the borders of Aramea. We lost our homes, our fields and our gods."

"How did you lose your gods?"

"My father taught me that Assyrians conquered our land, killed most of our fighters and leaders, and exiled all who could not be considered a threat to their power. In those days, our surviving wise men instructed our people that we were being exiled because our gods had abandoned us. They said we would be protected by new gods in a new land. The Assyrians intended to replace the defeated Israelites with my people. My tribe finally arrived in the territory of Samaria. They found empty cities and villages. They discovered abandoned altars to The One Whose Name Must Not Be Pronounced. He is the God of this place.

Israelites who managed to hide from the Assyrians and their policy of exile, old ones with many stories, told our wise men of the power of this God over another people in this place, the Canaanites. Over time, our people adopted this God and his rules, so that He would protect them from another exile."

"That makes no sense. It would seem that this God could not protect the Israelites; what makes you so sure he would protect your people?"

"Be careful, Judean! This One Whose Name Must Not Be Pronounced is the same God your people worshipped in Jerusalem."

"Exactly my point."

"Judah is going into exile because your kings, priests, and wealthy nobles abandoned Him. He did not abandon you."

"Where did you hear that?"

"Cursed be the rocks of this land," Eli said as he fell flat on his face, tripping over a rock he could not see in the fading moonlight.

"We are getting close to my village. Let's sit down and rest for a few moments. You need to know what is going on before we arrive so you don't say something or do something that will get you killed. The priests of Judah are hiding in my village. This is why your priest Ezekiel sent you to Mt Gerizim."

"Why are they hiding in your village?"

"Because my father is a tribal elder and chief. For the past five years he has been attempting to bring peace between our people and yours. He has even journeyed to Jerusalem to have conversations with your temple priests. He is returning their hospitality by granting them a safe haven from the Bavliim. But get this clear in your mind—our people are not happy that my father has done this. They are fearful that his harboring Judean fugitives will bring down the anger of the Bavliim upon us. In our village there are spies in the pay of the Bavliim. If you barge in with your story and your secret sack of Judean scrolls, they might turn you in for an extra reward."

"How do you know about the scrolls?"

"Please, Judean, do not take me for a fool. You told me yourself that you were on a mission. A mission means that some form of communication had to be on you. I searched you while you slept during our first day together. After only a few moments I found the priest, Ezekiel's letter and the scrolls."

"What are you planning to do with me?"

"First, I must make sure that you do not look like a Judean. Then I must find a way for my father to speak with us, away from the prying ears of the other elders."

"And how do you propose to do this?"

"By changing your appearance and introducing you as the daughter of my father's brother."

Chapter Fifteen

DATE: March 14, 2009

TIME: 10:40 P.M. Local Time

PLACE: Northern Talpiot, Jerusalem

Daniel Carlson continued to examine the scroll, letter by letter, for another hour. Keller wondered if this was how he came to be so near-sighted. Stone, Keller, and Margie Carlson stood in silence, not wishing to disturb the scholar's examination of the document. From time to time, the professor would make an indeterminate noise or sound, but there was no way to fathom what he was thinking. Finally, he set the lamp to one side and placed the magnifying glass down on the table.

"Well, Professor, is this scroll a real discovery, or a fake?" Keller looked at his watch and shifted his stance from foot to foot.

"At this point, before a serious laboratory examination, I can only say that I was unable to detect any of the tell-tale signs of forgery. The parchment looks and feels about right. The ink appears to be consistent with great antiquity."

"He means it's very old."

"Daniel, leave the Bible-speak at the door." Margie said.

"Abby is a student of Bible and antiquity. She understands the lingo. I am sure that Sergeant Keller can handle it as well."

"Thank you, Professor, for not thinking I am as dumb as I look." Keller said.

"What bothers me are the smudges."

"Smudges?" Keller asked.

"In a number of places in the text there are smears or smudges over the letters. It looks too regular to be random. Even under a magnifying glass I cannot tell what they are. One possibility might be that the scroll was not dry the first time it was rolled up. The wet ink might have adhered to the back of the scroll and then transferred to subsequent rows of letters. I just can't say for sure. We will need to try some trick photography to see whether the smudges mean anything."

"You mean like infrared photography?" Keller asked.

"That's exactly what I had in mind. I'm going to keep an open mind about all this until I can get the scroll into our lab and examine it with all of our expensive toys."

"If you don't mind, I think I would like to keep a close, personal eye on the scroll," Keller said.

"Professor Carlson is not going to steal your precious scroll," Stone said.

"No problem, Abby. I'm not offended. You're both welcome to observe the process. The HUC lab should be free early in the morning. Let's get a good night's sleep and set to work at dawn."

"How about something more like 8:00, dear?" Margie asked, sweetly.

"I guess you're right. Where are you guys staying?

"They are going to stay with us, of course," Margie said. "Abby can sleep on the couch in the second bedroom. Aaron,—May I call you Aaron? Aaron can sleep in the living room on the inflatable mattress."

Margie had no intention of waiting for Keller to respond. Keller was exhausted and, considering where he was less than 48 hours ago, an air mattress on a living room floor sounded delicious. For an instant, he almost thought it was great to be out of a war zone—and then he recalled that he was in the heart of Jerusalem, the oldest continuous war zone on the planet.

Church bells ringing from inside the walls of Old City woke Keller at 7:00 a.m. In that awkward moment of uncertainty when suddenly roused from a deep sleep, Keller thought he was home in South Carolina, listening to the Sunday choir of church bells sounding from every corner of Charleston. When his brain fog cleared, it was Sunday all right—cool, clear and crisp on the first day of the workweek—in the Holy City. Only Christians—residents, tourists, and pilgrims, were responding to the call of the bells.

Keller tapped lightly on the second bedroom door.

"Rabbi, you awake?"

"Of course I am, Gunny," Abby said as she tapped him on the shoulder from behind. He turned around very quickly with his right arm raised.

"Not a good idea to surprise a Marine from behind."

"Why are you so on edge?"

"I just want to get moving and see where this document thing is going."

"Me too, Sergeant, me, too."

Carlson insisted on driving them in his battered 1990 Peugot. Thirty minutes later, Sunday morning Jerusalem rush hour traffic was nearly at a standstill. Despite the professor's considerable maneuvering skills in weaving from lane to lane, the one-mile leg from the old train station to Liberty Park took the trio nearly twenty minutes. Along the way there were lots of colorful arm and hand gestures, a veritable ballet of road rage designed to alleviate the frustrations of driving in a city striving mightily to be a part of the 21st Century, but still suffering from traffic patterns established under the rule of Pontius Pilate and Suleiman the Magnificent. Finally reaching King David Street, they passed the stately grandfather of tourism in the Holy Land, the King David Hotel. They turned onto a side street, drove a couple of blocks, made a couple of more turns and parked the car in a lot that offered a wonderful view of the walls of the old city.

"Where are we?" Keller asked. The sun was directly in his eyes, but he stared anyway.

"We are actually at the back of Beit Shmuel," Stone replied. "This is a youth hostel that is sponsored by the World Union for Progressive Judaism. It is attached to the Hebrew Union College. We can grab a bit of breakfast and a cup of coffee on our way. There are always students and tourists staying here. It's a great deal, but you have to plan ahead. It's very popular."

Keller chuckled. "You sound like a tour guide."

"Actually, I used to work here on some weekends, greeting Americans and bringing them to the college chapel for Shabbat services."

Professor Carlson swiped his security ID card into a card reader and the door to the hostel unlocked. The security device replaced a security guard who would have had to inspect every visitor and any items they were bringing into the building. Beit Shmuel was actually part of a campus/compound. There were only two ways in or out, the main entrance on King David Street or this rear entrance near the staff parking lot.

The dining room of Beit Shmuel was almost without adornment. The walls were covered in neutral earth tones. The terrazzo floor was the same. The color scheme would not have clashed with the color designs of a wedding or bar mitzvah consultant.

"This space could have been a social hall in any synagogue anywhere around the world," Stone whispered.

Pointing to the buffet, Keller remarked, "I guess this is what my parents meant when they described an Israeli breakfast." There were massive amounts of vegetables, fruit, yogurts, sour cream, hard boiled eggs, baked goods, dry cereals, fresh preserves, butter, margarine, strong coffee and tea. Around twenty people were eating breakfast at scattered tables around the room.

"They look more like students than tourists," Keller said.

"Most of them are students," Stone said. With breakfast in hand, the trio followed the walkway from the hostel up to the college.

Stone continued in tour guide mode. "All of the buildings, even garden walls, are made out of Jerusalem limestone. The overall effect is peaceful and beautiful. In the 1920's the British Mandatory Authorities decided that all construction in Jerusalem would have mostly Jerusalem limestone exteriors."

Professor Carlson led them across the garden area to the entrance of the Museum. Tinted glass walls let in great amounts of light at the first floor entrance. Carlson swiped his ID card once again and invited Stone and Keller to follow him.

Carlson's office on the top floor was not really an office. It was more of a large workroom with broad tables in the center of a space that extended from exterior wall to exterior wall on one end of the museum building. Natural light flowed in from six floor-to-ceiling tinted windows. Extremely bright halogen lamps were suspended over the central work area. Floor to ceiling steel cabinets lined the wall to the left of Carlson's desk. A couple of them had six or seven trays, no higher than three inches each that were carefully labeled as to their contents.

Standing at the worktable was a short, very muscular man who appeared to be all torso and no legs. His body above the waist was narrow at the hips and immense at the shoulders. He had Schwartzenegger's chest and Danny Devito's legs. He was bent over a magnifying glass, one foot in diameter, suspended over the table by an articulating spring balanced metal arm. The object of his study was a fired earthen jar. It looked to be about a quart in volume. Without warning, the man grabbed the jar and hurled it to the floor, smashing it to dust.

"I saw Sean Connery do that in an *Indiana Jones* movie. I knew it was a fake. Now I can prove it." The pottery destroyer spoke English with an unusual Hebrew accent that carried a hint of Arabic.

"It's all about the color. The color is too perfect, too uniform. I could give these guys a lesson on how to fake 10th century Israelite pottery."

"Rabbi Stone, Sergeant Keller, I would like you to say hello to my very able assistant, Gadi Sagal. Did you know that the name Sagal is a Hebrew acronym, *s'gan l'kohein hagadol,* that means assistant to the high priest?" The professor did the introductions and commentary all in one breath, so no one had a chance to answer his question.

Sagal made a formal bow and smiled. His smile was not simply crooked. It was made up of randomly spaced and tobacco stained teeth.

"*Na-im m'od*, pleased to meet you." He shook hands with Keller but managed to avoid shaking hands with Stone. It was not an obvious slight. In fact it was very subtly done, as if his attention was suddenly diverted and he just forgot to observe the formalities. Keller missed it. Stone did not.

"Gadi, can you fire up the heavy microscope? I want to look at this scroll found in Fallujah by our brave American Marine."

"Fallujah, you say, as in Fallujah, Babylonia?" Gadi's voice seemed to tighten.

"Well I think they call it Iraq today, but yes," Carlson responded.

"Um, ah, how old do you think it is?" Gadi asked.

"That is precisely what we are trying to find out," Stone said. K e l l e r noticed the attitude and was at a loss to understand what was going on between Sagal and Stone.

Carlson unrolled the scroll, from the outer edge to the first seam. Gingerly, he placed two quarter inch thick, one foot by one foot glass plates, one above and one below the scroll. Moving slowly so as not to tear the scroll, he lifted the glass plates onto the viewing stage of the microscope. A twenty-four inch flat screen high definition computer monitor was attached to the side of the microscope. A keyboard rested on a stand below the monitor. Sagal began tapping commands on the keyboard. At first Hebrew letters appeared, then, the screen went blank. Then, just as suddenly, an image appeared, a dark shape against a parchment colored background. Sagal typed in a few more commands and the image changed. With each new keystroke command, a clicking sound could be heard.

"What are you doing?" Keller asked.

"I'm making digital images of each letter on the scroll, one letter at a time," Sagal said.

"When we have an image for each letter, we will be able to manipulate the image under several different wave lengths of light, both the visible spectrum and the invisible spectrum. There will not be much that will escape our examination. But we must be patient. As soon as Gadi has helped the microscope to learn what it is expected to do with this scroll, he will be able to let it work on its own, so to speak. It was designed by Russian émigrés, really quite clever," Carlson said.

"Shall I clip a bit for the Carbon 14 test?" Sagal asked.

"Hold on there," Keller said. "Won't that destroy the scroll?"

"Only a small part. We will take a parchment sample from the very end of the scroll, along with a letter sample for the ink. Before that happens, Gadi and his friendly photographing microscope will make a complete set of digital photographs of the scroll. I am going to give you back the scroll. I will keep the digital photographs in the college vault. The images will not leave my sight when they are out of the vault. I know cutting the scroll must make you nervous, but there is simply no other was to verify the age of the scroll."

"How long will this testing take?" Keller asked. "I'm supposed to be back with my unit by midnight, tonight, or I am AWOL.

"I think I can get both of us an extension," Stone said. "You definitely need more spiritual counseling."

"Spiritual counseling?" Sagal asked.

"Lieutenant J.G. Stone is a Navy Chaplain. She is Keller's Rabbi." Carlson explained.

"How—convenient!"

"Is there anything we can do while we wait for the results?" Keller asked.

Carslon nodded. "As a matter of fact, there is. While we are doing our thing, you need to make a short road trip to a very unique museum outside of Tel Aviv. It is a museum dedicated to the history of the Jews of Iraq. It includes, of course, their origins in Babylonia. I want you to show the scroll to Professor Shlomo Malik, the director of the museum. I want his professional opinion."

"The machine is finished with the scroll. We have what we need." Sagal announced as he carefully rewrapped the scroll in its leather cover and returned it to the towel."

"You think it's OK to carry it around like this?" Stone asked as she gently placed the scroll parcel into Keller's daypack.

"Now that you mention it, perhaps I should keep it here in the school's vault. It would be a shame to lose it or have it stolen. Let me make a photocopy of the scroll. Our copier has a good resolution. It should be very readable. If Professor Malik wishes to see the original, of course we will make that happen. Call me when you are on your way back. I may have some preliminary results for you by then." Carlson extended his hand toward Abby. She removed the towel-wrapped artifact from the daypack and carefully placed it in Carlson's hand

When the Rabbi and the Marine were safely out of earshot, Sagal could hold back no longer. A huge, and at the same time ugly, smile crossed his face.

"Did you see what I saw?"

"Even blurred it was possible to make them out. *Taggim!* Unbelieveable!"

"Do you even think it is possible?"

"That the traditions of your people are based on fact? Anything is possible."

"Why in the world did you give them a copy of the scroll and why did you send those two to Malik? He is the last person in the world we would want to get wind of this."

"The copy is meaningless. Without the original it has no value. Besides, I doubt the copy will fall into anyone's hands. I just couldn't think fast enough. When I saw the *Taggim*, Malik was the first person I thought of. It was on my lips before I realized what I was saying. I just sort of blurted it out.

"It may not be all bad. They might tell someone where they are going. Malik will sound like a plausible destination. One thing is for sure, we have to eliminate them and the copy."

"And how do you propose to do that?"

"The road from Jerusalem to Tel Aviv is always dangerous. You know how we drive. Fiery and spectacular accidents happen all the time. I will make a call to our friends in Holon."

Chapter Sixteen

DATE: Twentieth Day of the Fifth Month, in the Nineteenth year
             of the reign of King Nebuchadnezzar of Babylon

TIME: Noon

PLACE: On the Road to Samaria One-quarter Parsa from the
             Center of Shechem

Shoshana forgot the password. In truth, she never knew it in the
first place. When she left Samaria three weeks ago, there were no
lookouts and there was no need for a password. At the time, the Samaritans
believed they were secure. Now she sensed something had fundamentally
changed in her homeland.

The two Samaritan lookouts that challenged them were well hidden
behind a massive boulder on the south side of the road leading into Shechem.
From the instant of their first challenge, neither lookout was fooled by Eli's
masquerade as a girl. His masculine voice and heavy Jerusalem accent gave
him away.

These Samaritans were menacing, just as the local elders intended.
Their rough wool mantels were a nearly identical dark brown color, as
if they were intending to present themselves in uniform. A sand colored
sash of cloth was tied around their midsection. On the sash, each wore a

curved copper dagger. In a gesture meant to intimidate Eli and Shoshana, the Samaritan lookouts tossed stout, hand polished oak staffs, from hand to hand. The staffs were equal in length to the height of their owners. Eli was startled by their fair skin and the blond strands of hair that hung down over the forhead of first lookout. And then he saw the green eyes. He could not help but stare.

"What are you looking at, Judean dung face?" the second lookout said. His hair was light brown, but his eyes were as blue as the Western Sea.

"He means no harm. He's never seen a real Samaritan. Step aside! I am the daughter of Talmon ben Aram. He is expecting me." Shoshana stepped in front of Eli.

The lookouts did not know Shoshana bat Talmon by sight. At that moment, she did not look like the daughter of a tribal chief. She looked like the rough edged daughter of a Samaritan shepherd. They had no interest in her alleged family connections. They did accept her as a Samaritan, and that was all. Eli, unfortunately, did not fare as well.

The blue-eyed Samaritan grabbed Shoshana by her right arm and with very little effort, flung her to the ground. Before Shoshana could stand back up, the lookouts removed Eli's headscarf. His side curls proved what they had already surmised. Next, they stripped off his rags and roughly confirmed his sex. They bound his arms behind his back and dragged Eli along by his elbows, with his knees scraping the ground.

"Leave him be, you idiots! Don't touch him! He is under my protection. As I said before, I am the daughter of your chief, Talmon ben Aram. Here is his cord and seal. Look for yourselves. You are making a big mistake." She extended her hand palm side up, offering the cylinder seal and cord for their inspection.

"Listen, child, since we have never seen his cord and seal, we cannot verify if what you say is the truth. For all we know those could belong to the King of Bavel. We will have to present these to the tribal elders. Meanwhile, we will put your Judean friend in a safe place."

The Samaritans took him a distance of less than half a *parsa* down the road leading to Shechem. They dragged him off of the road to a small clearing. In the center of the clearing stood a small stone hut, about six cubits by six cubits by eight cubits high, with no windows and a huge round wheel stone for a door. They tossed him into the hut and rolled the wheel stone over the entrance. Air moved freely around the stone, so Eli had no trouble breathing. The four cubit high stone was one solid piece of rock. It must have weighed the equivalent of ten men. Only one or more men of enormous strength would be able to move the stone away from the entrance of the hut, and then, only with the very long and very strong iron pry-bar that the Samaritans produced from some hidden location near the hut. Eli knew then that he could not move the wheel stone by himself. In near total darkness he sat for what seemed like two days. He figured his time in the hut based on the changing patterns of light around the edges of the wheel stone. He passed the time by practicing his writing skills using his finger on the sandy floor.

As glimmers of light outlined the door wheel on the third day, Eli woke to the sound of the pry bar being applied to the stone. The sun shone directly on the entrance so Eli was blinded when the wheel shifted out of the way. He tried to stand but could not. He was weakened by starvation and thirst.

"On your feet, Judean. Our chief wants to speak with you."

Eli recognized the voice as belonging to one of the lookouts but still could not focus his light-starved eyes. At least the Samaritan did not call him "dung face." Perhaps that was a good sign. A cotton under-tunic, linen *ephod,* and soft woolen cloak and belt were thrown at him.

"Put these on. We can't have you meeting with our elders looking like a plucked chicken."

"These aren't mine!"

"Yours were too filthy to wash. We burned them. Be thankful you are getting these."

"In the name of the Holy One, what did you do with the scrolls?" Eli yelled. His mind suddenly cleared along with his eyes.

"Don't worry Judean, Talmon's daughter made sure we did not burn them. She took them and the letter to the house of the Judean priest. They are safe."

Eli took a deep breath and tried to calm himself. The new garments actually smelled good, but not as good as the three flat breads handed to him after he had finished dressing. He was so occupied with eating them as fast as he could, that he hardly noticed that there were no olives or beans or oil to go with them. He drank without pause from a large water skin the lookout provided.

The house of the Judean priest was located at the southern edge of the great Samaritan town of Shechem. The building style was very much like Judah stone structures coated with plaster on the outside and inner walls. The larger buildings were nothing more than groups of stone cubes, some placed side by side, others stacked on top of one another. The homes of the poorer inhabitants of Shechem were smaller and less likely to be plastered inside and out. In a way, they were more interesting because the stones were not all of one color. The better built homes all appeared one buff color. In all of Shechem there were only two structures that looked important. Both were surrounded by stone pillars that supported dressed stone beams. They announced power and strength. One was surrounded by a stonewall courtyard that reminded Eli of the Sacred House in Jerusalem. It was, in fact, the local temple, dedicated to the One-who-is-not-to-be-named. Eli presumed that the other house was the residence of some royal personage, but it certainly could not compare with the noble houses of the Holy City. This was not to be their destination. They had more walking to do. The Judean priest lived in the poor part of town. His was the only house that was plastered inside and out.

The blue-eyed Samaritan said nothing when he deposited Eli at the door to the priest's house. He simply turned and left. Eli saw the *mezzuzah* on the doorpost and relaxed, if but for an instant. At least this Judean had not forgotten the word of Shaddai, the God of Israel. Eli blessed himself and the house by placing his hand to the mezuzah and then to his mouth. Without warning, the door opened. A priest with regal bearing, dressed from *migbahat* to sandals in white, stood before him.

"Please come in, my son. I am Azaria ben Zevulun." He greeted Eli with a broad smile that was missing half of the teeth that should have been present.

"Have you eaten today? Did the Samaritans treat you roughly? Have you had any sleep since you left Jerusalem?"

As Eli entered he became aware of the presence of others. He heard their voices coming from another room, engaged in quiet conversation. The house was simple, neat and clean. The small entry way led to a square room, roughly ten cubits by ten cubits. Two small windows with simple iron screens allowed light in from the top of the walls. Reddish woven reed mats covered the hard dirt floor, nearly from wall to wall. A small table held a water pitcher and basin. There were small clay cups as well. Two men dressed as Judean priests were seated on cushions on the floor in the center of the room. They made no effort to stand when Eli entered.

"Brothers, this young man is Eli the scribe." The nearly toothless Azaria introduced him to the others. Every time someone referred to him as a scribe, Eli's chest puffed.

"He has risked his life to bring us the sacred scrolls of our people. I knew his father, Achituv ben Chanan." Azaria said this with a wistful far away look, as if he were at that very moment visualizing Eli's father.

"His memory will always be a blessing for us. He was more than a scribe. He was a talented artist with a quill pen, and an honest and good man. Ezekiel, our brother among the prisoners of Zion, is the one who sent Eli on this dangerous mission to us. Getting past bandits and Bavli patrols is not easy for a grown man, let alone a young one such as he. That he is still alive is a sign from the Holy One that our work here is important.

"In a note that came hidden with the scrolls, Ezekiel says that Eli has a sharp mind and a quick pen."

"How do you know that this clever boy-scribe did not forge Ezekiel's letter?" The accusation came from a priest with skin darkened by forty years of toil in the sun, and a longer than usual coarse and very black beard. "Our lives in Samaria hang by a thread. We are guests here. We must not take anything at face value. There are spies for the Bavliim everywhere," he continued.

"Avshalom, my brother, I take nothing at face value. Ezekiel left his secret mark on the parchment, on the back-side of the letter. It is his work and no one else's."

Avshalom grunted something unintelligible, which everyone appeared to take as his consent to proceed. Since Eli had not seen any marks on either side of the letter prepared by Ezekiel, he was anxious to know what the sign was. He would have to remember to ask.

"According to Ezekiel, this young man and his twin brother, Zadok, may have been the last two survivors of the destruction of the Sacred House. On orders from Akkub ben Shallum, may his memory be blessed, they rescued most of the hidden sacred scrolls. Ezekiel was concerned for the preservation of these scrolls. Ezekiel then divided them into two sets of scrolls. One set would be entrusted to Zadok and accompanied the exiles to Bavel and the other set would be sent into hiding with Eli among our people in Samaria."

"You call these scrolls sacred, yet I have never seen or heard of them before this. Why are they holy?" a heavyset priest asked.

"Menashe, although you have never actually seen these scrolls, their contents are very familiar to you. They were used for your training and education. They record the words that Moses heard from the mouth of the Holy One. They contain important rules for priestly consecration. They also contain stories of our covenant with the Holy One, as passed down through our ancestors. I have no doubt that your parents told you these stories as you were growing up. The very scribes who have copied these scrolls were your teachers. They were charged with copying and preserving the scrolls and with reading and explaining them to people like you, the children of the priestly families of the House of Aaron. In more peaceful times, some of these materials would only be shared with those likely to become High Priest. Now, with all of our brothers in hiding or in exile, these scrolls will be the beginning of our redemption from exile. That is why they are sacred."

"The four of us just might be the last living members of the Priestly house. I think it is time we all became familiar with these scrolls, beyond what we learned to recite in school. One of us could be the next in line," said Menashe.

"You are a fool, Menashe! There is no Sacred House. There is no priesthood. There is no king. In fact, there is no Israel and there is no Judah. We are fooling ourselves if we believe that the Holy One cares about our little band here at all. Either the Holy One is powerless in the face of the Bavliim, or the Holy One never cared for the House of Jacob at all or..."

"Do not give voice to your next thought, Avshalom." Azaria practically shouted at him.

"Denying the Holy One's existence lightens our own burden of guilt. Why are we here? We exist and survive because of the hospitality of a people we once scorned. The Samaritans embrace the Holy One without reservation. We, on the other hand, relentlessly question the Holy One.

"Our punishment for our faithlessness is just. We worshiped idols on every hilltop, even in the Sacred House itself. We allowed children to be sacrificed to a foreign god in order to prevent war. We acted like Canaanites and Philistines combining fornication and worship. We dare not deny it.

Our exile is our punishment. But the One who made a covenant with our ancestors will not abandon that agreement. When we have atoned through this horrible exile for our rebellion against the Holy One, He will take us back. This must be our faith. This must be our purpose. We must give the remnants of our people hope."

"And how do you propose to do that?" challenged Avshalom.

"The scrolls are the key to our redemption. Their safe arrival in our midst after being plucked from the very fires that destroyed the Sacred House is a sign from the Holy One. I also believe that we are here to learn a lesson from the Samaritans."

"What have they to teach us?" Avshalom asked.

"Few if any of the Samaritans know who they are or where they came from. They abandoned the traditions of their homeland and copied those of Israel. We cannot let that happen to us. We must never forget who we are and who is our God. Now we must make sure that the surviving remnant of Israel knows every word of those scrolls. All of our men, women, and children, shall all know of our eternal pact with the Holy One," Azaria said.

"You are an old fool, making pious noises like a prophet, Azaria," Menashe said. "Can you read the scrolls for yourself?"

"No, you know very well I cannot do so, and neither can you. But I have a plan."

"And what is your plan?"

"Eli, the scribe will teach all of us to read."

Chapter Seventeen

DATE: OCTOBER 26, 2008

TIME: 11:00 A.m. Local Time

PLACE: The Dan David Classroom Building Seminar Room 4B, Tel Aviv University

"Would one of you brilliant over-achievers please provide us with a synopsis of events surrounding the return of the Judeans from Babylonian exile? This will keep us on track toward our goal of beginning our discussion of the Books of Ezra and Nehemiah." Professor Malik had an impish grin on his face, which made the seminar participants suspicious. He would have made a horrible poker player. The trademark grin usually proceeded a "gotcha" moment.

"I'll give it a go." Sophia from Caesaria, a beautiful, tall blond, offered herself up as a sacrifice to Malik's question. Her fellow students nicknamed her "The Swede."

Sophia was not a dumb blond, not by a long shot, but she really had no business being in Malik's seminar. She really should have been in Professor Nimrod's seminar on nano-technology. But her fiancé and she agreed that they would share all aspects of their lives, even if it meant that her intended might flunk out of the seminar on artificial intelligence in the same semester that Sophia might flunk out of archeology. As usual, Malik chose to ignore her.

"How about you, Ruthie? This is one place where a traditional understanding can be very helpful."

Ruthie from Bnai Brak was the most Orthodox member of the seminar. She was the youngest of fourteen children of American-born parents, Herschel and Leah Rubinov. In the five weeks since the seminar began, Malik rarely missed an opportunity to chip away at her wall of religious certainty. At first, she deeply resented his hostility to her stalwart faith. After four sessions of browbeating, Ruthie was ready to complain to the head of the department. Then everything changed.

The topic at that time was the fall of Jerusalem in the year 586 Before the Common Era. Malik wanted the students to imagine themselves inside the courtyards of Solomon's Temple as the armies of Babylonia closed in for the kill. Ruthie had had enough.

"This is absurd—ridiculous!"

"Please explain yourself, *g'veret.*"

"Professor, no one knows what was going on inside the courtyards of Solomon's Temple."

"Use your imagination. You have one, don't you? The text at the end of the Book of Second Kings seems to know."

"Of course, but the fact is, the author of that account could not have been there because he describes the complete and total annihilation of all who were in that place at that time. He is writing from somewhere else, perhaps in Babylonia itself. For all we know, the entire presentation could be his imagination working overtime."

"What did Abraham say to his father, the idol maker?"

"Excuse me, Professor but I don't understand the relevance…"

"Abraham said, 'Let your ears hear what your lips are saying.' You are exactly correct, Ruthie. The account is not an eyewitness, contemporary, account. Remember this moment and ask yourself why you do not apply your brilliant analytical mind in the same way to the text of the Torah."

Malik's question went unanswered. Ruthie was determined to stick around until she could. Then she would storm out of the seminar room in a dramatic exit, worthy of the drama queen Malik imagined her to be. Meanwhile, she would continue to allow herself to serve as his Orthodox foil.

"Well, here goes," Ruthie began.

"Judean leadership is exiled in 586 BCE; actually a large number are already on the way to exile by 590 BCE. They endure the exile until Cyrus the Great overwhelms the Babylonians fifty years later, around 540 BCE. Cyrus allows the Judeans to return to Judea. They rebuild the Temple beginning around 520 BCE and dedicate it around 516 BCE. The Judeans hear Ezra read from the Torah and live happily ever after, until the arrival of Antiochus IV around 185 BCE."

"Any questions or comments?" Malik was often content to let others in the seminar do his demolition work.

"How about you, Akiba?"

"Well, it's not bad up to a point. Ruthie provided us with the account the sages of our tradition are most comfortable with."

Akiba Eltzur had thinning red hair, a very skinny build that was not improved by his choice of clothing, and a pronounced limp courtesy of an encounter with a Hezbollah grenade in Lebanon. Akiba saw himself as a true man of science. He was a dedicated archeologist despite the fact that archeology was riddled with holes of conjecture filled in with wishful thinking.

"And you can do better?" Malik threw down the challenge.

"I'll let you be the judge. A number of nagging questions from the period remain," Akiba said.

Ruthie scoweled. "Such as?"

"The Hebrew Scriptures preserve two accounts of the return from Babylonian exile: Ezra and Nehemiah," Akiba began.

"Actually, the two books were probably one text divided in a later period."

David Perach, the Haifa native who gave off constant vibes of superiority, was letting everyone else know he was very sharp on questions of Scripture.

"Thank you, David. I was going to get there. Now, if I may continue?" Akiba said sharply.

"By all means."

"The account that ends up being the Book of Ezra begins with a look back in time at the first return from exile."

"What do you mean, 'first return'? There was only one return, when Cyrus allowed them to go back around 540-539 BCE."

"And that is precisely my point, and I believe that is the point Professor Malik is trying to make as well. There were two returns. The first, as you say, was in 540-539 BCE. But that return failed. It did not take hold. The exiles that came back to Judah struggled to survive. They were attacked by local princes and clans. Many were not Judeans. It took the returnees nearly twenty years to start building something they could call a Temple. Four years later they managed to dedicate it.

"The text that becomes the Book of Nehemiah begins its narrative during the reign of a different Persian king. In fact, the author of Nehemiah begins seventy-one years after the first post-exile Temple is dedicated."

"*Rak regah*! Just a second! Hold on there! Now you casually change the Second Temple of the Household of Israel to the first post-exile Temple? You can't just get away with such a rewriting of Jewish history. You are implying that there was a second post-exile Temple."

"He is on the right track, Ruthie. In fact, there were three Temples constructed by the Jews after the exile. No one is quite sure how Herod the Great pulled it off, but he managed to build a completely new Temple on the site of post-exilic Temple number two."

"But our tradition speaks of only two Temples, one before and one after the exile."

"The truth is that the rabbinic tradition does speak of three Temples. For them, it is the prophet Ezekiel who envisions the third Temple. The power of his idealized vision of a divinely designed and constructed Temple puts our sages in an impossible position. They are members of the generations just before, during, and after the revolt against Rome in the year 70 CE. The Temple built by Herod is in ruins. The revolt is over and the people are in dire straits. Is it any wonder that the rabbis would latch onto the temple vision of Ezekiel in order to give the Jews hope? Since Ezekiel constantly refers to a new temple, it would not make sense to remind the people that there have been in fact three temples since the Temple of Solomon was destroyed by the Babylonians. Which temple then, is the one promised by their God?"

"He is your God too?"

"Thank you for that important correction." Akiba mimed a seated theatrical bow in Ruthie's direction.

"As I was saying, the Book of Nehemiah begins with a very bleak and depressing assessment of the state of Judea, the city of Jerusalem, and the

Temple itself. Nehemiah is serving a Persian king, Artaxerxes. In other words, Nehemiah is describing the condition of Judean life in Jerusalem and its surrounding areas ninety years after the Judeans return from their exile, and seventy-one years after the first post-exile temple is dedicated. This raises three questions.

"First, what happened to the Temple that they dedicated in 516? Second, why was Jerusalem in ruins so long after the exile was over? And third, what is the relationship between Ezra and Nehemiah, not as books in the Bible, but as leaders of the redeemed Jewish community?"

"Well done, Akiba, but I wish you had not used the word 'redeemed' to describe the community at that time." Malik raised his eyebrows. The only thing missing was the Groucho cigar.

"I used the word 'redeemed' deliberately."

"Where are you going with this?"

"I found an interesting article in a scholarly journal. It was written many years ago. The author states emphatically that around the year 485 BCE, the Judeans were attacked by a coalition of nations or tribes, led by the Samaritans and including Ammonites, Moabites, Phoenicians, Tyreans, Ashdodites and assorted others."

"Why did these nations attack Judah?"

"They attacked because they resented the special favors and status conferred upon the Judeans by Cyrus and his successors," Ruthie said.

"And just how do you know that?" David asked.

"It is right there in plain sight in the Book of Ezra. Most of those nations sought to join the Judeans in building a new temple. The leaders of the Judeans refused to allow them to play any role in the temple building project. I just sort of concluded that after they were rejected, they bided their time for the right moment to attack."

"So…you now accept the premise that Jerusalem and the Temple were destroyed after 516 BCE?"

"I didn't say that, Akiba. I'm working it through in my own mind."

"Now you are on to something," Malik said.

"If Persia was such a strong empire, these nations would never have dared to attack." Dan from the wastelands of the Wadi Arava joined in the discussion. He seldom joined in the discussion unless he was going to make some sort of dramatic contribution.

"Who woke you up? I thought you were on some other planet," Akiba said.

"When Akiba mentioned the year 485 BCE, an alarm went off in my brain."

"Alert Sky News!" Akiba said, trying to throw Dan off his stride.

"The Persians were at war with the Greeks in 485." Dan said.

"It would seem that the Persians were pre-occupied with the Greeks and did not have time to settle minor skirmishes in the outback of Judah."

"*M'tsuyan*...outstanding, Dan." Akiba said. "Your analysis is excellent.

"The local chiefs and princes know that Persia is busy with Athens and Sparta. They attack and plunder Jerusalem and do as much damage as possible before the Persians take notice. They take Judeans into captivity and decide to ransom them back to their families. There are psalms that speak of captivity and redemption, but they do not mention the Babylonians as the bad guys. They do not use terms like exile and return. They are two completely different events. Nehemiah rebuilds the city and Temple ruined by the neighborhood bullies, not the Babylonians."

"What caused this second post-exile Temple to endure when the first one was a failure?" Ruthie said.

"Let's start by asking what was wrong with the original returnees from Babylon?" Malik said.

"They were few in number."

"The local Judeans, those who never left Judah and thus did not experience exile, resented the new arrivals as foreigners."

"Maybe they were also viewed as collaborators with the enemy from the East."

"The left-behind Judeans were jealous of the privileges heaped upon the returning-exiled Judeans by the Persians."

"They immediately tried to revolt against Persia. At least that is the impression left by the writings of the prophet Zechariah. The Judeans who never left were afraid of another exile, one that would include them this time."

"And so...in summary?" Malik asked.

"There was no unity among the people. The new arrivals and the ones who never left didn't even speak the same language. Too many issues divided them."

"They probably did not even worship the same God." Ruthie whispered.

"Would you please share that provocative thought with everyone, *giveret*?"

"I said, 'They probably did not even worship the same God.' "

"Where did that come from?" Akiba asked.

"Once the Babylonians destroyed the first....I mean the Temple of Solomon, what did the Judeans who were left behind do, as far as their worship was concerned? Most if not all of their priests were taken into captivity. Who would lead them in worship? Where would they worship? The Book of Kings describes rampant idolatry at the time of the destruction. It is altogether possible that the Judeans who were not taken into exile continued to worship an assortment of deities. Maybe this is why Ezra and Nehemiah are so focused on wiping out intermarriage. Non-Judean women bring their foreign gods with them into the households they establish with Judean men."

"Thank you, Ruthie. The Office of the Chief Rabbi could not have said it better." Dan said.

"No, on this one she is more correct than she knows. There was nothing that held these people together, not common experience, social class, language, religion...nothing. The first, post-exilic Temple was built by a very small community. When it came under attack by the surrounding tribes and clans, the returnees who built it could not mount a vigorous defense. Judah would slip back into insignificance for forty bleak years," Akiba said

"So when Nehemiah and Ezra return...as you say, forty years later, what changed? What was different?" Malik said.

Ruthie provided the answer. "It was the Torah," she whispered. "The early returnees from exile in 540-539 BCE did not have the Torah." Then she repeated it for all to hear.

"It was the Torah."

"Where did it come from?"

Chapter Eighteen

DATE: Seventeenth Day of the Seventh Month, In the First Year
            Since the Destruction of Jerusalem

TIME: Mid Morning

PLACE: The City Gate of Shechem

Facing exile in Babylonia, some Judean priests sought refuge in Samaria. It was granted because the Samaritans wanted to know more about the Judean God. Long ago, when the Assyrians force-marched the Samaritans into Israelite territory, the God of the Israelites had become their God. That was what was expected. He was the god that protected the land. In time, they discovered that the neighboring Kingdom of Judah also worshipped the same God. Maintaining peace between Judeans and Samaritans was Talmon's responsibility. Eli and Shoshana put that peace in danger

Talmon may have been the overall leader of the people, but the Samaritan priests and elders were clearly in charge of all matters of justice and religious practice. When news of the arrival of Eli and Shoshana in Samaria had reached the elders, they immediately summoned Shoshana's father to appear before them and explain the reason for his young daughter being on her own for several weeks, in the company of a Judean boy. This was a clear violation of sacred tribal customs governing contact between unmarried men and women.

The court of Samaritan elders was in session this particular day because many people had come to the city on the eve of the full moon two days earlier to celebrate the harvest festival. The six elders were sitting, as was their custom, outside the newly plastered walls near the main gate of the city. Here is where they would pass judgment on Eli and Shoshana. The elders sat on simple stools, on an elevated earthen mound that allowed them to look out over the heads of the people. To shelter them from the late summer sun, a goat's hair canopy extended out from the wall to two stout tent poles.

Before the elders called Shoshana's father to answer their questions, three local disputes were presented and resolved. It was mid-morning when Talmon ben Aram came forward, still the proud tribal chief. He was accompanied by his bodyguards, his daughter Shoshana, and the scruffy Judean, who was clutching to his chest a very ordinary looking cloth sack. Behind the Judean, another of Talmon's men carried a pair of trestles and a flat thin board, about two cubits in length and one cubit in width.

"With your permission, my brothers, I have something you must see." He gestured to his man.

"Set up the table. This boy is a Judean scribe."

The elders, almost in unison, fixed Talmon with a skeptical expression on their faces.

"Yes, I know that sounds a bit far fetched, but I can affirm from personal observation that he is indeed a scribe, and a talented one at that. According to a letter he was carrying, the boy has been sent by a Judean priest, Ezekiel ben Buzi by name. This Ezekiel is now among the exiles to Babylon. When the boy encountered my daughter in the hills outside of Jericho, he was carrying parchment scrolls that he claims he personally rescued from the Sacred House in Jerusalem. The priest's letter also makes this claim. While the boy was being pursued by the Bavliim, my daughter took pity on him and rescued him. She agreed to help him because his mission was to seek out the Judean priests living here among us."

"Boy, is this your story?" demanded the chief elder.

Eli cleared his throat. "Yes."

"Hold on, please! I respectfully request permission to speak to the esteemed elders of Samaria."

"And you are…?" asked the chief elder. The chief elder was already well acquainted with Azaria, the new speaker.

Bowing very low, with his face toward the ground, Azaria spoke. "I am Azaria, the leader of the Judean priests in exile here in Samaria. First, I wish to express my thanks to all of the elders and the people of Samaria for their gracious hospitality. We shall not become a burden to you. We seek only to return to our homeland as soon as possible. Second, I will vouch for this boy-scribe's story. He is who he says he is, and he does carry with him scrolls rescued from the Sacred House of our people in Jerusalem."

"Show us the scrolls," another elder demanded.

Eli looked toward Azaria and silently sought his permission to bring out one of the scrolls. Azaria responded with a faint nod of his head. Eli then reached into the sack and brought out a single scroll. He placed it on the table, but the ends kept rolling up. Azaria must have been prepared for this moment, although Eli could not imagine how that could be. Out of nowhere Azaria produced four small flat stones and gently placed them on the four corners of the now unrolled scroll. All six of the elders came down from their shaded platform and walked around the scroll to inspect it from every possible angle.

"Did you write this, boy?" The chief elder asked.

"No sir, I did not."

"Can you write and read?" the chief elder asked.

"Yes sir, I can."

"Then show us, by reading from this scroll."

There was an audible gasp from the Judean priests standing nearby.

"Most honored and respected elders," Azaria said. "This scroll cannot be read aloud in public unless certain prayers are recited beforehand. The reader must be ritually clean and dressed..."

"Tell the boy to read from it now, or you and your people will be expelled from our land."

Azaria looked to his fellow priests for help. They nodded vigorously with their hands extended to strengthen him.

"Go ahead, Eli, the God whose name must not be pronounced, will forgive you. I will pronounce the prayer—then you read," Azaria said.

"Praised be You,———, to whom all praise is due."

When Azaria reached the point in the prayer he would have to pronounce the actual name of the God of the Judeans, his fellow priests and the rest of the Judeans who were present at the city gates, shouted over him and prevented the divine name from actually being heard.

"Praised be the One who is to be praised for all time," they declared.

Eli took a short length of reed in hand and used it as a pointer to guide his eyes along the lines of text. A brief smile broke out on his face as he realized that he had randomly chosen the scroll with the same passage he had sung to Shoshana in the wilderness. As he began to read, the thought occurred to him that this was no random event. His choice of scrolls was no accident.

At first, Eli read in a flat monotone, terrified as to what might come next from the stern and imposing elders of Samaria. But then as he experienced the rapt attention the elders and gathering crowd were giving him, he cleared his throat and began again—this time in the chant taught to him by his father. Except for the sounds of the chant, there was a powerful silence before the city gates, broken only by the flapping of the shade canopy moving with the gentle morning breeze. Tears started to fall from his eyes as he remembered his father teaching him and his brother Zadok in the proper chant for the Song of Moses at the Reed Sea. Tears were also falling down the cheeks of the Judean exiles, who heard in Eli's faithful rendering of the song of triumph a cruel reminder of all that they and their people had lost.

Eli reached the end of the scroll. The singular moment of near total silence was broken by shouts of "More! More!"

"That will be enough, for now," the chief elder said.

"If the Judean priests agree, we will arrange for further readings from the Judean scribe, at some appropriate time and place. Our purpose this morning, is to weigh the issue of this boy being alone in the wilderness with the daughter of Talmon son of Aram. Neither the boy nor the girl denies the facts in the matter. This is a very serious breach of the customs of both our peoples; yet it is the law of Samaria that will decide. The elders will now meet in the Gate Hall to render a decision. We invite the priests from Judea to speak and be heard on this matter. They may join in our deliberations."

Shoshana and Eli were not coerced to marry. In another time, they would have been forcibly joined as husband and wife because of a presumption that the two youngsters had intercourse during their journey.

The swirl of events surrounding Babylonian efforts to rule over

Samaria as well as Judah insured that these were not ordinary times. The Judean priests argued strenuously on Eli's behalf, that observing the tradition of forced marriage was not appropriate in this case. The two youngsters were thrown together by the circumstances of war. Eli was on a mission. His care of the sacred scrolls was proof of his dedication to his responsibilities.

Ultimately, the two older sisters of Talmon ben Aram would decide the matter. Upon careful inspection, they proclaimed that Shoshana had indeed remained a virgin. Besides, Judeans and Samaritans did not intermarry.

The truth of the matter was, his abilities as a scribe had saved Eli, but only for short while. Shoshana and Eli were destined to fall in love with each other. During the three years since his arrival in Samaria, their shared experience of survival had indeed brought them closer together. The constant needling of one another, based on their tribal identities, was more a sign of growing affection and the realization that together their differences made them stronger.

"Open your eyes, Talmon. The Judean has feelings for Shoshana." Asiya, Talmon's older sister was only expressing what Talmon already knew. This was not the first time they were having this conversation. But it was the first time that Talmon revealed what his was thinking.

"It is time for them to marry," said Talmon.

"What? Do you know what you are saying? A daughter of our people may not marry a Judean. If she did, you would no longer be *Melekh Shomron*.

"Sister, you are wise in most things. Wisdom comes to you from our mother. You wear it well like she did. It becomes you. But sometimes, wisdom is not enough. Sometimes courage must overtake wisdom."

"Not in this matter. Courage will lead to disaster. If the Bavliim hear that you have given your daughter to a Judean they will suspect you have larger ambitions."

"I can't control what the Bavliim suspect. But I am charged with the safety of our people."

"And this is how you protect us…by provoking them?"

The elders and I have discussed this matter many times. It is not the Bavliim we must fear. It is the Egyptians that would destroy us."

"I have heard the Bavliim boast of making the Nile a river of Bavel. We have seen what their armies can do. Egypt will be crushed by them," Asiya said.

"Perhaps, at first. But Egypt is a long way from Bavel. This is the greatest weakness of the Bavliim. They must supply their armies from here. That means they must have peace in Judah and Samaria. The Bavli Governor of this province told me as much last week. He confided that he was looking for a local *melekh* capable of keeping the peace between all the peoples of this land. I told him that I'm the *melekh* he is looking for."

"Your pride will get us all killed. How does Shoshana marrying the Judean insure our safety?"

"He has a name, my sister. Eli also has earned the respect of our people and the Judeans. By joining Samaritan and Judean within my own family, I will have demonstrated my ability to maintain the peace in this land."

"This is a dangerous game that you are playing, brother. I hope you are right."

The wedding was not a joyous affair. The absence of true and unfettered joy at the ceremony was due solely to the pall Jerusalem's destruction cast over the nearly four hundred Judean exiles in Samaria. There was no dancing, no music, and very little wine. No wedding coming so soon after the destruction of Jerusalem and the Sacred House could compensate for the loss of their spiritual heart.

"Azariah, I am deeply grateful that you stood as Eli's father beneath the canopy and prepared the wedding contract. I know it meant a great deal to him."

"My lord *Melekh*, you have graciously permitted us to dwell among your people in safety. This marriage is an important step in bringing Samaritan and Judean closer to one another. These are dangerous days."

Talmon provided the newlyweds with a home. The stone hut was not much larger than the one that imprisoned Eli when he arrived in Samaria. From the moment they crossed the threshold, Shoshana demonstrated great skill in making it feel like it was truly theirs.

Eli was woefully unprepared for his first sexual experience. This subject never came up in the school for scribes. It certainly did not come up in conversation with his father. Shoshana, on the other hand must have been receiving detailed and practical lessons in marital sexuality from her father's other wives. She knew what to do and when to do it.

Eli's status as one descended from a priest of a minor order did not impede his growing prominence within the inner circle of Judeans in Samaria. The reason for his acceptance was Azaria's plan for Eli and the community.

"The God who protects all Israel has sent you and the sacred scrolls to us for a reason," Azarah said.

"How can you be so sure?" Eli asked.

"Because I believe that our redemption from exile depends on what we do with the scrolls. First we must make many copies of each scroll. Then we must teach the contents of these scrolls to our people, all of the people, even the Samaritans. In that way we cannot forget who we are and where we came from."

"You and the elders keep telling me that I am the only scribe among our people here. I cannot undertake so great a task by myself."

"Other scribes will help you."

"What other scribes?"

"The ones you train."

Eli set about discovering which members of the exile community could read and write. Developing a cadre of teachers would be the first step. It was embarrassing for him to ask adults far older and wiser than he to demonstrate their abilities. It was embarrassing for those families who believed that their loved ones were literate, to discover that they were not. The language problem was more vexing.

The scrolls that Eli and Zadok rescued from the Hall of Scribes were written in the sacred language of the patriarchs, Abraham and Moses. The Bavliim referred to this language as the tongue of the Hebrews—the landless ones. In the ancient stories told by the Bavliim, the tribes known collectively as Israel, wandered into the land of Canaan as landless soldiers of fortune—no better than bandits and thieves. Their language was different but not unintelligible to the Bavliim.

Prior to the conquests of the Bavliim, the Kingdoms of Israel and Judah were subject to the harsh rule of Assur. The rulers of Assur imposed their language, Aramean, on all of their vassal kingdoms. Even Judah, struggling to maintain its independence, could not avoid paying homage to Assur by adopting their language. But in one place, the language of the Tribes of Israel was still heard—in the Sacred House. In daily sacrificial worship, the singing of the sons of Levi in the language of the ancestors was a bold act of defiance. Now, with the Sacred House in ruins, the tongue of the Hebrews was no longer heard in Judah or anywhere else. That was true until Eli the scribe and Azaria the priest, established their school.

Eli chose as teachers those priests whose writing skills were not in doubt and who could read from the sacred scrolls in Hebrew with confidence and ease. The plan called for the immediate creation of a school for the children of priests. From the age of three years and upward, these children would spend their days in school. They would start with alphabet and writing drills. From there, the students would advance to reading from the sacred scrolls themselves. Azaria was distressed to see the scrolls in the possession of mere children. He feared they might be damaged or destroyed as they passed from tiny hand to hand. The scrolls, after all, represented the heart and soul of the Judeans in exile.

Azaria was not wrong. Eli knew that his first responsibility was to begin the process of carefully copying each scroll. The priests had provided Eli with his own workroom. It was seven cubits by seven cubits. A window faced the rising sun and a makeshift scribal desk was placed next to the window for maximum light. Quills and ink were made available to him, along with expensive sheets of sheepskin parchment. Each morning, one of the priests would bring to Eli the sacred scroll he was currently copying, along with the parchment sheets, which bore his efforts. He was determined to avoid mistakes, so he worked very slowly, forming each letter in the style that his beloved teacher, Akkub son of Shallum, had taught him. He could only work during the time that light flooded into his window. He knew that if he worked in the presence of oil lamps, the parchment would become stained with soot. Each parchment sheet was capable of bearing forty lines of text carried in six columns, each column being about a handbreadth in width. At his current pace, Eli could only manage about one sheet per month. He was painfully aware that the whole process was taking too long. He needed help.

When the light was too poor for Eli to work, he would leave his room and walk the short dirt path to the school and observe the students and the teachers at their lessons. He was on a mission. Those who worked well with a stylus in sand or dirt were advanced to quill and ink on sheepskin. At each teaching level, Eli observed carefully for artistic talent. He was on the lookout for students to be chosen as apprentice scribes. There was no time to lose.

Chapter Nineteen

DATE: March 15, 2009

TIME: 11:15 a.m. Local Time

PLACE: Abu Ghosh On the Jerusalem—Tel Aviv Highway

The descent from Jerusalem was an adventure. Massive tour buses in riotous color schemes raced with each other down the steep inclines, oblivious to passenger cars and heavily laden trucks. Through the lightly tinted panoramic windows of one of the buses, it was possible to see the terrified faces of midwestern American tourists.

Keller's gaze fell to the steep water runoff channels just off the shoulder of the road. In more than a few of those channels were the burned out hulks of strange looking vehicles.

"Are those the tour buses that didn't make it around the curve."

"No, Gunny, those are remnants of the convoys destroyed in attempts to relieve the blockade of Jerusalem in 1948," Stone said. "They are monuments to the ones who died trying."

Abby insisted that she would drive them to the Babylonian Jewry Heritage Center in Or Yehudah, not as a way to remind Keller she outranked him, but because she wanted him to take in the scenery along the way.

"Here is the number for the museum. Call them and ask if we can see

Professor Malik around 2:30," Abby said, as she handed Keller a Post-it note.

"Do I have to do anything special as far as dialing the number?"

"No, just dial all the numbers in order. That will get you through. Israeli cell phones are more reliable than land lines."

There was something surreal about barreling down a multi-lane super highway through the hills of Judah at 80 Kilometers per hour making a cell phone call and at the same time, looking out at a landscape of stark power and beauty, virtually unchanged since Roman legions marched through these passes on their way from Caesarea to Jerusalem.

"Some things never change."

"How's that?"

"I am getting a recording in Hebrew. Even though I cannot speak a word, I know when an operator is telling me to press one for Hebrew and two for English." Keller pressed two.

"They're out to lunch until 2:00."

"That's what I figured. It will give us time to do some lunching on our own."

A sudden, bone-snapping jolt from the rear caused their heads to hit the head restraints. Stone and Keller heard their seatbelts lock before their bodies strained against the bands across their chests.

"What the hell was that?" Keller asked. He tried to lean forward to look into the passenger side mirror. A second jolt denied Stone the opportunity to respond. Her grip tightened on the wheel and she allowed herself a quick look in the rear view mirror.

"It's a huge dump truck."

"He's making another run. Brace yourself!" Keller put both of his arms on the dash and held them stiff. Under fire in Iraq, he often experienced a slowing of time and a sharpening of his senses. It's what kept him alive on more than one occasion. Now he focused on the visual information in the side mirror.

The driver was smiling and his dark eyes were very intense. He wore a dirty grey t-shirt with large dark sweat stains under his arms. The shirt bore a red crown design in the center. Keller could see that his muscles were well-defined. His smile revealed uneven tobacco stained teeth. His skin was dark brown. His hair was cut very close, almost a shaved head, but Keller could definitely see the shadow where the hair would be if he let it grow. The last detail Keller remembered was the smiling driver's size. He had the impression that he was short.

On the third crash contact, the dump truck did not strike the Subaru square across the rear bumper. That was not the driver's intent. He was now making every effort to spin the car out of control. Stone could not accelerate and get out of the truck's path, first, because they were heading down a steep incline and second, because there was a tour bus in the center lane and a tour bus directly in front of her. The guardrail was perilously close on the right.

The truck driver timed his move with near perfection. A scenic-overlook area was approaching, one of those turnouts that allow drivers to take in the spectacular scenery of the Judean hills. A low stone wall was all that stood between the sight seers and a sheer drop of nearly three hundred meters. The Subaru smashed into the low wall. The sedan's air bags deployed with a loud explosion and then deflated quickly. After being spun around, the rear of the car struck the wall. The rear axel hung out over the abyss. The car was caught up by its undercarriage. Very slowly it started to teeter with the front end rising and the rear end falling.

"Do not move a muscle!" Keller ordered. "We appear to be balanced on the edge—but only for the moment. The slightest weight shift might cause the car to flip over the edge."

"What next, Gunny?" Stone asked.

"Listen! I can hear sirens approaching. At least this did not happen in the middle of the night on a lonely road. Just sit tight."

The car scraped against the ground. It was still moving toward their doom.

"What was that?" Stone asked.

"The car is on the move again."

"No, I mean that music. Where is it coming from?"

"I think it's from the cell phone I rented along with the car. It's in the front pocket of my cargo pants."

"Don't even think about answering it! You'll get us both killed."

"I can reach it without shifting weight. Only Professor Carlson has this number. It might be important."

"Can't it wait until we are on firm ground?"

"All we can do is just sit here, anyway. I might as well answer it."

Keller slowly unsnapped the flap over the cargo pocket and slid the phone out.

"Keller, here!" He pushed the speakerphone button so Abby could listen.

"Keller, are you and Abby OK?"

"Well, ah—not exactly. But how do you know we are in trouble?"

"The scroll is gone!" Carlson ignored Keller's question.

"What do you mean, the scroll is gone?"

"I went downstairs for a coffee break, but I put the scroll in the safe and locked it. When I came back ten minutes later, the safe door was hanging wide open and the scroll was gone."

Carlson paused a moment. "I think Gadi took it."

"What makes you say that?"

"He and I are the only ones who have the combination to that safe."

"Listen, Professor, we are a little hung up at the moment," Stone said.

Keller winced at Abby's valiant effort to make light of their peril.

"A dump truck tried to run us off the highway at Abu Ghosh," Stone said. "We are barely balanced on a ledge."

"Where are the police?" Carlson asked.

"We can hear them on the way—at least we think we can hear them. We'll talk again as soon as we get out of this. Shalom, professor."

At that very moment, a shadow loomed in the driver's side window. It was a very attractive woman dressed in a powder blue shirt with dark blue epaulets. The embroidered emblem of a badge made it clear that she was a police officer. She had dyed blond hair cut short, which contrasted nicely with her dark eyes. The officer made a circular motion with her hand, signaling Abby to roll the window down.

In a rapid-fire stream of Hebrew, the officer gave Abby instructions. Immediately, she put the car in Neutral. There was a slight jolt when the gear shifted which caused involuntary gasps from Keller and Stone. The car held firm and then suddenly there was a forceful jolt from the front end. A tow cable had been attached to a canvas covered truck. A winch on the truck's front bumper was pulling the Subaru forward to solid ground. A double fatality on the Tel Aviv Jerusalem highway would not be the lead item on the evening news in Israel or anywhere else.

The rescued duo sat still and silent. Keller allowed himself a moment to look through the windshield. Maybe ten minutes had passed since the manic dump truck slammed into them. A sizeable crowd of onlookers surrounded the scenic lookout area. Five white Ford Fiestas with blue strobe lights flashing were blocking the westbound lanes of the highway. The tow operator removed the cable from the Subaru's undercarriage.

"Go ahead and move the car to the shoulder of the road behind that police car," Keller said.

Stone tried to relax her death grip on the steering wheel just long enough to key the ignition. Nothing happened. Her hands began to shake.

"Rabbi, it won't start because the car has a fuel cutoff switch. It should be in the trunk. I'll take care of it. Pop the trunk."

Keller had no trouble locating the fuel cutoff device and re-setting it. Stone started the car. Very slowly she moved the car onto the broad shoulder ahead of the scenic turnout.

"Wait here! I want to get a look at the undercarriage and see if there is any damage."

"I am not going anywhere," Stone said as she put the gearshift into Park. She laid her head back against the head restraint and closed her eyes.

Almost completely prone, Keller started at the rear end and proceeded to visually inspect the entire car.

"There's nothing leaking and nothing hanging down. We were lucky—sort of."

"Then let's get out of here!"

"Just sit tight. I think Officer Cohen or Shapiro or whatever her name is, will want a word with us."

Her name actually was Ramon, Gilat Ramon—Sergeant Gilat Ramon. When she learned that the car appeared to be in acceptable driving condition, she ordered Abby to follow her to the district police station. The station was about five kilometers from the accident sight and within view of the Jerusalem/Tel Aviv highway. The station was a stone fortress left over from the period of the British Mandate. Behind the station was a pleasant grove of orange trees. Beneath the shade of the trees were picnic tables. Sergeant Ramon invited Keller and Stone to sit at one of the tables.

An hour passed as Ramon conducted her interview. She had done her preparation well. She somehow managed to interview witnesses— drivers—at the scene. Now most of her questions were about the dump truck.

"Why do you think he was trying to push you off the road?"

"Maybe it was road-rage. Maybe he hates the American military."

"Are you in the military of the United States? And if you are, how would he know that?"

"I am a Gunnery Sergeant in the Marines Corps. This is Lt. J.G. Stone of the Navy. Maybe the guy followed us from Haifa where we came ashore." Keller reached for his military ID in his wallet and handed it over to Sgt. Ramon.

"That seems unlikely, but I will check it out. Lieutenant Stone, what do you do in the Navy?"

Abby responded in Hebrew. Whatever she said, the look on Sgt. Ramon's face was priceless. It was a combination smile and grimace and stare, all at once. Ramon cocked her head to one side and gave Abby a long, careful, visual once-over. Slowly her head started nodding. She conversed with Abby for another five minutes. Keller was feeling shut out.

"Lieutenant, what's going on?"

"I told her the truth—that I am a rabbi assigned to the Roosevelt as a military chaplain. She is having a little difficulty coping with the rabbi part. She has had virtually no contact with non-Orthodox rabbis, let alone female ones. Her family is originally from Morocco. She has broken with their traditions about the place of women in a man's world, but she says she is not ready for female rabbis."

Sergeant Ramon joined the conversation in softly accented English.

"Lieutenant Stone tells a fascinating story and I would love to continue a socially uplifting conversation over some espresso, but I need to know if the two of you can think of any reason why someone intended to kill you?'

"You don't believe it was road rage? Keller asked.

"All of the witnesses described the actions of the truck driver as deliberate and skillful. He intended to kill you both. Now why would he do that?"

"Sergeant, we have no idea. We are in Israel for a little rest and recreation."

"I just get the feeling that this driver wanted you dead for some specific reason, maybe one you are not even aware of. This interview is over. Thank you for your cooperation. I am filing a report with the Security Service. By law, any incident involving foreign military personnel must be reported to the *Shin Bet*. Lt. Stone, let me have your military ID card as well. You will get them right back. I need to make a copy of them for the file. Where are you staying while you are in Israel?"

"We are staying at the home of a friend in Jerusalem." Stone gave her the address and home phone number for the Carlsons. They shook hands and said their good-byes.

Stone and Keller were lost in thought and silence until they reached the outer edges of Tel Aviv.

"I need an espresso," Keller said flatly.

"Are you sure you need caffeine? Maybe a decaffe."

"OK, a decaffe it will be. "

"Where are we going now?"

"I know a bakery café on Dizengoff. No visit to Israel is complete without viewing the world from a street-side table on Dizengoff. We still have a good hour before Professor Malik will be back at the museum. We need to have a plan. What are we prepared to tell him? All we have is a copy of the scroll, not the scroll itself. He would be perfectly justified in thinking that we are a couple of kooks trying to peddle phony antiquities."

"Carlson gave me the distinct impression that he knows Malik personally. We will call Carlson and have him explain the situation directly to Malik. Right now, I can't think of anything else to do to convince him we have the goods."

Café Yuni was easier to find than a parking place. Stone settled for a very expensive parking lot or "car park" as the Israelis call it in the "King's English." The lot appeared to be the choice of the Audi and Mercedes drivers of Tel Aviv. Theodore Herzl would have been proud. The café was around the corner. From one end to the other, Dizengoff Street was a living, breathing organism. This was no Kibbutz. This was Paris and Venice and Rome and Amsterdam and London all rolled into one. Waves of stylishly dressed and overly made-up young women sauntered along the avenue. Young men in skin tight t-shirts and designer jeans appraised the passing scene from behind very dark and very expensive sunglasses. Mixed in with the walkers and the spectators were just enough soldiers in combat gear, carrying assault rifles and machine pistols, to remind the casual observer that this too was a front line in the war on terror.

The café bakery restored their energy with a Frisbee-sized glazed cinnamon disk that was delicious. The espresso gave a kick all its own. Stone put her hand on the cup and it shook so violently that the coffee was sloshing out the sides. Keller quickly placed his hand over Stone's and held it firmly. He looked directly into her eyes and saw tears forming in the corners.

"Lieutenant, you now know a small bit of what being in battle is like. The adrenaline crash after it's all over is a sign that it isn't all over. The sugar might help, but talking about it will help more."

"What is there to talk about? We both nearly got killed."

"Yes, but why did we become targets?"

"Isn't it obvious? There are people who do not want us to have the scroll."

"We really have no idea what the scroll represents. I mean, we know it contains a psalm, but why has it been protected and preserved for twenty-five hundred years?"

"I am more interested in why Sagal would risk everything to steal it. He has been a loyal member of the school staff for forty years. He will lose his position, his livelihood, his reputation—and for what? It does not make sense. Why is this scroll different from all other scrolls?"

"Maybe this scroll is more valuable."

"How would Sagal know that?"

"What if he saw something in the scroll that we missed."

"It's time to see what Professor Malik has to say."

Keller put down cash for the coffee and rolls and a generous tip. They returned to the parking lot and noticed that their Subaru was the least expensive car in the bunch. Following Stone's street-by-street directions, Keller drove to the Babylonian Jewry Heritage Center.

The building itself was a disappointment. It looked like the 1920's classic Bau Haus residence it once was. The original white exterior had accumulated sixty years of soot and grime. Most of it probably came from a coal-fired power plant in North Tel Aviv. Flower boxes filled with tulips flanked the main entrance. The flowers showed signs of great care. Keller tried the front door. It was unlocked. In security-obsessed Israel, this was almost shocking. They entered anyway. From down the hall they heard a shuffling of feet.

"*Rak rega*-Just a moment, I'm coming!"

Rounding a hall corner came a man dressed in Israeli Army fatigues that had almost as many wrinkles as his deeply tanned face. Slung across his shoulders was an Uzi machine gun. Keller's trained eye noticed it appeared to be unloaded. A magazine clip was taped to the short pistol grip. The man could have been anywhere from sixty to eighty years of age. He looked to be less than five and a half feet tall. He wore leather sandals on feet that had lots of mileage. His eyes were lively and black behind stainless-steel rimmed glasses that made him look like Harry Truman's Middle Eastern twin brother. He had a full head of salt and pepper hair cut to medium length. A black and white checkered knit *kipa* was perched on the back of his head, held in place by a bobby pin. Keller had to bite his tongue to keep from laughing out loud.

"*Mah yesh?* What's the matter? Never seen a seventy-nine year old watchman before?" Suddenly he adopted a martial arts stance—feet spread apart, arms in the ready position.

"Whoa, *Adoni*—take it easy there!" Stone put up her hands in front of her shoulders in a sign of openness.

"We're tourists. We just came to visit your museum. We intend no harm. We made an appointment to see Professor Malik. Is he in?"

"Are you here to see the museum or speak with the professor? Which is it? You are unusually bad liars. I expected better from the American military."

Keller and Stone exchanged looks. How did this guard know who they were? Then the answer became obvious. Keller extended his hand to the guard.

"It is an honor and pleasure to meet you Professor Malik. It would appear that Professor Carlson has informed you of our purpose in visiting you."

"You are pretty smart for a Marine. Yes, it is true. I'm Professor Malik. Please call me Shlomo. We do not waste a lot of time on formality here. Let's go into my office, shall we?"

His English was impeccable and carried a slight British accent—a gift from his years teaching Arabic at Oxford. Stone managed a Google search at Carlson's office while she was getting directions to the museum. She read the print out to Keller at the start of their ill-fated trip from Jerusalem to Tel Aviv.

"Malik was born in 1930, in Baghdad, Iraq," Stone said. "His parents were fairly well off by the standards of the day. They were distant cousins to the Sassoon family. He went to good schools, was sent to boarding school in England in 1947 then on to Oxford. In those days the British Empire wanted large numbers of diplomats and spies to study Arabic. Malik was a natural teacher.

When the State of Israel was born, the Jews of Iraq, especially in Baghdad, were in grave danger. Malik's parents were accused of being Israeli spies and hanged in a prison courtyard. His brothers and sisters managed to escape across the marshes of the lower Tigris and Euphrates rivers. They made their way into Iran and then ultimately into Israel. Malik was reunited with his family in Israel in 1952. He was sought out by Tel Aviv University and invited to become the Chairman of the Department of Semitic Languages. He was named Professor Emeritus in 1990 and since his retirement from academe, he had been dedicated to recovering all that was lost from the great Jewish community of Babylon."

Malik's current office was square, close to fifteen feet in length for each side. There were walls of shelves from floor to ceiling on each side and one wall of metal-framed windows. On every shelf were library storage boxes labeled in Hebrew. Presumably they contained materials on the Jews of "Babylon." A battered grey metal desk had its back to the window, and an old wooden armchair on wheels was behind the desk. The top of the desk was empty.

"Uh, Professor, who is going to guard the front door?" Stone inquired.

"Not to worry, no one ever comes here on a Monday. Besides, I can see the entrance from my desk. We will be safe. Carlson told me about your adventures on the highway. I understand your caution, but we will be OK here. Please, show me the copy of the scroll. I am anxious to see it."

Keller produced the single sheet scroll copy from his daypack. Malik pulled a magnifying glass from the top desk drawer and set about to examine the text. Keller noticed a tear fall from Malik's eye.

"Is anything wrong, Professor?"

"It does exist," Malik said in a hushed whisper. "I don't believe it. It does exist!"

"What exists?"

"The Ezra scroll."

Chapter Twenty

DATE: Fourth Day of the Fourth Month In the Tenth Year Since the Destruction of Jerusalem

TIME: Just Before Sunset

PLACE: The Scribal School of the Judeans On the Edge of Pumbedita In the Kingdom of Babylonia

The messenger from Samaria found Zadok in the supply storeroom of the school. The dust of extensive travel left a trail of dirt and dung with every step he took.

"I bring you this letter from Eli ben Achituv *hasofer*—the scribe."

Zadok's fingers trembled as he fumbled with the leather thong that held the scroll closed. Given the length of his journey, the messenger waited until he was well paid, but Zadok would not pay him until he was sure the letter was truly from his brother.

There was nothing routine about letters between Zadok and his beloved twin, Eli. The first letter came to Zadok nearly two years after the destruction of Jerusalem. A Judean priest found Zadok in the household of Ezekiel ben Buzi, just as Eli had predicted, when he handed the priest the letter scroll before his journey to Babylonia. It had been six months, an unusually long interval since Eli's last letter.

My dear brother:

Violence in our land is my reason for not writing to you sooner than this. A raiding party of sea peoples attacked Akko and held its inhabitants for ransom. My father-in-law bargained for the lives of the captured, paid the ransom, supervised their release and then sent the Sons of Z'vulun after the raiders. The Sea Peoples' reputation for skill in the art of sailing is over-rated. In half a day, the Sons of Z'vulun caught up with the raiders. The gold was returned. On orders from Talmon, the raiders were tied to the rails of their ship and holes were cut in the bottom of the boat. Talmon is a very strong governor. He is also a loving grandfather to our four children.

Have you become the father of two since your last letter? May you and Miryam continue to be blessed with strength and good fortune. My children all look like their mother—more Samaritan than Judean. That might not be such a bad thing in times of trouble.

Every time I think about your scribal school in Babylonia and the fact that I too am the leader of such a school in Samaria, I cannot help but ponder the special bonds of twins. The work on scroll copying goes slowly here. You at least had a number of professional scribes with you in exile. I was forced to start with nothing. I have been able to fully train only six competent scribes. The rest will serve our people well as literate teachers and leaders, but they lack the ability to make their writing absolutely uniform.

The Judean Priests in Samaria are continuing to object to my plan for all Judeans to achieve literacy. They see this as a danger and threat to their power and status. I have argued with them that as long as Judean leadership is unarmed and in exile, we will have to earn our redemption with the strength of our ideas and the word of our God. Hiding the word of God from the people will make their faith weaker not stronger.

There is so much more I have to say, but the cost of words grows with the distance they must travel. Our exile has given me purpose, but not wealth. In my next letter I will try and answer your questions about our worship of the God of Israel. I am working up the courage to explain it all to you.

May the God of our ancestors bless you and your household and all Israel with redemption and peace.

Eli.

Zadok read the letter scroll a second time. The light in the storeroom was weak but he had to savor each and every word before rolling the scroll back up into its leather cover. He came to the storeroom looking for an exercise scroll. Zadok was going to give the exercise scroll to his most vexing student. A short while ago, one of Zadok's instructors was at his wits end.

"Master. What shall we do with Bengeulah? We have never had a scribe write with his left hand. This is a big mistake," said Elisha.

"You must learn to be patient. Every student brings something different to our work. We just need to learn how to get the most out of him."

"Well, there is one advantage he has over the rest of us."

"What might that be?"

"When he writes he does not smear the letters as he goes like the rest of us."

"Perhaps we should all learn to write with the left hand."

"You are not serious, are you?"

"No, I'm not. But I have an exercise scroll that might help him to keep his letters from slanting in the wrong direction."

As Zadok continued unrolling and rolling scrolls on the storeroom shelf, he came across one that did not belong. The calligraphy was good, but clearly not the highest master scribe quality. The parchment was not bleached. In fact, it was dark, which made the act of reading from it very difficult. This was not a product of his school, he thought. This scroll might have been written before the destruction of Judah, but it was not one of the scrolls that he and Eli had saved from the burning Sacred House.

Over the past ten years he had memorized everything about those scrolls: their size, weight, color, thickness, length, calligraphy style, and content.

Each Judean scroll from the Sacred House told a story. Most of the stories Zadok already knew as a child. Relatives told stories of the Sons of Israel as evening entertainment. Each uncle or older cousin would embellish the stories as their enthusiasm and holding the attention of young listeners required. The first time Zadok read one of these stories from the scrolls was during the first month of the exile journey. He was actually disappointed. The scroll version was not as exciting as the storyteller's version he remembered from his childhood.

Now, as he began to read the unbleached scroll, he realized it was not a familiar story. In fact, he had never heard this story before—ever. With mounting excitement, in spite of the dim light, he read of the Eternal God of Israel instructing Moses to build a dwelling for God. It was to be a moveable sacred compound that would follow the Israelites wherever they sojourned. Artisans were to build it according to detailed descriptions presented by the Eternal to Moses. When the dwelling/*Mishkan* was completed, the actual presence of the Eternal God would come to reside within. Thereafter, it was to be the site of contact between the Eternal and Moses. Daily sacrifices and festival offerings would take place within the enclosed space. Sacred objects of bronze and gold, dedicated to the operation of the *Mishkan,* were also described in detail.

Straining to read the last words of the scroll in the disappearing twilight, Zadok was deeply moved by descriptions of the design of the sides of the huge compound. His childhood memories of the Sacred House in Jerusalem might have been distorted by his imagination, but as well as he could remember, the *Mishkan* enclosure was nearly as large as the area of the inner court of the Sacred House built by Solomon, son of David. His heart raced. He must show the scroll at once to his patron and mentor, Ezekiel the lead priest.

Ezekiel lived very well for an exile from Judea. His house was not large, but it was uphill and upwind. When it rained, water flowed away from the house. When the stench of rotting garbage was wafting through the neighborhood of exiles in Pumbedita, it usually wafted away from Ezekiel's house. The western wall of the house had no windows, so dust would not blow directly into the house from the desert. A small garden flanked the front entrance on the East side of the house. Ezekiel was bent over and pulling up weeds when Zadok ran through the gateless opening in the low mud-brick wall.

"Mar Ezekiel! Mar Ezekiel!" Zadok said. He stopped to catch his breath. "There is another scroll!"

"Zadok, take hold of yourself. Calm down. What are you talking about, another scroll?

"In the storeroom at the school, it is very old. I cannot understand why it was not noticed before. It must have gotten stuck between other scrolls or something."

"When did you find it?"

"I found it as the sun was just descending below the Temple of Marduk."

"Do you have the scroll with you?"

"Of course, my teacher. I would not let it out of my sight." His hand had reached inside of his tunic and drew out the end of the scroll for Ezekiel to see.

"Let's go into the house and take a look."

As Ezekiel entered, he began to light oil lamps along his way. He went into a room furnished with a table and two stools. The priest continued to light more oil lamps. He placed them all on a corner of the table. He then motioned silently for Zadok to hand him the scroll. He was very cautious in unrolling the parchment.

"It looks to be very old. We must be careful. It feels brittle. Now, let's see what you have found."

In what seemed like an eternity, the scroll was finally unrolled from end to end. Ezekiel read the scroll silently at first, and then continued out loud. Then he read it a second time, then a third time.

Zadok was puzzled but did not interrupt him. It was nearly the middle of the night when Ezekiel looked up at Zadok and said softly:

"This is just what our people need. This is a clear sign from the Eternal One, delivered by your hand. You just may have begun the redemption of Judah."

"How is that possible from a scroll, a good story at best, but still, just a story?"

"Zadok, our people are dying here! They lack hope and they lack faith in our eventual return to Judah. Not a day goes by when some old Judean family abandons the God of Abraham and Jacob and begins to make sacrifices to Tammuz, Ishtar or Marduk. They are forgetting who they are and what the Eternal One has promised."

"But surely you do not mean that the priests of the first watch have become idol worshippers?"

"The faithful ones gather in my home and in the homes of other Judean notables. They talk of return and renewal. They read a few lines from the rescued scrolls, tell a few stories of Judah and Jerusalem, heave deep and mournful sighs, and then return to the business of daily survival. But most of our people do nothing. When your generation dies, there will be no one left who actually remembers our land and sacred city."

Ezekiel then fell silent, closed his eyes and began breathing very slowly. He barely moved a muscle.

Zadok understood what Ezekiel was doing. He was seeking or having a vision from the Eternal God. On the road to exile, Zadok had watched as Ezekiel fell into this state. After a few moments he would start to speak, but not to anyone near him. It was as if he was speaking to God.

Since the first time Zadok had witnessed Ezekiel in this strange state, he tried to record Ezekiel's words as he was speaking. In most cases, his record was more babble than understandable. When the experience was over and Ezekiel opened his eyes, Zadok would read the words back to Ezekiel and the priest would explain and elaborate on their meaning.

Zadok grabbed a sheet of parchment, a quill and a bowl of ink from a wooden shelf in the corner. He took a seat opposite the priest.

In fits and starts, he was writing almost to the breaking of dawn. Over and over, Ezekiel repeated the same phrase: "You know, my God. You know, my God."

An hour after dawn, both of them were asleep at the table. A braying ass, responding to the lashing of its master, awakened them both. Ezekiel's eyes opened. They were bright and clear, as if he had completed a night of untroubled sleep. Zadok, on the other hand, was exhausted.

"Come, Zadok. Let's get some breakfast in the market."

"Are we not going to talk of what happened in the night?"

"What do you mean, what happened in the night? Rest easy! I am teasing you. Of course we will talk because we have much work to do. But first we must have food to give us strength. I think I now know what our God intends for us."

"Does it have something to do with the scroll?"

"It has everything to do with the scroll. But you must be patient. I need some olives, cheese and bread."

"The Eternal speaks to you and your first thought is food?"

"When the people hunger, they cannot hear the word of the Eternal."

"Did the Eternal tell you that?"

"No, I am telling you that. Go wash your face. It will wake you up."

There were only a few stalls open in the market of Pumbedita. It was not a market day, so farmers were not bringing food. Nevertheless, Ezekiel was able to locate the foods he sought and added to the purchases a clay flask of *sikaru*, a drink made from dates and honey. Zadok and the priest walked to the path that would lead them back to Ezekiel's house. A large tree with abundant shade marked the beginning of the path. They sat on the ground and ate.

"The Eternal has announced to me His intention to restore our people." Ezekiel tossed the leftover crumbs and scraps of their breakfast toward a mangy tan and white dog that had followed them from the market.

"But you have already had many such visions of our return."

"Yes, Zadok, but this was different. This vision was not about the rescue and return of Judah. The Eternal spoke to me about the whole house of Israel. The God of Israel has promised to reunite all of the sons of Israel, especially those who have disappeared."

"You know as well as I, they have not disappeared. Their great grandchildren walk among us. The Bavli point to them as an example of what they hope to accomplish with us. They want our talent and our treasure, but not our God. The Assyrians attempted to beat God out of Ephraim. They were successful. Not one of them attends our schools or meetings. They will have nothing to do with us."

"That's the point. They are cut off and they have no hope. This place is an empty wasteland for them and for us. The Eternal intends for Judah to give the whole house of Israel hope through us."

"And just how is that supposed to happen?"

"We are going to build a *mishkan* for the Eternal here in Bavel."

"The God of Abraham and Israel told you to build a sacred house in this land of idolaters?"

"Not a sacred house, a *mishkan* identical to the one described in the scroll: a moveable sanctuary."

"Last night, each time you read the scroll, I was astounded by the descriptions of the wealth of the former slaves of Egypt. I do not pretend to know where they amassed the wealth and the materials to make such a sacred place, but I do know that our people in Bavel have no storehouses of silver and gold."

"The God who brought our ancestors out of slavery will make our people's hearts willing to provide for the building of this sanctuary for the scattered remnants of Israel and Judah."

"And the Eternal said that?"

"Not in so many words. He made me to understand that a people without hope is like a corpse in the desert, doomed to disappear as dust. With something to live for, our people can be reborn, resurrected from the living death of exile. The building of this sanctuary will be the beginning of our return."

"Now you are sounding like a Persian priest, with your talk of resurrection."

"I only use the idea as a way of describing our situation. But, as your notes will show, that is what the Eternal showed to me: the dry bones of Israel in exile being resurrected to renewed life in Zion."

"How will this *mishkan* resurrect our people?"

"First, it will bring them together for a common purpose. Second, it will give us an opportunity to teach our people about the sacred scrolls and their content. They will come to understand that there will be an end to this exile. Third, it will provide us with a place to serve the Eternal, to worship our God in the midst of the Bavliim"

"Speaking of the Bavliim, how do you think they will respond to your plan?"

"Zadok, it is not my plan. It is the plan of the Eternal. The Bavliim have prohibited us from building a sacred house. We are not building a house. We are building a *mishkan*—a moveable sanctuary."

"Will the Bavliim understand the difference?"

"So long as our people follow their laws and make no attempt at rebellion, the Bavliim will respect our devotion to our God. That is what separates them from the Assyrians. The Bavliim honor the gods of their subjects. It's what gives them the strength to rule over a thousand distinct peoples. Allow a people their gods and they will not rebel. Take their gods from them and they will hate you forever. The Bavliim are masters at ruling an empire."

Ezekiel brushed crumbs from his tunic, yawned and stretched at the same time, then rose to his feet.

"Zadok, son of Achituv, it is time to call the Elders of Judah together. We have much work to do."

Chapter Twenty-One

DATE: March 15, 2009

TIME: 3:30 P.m. Local Time

PLACE: Café` Bavli, Or Yehudah, Israel

rofessor Malik struggled to keep himself from hyperventilating. Stone located a small refrigerator in the office and retrieved a bottle of water. After a few short sips, Malik waved his hands in a gesture that implied he was gaining control over his breathing.

"*B'seder*—I'm OK! I just did not expect to be so emotional. I need to hear from you every detail of your discovery. The details are important. They will help me to decide whether what you have discovered is the real article." His words came rapidly and with force.

"How about you tell us what the Ezra Scroll is, and then we'll tell you where I found it." Keller said.

"Gunny, what's wrong with you? Can't you see the man has suffered a shock? Give him some room to breathe. We came hear for information. If he needs to hear your story, then tell him."

"Not here, Sergeant. I need some good tea. I will introduce you to my favorite tea place in Or Yehudah." Malik was back in control. His normal voice had returned. His facial expression had softened.

Expecting an Israeli Starbucks for tea, Keller was disappointed by the austere hole-in-the-wall teashop at number 21 Bareket Street. A few grimy posters of Sri Lanka in better times graced the wall behind the counter. There were only two small tables for customers along the wall opposite the serving counter. One table was piled high with what looked to be accounting ledgers. The counter was a glass display case filled with glazed pottery jars. Each jar was carefully labeled in Hebrew, English, and some other language Keller could not identify. The labels, according to Professor Malik, revealed blends of tea.

Behind the counter was a beautiful woman in her late twenties with very dark brown skin and coal black eyes. She looked as if she belonged in one of the posters behind her. In Hebrew she asked the professor for his order. Malik pointed to a couple of the glass jars and then motioned for Stone and Keller to sit at the empty table. A few moments later, the woman brought over a teapot, three cups, a strainer, and a small container of milk. She strained and poured an initial cup for each of them and then returned to the counter.

"Thank you, Siri! I am sure it will be delicious."

Lowering his voice, Malik continued. "I wanted to come here to discuss our matter because I am never sure at the museum if someone isn't listening."

"Oh, Professor, you must be secure in your own museum," Stone said.

"In fact, I'm not so sure. There are several reasons why I do not feel my work is secure in the museum. First, the new Iraqi government has taken an interest in me because I have applied to the United Nations Cultural Legacy Commission for the immediate return of all artifacts that belonged to the Jewish community of Babylonia. Second, the Shiite Iraqi leadership believes that fellow Muslims are actually looting artifacts from our once glorious Iraqi Jewish community and smuggling them in to Israel. And third, the Iraqis are not pleased with my efforts to denounce their neglect of Jewish treasures in public. Did you happen to see my debut on Sixty Minutes last year?"

"Oh, gee—I was on patrol in Fallujah that day and my platoon forgot to set the TIVO. I missed it."

"You can find it on YouTube." Malik said without missing a beat.

"So, now tell me how you came to possess the Scroll."

For the next half hour, Keller detailed his accidental discovery of the *genizah* in the Al Jolan section of Fallujah.

"Do you think you could locate the house if you returned to the neighborhood?" Malik asked.

"Unless it was demolished after we left, I'm sure I could. You don't tend to forget those places where you might have died."

"We need to get back there and carefully document the location and then clear out the *genizah*."

"Other than more old books, what's the point?"

"Sergeant, would you describe the Dead Sea Scrolls as old books?"

"Of course not, but…"

"That *genizah* has been sealed up for nearly a thousand years. You may have literally stumbled upon what the Jews of Fallujah, my family, lovingly refer to as the Ezra Scroll. The Ezra Scroll may be the oldest document in there. I would say that the Ezra Scroll, if it is authentic, would be nearly five hundred years older than the Dead Sea Scrolls."

"Why would such a scroll from Ezra be preserved in Fallujah in the first place? Stone asked.

"Perhaps because Fallujah was the capital of Jewish life in Babylonia, in Ezra's day," Malik said.

"I never heard of any reference to Jewish life in Fallujah in all of my studies."

"Perhaps, Rabbi, because you knew Fallujah by another name, its Babylonian name: Pumbedita."

"Oh my God!"

"What's the big deal about that?" Keller asked.

"Fallujah or rather, Pumbedita was one of the great intellectual centers of Jewish life in the east for nearly a thousand years. Now a *genizah* hidden in Fallujah is beginning to make perfect sense. Professor Malik is right. We need to get to that storeroom.

"Did I mention the fact that the *genizah* is in a war zone? If I were crazy stupid I might go back there. Should you manage to convince me that a return to the *genizah* was essential, I might be able to work my way back there. But if you are along for the ride, the Iraqis might have a few questions about what an Israeli senior citizen is doing in an American patrol."

"You are not speaking to just any Israeli *'alte kocker.'*" Malik lowered his voice.

"Do not breathe a word to anyone. I am also Lieutenant Colonel Shlomo Malik of *Mossad*. For two years in the late 1950's I lived in the Sunni community of Bagdhad. Over the years I have made many visits to the land of my birth. I have kept up my contacts with a few current residents but they still do not know who I really am. My last trip to Baghdad was six weeks ago. You, Sergeant, will have more trouble getting around Iraq than I will. There—you know all of my secrets."

"Maybe, all but one. Tell us about the Ezra Scroll," Stone said.

"This may take a while. Have another cup of tea," Malik said.

Malik was anxious to talk. In a matter of minutes they returned to the table with fresh cups of tea and some dried figs.

"The community of Babylonian Jews now living in Israel believes that it is directly descended from the exiles of Judah. I am very much a part of that community. We are obsessed with genealogy. We believe that we can trace every true member of our community back to the days of the biblical Ezra and Nehemiah. Some can go even further back to families from Judah who were sent into exile in 586 BCE or even earlier. We pass the tradition of our genealogy from parent to child. It is as much a part of a bar mitzvah celebration as cake and wine. We learn to memorize lists of ancestors. We are the last names on the list. Most families have up to one hundred names on the list.

"My mother's side of the family traces its lineage back to Ezra the Scribe. I can see by the skepticism in your eyes that you think a lineage going back 2,500 years cannot be real."

"After 2,500 years we are all descended from Ezra." Stone said.

"For my family, such things are very real. The names are handed down in an oral tradition. My grandchildren learn these names like you would learn Mother Goose. They have a rhythm to them. When they are a part of your life for so long, they become easier and easier to recite. After the first five hundred years or so, the family gave out the names in a particular order. Once you master the eighteen names that are repeated, you only have to know how many times to recite the eighteen."

My list begins with Zadok ben Achituv Hasofer: Zadok the scribe, for short. He is the great-great-grandfather of Ezra the scribe."

"You're kidding right? You are descended from **the** Ezra?" Stone asked.

"Is that important?" Keller asked.

"Ezra is the biblical character who returns from exile and participates in the rebuilding of the Temple. If you have ever attended Rosh Hashana services, you may recall the traditional reading from the Book of Nehemiah. Chapter Eight describes Ezra reading from the Torah in front of the people from morning until noon. Then he tells everyone to have a good time," Stone said.

Malik raised his thick eyebrows. "You got most of it right, but God is in the details and you left a few of those out."

"The two biggest details you missed were: Ezra did not rebuild the Temple; and Ezra's reading of the Torah was the first time the people had ever heard anyone read from a document known as *sefer torat moshe*—the scroll of the Torah of Moses."

"If the people had never before heard words from a Torah of Moses, where did Ezra get the scroll?" Stone was now on full alert.

"Ezra wrote it." Malik said.

"You mean he copied it from some other document?"

"No, I mean he wrote it. He invented it. He edited it."

"Which did he do—write, invent, or edit?" Keller asked.

"He did all three. Without Ezra there would be no Torah."

"Moses didn't write it?"

"There may be parts of the Torah that reflect accurately what Moses said, but no—he did not write it."

"I have heard legends about the Ezra Scroll all my life. By the time I finished my doctoral degree I became convinced that if it was ever found, it would perhaps, lead to the discovery of the original Torah."

"Professor, what do you mean by 'original Torah,' the one Moses carried down from Sinai?" Stone asked.

"Please, Rabbi Stone, I'm not an idiot and neither are you. You are a graduate of an institution that has thrived on the Graf-Wellhausen hypothesis. You know as well as I do that the Torah is a composite work, drawing together different Israelite and Judean traditions. Moses did not write it, nor did the God of Israel.

"Since the Middle Ages, there have been rabbinic sages who have hinted and alluded to sections of the Torah that may not have been written or transcribed by Moses on Sinai. An obvious example of such a passage would be the last section of Deuteronomy. Did Moses write about his own death and burial? Some rabbis say that Moses took the words uttered by the Holy One down, as tears were streaming from his eyes. Others simply reasoned that Joshua wrote the description of Moses' death and burial and it became a part of Torah anyway. In the seventeenth century, Spinoza argued that the entire Hebrew Scriptures were a human product of interpretive history. The Jewish community of Amsterdam paid attention to his radical approach only long enough to excommunicate him.

"Two hundred years later, Julius Graf-Wellhausen a Protestant German Bible Scholar published a paper that divides the Torah into four distinct sources and an editor. His theory began with the unique ways in which the various names of God appear in the text. Sometimes God is referred to by the word *"Elohim,"* sometimes by the four-letter name of God which scholars pronounce *"Yahweh"*, and sometimes combining both of them together. Graf-Wellhausen believed that each such usage of a name for God represented a distinct and coherent tradition. If you could read only those sections where God is named *"Elohim,"* you would still be able follow a complete story line.

"The theory not only explains many difficulties in the Biblical text; it also provides a possible answer to the question of when the Torah was actually invented," Malik said.

"Invented—like in inventing the automobile or the computer? Keller asked.

"A better analogy you could not find. Automobiles and computers were invented from combinations of already existing technologies. The inventors bring these technologies together in a unique way and something new is the result. In the same way, the Torah is an invention. It brings together several distinct cultures and communities each with its own traditions and provides them with a unified story of their origins and relationships."

"So, when was Torah invented?" Keller asked.

"Between 586 and 540 BCE." Stone jumped in.

"Not bad for a Reform rabbi, Rabbi Stone." Stone bristled at the put down.

"But we may have to expand our time frame another ninety plus years. The important thing for us to remember is that when Ezra produces "a scroll of the Torah of Moses," and reads to the Judeans in front of the Water Gate on Rosh Hashana in the year 443 BCE, it is the first time that the text we know as the Torah has been presented as God's complete revelation to Israel."

"Ergo—the Torah was invented in Babylonia by the Judeans in exile, sometime between 586 and 443 BCE," Stone said. "Ezra was probably the inventor."

"I think you are on the trail of the truth. I believe that Ezra was not alone in his work, but he certainly played a major role in the invention of Torah."

"Back to the Ezra Scroll, Professor," Keller said.

"Yes, well—within my family, along with all of the names in the genealogical list, there is a tradition that describes Ezra's devotion to Torah. At the end of the story comes the following passage: *'Ezra the scribe sent a letter to Nehemiah, the Governor in Judah, informing him that the copy of the Scroll was finished. He also said he was bringing the copy with him to Jerusalem.'*

"Wouldn't this be the scroll he read on the New Year?" Keller asked.

"Many would agree with you but—" Malik shrugged.

"Wait a minute! The key word here is 'copy'. That could mean that there was some kind of 'original' Ezra was working from. What happened to the 'original'?" Stone asked.

"The ancients of my family believed that the original Torah never left Fallujah. Now, sad to say, I am one of those 'ancients.'"

"If this is such a great tradition in your family, why has the original Torah scroll not been discovered already? If community leaders used this *genizah* as a storehouse of sacred texts, it would seem logical that they would remember where their *genizah* is—wouldn't they?

"*Savlanut*—patience, Sergeant, patience. I am trying to get there. Each time I manage a visit to Fallujah, I try to locate that community *genizah*."

"It seems to me that all you would have to do is locate the community synagogue," Keller said.

"Easier said than done. The Iraqis have done a remarkably thorough job of erasing all traces of a Jewish past in Fallujah. And, there is no guarantee that the genizahh was ever in the synagogue. Nevertheless, on my last visit, at great risk to my Iraqi cover, I learned the possible reason why the *genizah* has been lost.

"At an outdoor coffee shop in Al Jolan I met a man who claimed he had been living in the Al Jolan neighborhood since he was born, eighty-two years ago. I asked him casually about whether there were any Jews living in the neighborhood when he was a kid. He said, with a great smile on his face, that the British bombed them to hell. Then he laughed. I wanted to kill him on the spot.

"After some extensive research, I figured out that the only time the British were directly involved in bombing Fallujah before 2003 was during the Second World War, in May of 1941. The old Iraqi was more right than he knew. In the midst of a struggle between Iraqi nationalists and their Nazi patrons on one side, and loyalist Iraqis and the British Air Force on the other side, Fallujah was attacked by a British bomber squadron trying to root out a rebel force that had established itself in the center of the town.

"With the help of some old friends in MI6, I was able to obtain an 'after action report' on the bombing. Buried deep in that report were a few terse words describing an explosion that destroyed a house with great loss of civilian life. It seems that all of the occupants of the house died in the basement."

Keller and Stone exchanged a glance. "That happens all the time in war. People take shelter from falling bombs in basements. So what's the point?" Keller said.

"Every victim in that basement was a respected leader of the Fallujah Jewish community. The British, seeking to deflect the blame for the civilian deaths, claimed that the rebels had herded the Jewish leaders into that basement for the purpose of liquidating them in order to please their Nazi advisors. But I have a different theory."

"And that is?" Stone asked.

"They were gathered at the sight of their *genizah*. They were all there to witness the storing and sealing up of their communal treasures. The Nazis had nothing directly to do with their deaths. They were part of the collateral damage of war, before we had such soothing euphemisms to wash away guilt. But that would also explain why no survivors from that time and community had any idea where the *genizah* was. The only ones who knew were dead.

"Sergeant, you may have fallen into the *genizah's* hiding place. You did not find the 'original' Torah. But the small scroll you did find may lead us to it. If it does, it would make the Dead Sea Scrolls pale by comparison."

"You can't be serious. You believe that an 'original copy' of the Torah in Ezra's own hand may exist in Fallujah, today, now?" Stone said.

"I realize that I was overcome with emotion back at the museum. This scroll brought back a lot of childhood memories. But let's not get ahead of ourselves. I am not even sure that this scroll is the Ezra Scroll. Before we get too excited, we should at least try and confirm that much. Let me see the copy of the leather scroll."

Malik examined the text one more time. It took him ten agonizing minutes before he was finished.

Stone and Keller sipped their tea and gazed out the front window of the shop. Traffic was light for the middle of the day.

"Well, well, well!" Malik mumbled to himself.

"What?" Keller asked.

"The scroll contains a hidden code."

The noise of the explosion was deafening. The tea-shop collapsed like a house of cards, along with three other small shops on the west side of the street. No one out on the street would be able to recall who had left the motorcycle with C4 loaded saddlebags. The Avihu family had just parked their Volvo wagon across the street from the teashop. They did notice the man walking quickly away from the cycle. He attracted their attention because of the unusual red crown in the center of his dirty grey t-shirt. The police would not know this. They would not be able to interview the Avihus. The family, all five of them, two adults and three children under seven years of age, were killed instantly. No terrorist group came forward to take credit for this latest blow to peace.

Chapter Twenty-Two

DATE: Tenth Day of the Ninth Month, In the Tenth Year Since
             the Destruction of Jerusalem

TIME: First Hour of the Third Watch

PLACE: The Scribal School of the Judeans On the Edge of
             Pumbedita In the Kingdom of Babylonia

Winter rains arrived early in lower Babylon. Grey skies made everything drab and colorless. Every pathway had been turned to yellow mud. The river was running fast and high. Mud brick houses required constant repair to prevent collapse. Zadok was on the top of a crudely made ladder placed against the side of his very ordinary house. Miryam was passing palm fronds up to him. Zadok was no craftsman.

"You should leave this work for a Bavli thatcher—they actually know what they're doing," Miryam said.

After going at this task for two hours in intermittent rain, Zadok started throwing fronds randomly on the roof and hoping for the best. "You're right," Zadok said. "My heart and mind are not in this work."

"Take your time, Zadok. You will leave holes and your sons will get wet. We cannot allow them to get sick with fever again. A dry house is a healthy house."

"What Bavli thatcher told you that one?"

"You know as well as I do that we cannot afford to have the roof re-thatched. I am just stating the obvious."

Miryam was the daughter of a Judean silversmith—a very talented silversmith. Part of her dowry was delicate silver filigree work. Extraordinary bracelets and necklaces, elaborate rings and earrings would make her appear, if she ever wore them in public, like Judean royalty and not the daughter of an artisan. Zadok had met her father Yonatan at one of the regular Sabbath meetings in the house of Ezekiel ben Buzi. In their initial conversation they discovered that both of their families were originally from Gezer. Zadok was too young when he left Gezer to remember any of the people there. Nevertheless, Yonatan took an interest in him. He admired Zadok's skills as a scribe and teacher. He would make someone a good husband; why not his eldest daughter Miryam?

Four years ago they had wed in Ezekiel's garden. They did not have the opportunity to fall in love. They grew in love. Each had a sense of humor despite exile and hardship. Each was an optimist in the face of a contradictory reality. Miryam was beautiful and modest, caring and kind. She knew how to get the most of the few coins Zadok earned as a scribe and teacher. They were better off than most Judeans in Babylon. They did not starve in winter.

In their four years of marriage, Miryam had already given birth to two healthy sons. The oldest was three years and six months and the youngest had just passed the one-year mark since his birth. The boys had their father's eyes and their mother's dark skin and straight black hair.

Bored with household duties and child rearing, Miryam insisted that Zadok teach her to read and write. The lessons almost ended their marriage. Zadok was not used to being interrupted by his students. He taught. They listened. When Zadok sought to instruct Miryam, he taught—she asked questions. She wanted to know every rule of grammar and spelling. She wanted to know the reason for everything. She accepted nothing on faith. Her desire to learn to read and write was also fed by her resentment of the way Judean customs treated women—bound to housework and childrearing. There had to be more to life than doing laundry and baking bread. Zadok could not say no to her. He loved her too much.

Miryam turned out to be a very adept pupil. In the course of a single year, she had exceeded the level of knowledge of Zadok's best third year students. She could prepare skins for parchment despite the considerable strength it took to stretch them on frames. She mastered the art of brewing ink, trimming feathers into quills, and shaping points on the end of the quills. Most of all, she had an artist's eye toward forming letters. She did not simply write letters; she drew them with uniform care. She was making herself into a true *soferet*/scribe. Her reading skills were equal to her scribal skills. After three years working with Zadok in her spare time, she had read all of the sacred scrolls preserved from the Sacred House and had even copied sections of them for practice.

"Hold the ladder steady. I'm coming down. Where are the boys?"

"Do you want me to hold the ladder or find the boys?"

"You know what I mean."

"They are at my father's work bench watching him melt silver or copper or something. It's always something with fire. He makes them think that he is a magician and they love it."

"I only hope that your father has enough sense to keep the boys from hurting themselves."

"Zadok, my father loves those boys almost as much as you do. Besides, being in his shed is not a bad thing on a cold and damp day.

"Zadok, there is something I must talk to you about."

"Of course, what is it?"

Before she could reveal her news, Yeshuah ben Yozadak, the priest of the second watch and Ezekiel's assistant, came riding up on a grey and black ass. Yeshuah was a heavy load even for this beast of burden. He was four cubits tall and four cubits wide. Zadok thought to himself that even without the offerings of a temple to feed them, none of the priests looked under-nourished. There was nothing elegant about a person sitting astride an ass. In most cases, the legs and feet of the rider were longer than the ass was tall. It gave the appearance that the rider was assisting the ass in walking. At any rate, the feet touched and scraped the ground.

"My lord scribe, I bring you a message from Ezekiel the High Priest," Yeshuah said. Zadok said nothing.

"My lord scribe, I bring you a message from Ezekiel the High Priest," Yeshuah said a second time.

"Since when did I become 'my lord scribe'—and when did Ezekiel become High Priest?" Zadok asked.

"The priestly council met last night and conferred the title upon him. In his acceptance of the office, he insisted to the council that you be made his official scribe. It is a great honor. He wishes to see you at once in order to confirm that you will accept."

Miryam bowed. "You must go and accept this great honor, my lord scribe. Please make sure you are back before sunset so you can finish thatching the roof, my lord scribe." She could restrain herself no longer and burst into fits of laughter.

"Please inform Mar Ezekiel, *Hacohein Hagadol*, that I shall be along presently, as soon as I can be sure that my roof is not leaking. His official scribe wants to make sure that when the meeting is over he will be returning to a dry house and a happy wife."

The dark of night was rapidly approaching. Yeshuah needled Zadok constantly about the need to set out immediately to Ezekiel's house. The roof was indeed thatched, finally. Zadok washed himself with the cold water from the basin next to the front door. He reached inside the door for a winter cloak. At last they were on the move. Yeshuah led the way. As Zadok approached Ezekiel's house, he saw a crowd gathered at the entrance to the small front garden.

"What's going on? Is something wrong? Is Mar Ezekiel not well?"

"You are a worrier, my lord Scribe. The community has gathered to congratulate our new High Priest." Yeshuah was wobbling from side to side on the long-suffering ass. Zadok walked about as fast as Yeshuah rode.

Zadok strode through the open gate with an air of purpose about him. Did he expect the people to stand aside and let him pass? They did just that. Other members of the community of Judean priests were standing at the front door. They too parted to allow Zadok to pass.

"Zadok, my scribe, my son! Thank you for coming so soon. I need you to get started."

"Get started doing what, Mar Ezekiel?"

"You will address the *Cohein Hagadol* with proper respect." The warning came from Yoel ben Azza. Zadok's only contact with ben Azza was to listen to him in community meetings complaining about the lax moral fiber of the younger generation. His wrinkled face was long and narrow. Zadok liked to imagine that his pinched personality was a result of having his face caught in a closing door.

"Yesterday, he was Mar Ezekiel. Today he is the *Cohein Hagadol*. It will take a while for me to get used to the idea, Mar Yoel." Zadok said with more than a hint of sarcasm.

"May the *Cohein Hagadol* speak for himself?" Ezekiel asked, a broad smile on his face.

"Of course, my lord." Yoel the weasel backed down immediately.

"Zadok, your discovery of the *Mishkan* scroll in the storeroom has changed everything. It is truly the hand of the God of our ancestors reaching out to us and showing us the path we must follow. Last night, when I read the scroll to the council of priests, their response was immediate and emphatic. They recognized that, like the Israelites in the Sinai, we too are in a wilderness—the wilderness of our exile. For the Israelites, their *Mishkan* was a visible sign of the presence of the God who set them free from bondage. It gave them hope and shored up their faith. The council, therefore, declared that we must build our own *Mishkan* in this wilderness of Bavel. We must do it now.

"They elected me *Cohein Hagadol* because it was necessary to have a unified leadership for this great task we have been called to perform. But I cannot do this work without you at my side. It was you who found the scroll. It has been you who has made it possible to maintain our scribal traditions. It is you I trust. I need you as the official scribe of the *Mishkan*. There will be so many tasks, records to keep, instructions to write and copy. You must accept this great honor. Our entire community needs your leadership, talent, and skill to insure our survival. We know that there will come a day when we shall return to Judah and Jerusalem. The *Mishkan* will hold us together and keep us ready for our redemption."

"My lord High Priest, did the God of Abraham come to you in a vision and declare this your duty?"

"The God of Abraham did not need to speak to me or give me visions for me to know what I must do. Ten years ago, he sent me a young boy who rescued the sacred scrolls of our people. That young boy taught us to cherish the words of Moses. That same person, now a man, found yet another sacred scroll that shows us the way to keep our nation together."

Zadok pressed on. "The *Mishkan* scroll describes the construction of the sanctuary in great detail. There are enormous quantities of gold and silver called for in the design. Where are we supposed to amass these materials? How can we pay for such a structure? Our community is practically starving. The Bavliim have already forbidden us the construction of our own Temple in exile. They have restricted the areas in which we might build our homes. What makes you think they will allow us to build this movable *Mishkan*? Do you actually intend to move it from place to place in this country of exile?" Zadok asked.

"Which question shall I answer first, Zadok? Let me begin at the beginning. When we set out on our exile, we asked everyone who was willing, to hide gold and silver and precious stones in their clothing. This gold and silver came from the Temple treasury. Many had to sell these objects to survive, but many still have them. If the hearts of Israel are willing, we shall have, like Moses, more materials than we can use.

"You also know as well as I do, that some of our fellow Judeans have prospered in this exile. We are going to insist that they participate in the building of the *Mishkan*. For them not to do so would be bad for their business.

"I have spoken with the *Pehcha* of our district. He has promised to take our request directly to the King. He has even offered to transport the *Mishkan* on his barges, for a fat fee of course. Did I mention that the *Mishkan* will be floating on the rivers of Bavel? I am sure Moses, in his own day, wished there were rivers in the desert."

Zadok was uneasy about the lack of a clear and unambiguous message from the God of Israel. But despite his doubts, Zadok was beginning to see the need for the *Mishkan*. Now he was working on his faith in the Judeans completing the task. About the only thing working in their favor was the fact that among the exiles were virtually all the artisans and craftsmen of Judah. There were more than enough skilled Judeans in Bavel to do the job—without help from the Bavliim. Some of the artisans had even served in the Sacred House in Jerusalem.

And so it was that Zadok, son of Achituv the Scribe, agreed to Ezekiel's urging and became on that day, the Chief Scribe of the Judeans in exile. The work on the *Mishkan* began on the same day.

With astonishing speed, the story of discovery of the scroll and the call to build a movable sanctuary for the God of Israel went out to every exile settlement. Judean artisans sought any excuse at all to travel to Pumbedita. They came with elaborate examples of their workmanship, hoping that the priests would commission them to provide their talents for the great, divinely inspired task.

As Ezekiel had foreseen, the work of building the *Mishkan* brought the Judeans in Bavel together and strengthened them. Each village and town where Judeans had been settled managed to send contributions of cloth, metal, thread and yarn. Of all the components to the *Mishkan*, none was more precious or difficult to obtain than wood. Bavel was not known for its forests. Date palms could not be worked in the same way that other woods could. The Lebanon with its cedar forests was out of reach financially and physically for the Judeans. If a piece of drift wood snagged on the shore of one of the great rivers, the race to extract it from the water took on the intensity of a rescue attempt for a drowning victim. When such wood was presented to the *Mishkan* builders, Zadok and his students would make a notation on an account scroll and carve a location number into the piece. It was the scarcity of lumber that conveyed to Ezekiel and the Judeans the simple fact that, try as they might, the *Mishkan* was not going to be an exact duplicate of the movable sanctuary described in the now-famous scroll.

Up and down the Euphrates there were small landings—clearings actually. These clearings were usually positioned on a level patch of ground just above the water's edge at the spring flood high water mark. The landings came in all sizes, based on the natural terrain. Within the first month of the *Mishkan* project, Ezekiel sought and received imperial permission to expand the landing closest to Pumbedita. Judeans gathered at all hours of the day between dawn and dusk to clear away the dense reeds and canes that grew along the river. Sometimes it would be only one worker. At other times, it felt as if every inhabitant of Pumbedita was engaged in the task.

The reeds and grass fell where they were cut. Heavy ox carts and wagons rolled back and forth to flatten the ground and dry it out at the same time. In a month, a square, flat area nearly 1000 cubits on each of four sides was the result. The trampled grass prevented the winter rains from turning the square into a quagmire. Here, Ezekiel directed the craftsmen to assemble the components of the *Mishkan*. He wanted the Judeans to be able to watch the progress of the work. He wanted them to pass by it on their daily journeys. He wanted Judeans in barges on the river to see it being built. He wanted no secrets from the Bavliim.

A master of diplomacy, Ezekiel managed to convince the authorities that the *Mishkan* would reflect the power and wisdom of the Bavliim in their dealings with foreign peoples living in their midst. As the first vertical wooden posts were set in place and tied to horizontal members, gold fittings were set upon them. These pieces, when viewed from the river, sparkled in the strong light before sunset, shooting off golden rays in all directions. Priest-Guards patrolled the site at all times, very much aware of the temptation to pilfer materials from the grand project. Because proper pieces of wood for the posts were very hard to come by, the work proceeded at a snail's pace.

The bulk of Zadok's labor was in recording the materials and supplies allotted to the craftsmen for the making of the elaborately woven fabric that formed the compound walls in between the posts. Then he would make a tally of craftwork completed. The weaving and sewing took place in individual homes. When a section was completed, it had to be brought before the priests for their approval and then before Zadok, who made a small mark in ink on one corner to insure that no one tried to receive payment for the same cloth twice. Once recorded and marked, the cloth was returned to the weaver for storage. At the appropriate time, all the pieces would be brought together and assembled. Metal objects were fabricated in villages throughout Bavel. When these were completed, they too would be presented to Ezekiel's priests and Zadok for recording.

From time to time, Zadok would be called to read from the *Mishkan* scroll to an assembly of craftsmen, gathered to hear and discuss the details of their work as described in the sacred text. He watched with fascination as they drew rough sketches in the dirt on the ground according to what they had heard from the scroll reading. The artists would argue over the interpretation of the text or the competing renditions on the floor, but eventually they would arrive at a consensus of the design or pattern called for. When that occurred, the best draftsman in the group would copy the accepted design several times onto sheets of papyrus. These were then taken to Ezekiel for his personal approval. If he approved, the copies were distributed among the artisans as their template for the work to be accomplished.

The *Mishkan* scroll was kept by Zadok in a leather pouch he wore across his chest. Although Ezekiel tried to persuade him to leave the scroll in a locked cabinet in the High Priest's house, Zadok insisted that valuable time would be saved if he were always able to refer to the text at a moment's notice.

Having the scroll with him at all times allowed Zadok to examine it carefully, in all kinds of light. Upon each examination, the scroll grew more precious to him. *Which of our forefathers held this scroll in his hands? How did it feel to write down the words of Moses?"* he thought.

He knew that the scroll was ancient. The parchment was so dark in color as to be nearly illegible in the light of an oil lamp. When he gazed at each letter, he noticed every detail: every arch and curve, every long and short line. *The scroll was not copied by a scribe,* he thought. There was little uniformity in the letters and spaces. It appeared to have been done very quickly. Zadok was able to make out the places where a knife or sharp edge was used to scrape off a letter and replace it with another. Each time he held the scroll, his hands would become black from contact.

In the last weeks before the consecration of the *Mishkan,* Zadok had more time on his hands. All of the interpretations and decisions had been made. He decided to examine the scroll one more time. He was curious about the staining of his hands from contact with the scroll. As he dragged his finger along the edge of the scroll, it came away with the dark stain. In that instant, he remembered his days as a scribe apprentice, watching with fascination as his teacher in the Sacred House was showing him how to clean a parchment scroll.

"Bread, Zadok—remember to use bread. You break it into a piece you can hold comfortably in your hand and then you start to rub the parchment, like this." To his amazement, the parchment was cleaned, but the letters were not damaged. Before his eyes, the text stood out sharply against the cleaner background.

Now, on the banks of the Euphrates, years and miles from Judah, Zadok obtained a piece of stale bread from a weaver who was resting in the shade of his mud-brick work hut. He was careful to try it out on an edge of the scroll. Immediately the scroll became brighter. Zadok next selected a section of writing near the beginning of the scroll. The same result: the scroll looked new. It looked too new. An ancient scroll would darken with age. Dirt could be removed, but the parchment would naturally darken and no amount of rubbing would restore it to its original color. The *Mishkan* scroll was anything but ancient.

Chapter Twenty-Three

DATE: March 17, 2009

TIME: 10:30 A.m. Local Time

PLACE: Trauma Unit, Souraski Medical Center Tel Aviv

The sound that brought Abby's mind back to consciousness was made by a sliding door slowly gliding in its track. She could not tell if it was opening or closing. The very next sound breaking through the thick sedative fog was a clicking and whooshing that came at very short intervals. A frightening realization pierced the fog.

Why am I on a respirator? She wondered. She tried moving her hands only to discover they were tied to the bed rails.

"Lieutenant, welcome back to the land of the living. You need to lie still for a few more minutes. A nurse and doctor are on their way. They will remove the breathing tube as soon as they are sure you will not need further assistance. For now, you need to force yourself to be calm."

Although she could not focus, the voice was familiar—even comforting. Very slowly, her vision cleared. It was Keller. She could see that she was in a hospital. Things looked relatively new and the usual beeping and monitors were state of the art. Back to gazing at Keller—he was injured.

Keller stood on the right side of the bed. He held her left hand. Stone focused on a four inch wide white bandage starting at the crown of Keller's head and continuing three inches down the left side. On him, a faded blue hospital gown was very un-Marine. Wherever Keller's skin was revealed from under the skimpy grown, small bruises and cuts were visible. Keller was holding on to a rolling IV pole. The plastic tubing snaked its way from his lower right arm to a flow monitor. It was controlling the drip rate of the colorless fluid suspended from the clear plastic bag at the top of the pole. Stone's face and eyes spoke to him. *What goes with the IV?*

"I think they will probably disconnect me from this IV as soon as they are sure I have taken in enough antibiotics. According to our Israeli docs, our biggest concern right now is infection. The debris from the blast was loaded with nasty, dirty stuff. If we didn't die from the explosion, we were supposed to die of lockjaw or something. Don't worry. The docs insist we are both going to make a full recovery.

"On another front—your boss is on his way up here to pay you a personal visit and wish you well. If you did not have that tube down your throat, I would caution you to say nothing about our current archeological adventure.

"While I'm on the subject, I received a message through the U.S. Embassy here in Tel Aviv. My commander in Fallujah, Major Subin, has given me a thirty-day R and R pass to recover from my injuries. He also informed me that I am to assist the Israeli investigators in their 'inquiries.' It all sounds so British, doesn't it?"

At that moment a doctor dressed in a crisp white lab coat over pale blue surgical scrubs opened the sliding door and entered Stone's room. He was followed immediately by an ICU nurse in blue scrubs. The doctor was in his mid-fifties. Random tufts of silver hair peeked out from under a bright yellow surgical scrubs cap. The nurse looked to be in her late thirties. Her smile was open and friendly.

"Shalom, Lietuenant Stone. I am Doctor Benyoshua. This is my assistant, Mrs. Rubinov. We are now going to remove the breathing tube and make you a whole lot more comfortable. I am going to ask your friend to step out while we do this. It will only take a moment." The doctor showed no trace of a Hebrew accent while speaking English, probably the result of so much medical education in English speaking countries. It definitely was not American. In fact, he sounded almost British. Reading Keller's mind, the doctor continued speaking as he was guiding him and his IV pole outside of the room.

"I am originally from Durban, South Africa. That is the source of my beautiful and flawless English," the doctor said. It was clear that he had dealt with American patients before.

Keller ran the wheels of the IV pole over the foot of a silver haired gentleman in a plain white shirt and khaki slacks, standing just outside Abby's room.

"Excuse me, I am so sor——-" Keller did his best to snap his right arm and hand in a properly formed Marine salute of a superior officer. The IV tube made that attempt futile.

"Stand easy, Gunny. There is no saluting here."

"Sorry, sir. I won't let it happen again, sir."

"How did you recognize me? I thought I was looking pretty ordinary."

"It's an old habit of mine, sir. I make sure that I get a chance to see photos of any commanding officer that has my life in his hands. Actually, I saw your photo in the chapel office, sir."

"How are you feeling, and how is Lt. Stone?"

"They are taking her off the respirator, as we speak, sir."

"That bad, huh?"

"No sir, I didn't mean to imply…"

"I'm just pulling your chain. I got a full report from the head of the ER this morning. If you don't mind, I would like to visit Lt. Stone for a couple of moments."

"Absolutely sir. I understand."

Captain Donald Shuster was an Annapolis grad with a distinguished flying record as a squadron commander in the first Gulf War. After the usual turn at mind-numbing Pentagon desk jobs, he was assigned as captain of the Theodore Roosevelt. The ship's crew was selected personally by him, including, Rabbi Lieutenant J.G. Stone.

The glass door slid open and Dr. Benyoshuah and Mrs. Rubinov came out, removing latex gloves and discarding them in a biohazard container next to the door. It seemed to Keller that Benyoshua and Shuster had met before. He directed his comments to the Captain without even waiting for a formal introduction.

"You can go in now. Her voice is going to be a little rough for a day or two. She took a pretty good hit on the head. The concussion will leave her with some significant headaches for a while. There is no permanent damage that we can see in the CAT scan. I would like to keep her here in a regular room for at least one more day. She and the Marine were very lucky. I've been doing trauma surgery for too many bomb victims over too many years. It could have been worse…a lot worse."

"Thank you, Doctor. I appreciate your candor."

"There is no HIPAA in Israel. I won't get sued. HIPAA would never work in Israel. Everyone knows everyone else's business anyway. The only confidence that will be kept is the fact that Keller and Stone are U.S. military personnel."

"How long before they can return to duty?"

Casting a glance in Keller's direction, Benyoshuah continued. "Keller is strong as an ox. The scars on his back and chest testify to a significant amount of combat time. I get the impression he does not like to be away from the action too long. Still, a couple of weeks off would not be a bad idea."

"Well, his own boss has given him a thirty day pass. That should do it. Again, Doctor, thank you for your great care."

"Glad to be of service."

Captain Shuster entered the room and walked to the bedside. He saw that Stone's eyes were closed. He hesitated for a moment.

"I'm not sleeping. What can I do for you? Are you going to interrogate me?"

"Lieutenant Stone, it's me—Captain Shuster."

"Sorry sir, I didn't recognize you." She made an attempt to sit upright but failed.

"Sir, might I ask you to find the controls for this bed and raise my head?"

"No problem." Shuster raised Stone to more of a sitting position.

"Thank you, sir."

"I know this is a dumb question, but how are you feeling?"

"Like shit, sir. Pardon my French."

"I have heard worse from the Baptist chaplain. Stone, I have to ask, what's going on?"

"I don't understand, sir."

"You failed to report back to the ship after shore leave. I sent out the bloodhounds to track you down. Twelve hours later, NCIS informed me that you and Keller were two of three survivors in a terrorist bomb attack that killed five Israelis in Tel Aviv.

Stone desperately tried to process her Captain's presentation of the terrible news. A bomb would explain the ER and Keller's wounds. But what did it all mean?

"Lieutenant, NCIS, The Israel National Police and two officers of the *Shin Bet* are sitting in the ER doctor's lounge. They are chomping at the bit for a chance to interrogate you and Keller. They were kind enough to inform me that this is the second attempt on your life—in a single day! So I'll repeat my question. What is going on? Chaplains are supposed to solve problems, not give me heartburn. Are you and Keller romantically involved?"

That question went right to the core of her confusion like a lightning bolt striking a tree.

"Whoa! Slow down, Captain, sir. I am not, I repeat, not romantically involved with Sergeant Keller. I am just helping him resolve a personal issue."

"Well, the issue must be very personal for a few other people, because they are trying to kill you."

For Stone, the dilemma was clear. How much could she reveal to her Captain, without telling the whole story. Her naval career was on the line here. With some difficulty, Stone tried to swallow and clear her sore throat.

"Sergeant Keller found an ancient Hebrew scroll in Fallujah," She said.

"The discovery might be of enormous importance to Jews and Jewish history. As you might imagine, the Iraqis have no interest in anything Jewish. They would simply bury and destroy Keller's discovery. When he learned that I was the closest to Iraq Navy rabbi-chaplain, he came to me asking for help. I agreed to introduce him to a professor of archeology, a teacher of mine. The professor referred us to a colleague of his in Tel Aviv, a Professor Malik. Oh my God! I forgot all about him! Is he OK? Is he alive?"

"Malik is very much alive. He is quite a character. He is in the waiting room anxious to see you. He walked away from the blast with only a temporary loss of hearing and a few scratches."

"Thank God!" Stone suddenly became aware of the thin ice she was walking on. If Captain Shuster had already met Malik, there was no telling what the professor might have told him. She could not lie to her commanding officer. At the same time, she could not tell him everything. Her biggest problem was in not knowing how much Shuster already knew.

"Lieutenant, according to the police and the Shin Bet, that bomb was meant for you and Keller. The media don't know that, but the Israelis are very sure."

"How can they be so sure? It's not like terror bombs never go off in Tel Aviv."

"One investigator put it this way: there is only one good thing that comes out of terror bombings. The bomber blows himself up in the process."

"So?"

"The bomber didn't blow himself up. He was not a suicide bomber. He got away.

"In any event, I cannot hang around to see how all of this will turn out. I have to get back to our ship. I am ordering you to be candid and forthright with the Israeli and NCIS investigators and tell them everything you know. Since your failure to report for duty after shore leave was not your fault, all disciplinary actions have been cancelled. You also have a thirty-day sick leave commencing now. Oh yes, and please, please call your mother. How she got my cell phone number I will never know."

"I am so sorry, sir. It will never happen again, sir. Please forgive me, sir. Thank you for the leave, sir."

"The pain-killers must have addled your brain. Chill out! I expect to see you back on board the Roosevelt thirty days from now, ready and fit for duty. Is that clear?"

"Aye Aye, sir!"

Shuster turned and left the room, leaving the sliding door open. Keller entered in his wake.

"Can we talk?" It was the worst Joan Rivers impersonation that Stone had ever heard, but it brought a smile to her face.

Keller assumed that the Israelis had bugged Stone's room in Intensive Care. That was the only possible explanation for why they were allowed to be together before they were interrogated. When he entered Stone's room, he held up a small piece of paper in the palm of his left hand. "The room is bugged," was the message.

Stone nodded.

Stone was moved to an ordinary patient room two floors above the ER and Intensive Care. A hospital lunch of chicken schnitzel, rice and asparagus was brought in. Stone finished picking at the meal and took a long drink of orange juice. Keller and Professor Malik were allowed to be present in Stone's room for the interview.

The questioning was a round-robin sort of affair. Two *Shin Bet* agents were joined by two NCIS investigators. The only surprise was the presence of two uniformed police officers from the national police service. Keller immediately recognized Sergeant Gilat Ramon from their adventure on the Jerusalem/Tel Aviv highway. Her colleague was introduced as Lt. Colonel Natan Lavi. All six of the interrogators seemed to work well together.

The interview took four hours. Ramon and Lavi were focusing in on the identity of the dump truck driver, which made no sense at all to Stone. Keller, on the other hand, was tuning into their train of thought.

"Wait a minute, you guys think that the truck driver and the bomber are one and the same person."

Shin Bet glanced at the police. The police looked at NCIS, and NCIS looked at *Shin Bet*.

"I'm right, aren't I? Come on, I got it, didn't I?"

"Nothing gets by you, Sergeant, does it?" Lt. Col. Lavi responded in a modulated baritone voice.

"Actually, there is no way we could make that theory stick. The best we could do would be to say that the two attacks might be connected, probably coming from the same source or organization. One eyewitness has come forward with a description of the presumed bomber that might link up with the truck driver. Both were wearing shirts with an unusual red crown logo."

"You know who these guys are, don't you?" Stone said.

"What we know so far is that this group is not, strictly speaking, a terror organization," Lavi said.

"They have never committed a violent act against anyone. They do not consider Israel or the Israeli government to be their enemy. They have no record of weapons trading or acquisition. Not one of their members or leaders has been arrested for anything more serious than trespassing. Since the end of the Six Day War in June of 1967, they have been an advocacy group for civil rights and recognition as a religious group under the Basic Laws of the State of Israel. From all that we know about this community, these two violent acts make no sense."

"So who are they?"

"They call themselves *Keter Shomron*," Lavi said.

Stone supplied the translation. "The Crown of Samaria—Oh my God, they're Samaritans!"

Chapter Twenty-Four

DATE: Second Day of the First Month, In the Thirteenth Year
Since The Destruction of Jerusalem

TIME: Last Hour of the Fifth Watch

PLACE: The Home of Ezekiel Ben Buzi High Priest of the Judeans
in Exile.

The excitement of completing the work of the *Mishkan* overwhelmed any misgivings Zadok had about the age of the scroll. He could be mistaken. There really was no way to establish the age of any parchment scroll. He needed to believe that the *Mishkan* scroll was God's word to the exiles. Doubt faded to the back of his mind.

The *Mishkan* in Bavel took two years and three months to complete. Zadok wondered at the abilities of the Israelites in the time of Moses. It seemed to him that the former slaves had managed the building of a moveable sanctuary in far less time. Perhaps the difference was the direct involvement of God. Ezekiel, the High Priest, set the consecration of the *Mishkan* for the New Moon observance for the first month, the month of Nisan. Zadok was working night and day to copy and send out official invitations to Judean leaders all over Bavel. This would mark the first time that Judeans would gather for a unified nationwide religious observance since the destruction of the Sacred House built by Solomon in Jerusalem. Bavli officials, without whose permission no gathering of Judeans would be tolerated, would be given places of honor and invited to observe the ceremony from a special viewing platform erected outside the sacred precinct but high enough to overlook the space. Building the platform cost a fortune in labor and materials, but Ezekiel was taking no chances to insure the continuing support of the Bavliim.

Ezekiel was very skilled at creating dramatic and powerful symbolic moments. If the *Mishkan* was to serve as a unifying symbol of Judean redemption, it was essential that all of the exiles in Bavel be present for the ceremony. They would all be summoned. The consecration celebration would involve all of the exiled families who served in the Sacred House in Jerusalem.

Two months before the consecration, Ezekiel assembled a large number of Sacred House musicians near the assembly site of the *Mishkan*. Ezekiel's network of informants made him aware that the Levite Guild of Sacred House musicians intended to challenge his authority as well as the *Mishkan* project itself. Thus, when he gathered them all together and requested new music for the ceremony, he already knew what their answer would be.

"My lord, High Priest. You know as well as we do that as long as the Sacred House is in ruins and Israel is in exile, we are not allowed to play our instruments for the worship of the God of our ancestors. That was our firm resolve as we stood by the waters of Bavel. We took an oath and the exiles bore witness to that oath. We will not sing, we will not play, until we are restored. By our sacred vow, we are bound."   Korach son of Izhar spoke for his fellow Levites.

"The Eternal has not ended our exile. You have gone too far without the hand of the God of Abraham to guide you."

Ezekiel answered in an unusually soft voice. "I am grateful for your reminder and respect your vows of loyalty to the Eternal one. Nevertheless, I ask you to take a good look around you. What do you see? They are your people. See what they have accomplished in this wasteland. Those loyal to the Eternal God have received an instruction from Him and built a sanctuary for Him to dwell among us in exile. Is not their very success in building a true sign that the Eternal is with them and favors this work?"

Korach seethed with rage and spoke with a clenched jaw. "We are sentenced to exile in this unholy land precisely because of kings and priests who so arrogantly assumed that they knew what was in the heart of God. Now, you and your fellow blasphemers follow their evil ways. My family and I will await the redemption of the God of our ancestors. We will have no part in this."

Korach and six of his sons and nephews stormed away from the *Mishkan*. Zadok started to go after them. Ezekiel grabbed his cloak and pulled him back.

"Zadok, I do not in any way agree with them, but this consecration cannot take place by force."

Ezekiel tilted his head toward the thirty or so Levites standing out of the sun beneath a goat hair canopy.

"We will work with the musicians who have remained. They understand how important this is for all of us."

Peace had been maintained before, during, and after the consecration. The people, by the thousands, celebrated their accomplishment. Ezekiel extolled the *Mishkan* as the divinely sanctioned vehicle of their atonement for sin, their redemption from exile, and their return to Judah. Twelve oxen had been sacrificed on an altar of rough-hewn stones, one for each tribe, including the ten vanished tribes of Israel. As he supervised the priests making the first offering, Ezekiel pronounced a prayer that captured the deep emotions of the day.

"Let this offering hasten the return of the entire house of Israel to its people and its land. May the One who placed us here in exile, redeem us in our own lifetime." He thanked the Bavli officials profusely for their gracious permission to build the sanctuary and pledged the loyalty of the Judeans to the king of Bavel.

Korach, who heard these words from a distance, spat on the ground in disgust. He and his sons turned away from the celebration and began their return journey to their home in exile, up the river Euphrates.

From that day forward, on the twenty-fourth day of each month, the *Mishkan* was packed up on a flat bottom barge and moved along the rivers of Bavel. Judean exiles gathered wherever it stopped and participated in its re-assembly. In most instances the assembly would be finished in time to celebrate the New Moon. At each river landing, Judeans would take an oath to abandon idolatry and worship exclusively the God of Abraham, Jacob, and Moses. Animal sacrifices would seal the oath. Music and singing would accompany the sacrifices.

In time, Judeans ceased their once forlorn attendance at the temples of Marduk and Ishtar. The Bavliim were actually relieved to see the Judeans developing a sense of self-respect. Before the *Mishkan* they were listless and without purpose. Now they moved with confidence and strength. Judeans were building a life for themselves in Bavel. Vineyards were planted, crops were sown, herds of sheep and goats were maintained. The people praised Ezekiel ben Buzi, their high priest. They saw great improvement in their daily lives and attributed it to the presence of the *Mishkan*.

On the third anniversary of the consecration of the *Mishkan*, Zadok was invited to a meeting of priests being held at Ezekiel's house. As Zadok crossed the threshold of the stately entrance and placed his hand on the doorpost for blessing, he reflected on how far both he and Ezekiel had come from the early days of exile. The home of the Judean High Priest had been completed the previous spring. It was the largest of all exile structures. The simple furniture was the work of Judean craftsmen and women. It was not ostentatious.

Zadok's own home had been enlarged and finally made watertight. Zadok's life as Chief Scribe to the High Priest was hectic and filled with nearly impossible demands. His one or rather two rays of sunshine were his boys who served the scribal schoolmaster as apprentice scribes. They reminded him of his own apprentice days in the Sacred House with his beloved brother, Eli. Each day he offered prayers of well being for Eli and his family in Samaria. He knew that Eli was doing the same for him in Bavel.

The meeting of priests was tedious and of little consequence, but, as always, Zadok made a complete record of the proceedings for Ezekiel. Almost too late he realized that he did not have enough papyrus to finish. Ezekiel told the priests to take a few moments for food and refreshment and they would resume as soon as Zadok retrieved enough papyrus for his assigned task.

"Zadok, I think there might be some papyrus in my old work room cabinet. You will find it on the middle shelf."

"I will be right back. Save me some figs."

As Zadok expected, there was no papyrus on the middle shelf or any other shelf in the cabinet. Ezekiel was notorious for misplacing anything of importance or use in his own home. Zadok noticed some parchment at the back of the cabinet. Parchment was expensive, but it would have to do. The parchment sheet on top of the pile was already prepared for writing and would save precious time. The meeting had gone on long enough. As he lifted the sheet and began to roll it into a scroll, he noticed familiar writing on the sheet beneath it. He was curious. As he brought the written sheet closer to the light of an oil lamp, he gasped. Although the text was Aramaic, the writing was identical to that of the *Mishkan* scroll. This was no sacred scrol. The content of the parchment sheet was a letter to a Bavli official. Zadok did not care about the message. He focused on the closing statement:

"I, Ezekiel ben Buzi now swear an oath before the god of my ancestors, that all I have written here is the truth."

Zadok was not mistaken. His first impression was correct. The letters of the words before the signature were identical to those in the *Mishkan* scroll. The meaning of his discovery was inescapable. His earlier suspicions began to make sense. Ezekiel, at the very least, was the copyist of the *Mishkan* scroll. If that were the extent of his involvement, Ezekiel could have explained away the "accidental" discovery of an original scroll. The priest had gone to a great deal of trouble to make the scroll appear as an ancient document. Zadok knew in his bones that Ezekiel was the author as well. The scribe suddenly became violently ill.

"Oh, Zadok, we were all so worried about you. You made a mess of Mar Ezekiel's writing room. You had such a fever. It broke only last night. You have been sleeping continuously for two whole days."

Through the haze of his mind Zadok knew that the voice was the voice of his wife, Miryam. He recognized her gentle touch as well. Questions—so many questions swirled as a whirlpool in the Euphrates. Had he been overwhelmed by a bad dream, a dream that gave life to his doubts? Did he actually see a scroll written by Ezekiel's hand? Was it indeed written by the same hand as the *Mishkan* scroll? Was the entire *Mishkan* project a huge lie put over on the exiles of Judah—playing on their desperate need for hope? Did Ezekiel realize that Zadok knew the *Mishkan* scroll was a forgery?

"Has Mar Ezekiel been here?

"Zadok, he has never left your side, except early this morning. There has been a tragedy—well, perhaps not a tragedy, but the news is bad, nonetheless. Ezekiel was called away because his own house caught on fire. It consumed everything he possessed."

"The sacred scrolls—what happened to them? Are they safe?"

"Zadok, you are still delirious. You know very well that the sacred scrolls are kept at the school for scribes. They are safe."

"I need to see Mar Ezekiel at once! Get me some fresh clothing, hurry!"

"Zadok, you are not strong enough to leave the bed."

"Just get me my clothes, please, Miryam. I must get to Mar Ezekiel's house now!"

By the time he arrived at what had once been the entrance gate to the High Priest's garden, Zadok was sweating and gasping for air. The stench of fire clogged the air immediately in front of the ruined house. The work of the fire was complete. It was obvious that nothing of value remained. Nothing.

"Zadok, what are you doing here? Go back to bed and preserve your strength."

"Mar Ezekiel, is it—gone?"

"Look around you, Zadok. Everything is gone, yes, including the *Mishkan* scroll."

Zadok stared into Ezekiel's eyes, searching for any indication of animosity or loss of trust. Did the High Priest realize what Zadok had come to know? His eyes revealed no emotion whatsoever. His voice was soft and steady, as usual. It was impossible for Zadok to detect any visible change in Ezekiel's demeanor toward him.

"It is fortunate that you and your students were able to make copies of the *Mishkan* scroll. We still have it as a precious possession among our people. The original was consumed in the fire but the *Mishkan* story still lives. My possessions are gone, but no lives were lost. For that we should give thanks, yes? Indeed we should."

Zadok's courage failed him. He could not bring himself to confront Ezekiel with his confirmed suspicions. The fire was no accident. Ezekiel knew exactly what Zadok had found. The letter with Ezekiel's signature must have been lying out on the writing table. The fire conveniently erased any possibility that Zadok could publicly accuse the High Priest of forgery and speaking that which God had not commanded.

The reality of what had transpired made Zadok dizzy. He grasped his walking staff for support. The whole *Mishkan* project was a clever invention—a lie of enormous proportions. Ezekiel used his imagination to create a myth about a moveable temple in the wilderness. His motives may have been honorable, but they were sustained by what amounted to blasphemy. The flames on the altar of the *Mishkan* consumed sacrifices meant to atone for the sins of the exiles. What could possibly atone for the very existence of the *Mishkan* in Bavel?

In the weeks that followed the fire, Zadok watched Ezekiel closely. He sought to detect any hostility or lack of trust directed toward him. There was no change. It did not take long before Zadok concluded that the lack of change in their relationship was itself a very ominous change. Why had Ezekiel not questioned him about the parchment letter on the table? There were no questions asked and there were no explanations offered. For Zadok, the lack of resolution was physically debilitating and spiritually draining.

On the twenty-fourth day of the sixth month, the month the Bavliim call Elul, the barges transporting the *Mishkan* arrived at the landing near Pumbedita. Ezekiel decided that the Judean community would join the Bavliim in a celebration of the reign of the king. In keeping with ancient Bavli tradition, each year, at the beginning of the seventh month, a massive national celebration would symbolically renew the reign of the king for another year. From the day they arrived in Bavel, Judean exiles were welcomed at the Temples of Ishtar and Marduk and invited to join in the celebration that featured much drinking of wine and beer and consumption of endless delicacies. Ezekiel was committed to weaning the Judeans away from the pagan temples by providing them celebrations of their own, centered around the *Mishkan*.

Coincident with the building of the *Mishkan*, Pumbedita was becoming the largest center of Judean life in Bavel. That was why Ezekiel had the

Mishkan return to the site of its consecration. The anticipated crowds would serve to impress the Bavli officials in attendance. Demonstrations of Judean loyalty to the Bavli king would be rewarded with a further lifting of the restrictions placed upon the exiles when they arrived. Most of those restrictions were annoying but not fatal. One prohibition did stand out.

Judeans were not permitted to bear arms. Ezekiel wanted to change that. He knew that ultimately, numbers of Judeans serving in the army of the Bavliim would reflect well on all of the Judeans. The Judeans' return to their homeland would be earned by the blood of their sons serving the king. When the time was ripe, Ezekiel would petition the king to allow the Judeans to return home as a proven, loyal military garrison protecting the empire's western flank.

Having managed the set-up of the *Mishkan* on six previous occasions, the Levites of the second watch, those responsible for this work, were becoming quite adept at its assembly. The pieces came together a little bit faster each month. With two days to go before the New Year of the King celebration, the *Mishkan* was standing and ready.

Their evening meal was substantial. Miryam had prepared a number of vegetable dishes and ground up beans with olive oil for dipping.

"Your feast was exceptional, as always," Zadok said.

"Stop with the false compliments. The only thing exceptional about the meal was the amount of it you consumed. What is it you desire, my husband?" Miryam walked to him and placed her arms around his waist

"You know me so well. I desire to lie down and take a nap."

"I have a better idea. You have been cooped up inside, bent over your desk for most of the day. Go take a walk. The evening air is cool and fresh. It will revive you."

"Revive me for what?"

Miryam just smiled.

"I think I will go and check on the *Mishkan*."

Third Watch Levites patrolled the outer wall in pairs. On their heads they wore white linen turbans. White robes with light blue sashes around their waists set them apart from the other Judeans who had the same idea as Zadok—an evening walk. Fifteen cubits from the walls and twenty cubits apart, a series of basin lamps circled the compound on the outside. Filled with olive oil and a large wick, the lamps cast dancing shadows on the *Mishkan*. Looking at the star filled sky, Zadok was impressed at how the *Mishkan* appeared to be an organic part of the landscape, as if it were meant to be there, on the banks of the river.

Perhaps the God of our ancestors truly did inspire Mar Ezekiel with a vision of this sacred place, he thought.

When the High Priest turned toward her front door, Miryam knew that something was terribly wrong.

"Mar Ezekiel, where is Zadok?"

"Miryam, I have some terrible…"

Before he could complete his sentence, Miryam had collapsed in a heap on the floor, just inside the doorway. Ezekiel lifted her into his arms and carried her to a bed in a connecting room. After a few moments, Miryam took one look at Ezekiel and tears and sobs overwhelmed her.

"What happened?" was all she could manage.

"A fisherman found his body snagged on a log at the edge of the river, about half a *parasang* from the landing where the *Mishkan* was assembled. Third watch Levites said they saw him walking around the outer portions of the *Mishkan*, but they neither saw nor heard anything. They brought his body to my house. He must have stumbled in the dark and fallen in. There is a deep wound to the left side of his head. The watchers have bathed him and prepared him. We must bury him tomorrow. Come with me to my house. You should be with him."

Suddenly, as if the implications of Ezekiel's story had just broken through the haze of grief, Miryam exclaimed, "My lord, High Priest, how could you allow yourself to be in contact with a corpse? You will be unable to perform your duties for a week."

"He is not a corpse, Miryam. He's like a son to me. I cannot stay away."

An hour later, Ezekiel had visitors. The shadows produced by the single, small oil lamp danced on the freshly plastered walls of Ezekiel's house. Evidence of the recent fire had all but disappeared. Ezekiel and the two Bavli rivermen sat around a small table in the center of the room that once had been his place of writing and study. A few more days work and repair and it would be worthy of his presence once again. Ezekiel seldom met with Bavliim—certainly not after sunset. But his business with them was urgent.

"Did you recover the letter?" Ezekiel said.

"We searched him thoroughly, before we placed him against the log. He had no letter on him. We are sure." A powerful stench came from the taller of the two hired killers. He reeked of dead fish and garlic. His robes looked as though they had never been washed—ever.

"How do you know he had a letter?" The smaller of the two smelled no better.

"I saw him writing one, yesterday. When he realized I was standing behind him, he hid it. I just know he was writing his brother in Samaria. I must get that letter back and destroy it. I must!"

"Even if he did write a letter, why are you so concerned? He writes his brother, so what? Getting a letter to Samaria is not something you can do easily. We will find it before it is delivered."

"Did he suffer?"

"No, my lord, one hard and swift blow was all it took. He was dead in an instant, as you commanded. Pay us and we will be gone."

Miryam leaned over the clay basin and looked into the water. She stared at her eyes, red with tears and swollen. She splashed water on her face then, grabbed the edge of her tunic and ripped it down the side.

"Blessed be the true Judge."

Her fingers ran along the edge of the tear, then reached inside the tunic to a pocket sewn into the front, but hidden from view. They withdrew the folded papyrus.

"You knew, my dear husband. You knew. Mar Ezekiel may kill you, but your brother shall have this letter. I swear this on oath to the God of our ancestors."

Chapter Twenty-Five

DATE: March17, 2009

TIME: 7:30 P.m. Local Time

PLACE: Souraski Medical Center Trauma Unit, Tel Aviv

"You have got to be kidding. Samaritans? Keller asked.

"In the States, we build hospitals in their honor. People who save lives are recognized with awards that bear their name. Here, they try to kill tourists by forcing them off the Jerusalem highway or throwing bombs at them. I don't get it."

"Sergeant, you're confused because of the story of the Good Samaritan from the New Testament." Professor Malik said "The so-called Good Samaritan is notable because, according to the prejudices of those times, there was no such thing as a 'good' Samaritan. Most ancient Judeans despised them. The feeling was mutual. The story gets noticed because someone, who by nature is supposed to hate Judeans, stops and provides assistance to a severely wounded Judean, whose own people—people who are supposed to have a high sense of morality—leave him dying in the middle of the road. It is not a bad lesson to learn. How we judge people should be based on their actions and not their race, religious affiliations or politics."

Sergeant Ramon lost patience. She sat on the window ledge, looking out at the lights of Tel Aviv, before getting up and looking at Stone and Keller.

"Maybe Rabbi Stone would like to incorporate that into her next sermon. Can we get back to the central problem? If we assume that our unknown killer or killers are Samaritans, why are they attacking you? They want you very dead very badly. What have you done to piss these people off? It has to have been something really big, because we have never had a problem with any of them before."

Stone, Keller, and Malik exchanged a look. Stone looked at Ramon, and then began to tell them the whole story, from the *genizah* in Fallujah to the teashop in Or Yehudah.

"I believe I paid close attention to your every word, Lieutenant. I still have no clue why anyone would want to kill you." NCIS Agent Nicholas Rigazzi said. "You do not possess the actual scroll, so, despite the fact that it may be priceless, they can't steal it from you. It feels as if their only intent was to prevent you from reading, understanding, or sharing it. Why would they try to prevent you from understanding an ancient scroll that, until a few days ago, did not exist?"

"As far as you are concerned, Agent Rigazzi, the scroll did not exist. But my family knew it existed. Half the Jews in Fallujah knew it existed," Malik explained.

"There are Jews in Fallujah?"

"There were before 1960. They told their children and grandchildren legends about its contents. It was an exceedingly dangerous time. The Jews of Iraq were struggling for survival. They could not celebrate Israel Independence. They made sure the community gave no offense to the government. The legend of the Ezra Scroll allowed them to feel pride at being Jews in the safety of their own homes. They believed that the Ezra Scroll, as we call it, will point the way to an original copy of the Torah—the Five Books of Moses."

"That still does not answer the question." Sergeant Ramon said.

"There must be something in that scroll that the Samaritans do not want revealed." The older *Shin Bet* agent spoke for the first time.

"And you are?" Keller asked in a hostile tone.

"Call me Rafi."

"Is that short for Rafael?" Stone asked.

"If that is what you wish," he said.

His English was careful with an accent of a *Sabra*. 'Rafi,' a mildly handsome forty-ish guy, was just under six feet tall, with the upper body of a person who worked out on a regular basis. He wore a white short-sleeved, open collar shirt, with epaulets. Khaki work pants and sandals without socks completed his "ordinary Israeli" look.

"And what shall we call your colleague?" Malik asked.

"Call me Omar." From his accent, Omar was a native Arabic speaker. He looked to be in his late thirties. He was no more that five feet eight inches tall and of slight build. He wore a faded navy blue polo shirt bloused out over olive green cargo pants. The bulge on his right hip was about the size of a nine millimeter Beretta or whatever the Israelis used as the semi-automatic pistol of choice. Omar's face was marked with deep craters on his cheeks, blemishes from a bad skin disease, skin grafts over a bad burn, or both. Overall, the effect was a bit menacing, probably helpful during an interrogation.

"Omar is a member of the Druse community."

"What's that?" Agent Rigazzi asked immediately.

"I'll explain it to you later," Stone replied. She was surprised when Omar stepped out of the shadows and took the lead in the conversation.

"We do not have any idea about what the *Shomronim* are trying to hide because we don't bother to cover them. To our office and our government they are an anachronism—a surviving remnant of a people forgotten by history and persecuted by everyone.

"The resurrection of dead individuals is the stuff that divides religious communities and starts holy wars. The existence of any Samaritans today is a miracle. Our second president, Yitzchak Ben Tzvi, was the catalyst for such a miracle. In 1948, Ben-Zvi founded The Institute for the Study of Oriental Jewish Communities in the Middle East. His scholarly works were devoted mainly to research on communities and sects of the land of Israel, its ancient populations, antiquities and traditions. The Samaritans of Holon became his pride and joy. When he first encountered them, a grand total of eighty-seven Samaritans lived in Holon. Ben Tzvi saw to it that the resources necessary to help the community grow would be supplied by the young State of Israel.

"Holon was the only enclave of Samaritans in the State of Israel. The original Samaritan community, numbering some 200 souls, was centered in and around Nablus on the West Bank, currently a part of the Palestinian Authority. From May of 1948 until June of 1967, hatred and war between Jews and Arabs kept the two Samaritan communities separated from each other.

"Six days of war in June of 1967 either saved the Samaritans from extinction or hastened it. It all depended on which community member or demographer you ask. With our occupation of the West Bank, including Nablus, the Samaritans were treated as a very special community. Unless there was a specific security situation that prevented it, the two Samaritan communities were able to travel freely back and forth across lines that still divide Arabs from Jews.

"Their quaint Biblical identity saved them from the constant scrutiny the Israelis directed towards Palestinian Arabs. They became an exhibit in a living museum. Christian pilgrims to the Holy Land wanted to physically touch the descendants of the 'Good Samaritan.' It was almost as good as touching Jesus. Jews flocked to the slopes of Mt. Gerizim on the eve of the Samaritan Passover to witness the slaughter and roasting of lambs, in accordance with the dictates of the Book of Exodus, instead of the Roman style *seder* meal designed by the rabbis. No Holy Land theme park could compare with the real live presence of Samaritans.

"The Samaritan twenty-somethings hated it. They wanted to determine their own course, not have it forced upon them—not by their ultra-conservative parents, not by the Israelis, and not by the Palestinians. A window of freedom opened when West Bank Samaritans were given unfettered access to Israel."

"How do you know all this stuff?" Keller asked.

"Omar is a cultural anthropologist who holds a PhD from Michigan State University," Rafi said. "He wrote his dissertation on the Samaritans."

"Michigan State, in East Lansing, is not exactly a hotbed of Near Eastern Studies."

"I know this is hard for a Wolverine to accept, but there are some things that are better at Michigan State than the University of Michigan."

Stone was not prepared for a Druse stranger making smart-ass remarks about her ties to Ann Arbor. It was clear that the security services had been studying her resume.

"Fifty years ago, the largest and possibly the only collection of ancient Samaritan documents in existence was donated to Michigan State. When I read about the collection, I had this crazy idea that somehow, in some way, my community was historically connected to the Samaritans. It did not take long for me to realize that this was not the case. In spite of that, I became fascinated with their story."

"Stop playing games with us," Keller said. "You knew the attacks were coming from someone connected with Samaritans. That's why it's such a 'coincidence' that you just happen to accompany Rafi. And, as for your not covering them, that's bullshit as well. You just happen to be an expert on a people, who according to your fable, do not matter in the larger scheme of things. I respect you guys and your reputation for toughness, tenacity, and preparation. What's going on—really?"

"As you wish, Sergeant Keller. I shall have to rely on your discretion. Nothing we say here gets out of this room," Rafi said.

"Omar, fill them in on our ancient friends' recent activities."

Omar nodded. "We started paying close attention to the *Shomronim*— the Samaritans, as you say, just after Hamas took control of Gaza," Omar began.

"Shall I call you Agent Omar or Professor Omar? Stone said. "What's Hamas have to do with Samaritans? Their strength has always been in Gaza."

"Patience, Rabbi, patience. I will get there. Hamas wants it all. They want to rule Gaza and the rest of Palestine for starters, on their way to destroying Israel and claiming all of it for an Islamic republic. Right now they are being heavily funded by Iran and supplied by Hezbollah. Their biggest weakness is the West Bank. The PA-Palestinian Authority has taken out its frustration over losing Gaza on the few Hamas supporters in Nablus, Ramallah, and Jenin. Our PA informants supply us with more intelligence than we need on Hamas, hoping that we will wipe them out.

"A year ago, Hamas approached a few young Samaritans living in Nablus. Playing on their sense of powerlessness, due to being tightly controlled and monitored by the PA, Hamas offered them a deal. If the Samaritans would support Hamas in its efforts to throw the PA out of the West Bank, then Hamas would guarantee the well being of the Samaritan community. The guarantee included designating tracts of land close to the sight of their ancient temple on Mt. Gerizim as Samaritan property, funding to build a new temple there, and land for housing and growing the community. Hamas even promised a one-time offer to resettle the Samaritans living in Israel back on the West Bank, at Hamas expense.

"These promises preyed directly on the Samaritan sense of impending doom. Most Samaritans on the West Bank believe that a Palestinian State has no room for them. The PA has always treated the Samaritans as spies for Israel. Should peace ever break out and include the international recognition of Palestine as a sovereign nation, the Samaritans expect the radicals in the PA to force their expulsion and confiscate what little property they still have. Even for a community that has lived on the edge of extinction for two thousand years, the young Samaritan radicals felt they had nothing left to lose. And so they formed *Keter Shomron,* the Crown of Samaria, to do Hamas' bidding."

"What possible help could *Keter Shomron* provide Hamas?" Professor Malik asked.

"There are two ways these young Samaritans can assist Hamas," Rafi said. "First, until we got wind of this whole deal, Samaritans went back and forth from Holon, in Israel to Nablus on the West Bank with little or no scrutiny from the Border Police or the PA. Although their Holon based cars have Israeli plates, they drive around the West Bank with a specially colored *kefiyeh* hanging from their rearview mirror. Both sides leave them pretty much alone. They have the potential to smuggle weapons parts, cell phones, electronic devices and messages for Hamas. Because we were blinded by their historic impotence, we never paid them any attention."

"And the second way?" Keller asked.

"Perceptions matter a great deal in the Middle East. They are often more important than truth. The second way the Samaritans could give aid and comfort to Hamas is to disrupt and challenge the Zionist version of history. Hamas has made serious efforts to de-legitimize Jewish claims to *Eretz Yisrael.* They enjoy playing with Western European guilt over the *Shoah.* In their propaganda, the Jews of Israel are no better than Nazis. Even mainstream Islam routinely asserts that the Jews distorted the text of the Bible. Hamas has never missed an opportunity to raise questions as to the accuracy of Biblical history, especially divine promises to Jews. For Hamas, the bottom line is that the Jews who settled here in the 19th and 20th centuries are imposters and are not the descendants of David and Solomon. Some go even further, with the aid and cover of European and American deconstructionist historians. They publish pseudo-scholarly articles in academic journals with impressive titles that claim there was no Biblical Israel at all, and that David and Solomon are figments of an over-active rabbinic imagination. Every doubt planted in the minds of ordinary Europeans make it easier to challenge Israel's favored political and economic status with the European Union."

Omar continued the analysis. Noises from the street below could not disrupt the quiet concentration of everyone in the room.

"The Samaritans are perfect foils for Hamas. They have always claimed that they are not Jews, that they were the true Israel, that only they are entitled to the land of Israel, because God put them on the land which the northern Kingdom of Israel forfeited through its disobedience and idolatry. They see themselves as the ever-faithful keepers of God's commandments. Whatever is contained in the Ezra Scroll, or whatever it may lead to, might be strong enough proof to deny the historical claims of the Samaritans and render them useless to Hamas."

"People are attacked and killed here over interpretations of history? Unbelievable!" Rigazzi shook his head.

"Welcome to our world, Rigazzi." Rafi could not resist.

"What a load of camel shit!"

All eyes turned toward Professor Malik.

"The analytical skills of the Shin Bet have deteriorated since I retired. What group of terrorist idiots wear logo imprinted t-shirts announcing their identity to surviving witnesses?" Malik asked.

Sergeant Ramon decided this line of speculation was getting ridiculous. "Maybe they don't wear t-shirts, but they have no problem phoning newspapers and taking credit for suicide bombing a crowded disco."

You have an answer, Professor?" Rafi asked.

"As much as it pains me to state the obvious, there is another player in this game. The killers may indeed be Samaritans. They may even believe that they are doing this as part of some deal with Hamas. But there is another hand being played by someone content to watch as the heat is applied to the *Shomronim*."

"So who is playing this hand?" Stone asked.

"I would put my money on the person or persons who are currently in possession of the scroll. And just so we are clear, I do not believe it to be the Samaritans. Nor is it Hamas. No, it must be someone who can actually read the scroll and decode it." Malik said.

"Now we're getting somewhere. That limits our field to how many?" Rigazzi said.

Let's see—every student of ancient Hebrew texts at the Hebrew University, Tel Aviv University, Bar Ilan University, Haifa University, Ben Gurion University, The American School for Oriental Research, The Pontifical Biblical Institute, Hebrew Union College School of Biblical Archeology, and the entire staff at the Shrine of the Book." Malik said.

"OK-OK! I get the picture," Rigazzi threw his hands up.

"Actually, we do have a clear starting place." Sergeant Ramon said.

"We need to go back to the theft of the scroll itself. At this point in our investigation, Gadi Sagal, an employee of the Hebrew Union College is the prime suspect. We need to start with him."

"Indeed, I agree. Gilat, get up to Jerusalem and see what is being done to locate Sagal and the scroll." Rafi said.

"Who died and left you in charge?" Keller asked.

"Actually, the Defense Minister put me in charge. Would you like his mobile number to confirm my orders?"

"You have his cell phone number?" Keller raised one eyebrow.

"On speed dial, Sergeant Keller. We are a small country. We are like a big rambunctious family. The Minister has taken a personal interest in this matter. Actually, your Secretary of the Navy phoned your Secretary of Defense who in turn phoned our Minister of Defense and asked what we were doing to protect American Naval personnel while on leave in Israel. We told him it was complicated. I was assigned to lead this band of warriors and uncomplicate things. Your safety is now my responsibility.

"You, Rabbi Stone, and Professor Malik will work on deciphering or decoding your copy of the Ezra Text. Any results you achieve you will share with me via text message. Here is my number. Put it into your phone, then destroy this card.

"Professor Malik, are you able to handle a couple of last minute house guests? They will be safer in your home than in a hotel."

"Colonel, it shall be my honor. My late wife, of blessed memory, always accused me of trying to turn our home into a *pensiyon*. That's like what you call a bed and breakfast in the States."

"Omar, please be so kind as to loan Sergeant Keller one of your Berettas. I will feel much better knowing that the United States Marines are providing security for our scholars. By the way, Sergeant, in case anyone asks, you did not get the weapon from us. You found it in a dumpster in Jaffa. It is, as you Americans say, clean. It cannot be traced to anyone. Need I remind you that it is only for your defense and nothing else?"

Keller nodded.

"Rabbi, as far as this hospital is concerned, you were never here. If for any reason you need the medical records of your stay, you will please contact Dr. Benyoshua directly."

"I understand," Stone said.

"Meanwhile, I would like to bring this group together again in twenty-four hours to see where we are in all of this. Let's meet at the Department Store at this time tomorrow. Agreed?"

"What's the Department Store?" Stone asked.

"I'll explain it to you later when we get settled at my home," Malik said.

"Agreed." They then responded, nearly in unison. The meeting broke up at 9:40 p.m.

Professor Malik's tan Opel was parked in the far corner of the parking lot restricted for patrons of the emergency room. The windshield was covered in hostile notices that the space was reserved. Malik tossed them into a nearby trashcan. Keller walked around the car with his hand on the body.

"Is something wrong Sergeant?"

"Not really, unless you count tiny bomb fragments embedded in the hood and doors. Your car was about as lucky as you were."

"Thank you for your concern. I would not have a car, had I not parked it around the corner from the tea shop."

"How far is the nearest *Hamashbir*?" Stone asked.

"What is *Hamashbir*?" Keller asked.

"It's a department store. When Rafi mentioned something about a Department Store, I decided I would not spend another minute in these borrowed scrubs. You should consider a shopping trip of your own."

"There is one less than five minutes from here and it's even on the way to my home."

"Are they open and do they have men's clothing?"

"Was Ezra a scribe?"

Stone emerged from the women's wear department dressing room sporting the Israeli version of the L.L. Bean look: dark khaki cargo pants, white cotton blouse, navy blue V-neck cotton sweater, Teva sandals. When she rode the escalator down to the main floor, she encountered Keller about to ride up. Malik started laughing. Customers passing by the three laughing shoppers did not think anything could be so funny. Stone and Keller were dressed in identical outfits, right down to the sandals.

"You have great taste, Lieutenant."

"So do you."

"I would say that it looks like the two of you were meant for each other," Malik said.

Stone raised her shopping bag as if she was about to clock him with it.

"I'm going back upstairs. They have a forest green sweater in the same brand. It will only take me a moment to exchange it."

Malik's home was the left side of a Bau Haus style duplex, a couple of blocks from the beach, on Jabotinsky Street in Tel Aviv. After years of neglect and indifference, this section of the first modern Jewish city established in Palestine was receiving a makeover by Israeli yuppies who discovered that these old buildings with the curved shapes and smooth lines were historically and practically very valuable. This particular duplex was coated in the soot of eighty plus years of Tel Aviv industrial smoke from the Reading Power Station in North Tel Aviv. The neighborhood had a nearly uniform gray patina to what might have been originally, smooth white stucco exteriors.

As they mounted the front steps, they could look directly into the window of a turret-shaped front room. The soft glow of a couple of lamps revealed a very colorful rug in an abstract pattern that left the impression that it was the aftermath of a Picasso and Chagall paint fight. The rug was centered on a cream-colored terrazzo floor. A flat, highly polished wooden desk stood against the front window, looking out on the street.

"Welcome to *beit* Malik! Let me show you around and get you settled, then we can have a bite to eat. You must be starving. I am not the cook my Aviva was. May her memory be for a blessing. But I can prepare frozen soup with the best of them."

"I'm not hungry," Stone said.

Ignoring her, Malik pointed out the location of the bathroom on the first floor and a guest room that was on the other side of the front room wall and also faced the street.

"I'm sorry, but the only light in here is provided by the reading lamps attached to the bed. Rabbi, you should be comfortable here."

"Stop worrying. If I can make do with a rack on an aircraft carrier, I can survive a down comforter. I'll be fine.

"Silly me, of course you can. Sergeant, you will have to make do on the leather couch next door. I will bring you some sheets and towels. Feel free to draw the front room curtains. We don't want our neighbors getting too excited. I will have some soup going in a moment."

Malik went into the kitchen. Stone and Keller dropped their backpacks in their respective sleeping spaces and joined the professor in the very modern kitchen. Everything in the kitchen appeared to be bright red: cabinets, refrigerator, and stove were all the color of a fire engine. True to his word, he was dumping a couple of frozen soup blocks into a pan of boiling water. In a few moments the fragrance of the soup filled the kitchen with an aroma of beef and barley and assorted vegetables. From a bread drawer Malik withdrew an uncut loaf of hard crust rye. He cut it into one inch thick slices and laid the pieces in a white plastic breadbasket. Out of the refrigerator came a tub of unsalted butter and a jar of Israeli strawberry preserves.

Malik disappeared for a moment, and then reappeared with two wine bottles in hand. "This is the finest vintage from the Golan. Are you permitted to drink from the produce of the occupied territories?"

"I could go for some Tennessee sour mash right now, but since that does not appear to be an option, the wine will more than compensate. I won't tell the State Department if you won't."

"And you, Rabbi Stone—may I pour you a glass?"

"By all means, Professor. It is just what I need on top of the painkillers from the hospital. I should be able to sleep like a baby."

Keller did not know what time it was when he became aware of a presence standing over him. Very slowly his right hand reached for the 9 mm. Beretta he had placed under the sheets at his side.

"You won't need the gun, Sergeant," Stone's voice was soft and calm.

"Are you OK? What's wrong?"

"I—I need a friend. Come with me." Stone extended her hand. Keller took it and stood up. Suddenly he was aware that he was standing, clothed only in his undershorts. He quickly withdrew his hand and grabbed at the sheets for some cover.

"That is so cute," Stone said. "I would very much appreciate it if you would join me in the guestroom. I don't want to sleep alone."

"Is that an order, ma'am?"

"Would it help if it was?"

"It wouldn't hurt."

"I don't want you to do anything you are not comfortable with."

"Truthfully, I've been imagining a moment like this since we met on the Roosevelt."

"Imagining or fantasizing?"

"Works for me either way. I just want to make sure that I'm not going to be drummed out of the corps for conduct unbecoming and sexual harassment."

"Let me put it this way, I need you by my side because I am having vivid flashbacks of the explosion. I can't get myself to close my eyes and I desperately want to sleep. There is no guarantee that you sharing my bed will lead to conduct unbecoming. I'm not saying it couldn't happen, but I'm not promising either.

"I am the one who can be brought up on charges of sexual harassment, not you. I am at your mercy, so to speak."

"I'm beginning to see the possibilities here."

"I thought you would."

"Is there any chance I could address you as Abby and you call me Ron? Verbal salutes kinda inhibit the likelihood of there being conduct unbecoming."

"You smooth talker you. Come to bed."

"Aye, Aye!"

Malik sat at the top of the stairs with his knees drawn up to his chin. A huge smile creased his weathered face.

That went well, he thought to himself.

BOOK TWO

In the first year of Cyrus king of Persia, in order to fulfill the word of YHWH by the mouth of Jeremiah, YHWH stirred up the spirit of Cyrus king of Persia, so that he sent a proclamation throughout all his kingdom, and also put it in writing, saying: "Thus says Cyrus king of Persia, 'YHWH, the God of heaven, has given me all the kingdoms of the earth and He has appointed me to build Him a house in Jerusalem, which is in Judah. Whoever there is among you of all His people, may his God be with him! Let him go up to Jerusalem which is in Judah and rebuild the house of YHWH, the God of Israel; He is the God who is in Jerusalem. Every survivor, at whatever place he may live, let the men of that place support him with silver and gold, with goods and cattle, together with a freewill offering for the house of God which is in Jerusalem.'" (Ezra 1:1-4)

Chapter Twenty-Six

DATE: Second Day of the Twelfth Month, In the Forty-Sixth Year
Since the Destruction of Jerusalem

TIME: First Hour of the Second Daylight Watch

PLACE: Pumbedita on the Eastern Bank of the Euphrates River

The survivors felt as if they were being mocked by the God of their
ancestors. Hilkiah and his grandmother, wife of Zadok the scribe,
were the only members of their immediate family still alive. Hilkiah stood
silently, watching his grandmother weep. At four years of age, he was too
young to actually comprehend what they had lost. He recalled his father's
stories of the deluge of Noah and wondered if the destruction caused by
the recent spring rains came close. He gripped Miryam's left hand tightly.
Everyone else was swept away. His father Shallum, his mother Aviva, and his
baby brother Chayim Ariel were among the hundreds from their community
who disappeared when a wall of water escaped the banks of the Euphrates
and smashed through Pumbedita.

An unusually warm spring sun brightly illuminated the devastation of
the flood. The once thriving community of Judeans in Pumbedita was all but
gone. The Bavliim had placed them at the edge of town in the flood plain. For
more than three decades the annual floods had been an annoyance. Judeans

coped as best they could, rebuilding with better materials and better designs each time. But not even fired brick could withstand the force of this year's flood. Was it any wonder that the *Mishkan* was also demolished and carried downstream? It would take three weeks before any flood survivors would speak openly about the place where they expected to encounter the God of their ancestors. The daily need for sacrifices and rites was overshadowed by the grim task of gathering family corpses and locating ground deemed high enough for proper burial. Some survivors suggested that the *Mishkan* was destroyed because God was angry with the Judeans for offering sacrifices outside of Jerusalem.

Only two days had passed since the floodwaters receded. The bodies of their dear ones were found together, tangled in the roots of a willow tree. At that terrible moment, Miryam demonstrated a determination that overcame the infirmity of her age. She was fierce in her efforts to give them a proper burial. With little Hilkiah picking up stones and broken mud bricks and tossing them out of the hole, they managed to finish digging the grave just before sunset. Miryam then climbed down three cubits into the six-cubit square, clay walled hole. Two adults and one very small child were wrapped in makeshift shrouds. She grasped the corpse of Shallum, her son, Hilkiah's father, and pushed it gently over the edge. The corpse made an awful sound when it landed on the floor of the grave. The vibrations coursed through her body and made her physically ill. She repeated the effort with Aviva and Chayim, placing Chayim on top of his mother, as if he lay in her arms.

"Blessed be God, the true Judge," Miryam whispered.

"Let's finish. Start pushing the soil into the grave."

"Won't the soil hurt them?"

"They cannot feel the soil, my precious grandson. It will be like a warm blanket for them."

"If they cannot feel the soil, how will they feel the warm blanket?"

"You are wise beyond your years. The truth is these bodies are only empty containers. What made them your father, your mother and little brother is not here. The breath of God that gives all things life has returned to God who gave it to them."

"Are they with God?"

"Yes."

The questions ended and the sad work continued. An hour later, with stones covering the mound of earth over the grave, Miryam stood back and gazed beyond the grave to the mud-brown waters of the Euphrates.

"Hilkiah, we are done here."

"Can we come back and visit them?"

"They are not here."

With tears welling up in her eyes, Miryam picked Hilkiah up into her arms and carried him down the hill and back to the random mounds of flood debris abandoned by the swollen river along the high water mark. When they arrived, well-dressed and well-fed Bavli officials were swarming all over the place. They came to see for themselves the devastation of the Judean community at the river's edge. Miryam assumed they would be concerned, not for the massive loss of life, but for the massive loss of tax revenue caused by the flood. At any event, they agreed that this flood was fifteen cubits higher than any flood of the Euphrates recorded in the annals of Babylon.

Beneath the watchful eyes of Bavli soldiers, and to the amusement of the tax collectors, there was shouting, grasping and shoving as the flood survivors scoured the riverbank for anything of value. Miryam did her own share of pushing and grabbing. She was determined to provide Hilkiah with some kind of shelter. Just before stars were visible in the night sky, she found the large square cloth panel. She was making her way down to the water's edge, when she stepped on the muddy cloth and nearly slid into the raging river. The cloth, nearly 4 by 6 cubits square, had been snagged on a scruffy looking willow. Miryam grasped at the cloth to stop her slide into the river. The cloth and the willow held firm.

By the ever-shifting light of a dozen cooking fires, Miryam stared at the woven cloth she had scavenged from the flood debris. It was as if she were seeing its design for the first time. In fact, she was. The caked mud obscured the pattern, but the outlines of the lions of Judah were still visible. How fitting. The wife and grandson of Zadok, the murdered scribe, would be sheltered under a panel from the now vanished *Mishkan*.

"Praised be the God of our ancestors, the protector of widows and orphans," she whispered.

Too bad Ezekiel died of a fever. He should have been swept away tangled up in his cursed Mishkan and dragged to the bottom of the river," she thought.

Fifteen years earlier, on the day of Shallum's thirteenth birthday, on the day her first born was bound to the observance of God's commandments, Miryam had made sure that he knew his father had been murdered at the command of the High Priest. Whenever Ezekiel's name was mentioned in her presence, she spat and uttered a simple curse, "May his name be erased from under the heavens."

Miryam taught Shallum to despise the *Mishkan* and all it stood for. It was a fraud. She made sure that he knew his father was murdered to keep him from exposing the priest's forgery. At the same time, Miryam made him swear an oath never to speak of his father's murder or the *Mishkan* scroll to anyone at anytime.

"How can he get away with these lies in the name of God? Shallum asked.

She remembered her answer back then. *This is a crime that God will not forgive. There will be a reckoning and accounting of this blasphemy. God's justice will occur in God's time, not ours.*

"Well, my beloved husband, I guess God's justice is swifter than I would have expected."

"*Savta*—Grandmother, who are you talking to?"

"I am talking to your grandfather."

"But he is dead. Can he hear you?"

"Yes, and so can your mother hear you. We speak with those we love who are not living, when we are troubled, unsure of what we should do next."

"Are you troubled, *Savta?*"

"I miss them all so much."

"I know what we should do next. We should make a tent and try to sleep." Was it simply childhood innocence that caused him to change the subject, or was he trying to offer comfort to his grief-stricken grandmother? Miryam was not sure, but she welcomed the opportunity to do something of practical value.

"Hilkiah, I hear the wisdom of your mother in your words. That is exactly what we shall do.

For the next hour they fumbled with the waterlogged cloth and random strands of rope, until they raised up a tent. Miryam then went on one last search of the flood debris for material that would serve as a covering for the damp ground beneath their tent. She rescued a tangled lump of cloth from under the broken remains of a wooden cabinet. The wood was so infused with water that Miryam could barely lift it up high enough to extract the soggy mess. She built a small fire in front of the tent and stretched the wet cloth over a makeshift drying frame. In a short while the cloth was dry. From the style of the weaving, the color, and the quality of the linen, Miryam believed that this garment was originally worn by a rather large Judean priest. After doubling it over and spreading it on the ground beneath the tent, she helped Hilkiah to find a spot close to the front opening of the tent and tucked him in, using her own cloak of goat's hair.

"Why does the sky glow orange, *Savta?*" Hilkiah caught Miryam by surprise. She looked up at the sky towards the east.

"It usually means there is a large fire burning."

"Will the fire burn us?"

"Of course not. The glow means the fire is far away from us. Now close your eyes, turn over, and let sleep overtake you."

Miryam knew, from the distance and direction of the glow and smoke that a large fire was burning in the area occupied by the government of the Bavliim. She was too physically and emotionally drained to care what the fire meant. She and her grandson had nothing more to lose.

Miryam and Hilkiah slept soundly. The hard ground that was their bed seemed to push the damp through the cloth spread beneath their tent. But they did not feel it, until they awoke with the first rays of sunlight. Both of them were stretching and groaning when the doddering old priest, Yeshuah ben Yozadak, arrived on an ass that looked older and more feeble than he did. At least age and loss of appetite had managed to reduce some of Yeshuah's weight. Nevertheless, he still looked well-fed. How was it possible for a priest to appear so well when the rest of the Judean community was expecting the destroying angel of death at any moment? Yeshuah stopped the animal beside the tent.

"How dare you steal from the *Mishkan* to make your tent. You shall be executed for desecration of God's dwelling."

"Who do you propose will carry out my sentence, old man? All of your brother priests perished in the flood. The only reason you survived is that you are too old to serve in the *Mishkan* and fat people float."

"Watch your words, old woman! Get on your feet, now!"

"I am too tired, old man. You will require the army of the Bavliim to get me on my feet."

"They are gone," Yeshuah said.

It took a moment for Miryam to make sense of Yeshuah's statement.

"What do you mean, 'gone'?"

"The Medes and Persians are now in charge. They took command of the Royal Palace last night. The elders and I have orders to assemble the leadership of our people for a meeting with the new rulers."

"So why come to me?"

"I am told by persons I trust, that in addition to your foul tongue, you are also a skilled scribe. Why your husband, may he find peaceful rest, taught you to be a scribe, I will never understand."

"Perhaps he taught me to be a scribe because exalted priests such as yourself were too stupid."

"One day your disrespect will cost you your life. I regret that today is not that day. In any event, a careful record must be made of the meeting between the Persians and our people. As much as it pains me to say so, it would appear that you are the only surviving scribe among our people."

"Is this an order or an invitation?"

"It is both. If you care for the future of your grandson, you will attend the meeting with your writing materials."

"I have no such materials. I have my grandson, the tent and the clothes on my back."

"Then we shall find some cold embers and some papyrus for you to use," Yeshuah said.

"The meeting will take place in two hours, down near the landing. Already there are rumors that the Emperor's barge will be docking there for this meeting."

"I will be there."

Miryam took Hilkiah to her cousin's tent and asked her to watch him while she attended the meeting. Then she walked down to the river, found a secluded spot, and bathed herself as best she could. She started with her clothes on, so she could wash them as well. Then she stripped and immersed totally and quickly in the waters, holding on to an overhanging tree branch so she would not be swept away. She prayed that the wet clothing would dry in the bright sunlight in the time that remained before the meeting.

The Judean reception party gathering at the landing was anything but impressive. Between thirty and forty flood survivors had been raised up to the rank of community leader. It was unclear to Miryam how this was accomplished. She was the only woman among them, which made her uncomfortable and anxious. They stared at her but did not openly challenge her presence. The staring stopped when Yeshuah arrived and handed her a writing box, a polished cedar wood container nearly three handbreadths in length by two handbreadths in width by a handbreadth in depth. The box had a compartment for papyrus sheets, a slanted top and a built in, copper lined inkwell. In that moment, the men at the landing understood Miryam's assigned task. Some muttered their disapproval, while others nodded their heads to no one in particular, as if to indicate that they almost admired her.

The newly appointed elders resumed gazing anxiously up river, trying to catch a glimpse of the royal barge. From the assorted smells being given off by the Judean assemblage, it was clear to Miryam that she was among the very few that took the time to bathe.

"I hope the Emperor has a strong stomach," she said.

Just then the royal barge appeared around a bend in the river. It was about fifty cubits long. Made of dark wood of a kind unfamiliar to Miryam, it seemed to gleam in the midday sun like a cut jewel in a mirrored setting. Five very strong oarsmen on each side of the barge stood with oars upraised at attention. A gigantic, very dark skinned helmsman manhandled the rudder back and forth and expertly guided the vessel to the rebuilt dock by the landing. Only one with much experience and great strength could have managed the docking without additional help.

In a sky blue robe that shimmered and reflected light from the sun, a tall stern looking man with shaved head and close cropped beard stepped onto the dock and strode purposefully toward the assembly of Judeans. Almost without thinking, they prostrated themselves on the muddy ground in a sign of submission and obedience to the new ruler.

An oarsman who came ashore ordered the assembly to rise.

"Rise, you fools! This is the local governor not the emperor. He now does speak with the authority of our great ruler, Cyrus of Persia."

"I must speak only with the leaders of the Judean community. The words of our great emperor are for them and them alone."

"Please, Most Exalted Governor, come into my tent." Yeshuah took it upon himself to represent the community. He extended his hand in the direction of a colorful tent situated on higher ground about three hundred cubits from the landing.

Miryam turned toward the designated tent and stared in disbelief. She struggled to control her compulsion to laugh. Yeshuah's tent was composed of sections of the covering that once lay over the so-called "holy of holies." It would appear that she was not the only Judean who had put to profane use that which had once been sacred and unapproachable.

Silver cups and pitchers of a watery beer were passed around by a few young boys, orphaned by the flood and in the care of Zera, the wife of Yeshuah. When Miryam learned of this act of compassion, her constant hostility toward him was softened. She allowed herself a slight smile to Yeshuah when he motioned for her to be seated at a small table placed in the front of the tent and behind the Persian governor. No one spoke. A few sipped the warm and slightly sweet beer. The governor rose to speak. When he did, everyone in the tent stood up.

"Be seated!" It was neither invitation nor command. He spoke Aramaic, the language of the Bavliim and also the language adopted by the Judeans.

"People of Judah, from the Province beyond the River: I am Memukan, as of now, the governor of this province of the greater empire of Persia. I speak with the authority and seal of His Majesty, Cyrus." He grasped a chord around his neck and held it out to show that a cylinder seal was attached to the chord.

"The catastrophic flood has wiped out almost all crops planted this winter for spring harvest. There will indeed be famine in this land. His Majesty seeks ways to insure that there will be enough food to get our land to the next planting and harvest. His Imperial Majesty, Cyrus of Media and Persia, has therefore decided to end your captivity. Your exile is at an end. You may return to the land of your ancestors."

All that could be heard was the sound of the river at full flood rushing by. The Judeans of Pumbedita were stunned into silence. They were prepared for higher taxes, forced work gangs made up of flood survivors, even orders to abandon what little property they had managed to scavenge. And then, like a flash flood washing down a *wadi*, the entire community erupted into a cascade of shouting, anguished voices expressing the terror and fear of the assembly.

"What does that mean?"

"What shall we use for food if we leave?"

"We're starving now."

"We are not fools. We shall die on the journey to save food stores for the mighty Persian army."

"This is their plan: Once we are far enough away from cities and towns they will massacre us along with our women and children. We will simply disappear."

"Judeans—enough!" It was not the voice of the governor. It was Yeshuah, shouting to be heard. The tent suddenly was filled with anxious silence.

"Have you no understanding at all? Are you all so blind as to be unable to see? This is not the decree of Cyrus. No! It is the fulfillment of the promise of our God, as prophesied by Ezekiel the High Priest, may peace be upon him.

This is what the Sovereign Eternal God says: I will take the Israelites out of the nations where they have gone. I will gather them from all around and bring them back into their own land.

"The redemption has begun!" Yeshuah shouted.

In an instant, the entire tent erupted.

Miryam put her stylus down on the writing box, turned away from the assembly, and then spat on the floor.

"May the name of the murderer priest be blotted out from under heaven."

Chapter Twenty-Seven

DATE: March 18, 2009

TIME: 9:00 A.M. Local Time

PLACE: Professor Malik's Home #24 Jabotinsky Street, Tel Aviv

The central principle of Marine training was repetition. If you trained to do an action enough times without the stress of battle, your body would perform properly under the worst of battlefield conditions. Given the length of his overseas deployment and the involuntary abstinence imposed by any sense of attraction to Iraqi women, Gunnery Sergeant Aaron Keller was quite pleased with his performance on the bed of battle—entangled combat with Lieutenant J.G. Abby Stone. There were a series of skirmishes, each ending in exhaustion and brief periods of sleep before the battle was joined once again.

Although he had no trouble wrapping his arms around Abby's beautiful body (who knew she was so well put together under all that amorphous clothing?) Aaron could not wrap his arms around the fact that he just had rough and tumble sweaty sex with his rabbi. He may have joked about his religious beliefs with friends and family, but lying in bed naked with Abby's head against his chest put him in a theological mood. *Is it a sin to fuck your rabbi? Is it a greater sin if you really, really enjoyed it? What does it mean if you get another hard-on while having these spiritual thoughts?*

Abby was not sleeping in Aaron's arms. She was, as Fagin put it in the musical, *OLIVER*, "reviewing the situation." Unlike Aaron, her first thought was directed toward how good she felt—not physically but emotionally. She was still feeling the after-effects of the bomb blast. What Aaron must have interpreted as moans of pleasure and orgasm were actually cries of pain each time a blast induced bruise was touched or a sore muscle was stretched. She ached throughout her entire body.

Emotionally, she felt no guilt, no second thoughts about having great sex with a grunt Marine. There were times on board the Roosevelt when she believed she understood the celibacy of Roman Catholic nuns. It was indeed, a choice. Shipboard romances are not confined to cruise ships. The sexually integrated Navy was a flotilla of casual sex. Dozens of officers including fighter jocks and wardroom adjutants found her very attractive. In ways subtle or crude, they let her know they would be honored to fuck her in a shaft alley or the anchor windless anytime she felt the urge. And she did have urges. She simply made a decision that casual sex was not for her. Fucking would be her decision on her terms with the man she chose. Aaron was even Jewish. Her mother would be pleased. Her father would rather not know about any of this.

"Why did you become a rabbi?"

"Why did you assume I was awake?

"Don't dodge the question."

"I became a rabbi because I knew that it would shock the hell out of my parents."

"Really? That's it?"

"It's a long story. I'm not sure you want to hear all the gory details."

"Try me."

"Becoming a rabbi was just something that felt right for me. I had no idea how my parents would react. The day my letter of acceptance arrived from Hebrew Union College-Jewish Institute of Religion, my mother was polite and wary and my father was in a state of disbelief. The whole becoming-a-rabbi thing came as a complete and total surprise.

"Once they started to look around and pay attention to the women rabbis of the Chicago area, they realized that women rabbis were doing OK. They all had families. Even the lesbian rabbis had families. They were respected in their communities and made a decent living. Most were married. My parents concluded that it was possible I might even find a nice Jewish husband—maybe a doctor or a lawyer."

"Does that mean that a Marine Gunnery Sergeant was not on their wish list?"

"Don't flatter yourself."

"Once you learned they were OK with you being a rabbi, then what?"

"Their acceptance of my career choice did not result in joy and happiness for me like I expected. All of a sudden I felt caged, boxed into a crate of conventionality. I could not stand the idea of being perceived as a member of the establishment, even the Jewish establishment."

"You don't strike me as anything but 'establishment.'"

"I don't look it now, but I spent my high school years in a perpetual state of rebellion against everything."

"This is not making sense. I can't be in bed with a rebel. I represent the U.S. of A."

"You have no idea. In Ann Arbor, I tried every destructive behavior short of dropping out or doing poorly in class. That would have gone completely against my grain. I even enjoyed freshman English."

"So what happened when the hippy arrived at the seminary?"

"I managed to rebel in non-rabbi-like ways. I pursued archeology as a major component of my career path. My parents got that message quickly. They understood. There would be no congregational life for their daughter. I was not going conform to their model rabbi scenario. I was not going to be a hatcher, match-er and dispatcher, as the saying went."

"Did they give up on you?"

"They tried very hard to convince me that it would be possible to serve a congregation from Rosh Hashana to Shavuot (roughly September to June), and then spend my summers on archeological digs in Israel."

"How did that work out?"

"I actually gave it my best shot. Their plan for me seemed reasonable. It almost worked. The only problem was actually finding a congregation that would buy in to my proposed schedule. With every job interview it became crystal clear to me that the rabbinic selection committees were very impressed with my talent, compassion, intelligence, and commitment."

"Did they have any problems with your ego?" Aaron asked.

"I'll pretend I didn't hear that remark," Abby said. "It was equally clear that those congregations believed they could remake me into their image of a rabbi who stayed and worked during the summer."

"What then?"

"For the first time in my life, I gave up. At the very end of interview season, on a Friday morning in May when the congregations were supposed to announce their choices, I walked into the Dean's office and announced that I was withdrawing from the process."

"Just like that, the Dean accepted your decision?"

"Yes, but."

"Yes, but what?"

"The Dean accepted my decision and then invited me for a cup of latte at the neighborhood Starbucks. That cup of coffee and Karla Schlesinger's gesture behind it saved me."

"Who's Karla Schlesinger?"

"She's the Dean."

"Women can become Deans in a rabbinical school?"

"You may have survived your tour so far in Fallujah, but you had better get with the program or you will not survive this day with me."

"Please proceed, Rabbi."

"I really did not know her all that well. Schlesinger was ten years older than I. She began our conversation by informing me that she was currently a reserve chaplain in the United States Navy. She chose the chaplaincy, she explained, as a way of buying time."

"Sounds a lot like you."

"She was. Schlesinger thought the Navy would organize her life and make all of the mundane daily decisions. It did all of that and more, but what was most valuable was that the Navy taught her how to separate the trivial from the important. World peace was important. Getting the right car to drive or a bigger house with larger payments were not.

"The latte` conversation changed my life. Rabbi Schlesinger was a woman who exuded self-confidence. She was smart, strong, independent, and capable—all the things I wanted to be. She painted a realistic portrait of Navy life for a woman rabbi. The negatives did not scare me. It was just the challenge I had been searching for."

"And the rest is history," Aaron said.

A soft tapping on the bedroom door ended the dialogue. "Uh, would either of you kids like some breakfast? We can have coffee and Danish here, or we can go out for something more substantial," Malik said, doing his best to make the whole situation seem perfectly normal.

"Thanks, Professor. I think we had better stay indoors. We wouldn't want to press our luck with Samaritan bombers. Give us a few moments."

Before Aaron was finished speaking, Abby grabbed the top sheet and wrapped it around herself, leaving Aaron exposed and cold. She turned her back on him and started to dress in the corner by the chair that held her clothing. His clothing was in a heap, two steps from the edge of the bed.

"You should use the head first. I can wait."

"Why thank you, Gunnery Sergeant Suh," Abby said in the dialect of a southern belle of her own imagination. "That's mighty Christian of you!"

"We have lots to do. Move yo *tuches*," Aaron's Yiddish pronunciation was actually worse than Abby's southern belle.

"I'm sorry, but living alone as I do, I do not own a proper coffee maker. We'll have to make do with these filter contraptions."

"Actually, Professor, I prefer them to the hazards of measuring out coffee." Abby began to pour boiling water into a cone-like device that stood atop her coffee mug. A pre-measured packet of coffee wrapped in its own filter was at the bottom of the cone. She had already poured a cup for Aaron.

"Hey, this is not bad. What is this called in Hebrew?"

"*Ca-fee fil-ter*," Malik said.

"It's tough to know when Hebrew is Hebrew and when Hebrew is Hinglish." Aaron moved to the kitchen table and sat down.

"You'll get the hang of it—in a few years." Malik grinned, and then turned serious. "Before the bomb went off at the tea shop, I said the scroll contained a hidden code. We need to go to my office. I know it still might be dangerous, but there are resources and references there which will help us decipher the Ezra scroll. We can't waste any more time. There are others probably following the same trail and they have a better copy of the text. Take your coffee with you, Sergeant. I will try not to turn too sharply."

Malik taped the copy of the text on a white board, and then stood back and stared at it in silence for what seemed like an eternity. He turned around and opened his top desk drawer and withdrew a rectangular magnifying glass on a black plastic handle. He moved the glass back and forth over the text slowly.

"This is no good. I cannot see enough detail. I'm not sure what I'm looking at. I don't know if they are smudges or intentional markings." With that Malik removed the text from the board and walked out of his office.

"Where are you going, Professor?"

"I am going across the street to the school. I need to borrow one of their science class microscopes."

Ten minutes later, with all three of them standing around Malik's desk, the text was positioned on the small platform below the lens of the microscope.

"Bring the desk lamp closer. I need more light. Aim it so the light shines from below."

Aaron complied, sliding the brass, goose necked lamp

"That helps."

"Well?" Abby asked.

"Take a look," Malik said.

Abby bent her head over the eyepiece. Her right hand was on the focus knob.

"What letter is this? I can't tell because the magnification brings it too close."

"It is an *ayin*." Malik replied.

"These shadows aren't smudges. They're *taggim!*" Abby exclaimed with rising excitement.

"What's that?" Aaron asked.

"We call them crowns," Malik said. "They are delicate, artistic, scribal ornamentation on the tops of letters. They only appear above certain letters. But this is all wrong!"

Abby stood. "What is all wrong?"

Malik turned around to the white board and picked up a dry-erase pen. With it he drew a line from one end of the board to the other, about five feet in length.

"This horizontal line represents time, Malik said. "Since we are having this conversation in English, let's say that time begins here on the left edge."

With that, he drew a vertical line at the left edge of the board that extended about three inches above and below the horizontal line.

"Is that the big bang?" Aaron asked.

"Bang, Shmang, it doesn't matter. What matters are these vertical lines."

About a foot and a half from the left edge, he drew three vertical lines, each about a foot apart and almost identical in length to the "big bang" line.

"This one represents the year 586 Before the Common Era. Judeans are taken into captivity by the Babylonians." As he said this he wrote '586 BCE' above the horizontal line, next to the vertical. Pointing to the next vertical he then wrote in '540-539 BCE.'

"And this one represents the year when Cyrus the Great of Persia allowed the Judeans to return to Judah." Another line, another caption.

"This one, 443 BCE, is the date some scholars, including me, believe that Ezra read to the people from the Torah for the very first time." Malik walked to the right edge of the board and drew a line and wrote in the date '750-850 CE.'

"This date, some twelve hundred years later, represents the first known appearance of *taggim*, crowns in a Torah text."

"So?" Aaron asked.

"Aaron, it means that the Ezra text is probably some kind of a forgery. Everything about it is wrong. Most scholars believe that *taggim* were created by the Masoretes. They were Babylonian Jewish scribes from the seventh or eighth century of the Common Era, not BCE. They dedicated their lives to copying the Hebrew Bible with great precision. The thinking is that these decorations were actually intended to serve as reminders of various popular interpretations of the text. Reluctant to actually change the sacred contents of the text, the Masoretes or Masters of the Tradition, if you will, sought to call attention to certain words. They were like signals to interpreters. It was as if they were saying: 'Consider this word carefully. It means more than you might think.' As far as we know, *taggim* were used only for Torah scrolls."

"I seem to be missing something," Aaron said.

"The earliest Masoretes were Jews from the seventh century of the Common Era. There is no evidence of these *taggim* before the beginning of that era and certainly not on documents written in Paleo-Hebrew. The location of the scroll is right but the timing is off by almost twelve centuries," Abby concluded.

Malik massaged his chin. "Maybe we should not be so hasty in our conclusions."

"How so?" Aaron asked.

"Well, consider this for a moment. There are no existing Babylonian documents or actual Hebrew texts of the Bible before the so-called earliest of the Masoretic texts. We do have the Dead Seas Scrolls, but nearly everyone agrees that they were Judean, not Babylonian. Arguments from silence are not proof of anything. Just because we have no actual evidence that *taggim* existed before the seventh century does not mean that they could not have been in use at that time. What if the *taggim* were a long-standing Babylonian tradition, far older than we ever imagined? If the parchment is genuine, and the ink is appropriate to the fifth or fourth century BCE, we may still have the real Ezra scroll."

"Except for the fact that we don't have the Ezra scroll," Aaron said.

"Professor, I'm familiar with the tradition of *taggim*, but I have never seen *taggim* with so many points."

"Points?" Aaron said.

"Did you ever go deer hunting, Sergeant?" Abby sounded like she was testing his testosterone level.

Aaron smiled. "A Carolina boy what don't hunt is a Carolina girl."

"What in the name of heaven are you two kids talking about?" Malik asked.

"Deer, antelope, what-have-you—have racks of antlers on their heads, at least the males do, anyway." Abby picked up the dry-erase marker and drew a crude deer head with antlers. Her illustration had six tips, which she circled with the marker.

"Even though these tagim look more like pine needles than crowns or antlers, these tips are the points. If you look closely at the *taggim*, they have 'points'—lots of them."

Malik returned to the microscope.

"Ahhh...yes, you are quite correct. These *taggim* are unlike any I have every seen before. Too many points," Malik said.

"How many is too many?" Aaron asked.

"I've never seen more than six or seven," Malik said.

"This letter has...thirteen, fourteen, fifteen, sixteen, seventeen!"

"Tell me, which letters have the crowns? Malik asked.

"Just the same ones found in Torah today." Abby was still checking.

"*Gimmel, Zayin, Tet, Nun, Ayin, Tsadi, Shin*......."

Aaron stood staring at the white board and the diagrams of letters with *taggim*. It seemed like a quarter of an hour had passed in silence. Then Aaron smiled.

"I have a crazy idea," he said.

"Try to find the rack with the greatest number of points."

"Good idea," Malik said. "You do it, Rabbi. You have younger eyes than mine."

Abby slowly shifted the copy of the Ezra text across the viewing stage of the microscope, all the while counting out loud.

"Twenty...twenty-one...twenty-two. So far none has more than twenty-two points," Abby said.

"Are there still twenty-two letters in the Hebrew alphabet?"

"We can begin your Hebrew lessons later," Abby said. Right now we don't have time for games."

"Really? Try this on for size," Aaron said. "What if the pine needles or *taggim* represent individual letters of the Hebrew alphabet? The number of points is the indicator of which letter it is. Do we know if the order of the letters was the same back then as it is now?"

Abby stepped back from the board and stared at the notes that filled the dry erase board. Her head was nodding slowly and after a few seconds, a big smile crossed her face.

"I will never refer to a Marine using the prefix 'dumb' ever again." Abby wrapped her arms around his neck and planted a wet one square on his lips.

Aaron was stunned.

Malik started laughing.

"You gave us the key to opening up the text. You did it!"

"Without the original scroll, our key has only entered the lock. It cannot open the door," Malik said.

"This copy is digital. There may be a few letters that stand out, but most are smudges and shadows. I'm not even sure that some of the points we are able to count are points at all. They could just be pixels. We can't read the message behind the text until we have the original."

"Now what?" Abby asked.

"We find the scroll and steal it back." Aaron said.

"It's time we arranged to meet our dear friends in the *Shin Bet*. I will make the call." Malik left his office and walked down the hall, opening his cell phone as he went.

"Do you think he has the Shin Bet on speed-dial?" Aaron asked.

"Actually, they probably have him on their own speed dial list. Malik is quite a character for an old guy. We need to keep ourselves alert and be ready for anything."

Malik returned after five minutes.

"The boys in the service would like us to come to their office as soon as possible."

"Do we go?"

"Sergeant Keller, when the *Shin Bet* requests a meeting, it is best to comply."

"Do you know where their office is?"

"Women's Wear—Plus Sizes."

"I beg your pardon." Aaron said.

"The top floor of *HAMASHBIR*, behind the dressing room for clothing designed for big women."

"You were in one," Abby said. "Remember where we got our current wardrobe? The department store. Still, it must look strange for all those toughs going into the dressing room to access the office."

"Some of our agents are women, you know. Actually, for reasons that have to do with religion and culture, that part of the store is almost always deserted. Who in this country wants to have themselves labeled as needing plus sizes?"

"How do you know all of this?"

"When I was a much younger man, I was the one who came up with the idea of de-centralizing and locating our offices in very ordinary places. *HAMASHBIR* was the first location of mine they accepted."

"Professor, you are a very strange man, indeed. Are you hiding any more secrets behind the old man disguise?"

"Sergeant, if I tell you…"

"I know—you will have to kill me. Ha, Ha," Aaron said.

This particular HAMASHBIR was easy to spot. The four-story cube, five hundred feet or so to each side, stood out from its neighbors in the Tel Aviv shopping district. Except for the posters with Hebrew lettering, the store looked pretty much like department stores in Chicago or South Carolina.

Malik, Aaron, and Abby located the escalator and rode to the fourth floor. The floor was deserted, as Malik had predicted. Each walked through the archway leading to the dressing rooms after making sure they were not being watched. Green heavy curtains covered a doorway at the rear of the dressing room area. Malik tapped twice on a steel door behind the curtains.

"Is that the Shin Bet secret knock?" Aaron asked.

"We do not have a secret knock because if you were not supposed to be here, you would have been immobilized immediately upon stepping off the escalator. The whole store is wired for video. We have been monitored since we came through the front door." Just as Malik finished his description of security in the store, a loud metallic click sounded and the metal door popped open.

Behind the door was a space so long that it must have run along an entire side of the four-story cube. Omar, the Druse expert on the Samaritans, extended his hand in greeting.

"Welcome to Plus Sizes! Follow me, and do not touch anything."

Along the inside wall was a counter nearly one hundred feet in length. Mounted on the wall above the counter were more than a dozen video monitors. Two young women were viewing the monitors and manipulating control sticks. They carried on a conversation in low tones. Abby could not make out all of what they were saying, but what she did catch did not sound like professionals screening for security threats.

Halfway down the length of the long main space, Omar opened a door and stood aside as they entered a square smaller room. A single, harsh fluorescent fixture lit up the center of the room. A round wooden table six feet across was below the light. Five plastic stack chairs were arranged around the table. A disposable aluminum foil ashtray with three cigarette butts was the only decoration on the table.

Rafi appeared suddenly. "Have a seat," he said.

"I commend you on your discovery of a code in the Ezra scroll. Good work! But it also means that the thieves are ahead of us because they have the original. Let me be clear. I'm not sure the *Shin Bet* should be a part of this adventure. Right now it is merely a police matter. Attempted murder and theft are the only charges we could present, assuming we catch the bastards.

"It's the Samaritan angle that has us concerned. The bomb was so out of character for them. We are still trying to figure out if they are at the center of all this or bit players in someone else's drama. Until we get all of these issues sorted out, we are going to partner with you in order to get the scroll back."

"Now we need for you to take a look at something," Omar said.

As if by magic, a screen dropped down from the ceiling at the front of the room. The screen was illuminated with images of Tel Aviv street life.

"That's the street outside the teashop," Malik said. "Based on the time stamp, this video was made just before the bomb blast."

"Be patient, Professor. *Savlanut! Savlanut!*"

As if on cue, a motorcycle appeared at the left side of the screen and moved slowly down the street. The cyclist reached into a saddlebag on his right side and removed a parcel wrapped in black plastic and secured with silver duct tape. In a split second there was a brilliant flash of light that obliterated any images on the street. Then the picture was restored just in time to record the devastation and panic taking place in front of the camera. There was an apparent editing cut in the video because the next image was from a different camera with a different angle on the same street. The focus was on a close up of the end of a row of small stores. A tall figure standing partially hidden in a shop doorway was engaged in a cell phone call in the midst of the chaos on the street.

"Do you recognize the man in the doorway?" Rafi asked.

"I can't make out his...Oh—my—God! It's your archeology professor, Carlson," Aaron said.

Chapter Twenty-Eight

TIME: First Hour of the Second Watch

DATE: Second Day of the Twelfth Month, in the Forty-Sixth Year
            Since the Destruction of Jerusalem

PLACE: Pumbedita, on the East Bank of the Euphrates River

Memukan, the *Pecha*—Governor, raised his hands to silence the group. It took quite a while, but he showed no impatience.

"In three weeks time, a group of river barges will arrive here from the north. They carry grain and olive oil. They are for you and the rest of the Judeans in Bavel. The armies of the Persian Empire are assembling a caravan of pack camels from Moab. Whatever you can carry in ox carts and wagons or load on the camels, you may take with you back to Judah. A contingent of that army is going to Judah with you. They shall be your escorts and protectors."

The only sound heard in the aftermath of the announcement was a collective gasp.

"We thank His Majesty for the enormous generosity, but we do not understand why he is doing this," Yeshuah asked.

"His Imperial Highness knows that those who receive gifts from his outstretched hand will be loyal and devoted servants. He is rebuilding the temples of the gods of many peoples in gratitude for the victories those gods have given him. He believes that the success of his military campaign in Judah, in pushing back the Egyptians, is because the god of Judah favors his cause. When the Emperor sought to reward this god he discovered that most of the people who claim him are exiles in Babylon. His diviners and magicians advised him that this is a clear sign that the god of the Judeans wants them returned to their ancestral land. The Great Cyrus sees the power of this god crossing the empty wasteland to bring his people home. He wants so powerful a god on his side. Sending you back to your god is Cyrus' gift to your god."

"The Emperor is wise as well as generous." Yeshuah said.

"Must we all go?"

The shout of the questioner came from behind the *Pehcha*. It was Miryam. The Judeans held their breath, fearing an outburst from the *Pehcha* for her impertinence.

To the surprise of those assembled, he answered her question without tones of anger or annoyance.

"Actually, some of you must stay as hostages."

"Hostages? Why?" Words recited in unison like a chorus of Levites in the Sacred House.

"Are we to be slaves here and soldiers against the Egyptians in Judah?" Yeshuah asked.

"Not slaves, but hostages, to make sure that the returning Judeans do not rise up in revolt against His Imperial Majesty. You shall have no ruler but Cyrus. You shall have no army but the army of Persia. You shall pay taxes to no one except Cyrus. He graciously allows you to rebuild your sacred house for your god and will permit you to raise money for the temple from your people as well.

"Who will lead us?"

"That shall be the decision of this body. That is what you must decide today. Just to be clear, no one descended from your last king in Judah shall serve as a leader of your nation. Cyrus knows that would be too strong a temptation for revolt."

The Governor watched silently as his soldier escort passed out small rough cloth sacks to the make-shift assembly. No one made any effort to open them.

"Go ahead and look inside. It won't hurt you."

Each sack contained a large, sky blue, shimmering garment that was as light as air itself. It felt smooth and slippery at the same time.

"What is this?" Yeshuah asked.

"His Imperial Majesty desires that all who lead the people in his realm shall wear these robes as a badge of office."

"No, I mean what is this material? It is unlike anything we have ever seen before."

"I'm told it is woven in a land close to where the sun rises. It is called silk. Some say it's produced by magicians. The truth is that it's produced by worms. It's very costly."

"You have seen these worms?"

"I have, but they died on the journey from their home to Persia. But enough of worms, it is time for you to choose your leadership. I shall return to the barge and await news of your decision. Choose wisely. Your journey home will not be easy."

For the next hour they discussed and argued. There was still great suspicion that the Emperor intended to do them harm. Much of the time was spent considering the matter of the hostages and who would go and who would stay. It was decided that the best way to designate who would remain as hostages would be to allow the people to make a choice whether to go or stay. The assembly would still have the final say. They knew that if those who chose to stay could not sustain themselves by their own skills and trades, then the hostages would perish or be vulnerable to attack and enslavement. The established goal was to have one-sixth of the exiles remain.

Choosing leadership provoked less tension than anyone would have imagined. Yeshuah ben Yozadak was elected High Priest. Since the Emperor had placed so much importance on the rebuilding of the Sacred House, who better to lead than those God declared responsible for the daily conduct of worship and care of the House.

The proposed order of leadership followed the rankings of the priests, Levites, musicians, guards, and scribes—all those who had served in the Sacred House before its fall. Many of them were but children when the House was destroyed, but the fact that they were not born into exile and had experienced the Sacred House in operation gave them at least a sense of their responsibility. The scribes or lack thereof would prove to be their most vexing problem.

In the aftermath of the flood, Miryam was simply the only scribe left alive in Pumbedita and she was more than seventy years of age. She would most likely never survive the journey to Judah. Yeshuah took charge of this part of the discussion.

"We have at least three weeks before we must leave. Let us send word up and down the river and see if we can locate additional scribes. If more than three can be located, we shall leave Miryam here with her grandson among the hostages."

"What about the sacred scrolls? Were they lost in the flood?" A young priest asked.

"They are safe for the moment, in my house," Yeshuah replied.

"They cannot go with you." Miryam said softly.

"And why not?" The question came from Asaph, the leader of the musicians.

"Miryam is right. They cannot go," Yeshuah sounded frustrated.

"They cannot go because we have no copies. All of the copies were destroyed. Two of my brother priests drowned while trying to protect them."

"It will take us months just to produce one careful copy. And that will be only possible if I am able to keep a steady hand at the work," Miryam said.

"The sacred scrolls must be returned to Jerusalem and the Sacred House. It will be a clear sign to the people that the God of our ancestors has caused our return from exile." Asaph said.

"And what if they are lost or destroyed on the journey?" Miryam countered. "The people will be cast adrift without them."

"The wife of Zadok Hasofer is correct. Here is what we must do. First, we must begin the search for additional scribes among our people. If we find but five or six, we shall leave three behind to assist Miryam in the copying of the sacred scrolls and training additional scribes. The rest of those additional scribes will make the journey with us. As soon as faithful copies are made, they shall be sent with an Imperial courier to Jerusalem for the Sacred House."

In two weeks time, five additional scribes had been located. All of them were from villages upriver from Pumbedita. Three were young enough to make the arduous journey. They learned their craft from Zadok from a time before Ezekiel's Mishkan existed. The other two were almost Miryam's age. Their abilities to practice their scribal art were reduced by stiffening joints and failing eyesight. Miryam convinced Yeshuah that they should not go on the return to Judah.

"We shall establish a school for scribes here. We will begin the process of copying the sacred scrolls. With these two old scribes we shall make a new beginning."

Yeshuah was forced to admit that Miryam's plan had merit. He took the idea to the new council of elders, a hastily formed group of twelve taken from those born in Judah before the exile. The youngest of these was nearly sixty years of age. The elders agreed.

The river barges carrying provisions for the journey to Judah arrived after four weeks. During the unexpected one-week delay, the Judeans speculated that the Emperor had changed his mind. Now, as the barges were unloaded a sense of confidence and trust began to build. For some, there was even a ray of hope for a new beginning. But more Judeans in exile were refusing to make the journey. They feared for their lives and the lives of their families. The elders were concerned that they would not be able to meet the numbers of returnees expected by the Persians. Yeshuah sent recruiters up and down the river to all of the surviving exile communities. He wrote a proclamation to be read to each community. The return, it proclaimed, was a sign of the power of the God of the Judeans, who reached across the wilderness to bring His people back.

Comfort, comfort my people, says your God. Speak tenderly to Jerusalem, and proclaim to her that her hard service has been completed, that her sin has been paid for, that she has received from God's hand double for all her sins.

A voice calls out: "In the desert prepare the way for God; make straight in the wilderness a highway for our God.

Why do you say, O Jacob, and complain, O Israel, "My way is hidden from the Eternal; my cause is disregarded by my God?" Do you not know? Have you not heard? The Eternal is the everlasting God, the Creator of the ends of the earth. He will not grow tired or weary, and his understanding no one can fathom. He gives strength to the weary and increases the power of the weak. Even youths grow tired and weary, and young men stumble and fall; but those who hope in the Eternal God will renew their strength. They will soar on wings like eagles; they will run and not grow weary; they will walk and not be faint.

One week after the supply barges arrived at Pumbedita, the *Pehcha* was taking his daily walk among the Judeans in order to guage the progress of their preparations for the return to their homeland. Having satisfied himself that the Judeans were very much engaged in the preparations, he asked Yeshuah about Miryam's location. Yeshuah was about to summon her to his tent when the *Pehcha* placed his hand on his shoulders as if to restrain him.

"I wish to see her at her work. Where can I find her?"

He was directed to the south side of the Judean encampment.

"Look for a ragged black tent with open sides. If there are children learning to become scribes beneath its shelter, there you will find her." One of Yeshuah's young Levites was eager to personally assist the *Pehcha* in finding it.

"I will find her. Please do not trouble yourself."

After a couple of false sightings, Memukan arrived at the tent in question. Under its shelter, children as young as Hilkiah, but none older than ten years of age, sat in a circle on the ground. Miryam held a pointed stick and wielded it like a pen cutting letters in the smooth floor of the tent. Memukan could make out the first ten letters of the alphabet. It was the writing of the old Judeans, Hebrew.

"Why do you teach them this Hebrew lettering? They will not be prepared for life in the new Empire," Memukan asked.

"My Lord *Pehcha*, they are not being prepared to serve the Empire. They are preparing to serve their God, the one whom your ruler has seen fit to honor."

"I hope you will teach them Aramaic as well. Perhaps your God also wishes to communicate with other nations."

"This is but the first step. Is there something I can do for you?"

"Please step outside for a moment."

"Why the need for privacy?"

Without giving Miryam an answer, he turned and walked outside. She followed him.

"This is for you." And so saying, Memukan handed her a leather bound scroll, tied with leather thongs and bearing an impressive red wax seal.

"The *Pehcha* of the Province Beyond the River has sent this to you. It is from your family in Samaria. I am instructed to inform you that you are to show its contents to no one. No, I do not know why there is need for secrecy." And with those last words, he turned on his heels and left.

After a long morning of lessons in the sand, Miryam's hands were inflamed with the pains of old age. As she struggled with the leather lace that secured the scroll, one of her fingers locked on her and she had to use all her strength to pry it open. Finally, she opened the scroll. One quick glance and she immediately recognized the writing as that of her brother-in-law, Eli. The letters were in the ancient style still favored by the Shomronim.

Beloved Sister:

Word has reached our province of the terrible flood that has destroyed much of the land of exile. Tell me please, although I fear the answer, is your family safe?

Miryam's eyes welled up.

How can I tell him that only Hilkiah and I survived? He is as old as I am. This news will kill him, she thought.

She continued reading.

Please take care of this letter. Do not show it to anyone you do not trust absolutely. Reply to me when you are able.

Zadok, may he rest in peace, would have been proud of me and the scribal school I have established and operated, lo these many years. A number of my students have gone beyond my skills and have produced the most beautiful copies of the sacred scrolls. My masters, the Judean priests, have decided that we will not adopt the writing form of the Bavli, or should I say the Parsi, because that could mean multiplying mistakes in the process of copying from one lettering form to another. Their decision has the support of the elders and exile community leaders. I believe they are correct in wanting all of the copies made of the sacred scrolls to look just as they did when they were rescued from the flames.

Before his death, Zadok asked about our service to the God of our ancestors.

I was ashamed to reply because I did not want the Judeans in Bavel to know that we are probably guilty of a grievous sin. You may recall that the Samaritans asked the Judean priests to tutor them in the service of the God of Israel. They may have done so, all too well. The Samaritans are an interesting people. They have built what they call a temple on Mt. Gerizim. It certainly lacks the beauty of the Sacred House, but they are very proud of it. They offer their sacrifices to the God of Israel. They are very scrupulous in keeping idolatry out of this sanctuary. Our priests began to participate in the offerings many months ago, in the guise of assisting the Samaritans to worship our God in the proper manner. Now the Judeans exiled in Samaria are looking to this sanctuary as their own. I fear they will forget the Sacred House in Jerusalem.

As if that were not bad enough, my efforts to encourage the Samaritans to allow me to train scribes for their own people has succeeded only too well. The death of the Samaritan high priest, Malik ben Shemen, has brought us a new problem. His successor, Avigdor ben Tsedek is insisting that the Judean priests make our sacred scrolls available to the Samaritan scribes so that they may make their own copies. So long as we are living under their protection, we are unable to refuse this request. If we did so, I fear that the high priest would make it a condition of our continued welcome. Ben Tsedek will not accept access to copies of the sacred scrolls. He is insisting on his scribes being allowed to make their own copies from our twelve scrolls. I cannot understand what he intends to do with his copies. What has become of the twelve scrolls in exile? Were they lost in the flood? If you have anything to do with watching over them, as the God of the entire house of Israel lives, make sure they are safe from those who seek to do us harm.

This letter must be understood as a clear and urgent warning to you and the exiles of Judah. It is being carried to you by the hand of a true friend of Israel. I cannot tell you what his office was here in Samaria, nor can I name him, for fear that those who do not pray for the redemption of Judah may cause him great harm. He has been called back to Bavel to assume a position of importance in the ruling council of the Persians. He tells me that when he carried official news of the imminent return of the exiles from Judah to the peoples who live in the Province Beyond The Rivers, they immediately began plotting various ways to make sure that Judean exiles would never arrive to threaten their hard won authority or favored status in the eyes of the new emperor.

You must tell your own priests to be very careful in their journey home. The land promised to Abraham will welcome them. The people who occupy its cities and villages will not.

I close this letter with the undying hope that you, your children, and your grandchildren will be among those who return to Zion in peace.

Eli.

Miryam dried the tears from her eyes with the edge of her apron. Carefully she rolled the scroll within the leather cover and hid it in a fold of her apron.

"Yeshuah must see this, at once!" She said out loud. Fortunately, no one was around to hear her outburst. The contents of the letter were secure. At least that is what Miryam believed.

Chapter Twenty-Nine

DATE: March 18, 2009

TIME: 3:30 P.m. Local Time

PLACE: 123 Shmuel Hanavi Street, Holon

Professor Carlson's face still bled from abrasions and cuts two days after the bombing on Bareket Street in Or Yehudah. He looked into the mirror behind the driver's side visor, repeatedly checking his appearance. This face would frighten both children and adults. Gingerly, he dabbed at the bleeding sores with the antiseptic pad, wincing with each burning touch. Shouting in rhythm with each dab seemed to help.

"Jesus H. Christ!"

"God that hurts!"

"Good Samaritans my ass!"

Sitting in the center of the largest concentration of Samaritans in Israel, it was fortunate that he left the windows up. Otherwise his shouts would have been heard all the way to Tel Aviv. Carlson tossed the pad onto the trash-strewn floor of his Peugot, and then checked the last screen on his GPS device. Having satisfied himself that he had arrived close to his destination, he shut off the engine.

A lifetime of digging in archeological sites had taught him to view the physical creations of human culture with a respectful reverence. Always at the back of his mind was the realization that someday, a thousand years from now, some future digger would reveal the scattered remains of the 21st Century. It kept him humble whenever he was about to cut loose with a heartfelt screed against modern society and its soulless architecture. This time however, reverence for the distant past did not save the structures he now faced from his withering analysis.

Yeacch—who the hell designed this abortion? he wondered.

Israeli apartment blocks built in the late 1950's were not intended to win architectural competitions. They were barely designed at all. This particularly depressing assembly of apartments was located in the heart of Holon, a suburb to the south of Tel Aviv proper. Concrete block, mortar, concrete/plaster overlay with a dash of beige for color, as if the country needed more beige, and that was it. The only real color in the neighborhood was provided by flapping laundry suspended on clotheslines from each apartment balcony. Apartment number 123 was surrounded by four identical buildings. With no effort at all, it became a totally anonymous structure in a painfully ordinary neighborhood.

Carlson was in this section of Holon to attend an urgent meeting with the young Samaritan militants responsible for the wounds on his face. The neighborhood was a vertical Samaritan village. No one entered or left the five building complex without being carefully scrutinized by the hyper-cautious saved remnant of the ancient Samaritans. The street numbers on each building had been lost or stolen forty years ago. Carlson knew that without help from residents it would be impossible to locate a specific apartment. The only question now was how to ask for help? He need not have concerned himself. His arrival in the neighborhood did not go unnoticed.

Focused on the apartment block across the street, Carlson failed to anticipate the sudden appearance of four burly young men at the rear of the Peugot. They began to pound mercilessly on the car.

"Enough! Go back home. He is a guest of mine. I'll vouch for him."

Carlson's savior emerged as if by magic, from the apartment block. He was of medium height, trim build, and very dark complexion. His close cropped hair was salt and pepper, mostly grey. His deep set eyes were a transparent kind of coffee color which gave his face a strikingly handsome appearance. He wore a t-shirt the color of his hair and a pair of olive green slacks. Open sandals were on his feet. His orders to the young toughs were barked in Hebrew, but there was some other kind of accent behind the Hebrew that indicated it was not his mother tongue.

"I am Tovya. Please forgive our young people. They do not observe the usual courtesies in the presence of strangers."

"Thank you for your timely arrival."

"Just so you know Professor, your presence was made known to me the moment you left the highway. We are not the only ones who watch the comings and goings of strangers. We must go inside quickly."

The man called Tovya led Carlson across the street and into an open stairwell of one of the apartment buildings set into the side of a hill. He started down the terrazzo paved stairs and continued for two flights below the level of the street. Four doors were on this lowest level, indicating four apartments. Carlson followed Tovya through the first door. All four apartments on this level were joined into one spacious, well-appointed, dwelling. One corner facing the street was furnished as an office with a sort of window wall and set of French doors closing it off from the rest of the room. Built-in bookshelves occupied the two walls that met in the corner with a desk built into the center. The wood of the bookshelves and desk was very light in color, probably Danish or Swedish pine. This contrasted nicely with the light brown color of the walls, trimmed in white. A small burgundy leather couch was against the wall with the door in it, the one opposite the desk. Tovya motioned to Carlson to take a seat on the couch. He sat opposite him in the ultra-modern, black desk chair with an ergonomically curved mesh back.

"Would you care for something to drink?"

"As a matter of fact, I would." Carlson said.

Tovya nodded his head ever so slightly to one of the toughs, who was standing just outside the office area. A few moments later he carried in a brass tray and set it down on the desk. An antique brass teapot with a long graceful spout, was flanked by two ceramic mugs, bearing the logo of the Macabbee Tel Aviv basketball team. Sugar packets and small containers of cream were scattered around the tray. A red packet of almond cookies, saved from some airline, completed the presentation. Tovya motioned to Carlson to help himself. When Carlson was settled back on the couch, Tovya poured himself some tea, added some cream and then opened the conversation.

"I owe you two apologies, Professor. First, that my man failed to eliminate our problem outside of Abu Ghosh, and second, that our effort to solve our dilemma at the teashop took the lives of an innocent family. We are not terrorists. We believe that God allows us to take a life to prevent the destruction of our community. But unlike the Arabs and the Jews, we do not have much practice in the lethal arts."

"You could have fooled me. You told me that if I arrived at the stone doorway by four o'clock, I would be able to witness the deaths of Malik and the two Americans and collect whatever copies of the Ezra text they had. I was still two meters from the safety of the doorway when I saw your man on the Yamaha toss his satchel. I dove for cover but it was the wrong doorway—filled with display glass, most of which became embedded in my face."

"As I said, Professor, you have my apologies. May you enjoy a complete healing from your wounds. Let's get down to the business at hand. You have in your possession the original text yes?"

"Let's just say it's in a safe place. From the moment I appropriated it from the Americans and decided to put it up for auction, my career as a once-respected archeologist came to a rapid conclusion. To be sure, I had grown tired of the summer fieldwork routine. It was indeed time for a change. But please be assured, my price for the scroll will be an amount that will guarantee a very comfortable retirement for me and my wife."

"Of course, that is how it should be, my friend."

"And while I am on the subject, my wife has already left Israel for our new retirement location. You will not be able to kidnap her or use her as leverage. You will get the scroll upon payment confirmation. You know the transaction details. Your failure to destroy the copies of the scroll means that someone else is in a position to discover its meaning and profit from it."

"Perhaps then, we should not concern ourselves with copies. What can you tell me about the scroll itself? Why are you so sure that it is an ancient Samaritan text."

"For starters, you must understand that the scroll is truly priceless, regardless of what it might or might not reveal. All of the usual tests confirm it is written on parchment prepared in the time of Ezra, around 450 BCE, plus or minus twenty years. The scroll therefore, is at least four hundred years older than the oldest texts of the Dead Sea Scrolls. That fact alone makes it an extraordinary find."

"But is it Samaritan?"

"As I explained in my email, it is a carefully crafted version of Psalm 137. Line for line it is nearly identical with the oldest known written version of that psalm in the Aleppo Codex, from thirteen hundred years later. The lettering is also consistent with the 450 BCE date, but with an interesting twist. It was the style of the Hebrew letters that prompted me to contact you in the first place. The lettering is consistent with Samaritan inscriptions of the period and not Jewish ones."

"So what is the problem with that?"

"Although we have no other texts from that time, inscriptions and ostraca of the period are unanimous in indicating that the Babylonian Jews used Aramaic script instead of so called paleo-Hebrew. Therefore, we need to answer this question. What is a Samaritan copy of Psalm 137, a psalm with a clear connection to the exiles of Judah, doing in Babylonia? Most of the modern research of this period assumes a great deal of enmity existed between Jews and Samaritans. The Marine and his Navy rabbi claim the scroll was part of a *genizah* in Fallujah. If this is true, it means that a scroll produced by a Samaritan scribe was preserved by a Jewish community in Babylonia. Why? Even if we cannot answer the question, the scroll is positive proof that some kind of contact existed between the Samaritans and the Jews."

"I have been expecting this news. My dear Professor, there is no problem."

"There isn't?"

"In fact, this is the information that confirms one of our oldest Samaritan traditions."

"And that would be…?"

"That someone from Samaria was in contact with the Jews of Babylonia around the time of Ezra."

"This text indicates more than just contact. What else does your tradition have to say?"

"Let me quote from a story my sainted grandfather relayed to me. 'Behold, from Mount Gerizim the scroll of the Torah of Moses was given.'"

"That is not the Sunday School version."

"Why should you be any different than the rest of the so-called Judeo-Christian world? This Samaritan tradition has been denounced and ridiculed down through the ages. The single most disputed part of that tradition is the one that holds that the actual Torah belonged to us first. Our scribes brought it together. Our scribes made it known to our people and so, perhaps, one of our scribes sent a copy of that Torah to the Jews in Babylonia."

"And what do the skeptics say?"

"The skeptics say that the first time my ancestors encountered the Torah was during the period of the Hasmoneans, the Maccabees—about four hundred years later. Then, as enmity grew between the Samaritans and the Maccabees, our priests altered the original text to give emphasis to Mount Gerizim as God's chosen mountain instead of Jerusalem and Mount Moriah."

"So the scroll might lead to proof that the Torah was produced by the Samaritans and later given to the Jews?"

"Now you understand, Professor, why it is so important that we decipher this text. What it contains may lift my people from the dung heap of history. Instead of being the unwanted backward stepchild of Judaism and Christianity, we become the authors of the one text that inspires all of Western religious tradition. Without our ancestors there would be no Hebrew Scriptures, no New Testament, no Koran."

"You said that your tradition allows the taking of human life if your community is threatened, " Carlson said. "How does this scroll discovery threaten your community? If the scroll disappears today, nothing changes. The status quo remains."

"For my people, the status quo means our extinction. Our numbers are so small that in recent years our priests have given permission for our men to marry Jewish women, so long as they adopt our religion. We are living artifacts, known only to a few dedicated scholars. International assistance programs pass us by with regularity. We are trapped between the rock of Israel and the hard place of Palestine. Beyond those who wish to preserve us like some specimen in a petri dish and study us under a microscope, we are actually seen as an inconvenience. The Israelis think we receive too much welfare from them. The Palestinians covet our lands around Nablus. We need to upset the status quo. Right now it is killing us. Israeli politics have become totally dependent on placating the Black Hats, the Ultra Orthodox. If the Israelis decipher the scroll first and come to realize what it actually means, they will bury it in some obscure cabinet at the Israel Museum, rather than incur the fierce wrath of the rabbis."

"But the Israeli government is not involved in this scroll business."

"How naïve you are, Professor. Do you imagine that after two failed attempts on the lives of the Americans, the Israeli security services have not become involved? As I see it, they have two problems. First, how to steal the scroll copies from the Americans. Second, how to steal back the original scroll from you. When I get the scroll from you, it is no longer your worry. It will be all mine."

"You will need me to help you decipher the text, even after you have the scroll."

"That is where you are wrong. We have our own experts."

The young Samaritan who had brought in the brass tray knocked on the French doors. Tovya waved him in.

"This email just arrived from the Bank of the Cayman Islands," he said with a knowing smile on his face."

"Thank you, Amram." Tovya said softly in reply. He passed the paper across to Carlson.

"As you can see, the ten million Euros have been deposited into your island account. And now, if you don't mind, the location of the scroll please."

"Give me a moment so I can confirm the transaction. Anyone can send a convincing email." Carlson produced a smartphone from his pocket and entered a few keystrokes. "It is confirmed. Thank you so much. You or your men will find the scroll in the guest safe of room 502 of the Carleton Hotel, on the beach in Tel Aviv. When I am safely away from Holon, I will call you on your cell phone and give you the four number code for the safe. Here are the keys to the room. I checked in using my own name. The room is mine until noon tomorrow."

"Professor, if you betray me and my people in this matter, and do not call with that code within the hour, we shall track you down and kill you, your wife and anyone else that is close to you."

"Tovya, you need not threaten me. I want you to have that scroll. I will make the call."

Carlson's voice was crystal clear, emanating from two powerful yet small speakers, mounted on the wall of the Shin Bet conference room. Abby,

Aaron, Malik, and the two Shin Bet agents Rafi and Omar, heard every word of the meeting between Professor Carlson and the Samaritan known as Tovya. They were all still on the fourth floor of the department store in downtown Tel Aviv.

Rafi and Omar did not bother to explain the means by which the bug or bugs had been planted on Carlson or Tovya or both of them. Aaron just assumed they had a Shin Bet agent working inside the Keter Shomron organization.

"We need to get to the Hotel first and make sure the scroll lands in our hands." Abby said.

"Rabbi, we are way ahead of you. Our team is only one minute out from the hotel. If Tovya intends on using Carlson's room key, it will take him at least thirty minutes to get it here from Holon. Besides, the one unknown in all of this is how soon Carlson calls him with the code. That could work in our favor, buying us a little more time. We need to get our people there now and make things look as normal as possible. Tovya is no fool. He will be on high alert." As he said this, Rafi was putting on a light windbreaker to conceal his waist holstered 9 millimeter Barretta.

"The three of you will go with Omar." Rafi nodded in the direction of Abby, Aaron, and Malik.

"He will be your host at the ice cream parlor behind the Carleton Hotel. You will be close enough to respond when we need you and far enough away to be safe."

"What do you need us for, inasmuch as you are going to bury or destroy the scroll anyway?" Abby asked.

"The scroll is not our concern, no matter what Carlson thinks." Omar said.

"It never has been. You have given us an opportunity to shut down an organization that has killed innocent civilians and serves as a conduit to Palestinian extremists. Once we have it, we will turn the scroll back to your custody. It is not an artifact found here in the State of Israel. It is not our property. The Iraqis may have something to say about it, however.

"Besides, there is so much suspicion and mistrust among archeologists and scholars of the Bible, it will take ten years before more than twenty people in the world understand the implications of your amazing discovery. It will take another twenty years for the conspiracy theorists to run out of boogey men and forgers who they will accuse of inventing the scroll altogether. And I haven't even mentioned the wrath of God brought down from Sinai, Mount Gerizim and Mount Moriah by the religious fanatics who will put out contracts on the lives of anyone associated with the blasphemy represented by the scroll. As far as the Israeli government is concerned, the sooner you have it, the better."

Now when the enemies of Judah and Benjamin heard that the people of the exile were building a temple to the Eternal One, God of Israel, they approached Zerubbabel and the chiefs of the clans, and said to them, "Let us build with you, for we, like you, seek your God; and we have been sacrificing to Him since the days of Esarhaddon king of Assyria, who brought us up here." But Zerubbabel and Yeshua and the rest of the chiefs of the clans of Israel said to them, "You have nothing in common with us in building a house to our God; but we ourselves will together build to the Eternal One, God of Israel, as King Cyrus, the king of Persia has commanded us." Then the people of the land discouraged the people of Judah, and frightened them from building, and hired counselors against them to frustrate their counsel all the days of Cyrus king of Persia, even until the reign of Darius king of Persia. (Ezra 4:1-4)

Chapter Thirty

DATE: Second Day of the Twelfth Month, In the Sixty-Eight Year Since the Destruction of Jerusalem

TIME: Second Hour of the First Watch

PLACE: Five Parasangs South of Shiloh, In the Persian Territory Known as The Province Beyond the River

"Take a good look at yourselves! The Samaritans have taken everything from us: our dwellings, household goods, domestic animals, stored grain, bolts of rough woven cloth, craft and farming tools and sacred scrolls.

"Hear my words, you lost sheep of Judah! The God of our ancestors is punishing all of us. When the great Cyrus of Persia allowed our brothers in exile to return to Jerusalem and rebuild the Sacred House, what did we do?

"Did we meet them on the road from Damascus?

"Did we offer them food and drink after their long journey from Bavel?

"Did we join them in Jerusalem and celebrate our redemption?

"Did we lift the fallen stones of the forsaken sanctuary and place them in the wall of the Sacred House?

"We did nothing! We chose to remain close to our vines and fig trees in the comforting shadow of Mount Gerizim. This new exile is our punishment. It is justly deserved, you still-born cubs of Judah."

Standing on a high and rough boulder, the speaker was Naftali ben Ami, the shepherd. Under ordinary circumstances, Naftali had the look of a mad man: filthy and disheveled clothing, unkempt, straggly, salt and pepper, crumb-filled beard, piercing dark eyes beneath full and thick eyebrows that started on one side of his face at the brow ridge and crossed to the other side. Today, he looked and acted the part of a prophet of God.

"Naftali, what have <u>you</u> lost—a couple of mangy sheep? You have nothing. So you lost nothing. Perhaps you should hold your tongue in the presence of those who have lost much." Shifra, the widow of Malachi the baker, shouted her comments as she passed by beneath Naftali's stone *bimah*.

"Why must you torment us with your words?" she asked.

"I bring not words of torment. I bring words of comfort." He sang this answer as a parent sings a lullaby.

"When we get to Jerusalem all will be well. We shall have food and shelter and security."

"Are you…an agent…of the governor…Naftali…. that you bring us these assurances?…My trading partners…in Judah…. tell me that the current governor…is a descendant…of the House of David…. They tell me that he looks upon us…as traitors. Anytime…there is mention in his court of the Judeans…in Samaria, he spits and curses…every one of us."

Avner ben Micah, a merchant well known throughout the Province Beyond the River, was the source of the rumors from Judah. He was out of breath and completely hidden beneath his enormous pack. While most of the refugees were carrying their precious personal possessions, Avner was hauling the inventory of his business.

"Avner, at the rate you are going, you will never make it to Judah to find out. I think the Samaritans intended you to leave at least some of your goods behind."

Naftali's sharp tongue caused those who heard the exchange to laugh in spite of themselves.

A Judean, in threadbare priestly robes, stopped below Naftali and set down a large clay jar. He produced a small wooden ladle and dipped it into the jar. He offered water to all of the exiles within his reach as well as those passing by.

"Now that is comfort that is real." Avner took a long sip.

"Thank you, son of Aaron."

"We all must reach the shelter of En-Tappuah by dark. This is the only way we can protect the little ones from thieves and killers. Drink and keep moving. Give help to the weak." The priest was referring to the village that would be their stopping place for this first night of what would probably be a four-day journey.

"Son of Aaron, why do you think we were expelled from Samaria?" asked Shifra, widow of Malachi."

"Naftali is partially correct. I do believe we are being punished for not participating in the redemption of the Household of Israel and the Sacred House. But I also know that our Judean brothers and sisters are about to dedicate a new Sacred House. They have been building it for more than four years."

"May the God of our ancestors be praised! That is great news for us. But what does that have to do with our exile from Samaria?"

"When the work on the new Sacred House began, the Samaritans and the other peoples of the land journeyed to Judah to ask the Judean leaders to allow them to participate alongside the returned exiles, in the building of the House."

"Did they accept their offer?"

"The redeemed ones harshly rejected their offer of help. The Samaritans worship the God of Israel, just like we do. They were hurt and angered by this rejection."

"That was nearly four years ago. Nothing came of their anger, did it?"

"The Samaritans and their friends made sure that the work on the Judean Sacred House did not go swiftly. They flooded the Emperor with accusations of treason and complaints of corruption. There were delays, but the rebuilding continued. And then, three days ago, came word of the actual rededication of the Sacred House. We could hear the Samaritan elders shouting from the other side of the mountain. They had decided to expel all of the Judeans in Samaria. They may not have been of the seed of Israel, but together our peoples would have been a strong nation, capable of standing on its own. Now we are weak and subject to the blinding dust and capricious winds of the desert.

"Here, dear sister, drink deep and conserve your strength," said the priest as he offered her another cup of water."

As she lifted the cup to her lips, her eyes locked with the eyes of the priest. The cup dropped from her hands. She fell to her knees and grabbed the hem of his robe, careful not to touch any part consecrated to divine worship.

"High Priest of the Most High: Forgive me! I did not know it was you!"

"Save your strength, dear sister. On this road, God has chosen to humble us all. I am now High Priest of nothing. The priests in Jerusalem will most likely burn me to death for blasphemy."

"What act of blasphemy have you committed?"

"I offered sacrifices to our God on the altar of the Samaritans. That will be enough to get me killed."

"Your people will not let that happen!"

"Your words of comfort bring me peace, but they will not save my life."

"Then why do you return to Judah and your death?"

"I must complete a sacred task given to me by my father. I swore an oath to fulfill his promise at the time the God of our ancestors redeems the Household of Israel. Now, with the Sacred House nearly restored, I have the honor and obligation of fulfilling the oath I swore to my father when I was eighteen years old."

"And the honor of dying for it," Shifra shook her head in disgust.

The priest hoisted the water jar on his shoulder and walked on down the line of exiles. As he passed the water around to the next group on the road, his thoughts began to drift to the events which brought them all to this sad state. Only twenty-four hours earlier, the Samaritan order of expulsion arrived at Mt Gerizim.

"Pack whatever you can carry and be gone before the sun is overhead." Samaritan priests had delivered the order in person and not by messenger. Their facial expressions revealed nothing, neither anger nor sadness. They accepted no pleas for more time. "Leave now!" was their united refrain. Since these exiled Judeans had lived nearly four decades among the Samaritans, there was disappointment but not anger, acceptance and not rebellion.

That night, Judean priests convened at the home of their designated leader, Yeshai ben Gilad, to discuss the expulsion order and what to do about it. For a High Priest, Yeshai was quite young. He was born thirty-eight years before, in Samaria, to Judean exile parents. His maternal grandmother, however, was a Samaritan, daughter of a Samaritan tribal chief.

Yeshai came to his leadership position two months ago after the untimely death, due to fever, of his father, the previous Judean High priest.

Yeshai was strongly built and of average height. Although his priestly headdress covered his hair, it was dark brown and very straight. His eyes were dark brown as well, but they were often obscured by the narrowness of the openings, giving him the appearance of some of the tribes from the distant east. As a boy, whenever he encountered Persian soldiers he had the strange feeling that he was looking at people who could have been his relatives. His hands were not large but his fingers were slender and long. Writing quills seemed to disappear in his grip.

Before he had been chosen for training as a priest, Yeshai had studied the scribal arts. His teachers always compared his work, for better or worse, with that of his grandfather Eliezer. It was not an accident. His grandfather had placed a quill in his hands when Yeshai was two. Writing and calligraphy were in his blood. But they would not determine his life. The Judean community had greater need of him as a member of its priesthood than as another talented scribe.

Yeshai's training as a priest was made easier and he advanced faster because he had an advantage over his classmates. Yeshai could read and write from the time he was three. While the other young priests had to spend hours listening to their teachers drone on and on with the rules and responsibilities of their office, Yeshai could sit down with copies of the twelve sacred scrolls and read and study the rules by himself. He was only vaguely aware of the story that placed his grandfather Eliezer at the center of the rescue of the twelve sacred scrolls. The irony of his ability to study the scrolls two generations later was lost on him.

In the last year of his training, when he was eighteen years old, his life changed. One very hot and sunny day, his teacher Azariah, a priest of indeterminate age and foul breath, took him to the place where the twelve sacred scrolls were kept. The location was not hidden, but it was well guarded day and night by armed young priests. It was a small stone hut that looked like it was attached to the home of the High Priest of that time, but was not.

With barely a nod to the guards flanking the door to the hut, Azariah produced a large iron key attached to a thong around his neck and unlocked the heavily reinforced oak plank door. From a ledge just inside the door, Azariah retrieved a simple clay oil lamp. He lit the small lamp from a large one placed outside the hut. For just this purpose, the guards maintained the lamp. In the middle of the day it was still necessary to carry an oil lamp into the hut.

Despite the oppressive heat outside, it was cool in the hut. Perhaps this was due to the depth of the walls, nearly three cubits thick in all. There was no external light source. On the wall to the left of the entrance were three rough-hewn upright wooden posts. It appeared as though the posts were buried deep into the compacted earthen floor. The posts were set two cubits apart, starting at the walls. Each post served as a support to three shelves that went from wall to wall on that side of the hut. The shelves began at a height of two cubits and were set two cubits apart from each other. On each shelf were four scrolls. Each was tied with leather chords.

"Take a close look, Yeshai. These are the sacred scrolls of our people."

"What makes them sacred?"

"They contain the words of the God of our ancestors."

"Who wrote these scrolls?"

"Scribes who served in the Sacred House before the Bavliim destroyed it."

"Did you serve in the Sacred House?"

"I was just a baby when the House was destroyed. But your grandfather Eliezer and your uncle, Zadok…"

"The one taken into captivity in Bavel?"

"Yes, that one. Eliezer and Zadok were apprenticed to the scribes of the Sacred House. They started their studies just before the Bavliim invaded Judah. In the midst of this terrible tragedy, they both risked their lives to rescue twenty-four scrolls from the flames that ultimately would destroy the Sacred House and the rest of Jerusalem. In the middle of the night, with soldiers searching and killing Judeans on sight, Zadok and Eliezer made their way out of the burning city and joined the exiles in their forced march down to Jericho.

"You said they rescued twenty-four scrolls. I see only twelve here. What happened to the rest?"

"It was a time of danger and great uncertainty. No one knew what the future would bring to the descendants of Judah. It was decided by the leader of the exiles, the great priest, Ezekiel ben Buzzi, that your grandfather, Eliezer should take half of the scrolls and make his escape to Samaria in the North. Your great-uncle Zadok would guard the rest of the scrolls as they joined the Judeans in exile."

"Did my great-uncle survive?"

"Not only did he survive, but he lived a life very similar to that of your grandfather."

"How do you know all of this?"

"Because this is what your grandfather told me. Two or three times each year, the brothers exchanged letters and wrote about their lives in exile. Both of them were certain that God had given them the task of returning the scrolls to Judah. Both became scribal teachers and very learned in the contents of the sacred scrolls. Both made sure that there would be succeeding generations of Judean scribes who could read, and yes, even chant, the sacred scrolls."

"When did Zadok die?" Yeshai asked. He wanted to know if anyone outside of the family knew that Zadok was murdered by the High Priest Ezekiel.

"He had an accident and fell into the great river. He was a young man... such a tragedy for his family. His wife Miryam lived into her nineties. She taught generations of exiled Judean scribes and made sure there were ample copies of the twelve scrolls, that is, the twelve scrolls under her care."

"Can we unroll them and read from them?"

"There is no need. You have been reading copies of the scrolls throughout your training."

"I want to see the writing. I want to think about the scribe who put his quill to the parchment. I want to touch them."

"God willing, you will have ample time touch and read from them. But I must complete my charge, now. Your father ordered me to bring you here and show you the sacred scrolls and something more important than the twelve scrolls."

"What could be more important than the sacred scrolls?"

"Watch."

Azariah placed his right hand on the upright post nearest the entrance. With care he moved it downward, feeling for something on the back of the post with his fingertips. With his hand just above the first shelf, he stopped.

"Give me your quill knife, Yeshai."

"How did you know I had a knife?"

"You are a scribe, aren't you?"

About as long as his hand was wide, the knife Yeshai removed from the side pocket in his robe, was a near razor sharp flake of flint bound into a notch in a polished piece of olive wood. The flake was sharp at the edges but was not thin down its center. It would not break easily. This was fortunate, because Azariah took the knife and started using it to scrape along the backside of the post. Suddenly, a quarter cubit section of the post popped out onto the shelf.

"What is that?"

"Be patient, Yeshai and you shall see."

Azaria reached his fingers into the opening in the post and slowly withdrew a leather bound scroll. It was almost the same length as the sacred scrolls. He moved two of the scrolls on the center shelf to make room for the hidden scroll. He untied its binding and unrolled the scroll within.

"It is time for you to read, Yeshai. I must leave now."

"Leave? Leave me alone with the sacred scrolls?"

"I swore an oath to your father that I would not read the hidden scroll. You will be safe. They are in as sure hands with you now, as they were from the day your grandfather and great uncle removed them from the Sacred House. If they are not secure with you, then they are safe with no one. The guards will protect you. They will lock the hut when you have finished. Make sure that you replace the scroll in the post, just as we found it."

Azariah turned abruptly and left the hut.

Yeshai's eyes settled on the scroll spread out on the shelf. The writing was very small. Whoever wrote this scroll wanted to fit a great deal of text in a minimum amount of space. There was very little separation between the letters.

The text was not from one of the sacred scrolls. If it had been, he would have had an easier time reading. Slowly at first, then with growing confidence, he started to sound out his word guesses. The language was Hebrew. The letters were written in the style of the sacred scrolls. The first line of letters described creation beginning with formless emptiness. As he continued to make his way, line-by-line, he found himself pausing and repeating what he believed were the sentences formed by the letters. Without writing implements, Yeshai was forced to commit his reading to memory. When his muscles became fatigued, he would walk to the door and step outside to stretch, noting the position of the sun in the sky and track his time in the hut. He could not bring himself to stop reading, despite his growing aches and pains. And then, the reading became familiar. He was reading words he had memorized long ago from the twelve sacred scrolls. Had the sacred scroll writer joined material from some another source?

After hours of reading, Yeshai was emotionally and physically exhausted. Reluctantly, he began to roll the scroll and prepared to return it to its hiding place. As the scroll was being rolled, a small piece of parchment fell out on the floor of the hut. More writing. Same style. Same author? This time, it was clearly in the form of a letter. Yeshai had no trouble reading it.

May the God who preserved our people from harm during years of exile and atonement and returned the remnant of Judah to their land, see that this scroll finds safety in the hands of my grandson or his children.

My name is Eliezer. I am the son of Achituv the priest and scribe from the town of Gezer. I am the twin brother of Zadok. Together, we were chosen by our teacher to preserve the sacred stories of our people and our relationship to the God of Israel. These stories were written on twenty-four parchment scrolls. We divided the scrolls between us. I went into exile in Samaria. My brother carried his twelve scrolls with him to Bavel.

A singer of our people once said: "The days of our years are sixty plus ten, or by reason of strength eighty years." When I reached my seventieth year of life I began to have deep feelings of regret that I had not found a way to teach my young and impetuous grandson about his people and their story. And then the way was shown to me from one of the scrolls I had carried into exile in Samaria. That scroll describes when Moses' tribe of Levi and the tribes of Judah and Benjamin were freed from Egyptian slavery. The scribe says that Moses wanted the tribes to remember the moment they were free, by celebrating a festival each year on the very day of freedom.

"You shall tell your children on that day, our freedom is due to the God of our ancestors who sent us out of Egyptian slavery. We were slaves in the land of Egypt."

I am following the words of Moses. In the hidden scroll you must have unrolled, I am telling you about our ancestors, our journey from slavery to kingship, our covenant with the God who freed us, and our worship of gods who had no power and no existence.

Your grandmother, Shoshanna bat Talmon, may eternal peace be upon her, my beautiful wife, was the daughter of a Samaritan tribal chief. She was also a very talented weaver of cloth. For years, I watched her take individual threads of many colors and place them on the loom. Slowly, with each pass of the shuttle, a pattern would emerge. The finished cloth, when held at arms length, shows the intended design. The individual threads became something greater when joined together.

This was my plan for the scrolls. If you know well the content of the twelve scrolls, then you will know where I have used my own words or the stories of others as the loom on which the wondrous pattern of the story of our people emerges. Do not spend your life looking so closely at my added words and the colorful tales of our tribes and clans. They are only the individual threads. If you do so, you will miss the pattern and power of our story.

The hidden scroll you now possess includes every word of the twelve sacred scrolls. For the future of our people and their continued loyalty to the God who brought them back from the sure extinction of exile, I now call upon you to swear an oath before the God of our ancestors, that you will do as I now command.

You must swear before God that you will destroy the twelve sacred scrolls in your possession. Burn them to ash and then bury them in consecrated ground. Let the hidden scroll that lies open before you become the Sefer Torat Moshe—the Scroll of the Revelation of Moses.

"Yeshai, do you so swear?"

"What?" Yeshai looked up from the letter with a start. His imagination got the better of him. He thought his grandfather had arisen from the dead and had joined him in the hut to make him swear the oath. The truth was nothing so wondrous or dramatic. His father Gilad had entered the hut while he was totally involved in the reading of the letter from his grandfather.

"It is a simple question. Do you swear the oath my father demands?"

"As God lives, I so swear."

"Will you do as he says in his letter?"

"I will."

"Now?"

"Now."

As High Priest, Gilad had the authority to dismiss the guards from their posts. He told them to get something to eat and then return to the hut. Yeshai discovered that his father was well prepared to carry out the destruction of the twelve sacred scrolls. Standing to the left of the hut entrance was a large clay pot with a broad opening at the top and three narrow openings around the sides at the bottom. The openings at the bottom would serve as vents to increase the temperature of any fire set within.

One scroll at a time, Yeshai set a corner of the parchment on fire with the flame from the oil lamp. Gently he lowered the scroll into the pot and stood silently as it was totally consumed in flames. In all, it took an hour for the twelve scrolls to be reduced to ash. Gilad used his staff of office to stir the ashes at the bottom of the pot. Another half hour would pass before the pot was cool enough to lift and carry. The night was dark and cool.

"What did Saba mean by consecrated ground?"

"I know where they belong."

In a quarter of an hour they walked beyond the boundaries of their village, to the Judean exile cemetery. Gilad went straight to the burial cave of his father, Eliezer. Even in the complete darkness, he knew where to find the bone box that contained the remains of Eliezer ben Achituv. The Bone box for his grandmother, Shoshana bat Talmon was right next to it. He lifted that box from the shelf.

"Give me your knife, Yeshai."

With the flint knife, Gilad opened a small hole in the sealed clay top of the bone box. In daylight they might have been able to see Shoshana's name written in thick ink, on the front side of the box. When the hole was finished, Yeshai lifted the clay pot and carefully poured the ashes of the twelve sacred scrolls into the opening. Gilad placed fresh clay over the hole and restored the box to its original position on the top shelf of the man made cave.

Yeshai had fulfilled his oath. The twelve sacred scrolls were no more. Their words now lived within the *Sefer Torat Moshe*.

Chapter Thirty-One

DATE: March 18, 2009

TIME: 5:45 P.M. Local Time

PLACE: On the Beach Behind The Carelton Hotel, 10 Eliezer Peri
                 Street, Tel Aviv

The sunset over the steel gray Mediterranean was spectacular. The clouds in the west were perfectly aligned across the sun, producing long and wide beams of light radiating above and below the formation. The total effect was almost spiritual, but the beauty of the moment was about to be shattered.

Launching an anti-terror operation from an ALDO ice cream parlor was not in any Marine Corps manual Gunnery Sgt. Aaron Keller had studied. The shop was a part of a very popular chain in Israel, declared by the guidebooks as having the best ice cream in Israel. This one was located directly behind the Carlton Hotel and at the beginning of the *Tayelet,* the Tel Aviv Beach Promenade. The *Tayelet* was a broad concrete walkway with swirling mosaic like designs that framed the beach. From the Carlton, the walkway extended south nearly four kilometers to the outskirts of Jaffa.

Aaron could not keep his legs still beneath the simulated wood topped plastic table. The anatomically shaped plastic chair must have been molded for a civilian with a much smaller behind. He begged Rafi and Omar to be a part of the take-down in Room 502. Omar simply laughed and walked away. Rafi was polite enough to explain to Keller about Israeli liability laws, should an innocent bystander get hurt in the operation and more importantly, the magnitude of probable fallout should an American Marine get hurt or killed. Aaron passed the time closely observing Abby licking a sugar cone single dip of the Israeli version of mint chocolate chip. The image was very sexy.

"You should try the pistachio, Sergeant. It is always excellent!" Malik said. "You can tell a lot about a person by the way they eat an ice cream cone. Some like the long slow lick. Others bite into the ice cream with great violence. Others seek to prolong the experience by taking dainty licks like a kitten."

"Do you mind, Professor, I am trying to concentrate here."

"Concentrate on what? There is nothing for us to do but wait patiently for the *Shin Bet* to retrieve our scroll. Have an ice cream, it will calm your nerves."

"My nerves are calm."

"Yes, I can see just how calm you are."

"You two should take this show on the road. Let's just make sure that we do as Rafi ordered and keep our eyes on the rear beach level service doors to the hotel." Abby said all of this, never taking her eyes off the door in question.

A young man and a woman sat on a small bench to the left side of the door. A full sized baby carriage was between them. They were *Shin Bet* operatives guarding the exit. From time to time, the man or the woman would lift their hand to their mouth and speak into the end of their sleeve. An occasional nod towards the window of the ice cream parlor was all Abby was receiving to indicate whether there was any progress in the operation.

Malik suddenly stood up and violently tossed his ice cream cone into the trash.

"Shit, this is all wrong! Sergeant, use the radio and get them out of that hotel room—now!"

"They never gave me a radio. What's the matter?"

"The ten million euros. That's what's the matter."

"Right, they were deposited in the numbered account. So?"

"The Israel-based Samaritans are a modestly successful community, but they do not have the resources to wire transfer ten million euros around the world. Where did they get the money?" Abby asked, her eyes still locked on the rear exit.

"You are a very clever rabbi. You remind me of my teacher in Baghdad."

"Your teacher in Baghdad had a beard and a life style from the twelfth century. Where do you think they got the money, Professor?"

"From the Palestinians or the black hats. My money is on the black hats."

"Black hats?" Aaron asked, a puzzled look on his face.

"The Ultra-Orthodox with their American backers on the right wing fringe," Abby said.

"So, I say again, what's the problem?"

"Outside investors means outside muscle making sure that an investment of that magnitude is going to pay off. The Samaritans may be the ones taking custody of the scroll, but the investors will be there to back them up."

"How would they know what is happening and how could they be in place so fast?"

"I would imagine that electronic surveillance of the Samaritans was set up with their assistance and full knowledge. We must assume that they got in place just as we got in place. Their goal would be to block any move on our part to obtain the scroll."

Abby heard no gunshots. She saw the couple with the baby carriage slump forward and then fall from the bench. Dark stains of blood appeared on their light colored windbreakers. She was on the move immediately, running from the ice cream parlor directly toward the hotel exit.

"Abby, where are you going...?" Aaron yelled, then spotted the *Shin Bet* couple on the ground.

"Get down! You don't have a vest or a gun. We don't know what is going on yet. Stop, for God's sakes! You'll get hurt."

By the time Aaron uttered those last words he had caught up with Abby and tackled her from behind.

"We've got to do something! We can't just sit here. Get off of me!"

"Your getting killed is not exactly a solution. First, we need to assess the situation. Did you see anyone come out of the door?"

"Not really. I think I saw the door open a crack and then the couple fell off the bench. We have to help them. They might still be alive!"

"Not a chance. Whoever put them down is a pro. No noise. Silencer. At the most, two shots. They are waiting to see if there is any follow-up action—any agents coming to their rescue. They might not have seen you bolting from the shop. We need to move down the beach and when we are sure they can't see us, work our way back to the wall of the hotel. If they don't know we are here, they might try and use the beach as their escape route. I have a nine mil, but it only has fifteen in the mag. Are you OK?"

"Covered in sand, but aside from having the wind knocked out of me, I'll survive. Let's get moving. Oh, where is the professor?"

Aaron turned around to look at the ice cream parlor window. The shop lights were on in anticipation of nightfall. Malik was standing in the window looking in their direction and talking on his cell phone at the same time. With his free hand he gave a 'thumbs up' and then moved his hand in a vigorous 'get moving' wave.

"I think he's made contact with Rafi and Omar. He's signaling us to get off the beach in a hurry."

Abby and Aaron made a dash for the hotel wall, Abby in the lead and Aaron right behind her. Two thoughts entered Aaron's mind during the one hundred yard dash. First, that Abby ran fast, very fast, track star fast. And second, that he really enjoyed the view of her in motion.

There was no evidence that they had been observed, no sand kicking up from gunshots, only the sound of the nearby surf at high tide. At the wall they flattened themselves against the rough concrete and caught their breath. Aaron was pissed that it took him longer to catch his breath than it did for Abby to catch hers.

"Did you run track or something? You were really moving."

"Field Hockey, right forward. I'm dangerous with a stick in my hand."

"Sorry, I'm not carrying any sticks today. As we move along this wall toward the door, stay glued to the wall and behind me. We need to give them as small a target as possible."

"Aye aye, Gunnery Sergeant!"

"Uh, excuse me, ma'am. No disrespect intended."

"You are the one with urban combat experience, not me. I yield to your expertise in this area."

The total elapsed time, from the death of the two *Shin Bet* agents to the moment when Aaron and Abby were three feet from the hotel exit, was less than four minutes. There was still no sign of movement from inside the hotel. Neither Abby nor Aaron was comfortable with the total lack of intel as to what was happening inside. The hotel service doors suddenly burst open and two men, dressed all in black, made a dash for the service driveway that connected to Eliezer Peri Street.

Aaron took up a firing stance with the pistol firmly in both hands and squeezed off six shots. Both runners went down. One did not move and did not make a sound. The second runner was grabbing his ass with both hands and moaning and wailing from alternating waves of pain.

"You are truly dangerous, Gunny. I think one of them is dead."

"Get back against the wall. We don't know if this is over yet."

A firm hand grasped Aaron's shoulder. He spun around ready to fire.

"*Rak Rega* Marine! Hold on, don't shoot me, hombre."

It was Malik doing a Hebrew accented John Wayne impression.

"That was some mighty nice shootin'. I just heard from the *Shin Bet* boys. It's over. Rafi too sensed that something was not kosher about the ten million. Rafi did bring extra people, but they failed to spot one of the Palestinians and he was the one who killed our agents. It's a real loss. I know their parents."

"Did anyone get the killer?" Abby asked.

"Sergeant Keller dropped him. He's not the dead one. He's the one grabbing his ass and crying for *Emah*."

"Who is he?"

"Too soon to tell. One thing for sure, he's no Samaritan. He's a Palestinian. My guess, he was hired by whoever put up the ten million."

With flashing lights from ambulances and police vans and camera strobes going off every few seconds, the scene at the side of the hotel was like a cop show movie set. Aaron and Abby sat patiently on a stone ledge taking it all in. Malik was deeply engaged in conversation with a familiar looking uniformed police commander. And then Aaron made the connection. He was the district commander for terrorism that was involved in the meeting at the hospital. Malik broke away and walked toward Aaron and Abby. The police commander was right behind him.

"Sergeant Keller, may I have your weapon please?" Lt. Colonel Natan Lavi asked.

"To be perfectly honest, Colonel, it was given to me by the *Shin Bet* agent known to me as Rafi. I think it is his." Aaron removed the pistol from his windbreaker pocket, gripping it from the barrel and slowly offering it to Lavi.

"Rafi has made me aware of his gift to you. I suppose I should thank you for making sure that the criminals did not get away, but now I am faced with a mountain of forms and paperwork that will have to make sense out of an American Marine killing a criminal on the streets of Tel Aviv with a weapon provided by our security service. Since it would appear that you are still in danger, please take this Beretta as a replacement. Take good care of it. It's one of my favorites." Lavi handed Keller the compact automatic.

"Might I make a suggestion, Colonel?"

"Of course, Professor, this is your operation. It's your call."

"Why don't you write this up as a tribute to the bravery of Yael and Gidon who, although making the ultimate sacrifice with their lives, were able to bring down two of the criminals. It might bring some peace to their parents."

"I can do that, just so long as you are able to make sure that all of this forensic evidence being gathered here, gets lost—permanently."

"At my age, I am an expert at losing things and forgetting where I put them."

Abby and Aaron both stared at Malik.

"What did he mean, 'This is your operation.'?"

"I suppose he meant that the *Shin Bet* boys and girls were working to obtain something that belongs to us."

"You can only shmooze us for so long and then we catch on. You are more to Colonel Lavi and the *Shin Bet* than a history professor." Stone said.

"I am just a retired *Mossad* field commander calling in a few favors. Nothing more."

Aaron stared at Malik a long moment.

"Now what?" Abby asked.

"Here comes Omar. Maybe he can tell us what happened inside.

Perspiration dripped down his face. Dressed from head to toe in black and wearing a black Kevlar vest, Omar carried a deadly looking assault rifle slung over his shoulder. His hair was sweaty and matted, probably from wearing a helmet.

"Rafi will be out in a moment. He is asking one of the Samaritans a few questions. He also has the scroll. It's safe and undamaged, as far as I can see."

"Anyone else hurt inside?" Malik asked.

"No one was hurt during the actual operation. The shooting came later. We grabbed the Samaritans in the hotel room. Someone else starting shooting into the room through the door using a silencer. We returned fire and chased them down five flights of stairs and lost them on the first floor of the hotel. They must have found cover somewhere along the way, because the next thing we knew they were shooting their way out the back. The rest you already know."

"Do you know who the shooters were?" Aaron asked.

"They are Palestinians, but not terrorists, just criminals."

"What's the difference?"

"Rabbi, do I really need to explain that to you?"

"What I meant to say, is how do you know they're just criminals?"

"According to Colonel Lavi, one has been arrested before as part of an undercover operation against a car theft syndicate operating on the West Bank. It was a simple operation. Steal the fancy cars from Tel Aviv suburbs and then strip the parts in Nablus."

"So you think that is how the Samaritans and the Palestinians hooked up?"

"Actually, Rabbi, we are not sure. When the shooting started, it was very clear to us that the Samaritans were taken by surprise as well. They started yelling at us to tell our men to stop shooting. When we informed them that all of our men were either in the room or accounted for, they had a look of real terror in their eyes. They definitely were not expecting someone to attempt to rescue them."

"We need to have a chat with the momma's boy." Malik said.

"While I doubt that he is any kind of mastermind, he just might point us in the right direction."

"Based on his cries of pain, I think we will manage to obtain all we can from him with only a brief amount of water-boarding."

"Omar, you can't!"

"Relax, Rabbi. I was only kidding. You Americans are so programmed to believe the worst about Israel. Actually, we are going to have Sergeant

Keller's bullet pulled from his *tuches*, as your Ashkenazic relatives would say, and then we will take him to the Spa for a massage and a facial."

"No, really—what will happen to him?"

"The 'SPA' is an acronym for ***Shirut hei-Feir Oivim***. The translation is kind of forced but it means the Service for Frustrating Enemies. The acronym guys loved the idea of calling it the SPA, so that's what it is. It is where all of our intelligence agencies meet to share information. In a few hours we should know who is paying this guy." Before Omar had finished, Rafi, dressed identically with Omar, was at his side. He extended his hand to Abby. The scroll was still in the Marine issue towel Keller had originally placed it in.

"I believe you will want this." Rafi said, extending his hand.

"Now it is even more precious. It has cost two Israeli lives. Take good care of it. I hope what you learn from it will be worth the cost."

"So do we, Rafi, so do we. Thank you!"

Malik, Abby, and Aaron returned to Malik's home. It was 8:30 p.m. The streets of Tel Aviv were full of traffic. The trio decided to make do with a meal from Malik's pantry. It was more breakfast than dinner, but the fresh bread and strong coffee pushed away any fatigue. After cleaning up, Malik pulled the drawstrings on the kitchen garbage bag and walked to the back door.

"Where are you going?" Aaron said.

"Where does it look like I'm going? You see, this is garbage and what we do with it is put it in the garbage can at the back of the house so the rats and cats can battle all night for their share."

"I'm coming with you."

"I'll be fine. Relax."

A few moments later, Malik returned, without incident.

"For the moment we are safe. It will take a day or so for whoever sent the criminals to figure out their next move. Meanwhile we have to use this time to figure out what the scroll means or contains."

"Well, we can't go back to Hebrew Union's lab. That's for sure. I never imagined that Gadi Sagal or Professor Carlson could be thieves."

"Every rabbi I ever met was always too trusting, something about faith in the basic goodness of humanity. Maybe it was a direct result of Jews not believing in original sin," Aaron suggested.

"Where do you get this nonsense and how many rabbis have you known?

"I think I read it in *Judaism for Dummies*. And you are only the second rabbi I have known. But both rabbis made a big impression on me."

"Children, could we recover our focus long enough to return to the question of the scrolls?"

"Of course, professor." Abby was tired and sounded it.

"It's been a long day. Let's get a fresh start in the morning—early in the morning, say departing here at 7:00 a.m.?"

"That's two hours later than I usually arise, but that will work." Aaron did not wait for Abby to answer. He was halfway to the bedroom.

Malik went to bed with his own loaded Beretta beneath his pillow. Despite his efforts to calm Aaron, he was taking no chances. Whoever was bankrolling the Samaritans was not someone to take for granted.

Around 3:20 a.m., the sound of something solid and heavy hitting the floor woke Malik with a start. He grabbed his gun and threw on a robe—he did have guests in the house after all. While the sight of a nude *alte kocker* might frighten away the bad guys, he did not want to end up shot by Keller, nude on the floor. The thought of his demise captured on digital cameras and downloaded on Facebook was about as terrifying as anything he had endured in his 79 years of life, including torture at the hands of the Iraqis.

With silent steps, he padded his way down the hall and placed his ear on the door to what had become Keller and Stone's room. From the sounds within, either the Americans were wrestling with an intruder, or more likely, they were wrestling with each other. Either way, there was a lot of panting and groaning. Malik decided that the noise was the sound of Keller's replacement weapon hitting the floor.

"Thank God no one got shot!" Malik said to no one in particular, as he made his way back to his room. Lovemaking was such a life-affirming act. With that thought, he slept like a baby until his alarm went off at 6:00 a.m.

Chapter Thirty-Two

DATE: The Twenty-Second Day of the Twelfth Month, In the
            Sixty-Eighth Year since the Destruction of Jerusalem

TIME: First Hour of the Third Watch

PLACE: City of David, Jerusalem

The makeshift prison compound was built in the neighborhood known
as the City of David. The relationship to David may have been legend,
but this was clearly no city. At best it was a slum. It bore a closer resemblance
to a refuse pile. The natural sloping topography going downward from the
well-named "Dung Gate" meant that anything discarded from Jerusalem
would eventually end up there. Yeshai, son of Gilad, son of Eliezer, son of
Achituv, the priest, had become part of the refuse routinely dumped outside
of the city's gates.

Yeshai's hands were tied above his head to a stout tent pole anchored
deep into the dirt floor. His feet were bound together in front of him. He
sat on the ground with his back against the rough-hewn pole. The goat-hair
canopy kept the steady rain from falling directly on his head, but did not
stop the rivulets of runoff from passing beneath his buttocks. He could not
stop shivering, except when his pride got the better of him. Whenever the
interrogators would enter the tent, he would make a valiant effort to control

the shivering. Anger gave him the inner strength to control his body. He was a *cohein,* a priest. They had no right or cause to treat him like a common criminal.

Two weeks had passed since Yeshai's arrival in Jerusalem. Heavy rains caused a fatal slow-down of the shabby caravan of exiles from Samaria. Ten infants and fourteen older adults developed fevers and had died as a result of the cold and damp. After the exhausting four-day journey had become a five- day journey, the Judean refugees from Samaria were not greeted as long lost tribal brothers and sisters. They were treated as traitors, spies, or worst of all, Samaritans. Each one was questioned extensively before being admitted to the city. Yeshai's treatment at the hands of Levite guards was the harshest of all.

"You wear the headdress of a priest. Who did you steal it from?"

Each question was punctuated by a stinging blow to Yeshai's upper arms. The interrogator was a young and burly Levite. He was not interested in anything Yeshai had to say.

"I stole it from no one. It is mine. I am the elected chief priest of the Judeans in Samaria."

"You are a blasphemer and a traitor."

"I am your kinsman from Judah. The only thing that separates you and me is the location of our exile—you in Bavel and me in Samaria."

"You arrogant piece of dung. You are no better than the ones the Bavliim left behind. You're all the same. You claim to be descendants of Judah, but you are all liars. I will never understand why we waste our time with questions and trials. You all deserve death. You have violated the purity of Judah by marrying the whores of the land. Your children's eyes testify to your rebellion against God."

"We are all one people dedicated to the one and only living God. Why are you doing this?"

Yeshai never heard the Levites answer. The blow that followed his question was directed to his head and rendered him unconscious. It was the sound of heavy rain that brought him back. Was it minutes or hours later? He had no way of knowing. As his eyes cleared, he could see that someone had entered the tent.

The rain, driven by a strong westerly wind, began pouring into the makeshift prison. Yeshai turned to face his next tormentor. Two large torch bearing Levite guards dressed in identical dark brown tunics entered and took up positions at opposite ends of the twelve cubit by eight cubit tent. The torches cast shadows of dancing flames against the sidewalls.

A third Levite wearing a red wool over-tunic with black and white stripes at the edges entered and approached Yeshai with a drawn dagger made of expensive bronze. Yeshai held his breath and stared directly into the eyes of his murderer. If he was going to die, he was not going to close his eyes. He would make sure that his last image in life would be the eyes of his executioner. The dagger passed the right side of Yeshai's face and began to cut the ropes binding him to the center pole. The ropes around his feet were severed next.

"Stand up!" The dagger bearer commanded. He was almost the same height as Yeshai but looked as if he weighed twice as much. He tossed a bundle made from coarse cloth and tied with thin string at Yeshai's feet.

"Put them on. Hurry, we don't have all night!"

Yeshai untied the bundle. There were two garments. One was an undergarment with a drawstring sewn in at the top and the other was a simple un-dyed wool over- tunic. Worn leather sandals were at the bottom of the bundle. Both garments were loose fitting and very coarse. They were dry and that is all that mattered to him.

"Follow me!" The Levite in charge ordered.

"Where are you taking me?"

"Where you truly do not belong, Samaritan. Do not ask me any more questions. We haven't time." He spat out the word Samaritan as if he had eaten something foul and diseased.

An amazing sight greeted them when they exited the tent. The rain had stopped. The sky was free from clouds. The storm had passed and the stars, the host of heaven, were all in attendance. The Judean hills were coated in a thin film of ice. The waning quarter of the moon cast enough light to make the ground appear to be pure silver. Had it not been so cold, they would have continued to stare at the incredible view.

The Levite officer led the way up a narrow path. It might have been a true road before the destruction of Jerusalem. It was possible to make out the line where edging stones had once defined the roadway. Now most of the space was covered in debris and rubble. Fifty years before, the Bavliim had forced the left-behind Judean farmers to take apart the once great city walls, stone by stone, and block by block. Judging by the size of the stones and blocks clogging the roadway, Yeshai concluded that they must be close to the location of the Sacred House. The presence of many Levites bearing torches and the activity level of the area seemed to confirm this observation.

The small procession arrived at a compound defined by cloth stretched between posts that were each twelve cubits apart. An undulating goats hair canopy, held aloft by thick poles four cubits high, created an impressive interior space. Yeshai estimated it was as large in area as the Samaritan Temple courtyard. The entire interior space was covered in woven reed mats. Each mat had unique geometric designs. At the end opposite the entrance was a raised platform covered in carpets of intricate design. Cushions were placed on the platform for seating. Next to one of the cushions, on a frame made of wood, was a stretched sheet of parchment. A detailed drawing took up most of the space on the parchment. Yeshai studied the parchment, looking at designs for the Temple restoration. Alone on the platform was a heavily bearded priest dressed entirely in what must have been expensive white linen. A blue linen turban sat upon his head. Across his shoulders was a sky blue robe made from a very unusual material that appeared to move like water flows.

"Come here that I may see your eyes," ordered the priest.

"What is your name?" The priest was speaking Hebrew very carefully.

"I am Yeshai, son of Gilad, son of Eliezer, son of Achituv from Gezer. I am the Chief Priest of the Judeans in Samaria."

"O-ho, so you say, so you say." The priest muttered in Aramaic to himself.

"Look at me directly!" he said.

Not surprised by the coldness in the priest's eyes, Yeshai stared at the tent wall behind the priest on the platform.

"I am Yayshua ben Yo-tsadak, a direct descendant of Zadok the High Priest in the generation of the anointed of the Almighty, King David."

Yeshai got down on his hands and knees and prostrated himself on the reed mat floor.

"At least you show decent manners for a Samaritan, I'll give you that."

"I am not a Samaritan. My grandfather, Eliezer, was an apprentice scribe in the Sacred House that stood in this place."

"Actually, I know that. Get up. I also know that your grandfather and his brother, Zadok rescued the sacred scrolls of our people from the hands of the Bavli. Do not look so surprised. We know all about you priests and scribes in Samaria. We also know that your grandmother was Shoshana bat Talmon, a Samaritan whore."

Yeshai lunged at the priest. From out of nowhere, two Levite guards grabbed him from behind and pushed his face, once again, into the floor.

"Let him up." Yayshua ben Yo-tsadak said.

"My grandmother was but a child when your brother priest, Ezekiel ben Buzi enlisted her as a messenger to the Samaritans. Without her, the sacred scrolls would have been destroyed by the Bavliim."

"Yes, yes, that is all well and good. We are well informed of the fable of Judeans living in Samaria."

"What do you mean, 'fable'?"

"You know as well as I do that the Judeans who escaped exile by running to Samaria were all deserters. Your heroic tale was concocted by your grandparents in order to erase their shame. The One who promised this land to our ancestors intended that the entire House of Judah would suffer exile. This was our punishment. Only through exile could we atone for our sins. You deserters have not suffered as we have suffered. Therefore, you have not participated in the atonement."

"As I look around this place, you and your host of Levites do not look as if you have suffered all that much. How is your own atonement progressing?"

"Your impudence will cost you, polluter of the seed of Aaron."

"Why am I here?"

The priest, Yashuah shifted on his cushion. He gazed about the pavilion, and then ordered the Levite guards to leave his presence. They protested, but he was insistent. He then lowered his voice, practically to a whisper.

"Where are the sacred scrolls?"

"The clan chiefs of the Samaritans stole them from us before they drove us out of Samaria."

"Do you think I am a fool? Our spies inform us that the Samaritans confiscated numerous copies of the sacred scrolls. The sacred scrolls themselves remain hidden. Where are they?"

"I have heard that rumor as well."

"Do not make me force this information from you."

"You cannot force from me what I do not know."

"You were their lead priest. The scrolls were in your custody. The spies say that the stone hut in which the scrolls were preserved and guarded was empty by the time your people left Samaria. You, of all people, would not have left them behind."

"Why? Do you now acknowledge the truth of the fable? Every sacred scroll copy was confiscated by the Samaritans. They barely let us leave with the rags on our bodies."

"You are a liar! People will die because of your stubbornness."

"I have told the truth. Here is more truth. My grandfather Eliezer ben Achituv made me swear an oath that I would destroy the original sacred scrolls."

"More lies!"

"It is the absolute truth." Yeshai left out the part about destroying the original scrolls long before the Samaritans expelled the Judean community from Mt. Gerizim. He also failed to mention the hidden scroll, the *sefer torat moshe.*

"Why would Eliezer the famous rescuer of the scrolls demand their destruction?"

"He did not want the Samaritans to claim the scrolls as their own heritage. Without the originals, they could not do this."

"Who could be sure what is original and what is a copy?"

"Have you seen the original scrolls?"

"Of course not." This answer would help Yeshai compose his fable. He proceeded to do so.

"Each scroll bears a wax seal at the end of the last column of text. This wax seal bears the imprint of the cylinder seal of the High Priest serving at the time they were written." It sounded so reasonable, even Yeshai was inclined to believe it.

"Only scrolls with those seals are authentic. Those are the ones I reduced to ashes. They exist no more."

"Your grandfather was a madman, and you have committed blasphemy." Yayshua ben Yo-tsadak arose from the platform and began walking back and forth in front of Yeshai, stroking his beard and reflecting on what he had just heard.

This much he knew. The returnees from Bavel carried with them copies of the sacred scrolls. Leaders of the Judeans in Bavel refused to allow the originals to make the journey to Jerusalem. To verify the story of the Judean from Samaria would take a month or two of correspondence with Pumbedita...and then what?

Yayshua ben Yo-tsadak made it his personal mission to locate the sacred scrolls and insure their safekeeping. Nevertheless, he could not fulfill this task. There was no secure way for him to send Judeans north to Samaria. The political climate was deadly, and the Samaritans wanted the Judeans to return to Bavel. They did not like sharing the Province Beyond the Rivers with the returning exiles. At that very moment, marauding bands of Samaritan soldiers were killing Judeans from the south on sight. They were even so bold as to conduct night raids on Jerusalem, in order to disrupt the rebuilding of the Sacred House. If this young so-called priest was to be believed, the sacred scrolls once preserved in Samaria were gone forever. But was he telling the truth?

"Set me free. I have done nothing wrong."

"Nothing wrong? By your own words, you have admitted destroying the sacred word of the God of our ancestors. Your own people have witnessed you worshipping in the sanctuary of the Samaritans and offering sacrifices there." Yayshua wished to be done with the matter. He had better things to do than chase after scrolls that didn't exist. His path was now clear.

"You shall be made an example, burned at the stake for your crimes."

"Guards! Take this *mamzer* back to the tent of confinement. Bind him securely and do not let him out of your sight. Tomorrow, he will die for his insults to the God who redeemed us from exile."

Late into the night, Yeshai prayed for deliverance from his sentence. Two hours before dawn he heard a noise outside the tent. Suddenly the entrance flap parted and a tall, dark skinned Persian officer dressed entirely in shimmering black robes, entered the tent and immediately cut Yeshai's bonds with a short, slim silver dagger.

"Who are you?"

"I am Memukan, *Pecha* of Bavel and personal messenger of the Emperor. We have no time to waste. Follow me!"

As they exited the tent, Yeshai looked upon the Levite Guards, motionless on the ground.

"Are they dead?"

"They will awaken when we are far away from here. Now hurry! Our horses are below. Follow the path as quickly as you can."

Yeshai realized that they were following the road to Jericho. They were riding on four magnificent Persian horses, each the color of the night sky. They rode in complete silence for an hour. Rays of light crept over the eastern horizon. The man called Memukan ordered his escorts to stop and rest the horses. A winter stream paralleling the road had captured water from the rain of the previous evening. Everyone including the horses drank their fill. The water was clear and cool. For Yeshai, it was time to get some answers. He cleared his throat and began haltingly in Aramaic, the language of the Empire.

"Who sent you and why are you doing this? Am I your prisoner?"

"Your cousin Hilkiah ben Shallum ben Zadok in Pumbedita sent me to bring you to him. For two months we have been riding all over Samaria and Judah looking for you. You were a hard man to locate. You have many friends in Pumbedita, most of them are your relatives. They want the sacred scrolls."

"Now you? It would seem that I am only worthy of rescue because of the scrolls. Well, I have some difficult news for you. The scrolls no longer exist. And about this I am not lying. That is why the returned priests wanted to kill me. I gave them the same news. You might as well kill me and get it over with."

"We are not here to kill you. There were two parts to our mission: first, find the scrolls and second, bring you to Pumbedita."

"I still do not understand."

"Your family needs you and the Emperor agrees. Your place is in Bavel. A disaster has befallen your family. By the time we return, Hilkiah may already be dead. You are the last of the Ben Achituv scribes."

"What is that supposed to mean?"

"Exactly what it sounds like it means. You are, as far as we know, the last in a line of scribes descended from Achituv from Gezer. You are needed in the community of Judeans of Bavel."

"The leaders of that community in Judah were about to have me burned at the stake. Why would I want to place myself under their rule?"

"Perhaps in order to remove the sentence of death which hangs over you. I carry the Emperor's seal. His Median priests have prophesied that Judah must be restored before the throne of Persia will be secure."

"What does that have to do with Judean scribes?"

"In the days of Cyrus, your great aunt Miryam, wife of Zadok ben Achituv, created scribal schools among the Judeans in Bavel. The Emperor was greatly impressed with her skill and dedication. Four months after the Judeans left for their return journey to Jerusalem, the Emperor visited the city of Pumbedita, along with the schools set up by Miryam. He took note of her care for the sacred scrolls. He asked her to read to him from the scrolls. Over the course of several days, she read to His Majesty from the scrolls of your people."

"I still do not see what the traditions of my people have to do with the exalted Emperor of Persia."

"The Emperor developed great respect for your God. He believed that his victories over the Bavliim were because of the power of the God of Judah. He inquired of Miryam as to what steps he should take to secure his throne. She saw this as a moment of great opportunity, so she responded that the Emperor must protect the Judeans and their sacred scrolls, both in Judah and in Bavel. You are needed in Bavel to continue copying, protecting, and preserving those scrolls and the scribal schools as well."

"Surely my Bavli cousins have trained many capable scribes, just as my family had done in Samaria."

"That may be so, but in the shadow of the illness that has befallen Hilkiah, your scribes in Bavel have divided into factions. Some wish to continue their life in Bavel, but others insist that there is only one place for Judeans and that is in Judah."

"But that is a dispute for Judeans, not Persians."

"It is not so simple. Have you not heard of the many gifts the empire has bestowed upon the Judeans for the building of their Sacred House and their nation? Do you think those gifts come without a price? The return of the Judeans from exile was not just a sign of Cyrus's respect for your God. He expected Judean loyalty in return. Judeans were expected to guard the empire against the grand ambitions of the Egyptians. Only a united Judean people can hope to stand against the mighty pharaohs."

"They cannot even stand up to the might of Samaria; how are they supposed to stand up to Egypt?"

"Our enemies wish to encourage divisions among the nations of the empire, to weaken the power of the sons of Cyrus. Your cousin Hilkiah saw great danger; should it happen that because of their lack of unity and purpose, the Judeans would be blamed for the defeat of the Empire by Egypt. He believed that only one such as you, trained in the sacred scrolls, could bring the factions back together."

"He never knew me. I never even met him!"

"He believed that because you lived in Samaria, you were unpolluted by the stench of exile. Hilkiah was just able to convince the assembly of Judeans in Bavel to send for you. The Emperor was pleased by their decision. It was the first time in many months when they managed to agree on anything."

"Why is it you and not some Judean sent to find me?"

"Here is Hilkiah's seal. I am his friend. He made me swear by my gods that I would search for you and bring you back. I hope he is still alive when we return."

Yeshai rubbed the cylinder seal between his thumb and first finger. Then he looked carefully at the carved impression. He reached for his water skin and poured out a palm full of water on the ground, then worked the wet soil into a flat, smooth surface. Finally, he rolled the cylinder seal through the damp flattened earth. The seal quickly revealed its owner's identity.

Hilkiah ben Shallum ben Zadok ben Achituv M'gezer—Shomer Sefer Torat Moshe. The seal belonged to Hilkiah. This was certain. But the phrase which followed his name took Yeshai's breath away—"Guardian of the scroll of the teaching of Moses." Yeshai's mind was made up.

"I will go with you on one condition."

"Priest, you are in no position to make demands. Get on your horse, now!"

"I will go with you, but first we must turn around and head north to the town of Anatoth." Yeshai was insistent.

"You will place yourself in the territory of the very people who would have you roasted on a stake. You said so yourself."

"Listen to me," Yeshai said.

"Yes, I destroyed the twelve sacred scrolls, as my grandfather made me swear to do. But you need to know that there is still a sacred scroll hidden in

Samaria. The contents of the twelve other scrolls are contained within that single scroll. Over the course of many weeks, I made a copy of that scroll. The original I returned to its hiding place. It is secure. The copy I took with me when the Samaritans expelled us from their land. As we drew near to Jerusalem, I realized that the possession of that single scroll would be my death warrant, so I gave it to the priests of Anatoth for safe keeping."

"Just like that you gave it to other priests?" Memukan was having difficulty believing Yeshai's tale.

"The priests of Anatoth are trustworthy. They never sank into the idol worship of the Jerusalem priests. I knew that they would not hand the scroll over to the Jerusalem priests. There has been enmity between Anatoth and Jerusalem since the days of the prophet Jeremiah."

"Who?"

"Never mind. Will you take me to Anatoth?

"Take these." Memukan handed Yeshai a short bronze dagger and a bronze curved sword.

"We may have to fight our way out of Anatoth. I hope this scroll is worth it."

"It is the word of our God through Moses his prophet."

The king of Assyria brought men from Babylon and from Cuthah and from Avva and from Hamath and Sepharvaim, and settled them in the cities of Samaria in place of the sons of Israel. So they possessed Samaria and lived in its cities. At the beginning of their living there, they did not fear the Eternal; therefore the Eternal sent lions among them, which killed some of them. So they spoke to the king of Assyria, saying, "The nations whom you have carried away into exile in the cities of Samaria do not know the custom of the god of the land; so he has sent lions among them, and behold, they kill them because they do not know the custom of the god of the land." Then the king of Assyria commanded, saying, "Take there one of the priests whom you carried away into exile and let him go and live there; and let him teach them the custom of the god of the land." So one of the priests whom they had carried away into exile from Samaria came and lived at Bethel, and taught them how they should fear the Eternal. (II Kings 17:24-28)

Chapter Thirty-Three

DATE: March 19, 2009

TIME: 7:30 A.M. Local Time

PLACE: Archeology Building, Tel Aviv University

Strong coffee and fresh pastries from the *A Roma* Café gave Malik, Keller and Stone an alertness that would have to see them through the day. At 7:30 a.m., in front of the Archeology Building at Tel Aviv University, they met up with a grad student of Professor Malik.

"Permit me to introduce one of my students, Akiba Eltsur. He is an accomplished archeologist in his own right. In a few short weeks he will be defending his doctoral thesis. Then he will be unemployed."

"Thank you so much, Professor!"

"Think nothing of it. Is the equipment ready?"

"It's all set up. The imaging lab is in the basement. Follow me."

They took the stairs just inside the entrance and descended into a basement that was empty except for a pair of steel doors at the far end. A small sign in Hebrew, English and Arabic declared this to be the entrance to the Archeology Laboratory.

"How come this is hidden away in the basement?" Keller asked.

"For some, archeology is the science of desecrating ancient cemeteries.

The Ultra-orthodox enjoy demonstrating in front of this building because the word ARCHEOLOGY shows up well on the evening news. It is a precaution well worth taking. The equipment behind these doors is expensive. This department rarely gets a second chance at big-ticket items," Akiba said.

He swiped a card in front of an electronic lock and the light on the lock changed from red to green. Akiba opened the door, switched on the lights and invited the trio to follow. The room was square, about 25 feet by 25 feet. The lighting was subdued. Since the room was filled with a variety of monitors attached to larger machines, it probably made sense to keep the lighting at a minimum to enhance viewing at the monitors.

Akiba sat at a machine that straddled a corner of the counter opposite the doors. With a few keystrokes the system began booting up.

"May I have the document in question?" Akiba asked.

"I have it, Akiba." Aaron placed the towel-wrapped package on the end of the counter, removed the cloth and revealed the leather roll. Akiba carefully untied the leather straps and began peeling the cover away from the scroll.

"Sorry, I got so excited; I almost forgot." With that, he reached for a small box on a shelf above the counter and removed a pair of white cotton gloves.

"The last thing I want to do is damage the scroll or contaminate the image."

In a manner almost identical to the technique employed by Carlson, Akiba continued peeling the cover away. A minute later the scroll was free from the cover. Akiba took a lot longer to open the scroll.

"It is truly beautiful! The lettering is amazing. Where did you get this?"

"If we tell you, we will have to kill you or simply tell the bad guys you have read the document and they will have to kill you," Malik said.

"You're kidding, right professor?"

"Just get it under the screen, Akiba."

"I'm going to put this on the wall monitor." Akiba hit a couple of keys and an enormous LCD flat screen came to life on the wall above the utility shelf.

"I know a great little sports bar in Charleston that would kill to have a TV like that."

"Sergeant, there has been far too much killing already."

"Rabbi, you are right there."

Akiba turned to look at Abby.

"I'll make introductions later, Akiba." Malik said.

"It will be up in just a…there it is!"

The quality of the image was extraordinary. Every stroke of the pen was now revealed with a clarity that showed every start and stop in the penmanship of the scribe.

"Akiba, let's see the whole scroll as one image, first," Malik said.

"Right," Akiba enlarged the image.

The edges of each line of the text were almost as perfect under magnification as they were without electronic devices.

"I have never seen so many *Taggim*. They're all over the place."

"And so they are. Sergeant Keller was absolutely correct. We can now confirm that there are no more than twenty-two points.

"It's a letter substitution code, Professor."

"We already concluded that, Akiba. Now we need to view the scroll, one letter at a time, so we can list the crown letters in order. It's not a sophisticated cipher, but it would have been very effective if it was simply passed off as decorated scroll and nothing more."

For the next hour and a half, Akiba, Malik, and Abby, patiently moved from letter to letter and counted the points and converted them into letters. Aaron, contented himself with watching the code unfold.

"Why are you not putting spaces between the words, Abby…uh Lieutenant?" Aaron asked.

"Because Hebrew, at the time this scroll was written, did not put spaces between words. We want to see what the letters looked like without making assumptions about what words they formed."

"This is where a committee might come in handy," Malik said.

"How so?"

"We shall vote on whether a word is a word. Majority wins."

"You can't be serious."

"Do you have a more accurate way of doing it, Sergeant?"

"Proceed, Professor."

"So, what does it all mean?" Aaron asked.

"*Savlanut*! Sergeant, *Savlanut*! Be patient and we shall have our answer."

"I'm already having trouble with making out the first word," Abby said.

"What word beings with *samech hey kuph*? I believe the second word is *bateivah*—'in a box' or 'in the box'."

"Rabbi, I agree with your second word. But I am having trouble with these three letters. They don't make sense," said Akiba.

"They don't make sense because they might be the first historical example of an abbreviation in the Hebrew language. *Samech, hey, kuph*… How about *sefer hakodesh*?" Malik said.

"Brilliant!" Abby exclaimed.

"How about letting a dumb Marine in on the word?"

"It's not **a** word. It's two words. *Sefer hakodesh* means: 'The sacred scroll'. If the professor is correct, it is trying to tell us where the sacred scroll is.

"So, where is it?"

"The sacred scroll is in the box."

"What box?"

"If you will be patient, we need to work out the rest of the message carefully so we do not make any stupid mistakes. With Hebrew this is not hard to do."

"Whatever you say, Rabbi."

Two more hours of painstaking analysis produced a message that was not all that transparent. Akiba was kind enough to write a translation below the Hebrew. The translation read:

THE SACRED SCROLL IS IN THE BOX BENEATH SHOSHANA BAT TALMON, WIFE OF ELIEZER BEN ACHITUV, IN THE SACRED CAVE NEXT TO, (IN FRONT OF, BESIDE, OPPOSITE) MT GERIZIM.

D/E/H/S.

"What do you think *dalet aleph hey samech* mean?"

"Try this. *Divrei Ezra Hasofer*—The words of Ezra the Scribe."

"That might be wishful thinking."

"Wait a minute!" exclaimed Akiba. "You're not saying that this scroll was written by the biblical Ezra himself...are you? You are! *Oi vavoi!*" Akiba's mouth hung open.

"Calm down, Akiba, you are getting way ahead of us. This is just a working hypothesis."

"Give me your best guess so far, Rabbi." Malik said.

"I do not know who these named people are, but I think it has something to do with a burial site."

"How did you get to that?"

"The reference to a sacred cave may be referring to a burial cave. Ancient Israelite custom was to locate a natural cave or carve one out of limestone and use it for the final resting place of human remains."

"You mean like the cave at Machpelah, the so-called Tomb of the Patriarchs?"

"Sergeant, you never cease to surprise me. Just when I assume that you have been raised with the barest minimum of a Jewish education, you demonstrate that you must have been listening a few times in Hebrew School."

"The story of the death of Sarah was my Bar Mitzvah Torah portion. Genesis: Chapter Twenty-three. Abraham purchases the cave at Machpelah to bury his wife. Didn't they dig a hole in the floor of the cave and just bury her there?"

"It wasn't that simple. They would make stone shelves or niches against the walls and lay the bodies on the shelves, wrapped in linen shrouds or whatever. The bodies would be allowed to decay naturally, and then family members would return to the cave and gather the bones of the deceased and place them in clay or stone bone boxes. Archeologists refer to them as ossuaries. The boxes would have the names of the deceased inscribed on a side of the box. The boxes would then be placed on a shelf, probably an upper shelf."

"Wait a minute! I remember a story about one of these boxes on a NatGeo special."

"What is NatGeo, Sergeant?"

"It's a cable channel in the States. It's the National Geographic Channel. They do stories about all kinds of cultural stuff from around the world. The story they did was about a bone box, like Lieutenant Stone described."

"Lieutenant Stone? Is that the same as Rabbi Stone?" Akiba was now totally confused.

"Akiba, I told you I would make introductions later. We don't have time for this. Go on."

"Well, the box had an inscription: "James brother of Jesus" carved into the side."

"It's a fake," Malik said.

"You already knew the story."

"I did not know where you were going with it. The guy who allegedly discovered the box is a known antiquities forger. He knew exactly what would get the fundamentalist Christians' bowels in an uproar. They went for it like it was the loincloth of Jesus. No evidence could dissuade them from their conviction that this was proof positive that Jesus was an actual person."

"He wasn't?"

"We shall speak of that later, if at all. Now we need to concentrate on this message."

"So, Rabbi, you think that we are being directed to a burial cave near Mt Gerizim?" Malik asked.

"It does not make historical sense."

"What is that supposed to mean?"

"There were no Judeans in Samaria at that time."

"What makes you so sure?"

"Well, everything I have read about the period in question seems to indicate that there was no love lost between Judeans and Samaritans."

"Isn't that a curious turn of phrase?" Malik asked.

"Actually, I believe there **was** love lost between the Samaritans and the Judeans. If you remember, the Second Book of Kings records that when the Assyrians brought in replacement peoples for the exiled ten northern tribes, the newly arrived peoples from the east made a request of the Assyrian king. They asked for an Israelite priest to be returned to Samaria so that he would teach them about the god of the territory. But I have never been convinced that is what happened."

"OK, what happened then?" Aaron asked.

"They invited Judeans, not Israelites, to Samaria to teach them," Abby said.

"The new arrivals sought out Judean priests because they were seen as being favored by their god."

"You know, for a rabbi, you're very smart."

"I try."

"Professor, didn't you theorize in that god-awful seminar on Ezra that when the Temple of Solomon was destroyed, not all of the Judeans went into exile in Babylonia?"

"I am still one of the referees on your thesis. I would be careful how I criticized courses dear to the *alte kocker*."

"I apologize. But if that was the case, why would the Book of Kings say specifically it was an exiled Israelite priest that was returned to Samaria?"

"The answer to that is bound up with the answer to a more important question: Who are the editors of the *sefer torat moshe*? I am in complete agreement with those who point to a Babylonian source for the Torah. I am also convinced that the text they produced was more than Genesis through Deuteronomy."

"Right; you said it was actually Genesis through Kings."

"Thank you for remembering, Akiba."

"I believe that the tradition of the Samaritans requesting a Judean priest was altered by the Judean editors of those texts to read 'Israelite priest', in order to further discredit the Samaritans," Malik said.

"How did that work?" Aaron asked.

"A major piece of Judean theology, after the exile in Babylon, was that the Northern Kingdom of Israel was exiled one hundred thirty-six years earlier because of their rampant idolatry. If the priestly tutor to the Samaritans was from the North, his faithfulness to the God of Abraham would have been suspect. As a result, the Samaritans' understanding of God would have been seen as flawed. I think the Judeans were uncomfortable with the truth, that one of their own priests instructed the Samaritans."

"Now, it could be that your theory has support from the evidence," Akiba said.

"The Ezra scroll is not evidence...yet. We have to see where it takes us. Still, I am flattered that you remembered. You are essentially correct. It is my conviction that many Judeans escaped the annihilation of Jerusalem, capture, and exile, by running north into Samaria. If there was already a resident small contingent of *cohanim*/priests, they might have persuaded the

Samaritans to allow them to make a permanent settlement there and admit the recent Judean refugees to remain as well."

"How did you ever come up with this idea?" Aaron asked.

"Do you recall my conversation with you about memorizing the genealogy of my family?"

"It's about the last thing I remember, before the bomb went off outside the tea shop."

"The first three names on that list are Achituv, then Zadok ben Achituv, then Eliezer ben Achtuv *m'shomron*. All of them were from a priestly clan, but Eliezer is the only one known as 'from Samaria'. My family tradition says he settled in Samaria. I believe that tradition. Eliezer is the brother of Zadok. Zadok ben Achituv went into exile in Babylonia."

"How do you know that?"

"Because, Sergeant, I am descended from Ezra, and Ezra is descended from Zadok. His—my genealogy is all there in the book of Ezra."

"Let me see if I am getting this." Abby began to outline a sequence of events.

"You are saying that:

1. In 586 BCE, some Judeans go into hiding or exile in Samaria.

2. While waiting for their exile to end, one or more of the Judeans hides something in Samaria.

3. More than a century later, around 445 BCE, Ezra actually knows where this object is hidden.

4. Ezra writes a coded text describing the location of the object in question.

5. The location of the object is a bone box in a burial cave in Samaria."

"That is it, essentially." Malik said.

"OK, Professor, what do you think this hidden object is?" Akiba asked.

"An original Torah."

"You mean an early copy of the Torah, don't you?"

"No, I meant precisely an original Torah. There is a great deal of circumstantial evidence that points to Ezra as the actual editor of the original Torah. While there were many sacred traditions and stories written before Ezra, no coherent Torah with a national story and theology existed. I believe that the Ezra scroll is telling us where this original Torah may be found."

"Wow!"

"Wow, indeed!"

"Wait a minute! Your theory cannot be right. If the original Torah is hidden in a bone box in Samaria, Ezra could not have brought it back from the Babylonian exile," Aaron said.

Malik nodded. "When you are right, Sergeant, you are right."

"What if there were two Torahs?" Abby asked.

"Go on."

"Well, what if the Samaritan-based Judean exiles wrote their own Torah or, better yet, what if they had written the first Torah and then shared it with the Judean exiles in Babylonia?"

"I see what you are saying. The Judeans in Samaria maintain contact with the exiles in Babylonia. They write their national story and send a copy to their fellow exiles."

"Why does Ezra want anyone to know the location of the first Torah?" Akiba asked.

"Maybe it was his way of giving authenticity to his own Torah," Abby said. "It's like he's saying my Torah is just a copy of the original, and that original is hidden in Samaria."

"This is getting way too complicated. We need to operate on what we actually know," Malik said.

"There may be issues we can never resolve," Abby said. "Just for the sake of argument, let us suppose that one or more Judeans living in Samaria invents a Torah."

"Invents?"

"Exactly. Using existing materials, stories, legends, traditions, and things made up on the spot, he, she, they put together a theological history of the household of Israel."

"Let's assume the inventor is proud of his work," Abby said. "He sends a copy to someone he trusts. In the course of time, perhaps fifty or ninety years later, the Torah invention finds its way into the possession of Ezra, the priest and scribe—yes, that Ezra, Professor Malik's grandfather fifty generations removed. At some point, Ezra realizes that the Torah invention might be a valuable asset in his battle to unify the Judeans and restore the Household of Israel to its former glory. He edits, writes, invents, his own version. Maybe it's the same. Maybe it's different. He presents it to the people as the scroll of the Teaching of Moses."

"And they buy it? Just like that?" Aaron asked.

"Sergeant, if you read the beginning of the Book of Nehemiah, it paints a bleak picture of life in the exile," Malik said. "Every nation needs its founding myth. George Washington never lied and so forth. In a time of desperation, people cling to hope and pride. The Torah would give them the sense that indeed their exile is over and they have a sacred purpose."

"I still don't understand why Ezra wanted to inform someone about the existence of the first Torah."

"Get him on the phone and ask him," Malik said.

"It's a fair question," Aaron said.

Malik nodded. "I'm just agreeing with Rabbi Stone. There are some issues we may never resolve. Our next task is to try and locate the Samaritan bone box."

"Good luck with that one." Akiba was not hopeful.

"Is that laptop connected to the web?" Abby asked.

"Sure, it's already on line through the university." Akiba said.

"What are you doing?" Malik asked.

"I am Googling 'Samaritan Ossuaries.'"

"Rabbi, you are also giving our enemies a roadmap to our intentions."

"They're not that hip, Professor."

"I would not bet my life on that, Sergeant."

"Got it!" Abby shouted in triumph.

"Here is an article in the Biblical Archeology Review describing the excavation of a fourth century BCE burial cave near Mount Gerizim. And I quote:

"The most exciting find was a collection of ossuries located on a high shelf in the deepest part of the burial chamber. The Ministry of Antiquities claimed these ossuaries on behalf of the Israel Museum."

"We can't be that lucky," Aaron said.

"Have some faith, Sergeant," Malik said.

"What are you going to do now?" Akiba asked.

"In keeping with the advances of modern information technology, I'm going to SKYPE a colleague at the museum. Perhaps she knows the location of these bone boxes."

At that moment, the first two musical phrases of *Hatikvah*, the Israel national anthem, sounded in the lab basement. It was Malik's cell phone ring tone. Malik dug his phone from his pocket and pushed the receive buton.

"Professor, this is Lieutenant Colonel Lavi. I need to speak with you and your American friends. Bring Keller and Stone with you to the Tel Aviv District Headquarters. There is some information you need to have right now!"

Chapter Thirty-Four

DATE: The Twenty-Third Day of the Twelfth Month, In the Sixty-Eighth Year since the Destruction of Jerusalem

TIME: Second Hour of the First Watch

PLACE: On The Beit El Road North of Jerusalem

"Shave your head!" Memukan was used to giving orders. He gave this order as the quartet of Persian soldiers and their rescued Judean rode slowly on the Beit El road. Yeshai rode alongside Memukan on his left.

"I must not."

"It is the only way to insure that the Judean priests will ignore you."

"I am a Nazirite."

"What does that mean."

"It means I have sworn an oath before the God of my ancestors. I made a promise to Him."

"Why would you do that?"

Why indeed? Yeshai thought. "I wanted my wife and son to live."

Memukan turned his head toward Yeshai and looked him directly in the eyes. He saw tears welling up and flowing in streaks down his road-dusted cheeks. Yeshai continued to speak, but his tone was lifeless and flat.

"When a Judean seeks the help of the Almighty for a personal reason, he takes a Nazirite oath. He gives up all manner of strong drink and is not allowed to cut his hair. Other Judeans, when they see such a person, know immediately that he has taken the Nazirite oath. In most cases they show him great respect."

"Did your god respect your oath? Did your wife and son live?" Memukan asked.

"No," Yeshai whispered.

"I do not know about all of your Judean customs, but where I come from, if the gods do not do as you have begged them to do, you are released from your oath. When did they die?"

"Two years, seven months, and fourteen days ago." The words lodged in Yeshai's throat as if he was swallowing a stick from a thorn bush. Memukan changed the subject.

"Is this sacred scroll you seek important to your god?"

"I believe it is. Yes."

"Do you also believe that your god wants you to carry it to your family in Bavel?"

"I do."

"So, until you deliver the scroll, your god wants you alive, correct?"

"That would make sense."

"The only way you are going to arrive in Bavel alive is if you disguise yourself as one of my people. If you intend to ride with my men and me, then you must look like us. Shave your head!"

Before the sun reached its highest elevation overhead, the riders dismounted and walked their horses to a wadi filled with rushing rainwater from the previous evening's storm. Memukan handed Yeshai two knives. The first had a polished olive wood handle. It was a straight flint blade half a handbreadth long. This was for cutting the hair close to the head before shaving. The second knife was a small curved flint knife with a razor sharp edge. This was for the actual shaving of the head.

Yeshai was surprised at how well the knives worked. Memukan advised him to wet his hair completely. This made the shaving easier and less painful. In less than an hour, his head was mostly smooth and slick, except for the cuts above the back of his neck. One of Memukan's soldiers had to finish that part of the task. Memukan looked Yeshai over carefully, walking a circle around him.

"Not bad for a Judean. You must have some Persian blood in you. Here, put these on." Memukan handed Yeshai a black cotton tunic and a heavy leather Persian breastplate and back piece.

"My father's mother was a Samaritan. Some of them believe they are originally from Persia," Yeshai said. The armor overwhelmed him.

"You'll get used to it. It might even save your life. Remember, when we are among the Judeans, you must only speak Aramaic. Out here, no one is going to test your knowledge of Persian."

"Shaving the head is anathema for any Judean. They could not ever conceive of one of their own shaving the head. It just is not done."

"As I said, your smooth head will keep you alive."

When Memukan and his soldiers arrived in Anatoth three hours later, Yeshai looked as if he had been in the Emperor's service his entire life. Memukan barked a few words in Persian and the real Persian soldiers dismounted. Yeshai followed their lead.

The Judean priests of Anatoth paid no attention to Yeshai. They were totally absorbed in greeting the important representative of the Emperor. So it was that their jaws dropped open in shock when the last Persian to dismount began speaking to them in flawless Hebrew.

"It's me, Yeshai ben Gilad, your brother priest!"

The priests of Anatoth shook their heads slowly in disgust and disbelief. After a few very tense moments, including Yeshai's explanation for his appearance, their manners and commitment to caring for sojourners overcame their unease with the change in Yeshai. The wayfarers were invited to bathe and refresh themselves. A simple meal was prepared for them. They spent the night sleeping in the home of the chief priest of the town. When dawn arose, the copy of the scroll written by Eliezer ben Achituv was produced by their host and presented to Yeshai. The wax seal binding the scroll was not broken. No one had read or copied the scroll. After a light morning meal, the chief priest walked with Yeshai and the Persians to the northeastern edge of their town.

Walking alongside Yeshai who was mounted on his horse, the chief priest unexpectedly pressed a small scroll into Yeshai's hands. The position of his horse prevented the passing of the small scroll from being witnessed by the other riders.

"Take this with you to the Judeans still in exile." He said quietly.

"What is it?"

"These are the words of prophecy pronounced by our brother, Yeremiyahu. In the days of the last kings of Judah, the God of our ancestors revealed to Yermiyahu what would befall Jerusalem and Judah. Perhaps this scroll and its message will help our brothers in Bavel remain faithful to the Creator of the world. I fear that the priests now in control of rebuilding Jerusalem are failing. They are becoming lazy in their service to our God. There will be more disasters to follow. May the God of our ancestors keep you safe on your journey."

Before Yeshai could question the priest further about the scroll or his concerns for the rebuilding of Jerusalem, Memukan ordered the party forward on the road out of Anatoth.

The Aramean flat-bottomed vessel put into shore at the landing below Pumbedita. One month and four days had passed since Memukan, Yeshai, and Memukan's soldiers departed from Anatoth in Judah. Yeshai's head was still clean-shaven. Caution protected them on their journey as much as their prayers. They avoided contact with local populations whenever possible. Now it was time for Yeshai to face his cousins. How would be received among the Judeans still in Bavel?

From the middle of the river, Yeshai could feel the energy of the bustling waterfront. It seemed even more alive when his feet touched dry ground. Woven reed structures built on stilts that were at least four cubits high contained a dizzying variety of goods. Grain and produce seemed to occupy most of the sheltered space visible from the river. Once the boat had landed, it would take some time for the crew of the boat to unload the horses and baggage of the Persians.

"Wait for us at the gate to the city. Do not enter on your own," Memukan said.

"I just want to stretch my legs. I will do as you have ordered."

Whatever personal rapport developed between Yeshai and Memukan on the journey disappeared the moment the boarding ramp was lowered to the shore. Memukan was once again a high-ranking official of the Emperor.

Yeshai approached a wide street that appeared to be headed in the direction of the walled city. The distance from the riverfront to the walls was almost a full parasang. Yeshai learned from a local resident who was a passenger on the boat that the town had suffered a devastating flood some years before and was so completely destroyed that the local notables decided to rebuild the city on much higher ground. Tall grasses and reeds growing in abundance were confirmation that this part of Pumbedita was indeed a flood zone.

Walls of reddish-brown mud brick and not stone surrounded the main city gate and went on for a great distance in both directions away from the gate. Enormous and beautifully carved sandstone lions stood as sentinels atop the towers that formed the gate.

Memukan and his soldiers caught up with Yeshai. They were leading his horse. Yeshai mounted and looked to Memukan for assurance that his Persian disguise was still capable of fooling the locals. Memukan said nothing and rode on at the head of the small party.

Yeshai was captivated by the sights and sounds as he entered the largest city he had ever seen. The lushness and wealth on display in Pumbedita was impressive. The color of the structures was the same as that of the ground beneath their feet. Bright colors could be glimpsed from clothing or cloth suspended on ropes behind each house, drying in the soft breeze from the East. Each home had its own vegetable garden in front and small stable in the back. Yeshai was surprised at the number of Judeans present at every turn. He recognized them because the Judeans dressed in a similar manner to their brothers and sisters in Judah. There were differences, however, in small bits and pieces of gold and silver jewelry on open but modest display. The palpable social and political tensions of the Land of Israel were absent. It was a wonder to Yeshai to ride among a people who were not afraid, not even of Persian soldiers.

"Son of Gilad, our journey together ends here." Memukan announced with no hint of interest or concern. The group halted at the head of a street that led away from a small open square. There was nothing particularly distinguishing about the street or the square, which made Yeshai curious as to why Memukan chose to stop in this particular place.

"Should you not accompany me to the home of my cousin, so that his people will be assured that I am who I say I am?"

"Yahud, your scribal skills and your knowledge of your family will gain you their acceptance. Besides, you bear a strong family resemblance to your cousin. Go now! It is the fourth house ahead, on your left. May the god who protected you on your journey, keep you all the days of your life."

"May He do so also for you. How may I adequately thank you for saving my life?"

"You may not. It is the Emperor you must thank." And with that, Memukan and his soldiers wheeled and turned in the opposite direction and rode away.

Yeshai dismounted and led his horse toward the home of Hilkiah his cousin. It was identical in size and shape to all of the other houses on the narrow street. An arched gate marked the entrance. Yeshai tethered his horse to an iron ring attached to the frame of the arch. There was no actual gate. The hinges where once a gate might have been attached were red with rust. It was difficult for Yeshai to imagine a place where gates were not required for protection from thieves and bandits.

A short stone path led to the front door. The small niche about the size of a human finger was hollowed out of the right doorpost. A delicate, fired-clay filigree concealed the presence of a tiny scroll. The simple *mezzuzah* on the doorpost announced that at the very least, this was the home of a Judean who still maintained the traditions of his ancestors. Yeshai let his fingers linger on the small scroll container, then slowly and deliberately brought them to his lips. In a silent prayer he thanked the God of his ancestors for seeing him safely to the home of his family in Bavel. At least he hoped it was the home of his family. Before he could announce his presence, the heavy door with wrought iron hinges opened before him.

"My lord, your presence brings honor on this household. May I inquire as to the purpose of your visit?" The words in Aramaic belonged to a man in his sixties. His cloak was cut from dark brown goat's hair with a light cream-colored goat's hair trim at the sleeves and hem. A nearly white beard covered most of his lower face but the smile was warm and genuine.

Yeshai replied in Aramaic. He wanted to make sure that he was in the right place before revealing his identity.

"Is this the house of Hilkiah son of Shallum son of Zadok?"

"It is."

"Are you Hilkiah?"

"I am Elimelech, his *m'chutan*—the father of, I regret to say, his widow."

"Widow?"

"He passed away from fever three days ago. Since he has no living relatives, I am here to take charge of his affairs on behalf of my daughter. May I ask who you are and what brings you to this house of mourning?"

"May the God of Abraham comfort you in your loss. I am Yeshai son of Gilad son of Eliezer, priest and scribe of the Judeans living in Samaria. We are both descended from Achituv of Gezer. I am Hilkiah's cousin."

The man called Elimelech fainted dead away. Yeshai rushed to offer aid but was pushed aside by a woman who appeared out of nowhere, wearing the garments of a mourner. He could not see her face but he could feel her strength.

"Give us room, Persian. Don't touch him!" She practically shouted in Aramaic.

"I am not a Persian!" Yeshai replied in Hebrew.

"You are not Persian and I am the widow of King David." The woman caught her breath as she realized that they were conversing in Hebrew.

"Who taught you to speak our tongue?" She asked in a near whisper as she attempted to unfold her father and lay him flat on the ground.

"My parents, of course. As I was trying to explain to your father, I am a Judean from the community of exiles in Samaria. I am your husband's cousin, Yeshai son of Gilad."

"Then why are you dressed and bald as a Persian?"

"To save my life, but that is a very long story. Is your father all right?"

"Help me to lift his legs over his head. He will recover quickly. If you are the cousin of my husband, then you are welcome in our home. But my father and I will demand proof that you are who you say you are. Now, help me to carry him into the house."

After a few sips of cool water, Elimelech made a rapid recovery but was still having difficulty comprehending Yeshai's story. He sipped the water from an earthenware cup and wiped beads of sweat from his forehead.

"I see you have met my daughter, Ruth." His head nodded in the direction of the widow sitting in the corner of the main room of the house.

"That's not a Judean name, is it?"

"My mother was a daughter of Moab." There was a sharpness to her reply.

"I did not mean to make you angry. I merely asked."

"Ruth, go into the work room and bring us some papyrus and quill and ink. I want to see if this man is indeed a scribe as he pretends to be."

"Of course, Father." In a moment she returned with the implements of a scribe. Ruth did not bring a quill prepared for writing. Instead, she handed Yeshai a handful of feathers of various sizes and a small scribe's knife. She placed a clay inkpot and papayrus sheets on the wooden table before them. She watched Yeshai as he first examined each of the feathers and selected a single light brown one. With a few simple strokes of the very sharp knife, he cleared the shaft and cut a point then held the quill in his hands to get a sense of the balance point before he made a cut and shortened the shaft. Her beloved Hilkiah worked the quills in exactly the same manner. But this proved nothing. He may have been a scribe, or at the very least, taught how to write by a scribal master. It did not make him a relative.

"You say you are Hilkiah's cousin. How much then do you know of the story of the rescue of the sacred scrolls?" Elimelech sought ways to expose Yeshai as a fake.

"It was told to me by my grandfather, Eliezer."

"Did your grandfather have any other brothers or sisters?"

"He had a twin brother Zadok who went into exile, here in Bavel."

"If you are a pretender, someone has instructed you well. Now write something that was contained in the sacred scrolls."

The thick ink was quickly absorbed into the dry papyrus sheet, but Yeshai began to put less and less ink on the tip of the quill. Elimelech glanced toward Ruth. She was fixed on Yeshai's hands and each stroke of the pen. There was no hesitation, no pausing to recall words of text. Yeshai was writing from memory and the memory was a part of him, not something learned in recent days. He filled the page with the Song of Moses at the Sea of Reeds. When he finished, he turned the page towards the father and daughter for their inspection.

"Not only are you indeed a scribe of our people, but you are an artist as well." Elimelech said, unable to hide his rising hope and admiration.

"That does not make him our kinsman." Ruth said.

"My Persian escort, the court official, Memukan, said that I bear a strong resemblance to your beloved husband, may peace be upon him. Look at me!"

Tears welled up in Ruth's eyes. She ran from the room.

"Your shaved head distorted your appearance for a while, but it was impossible to deny your resemblance to Hilkiah. You could have been twins. Dear cousin Yeshai, son of Gilad, the door of our home is open to you in blessing. I ask that you join us at our table tonight. You are welcome to stay with us for as long as your journey permits."

"I am not sure how long that will be. I am not even sure what I am doing here. Memukan made it seem as though the Emperor himself had ordered me to Hilkiah's house. But for what actual purpose, I know not."

"There is an expression current among the Judeans in Bavel. 'The God of Israel commands and the Emperor acts.' I have no doubt that you have been sent by our God to this house to preserve and protect the sacred scrolls of our people."

"There is yet more to my story than what I shared with you. I spoke of my journey here, but I did not tell you the story of the twelve sacred scrolls that Eliezer my grandather protected in Samaria."

For the next hour, Yeshai explained to Elimelech in great detail the story of the Judean priests in Samaria, the scribal school established by Eliezer, the mass copying of the scrolls, and finally, Eliezer's single scroll attempt to bring the twelve scrolls together in one narrative.

"I am a simple Judean in the Exile. So, I may not understand the meaning of all you have told me. But I do know, with certainty that God has sent you to this house. God has sent you to marry my daughter and give Hilkiah, peace be upon him, a son. You are the nearest, and it would seem only, living relative of Hilkiah ben Shallum. As a consecrated priest you are well aware that according to the laws of our people, it is your sacred duty to fulfill the obligation of the *Levir*, so that Hilkiah's name will not be erased from under heaven."

Yeshai was speechless. The pain of the loss of his own family was still an open wound that gave him no peace. Now he was about to be coerced into marrying a grieving widow in order to plant his seed, to produce an heir for the recently deceased cousin he never met.

"You must be exhausted from your journey. Take this reed mat to the roof of our home. Under the palm frond canopy you will find cool afternoon breezes that will aid in your rest. I will call you when it is time for the evening prayer."

"The evening prayer? What is that?"

"Forgive me. You Judeans have the Sacred House. We Judeans living in exile, do not. We offer prayers each day at times that mark the sacrifices taking place in Jerusalem."

"I see," Yeshai said as he followed Elimelech to an external stairway that was at the rear of the house. The steps ended on a flat roof that matched the dimensions of the house below. On the west side of the roof was a square canopy with ample shade beneath. Yeshai unrolled the reed mat, set his leather saddle pouch on the ground next to it, then struggled to remove the Persian armor. As he was doing so, he caught sight of the small scroll now visible from a corner of the pouch. He had forgotten the scroll, pressed into his hands at the last moment by the priest of Anatoth. He removed the scroll and then positioned the pouch to serve as a pillow beneath his head. Carefully, he unrolled the parchment and began to read: *"The words of Yeremiyahu son of Hilkiah, one of the priests at Anathoth in the territory of Benjamin."* 'Benjamin' was the last word he was able to read before falling into a deep and undisturbed sleep.

BOOK THREE

Chapter Thirty-Five

DATE: March 19, 2009

TIME: 7:30 A.M. Local Time

PLACE: Tel Aviv District Police Headquarters, Shalma Street

On a good day it takes twenty minutes to go from Tel Aviv University to the Tel Aviv District Police Headquarters building on Shalma Street. With Professor Malik driving, they made it in twelve.

The police building was a five-story office rotunda. In the post 9/11 world, whether in Israel or the United States, parking within a hundred feet of a major government facility was supposed to be an impossibility. This complex was no exception. Surrounding the facility, every meter and a half, a reinforced concrete post stood sentinel at the edge of the street and insured that no car truck, bus, or tank, would dare park in front of this symbol of law and order. Malik found a space on Shalma Street, directly across from the canopied entrance to police headquarters, but one hundred and fifty feet away.

S'gan Aluf Lavi met them at the front entrance security desk and asked them for their I.D. For Malik, it was his Israeli identity card. For Stone and Keller, it was their passports.

"You'll get them back when you leave. They're safe with us. Follow me."

Lavi turned and walked out the front door and made a left turn at the street. They proceeded to walk down a quiet shaded side street that paralleled the District HQ. The street was lined with stately semi-detached homes built in the 1930's and 40's. Lavi led them down the front path of the fourth such home on the street. Like the others in the neighborhood, this one was a Bau Haus exemplar in a pastel green that looked rather handsome when contrasted with the cream colored trim around the windows. Lavi knocked lightly on the solid oak door.

A stocky woman with silver hair wearing a frumpy housedress opened the door. She was about to speak but spotted Lavi and silently stepped aside. The police commander led the way. The group moved to a door located beneath the front hall stairway.

"This way. Watch your step," Lavi said.

"Was that woman going for the Golda Meir look or what? Who lives here anyway?" Aaron asked.

"Her name is Olga, if you must know, Sergeant. Did you notice her left hand? It was wrapped around a Sig Sauer nine millimeter with an expanded magazine. When we found out she was expelled from the Soviet GRU because she happened to be Jewish, we thought we might make some use of her talents. She is a first rate interrogator. As to your second question, the house is an elaborate cover," Malik said.

"No time for house tours, *Chevre*. This way."

At the bottom of the carpeted stairway was an interior solid oak door with beautiful and highly polished brass hardware. Lavi slipped a plastic electronic key into a cleverly hidden slot built into the doorjamb. The oak door released and opened. They stood at the end of a long hallway. The walls were grey concrete. Every four meters there was a heavy gage steel door. It had the look and feel of some sort of prison.

"How many guests do you have today, Natan?"

"Only one, professor. Tovya Tsadka, the Samaritan council president. He wants to share some information with us."

"Did he always want to share this information or did he have to be persuaded?" Abby said.

"Fear not, Rabbi. He very much wants to cooperate, but you can judge for yourself."

The fourth door on the left hand side of the prison-like corridor was not closed. Lavi walked in followed by Malik, Abby, and Aaron. Tsadka was seated at a metal-topped table. The Samaritan was wearing a plain white t-shirt and loose fitting khaki slacks with a drawstring at the waist.

"Permit me to introduce you to Tovya Tsadka, leader of the Crown of Samaria—*Keter Shomron* and president of the Samaritan community council."

Lavi introduced everyone to Tsadka. He used Aaron's military rank in his introduction and did the same for Abby. Abby was beginning to wonder just when it was possible for Israelis to consider her a rabbi and when it was not. Only Omar the Druze insisted on calling her "Rabbi."

"Let me start with an apology to you for the attempts on your lives." Tsadka's English was fluent and clear.

"You were not supposed to get hurt. No one was supposed to get hurt. I only agreed to scare you away from the Ezra Scroll so you would not be able to decipher its meaning. You need to know that the murderers were not from my own people. They were not even hired by me."

"The apology and explanation will not restore a murdered family," Abby said.

"I am acutely aware of that fact, Rabbi. And yes, I do know you are a rabbi. Professor Carlson is quite taken with you. He told me you were his best student."

"I don't give a damn for what Carlson thinks of me!"

"Please, I may receive a reduced sentence for my part in this disaster because of my cooperation, but I will grieve for that family every day of my life."

"When did you first meet with Carlson?" Without any preliminaries, Lavi began the questioning.

"He contacted me by email and asked to meet with me."

"When was that?" Malik sat down close to Tsadka and turned his body, facing the Samaritan straight on.

"About two years ago."

"Woa! Hold on there! I only found the scroll a few days ago." Aaron said.

"Let Tsadka continue, Sergeant. I believe you will find this fascinating. This violence is not about your precious scroll. Lavi explained.

Receiving a nod from Lavi, Tsadka continued.

"I met Carlson at the YMCA in Jerusalem. It was a Thursday afternoon, I think. I am really not that sure about the date. Anyway, we had lunch."

"What was the stated purpose for his meeting with you?" Malik asked.

"He said he was deeply interested in the history of the Samaritan Torah. He wanted to view our most ancient documents. I told him those were in East Lansing, at Michigan State University."

"Were you suspicious then?"

"Suspicious about what?

"Suspicious about his lack of basic knowledge about the Samaritan Torah and its current location. Anyone sincerely interested should have known that."

"I guess I wasn't at the time. He then requested access to the excavation of our ancient Temple on Mt. Gerizim."

"How did you respond?"

"Since he was a serious archeologist and came with glowing recommendations from colleagues, I thought that there was nothing wrong with giving him the access he requested. There was nothing extraordinary or unusual about it. I told him that we would probably grant him the permission he sought. Our council of elders would have to give their approval, but I thought it was a very doable request."

"Was that it?"

"No, not really. He then asked to visit our communities in Holon and in Nablus."

"Not just the archeological sites?"

"He claimed to want to get to know the people. Since he was an American and not Jewish, I thought I could accomplish his request. We set a date for his visits two weeks later and they went off without a hitch."

"What did he do during those visits to Nablus and Holon?"

"He took an extraordinary number of photographs with his digital camera. The elder who served as his guide in Nablus reported to me that he was doing very detailed studies of the site and the surface artifacts, as if he was trying to make a map of the topography."

"Then what happened?"

"Nothing. About a month or so passed, and then he called me and again asked to meet with me in Jerusalem at the YMCA, again for lunch."

"What was that lunch all about?"

"He wanted to discuss with the elders of our community the possibility of conducting his own excavations on the site of the ancient Samaritan Temple."

"Did you agree to his request?"

"I said I would have to think about it. At that time, all I could promise was to arrange for him to meet with the elders of the community."

"Was he satisfied with your answer?"

"Actually, he became hostile and agitated. He started making demands."

"How did you respond?"

"I responded the same way we Samaritans always respond to the outside world, when that world believes it has the right to treat our communities like museum pieces."

"And what way is that?"

"I told him that permission for a special archeological excavation would require two things: first, a formal request from an accredited academic institution with an archeology program, and second, a great deal of money."

"And how did he take it?"

"He suddenly calmed down and then asked, 'How much?'"

"Just like that?"

"Yes, just like that."

"What did you tell him?"

"Well, just so you understand, we Samaritans figure if we want our peace and quiet we should make the price for access high enough so that if the people making the request take us up on it, it will be truly worth the trouble the intrusion it will bring."

"So what did you tell him?"

"Twenty million Euros." A small smile broke out on Tsadka's face.

"You cannot be serious!" Aaron said.

"Oh, Sergeant, I was very serious."

"Then what happened?" Malik asked.

"Carlson just nodded his head, got up, and walked out of the restaurant. And that's when I knew that something was definitely not kosher."

"Why?" Malik asked.

"Professor, this is the Middle East. You might say that at that moment, Carlson and I were in the *Souq*—the market. He should have countered with a ridiculous number, say five hundred thousand. It's in our blood. It's in the very air we breathe. It is our national sport. We love to haggle over the price of everything. Carlson just nodded and left, like we had agreed at a number. It was way too easy."

"What did you conclude from this?"

"I figured his backers possessed very deep pockets."

"Then what did you do?" Abby asked.

"I went home and checked into Carlson's background. I was searching for any indication of who his backers might be."

"How did you do that?"

"I Googled him a second time. I was looking for fundraising footprints."

"What did you find?" Keller asked.

"A single reference to a group called 'The Builders'. The strange thing is, there was absolutely no information about the group anywhere on-line. Pardon the pun, but that did not compute."

"What did you do next?" Lavi asked.

"The lack of on-line information about The Builders gave me an idea. I decided to, as you say in poker, bluff him. I called Carlson and told him I knew who his backers were and that I needed to meet with them. I told him that my community could not risk putting the excavation of our most ancient and sacred sites in the hands of fanatics, terrorists, or amateurs."

"How did he respond?"

"After some perfunctory denials, he said he would arrange it and asked if the meeting could be held in the Old City, the next day. We agreed to meet for lunch at Papa Andrea's, a rooftop restaurant in the Christian Quarter. You can see the Church of the Holy Sepulchre from there."

"How nice!" Abby said.

"Tell us about that meeting," Malik asked. "We need as many details as you can remember. It is very important."

"Can I get a fresh bottle of water, first?"

"No problem. This would be a good time for a break. Give us a few moments." Lavi stood up.

From a well-concealed passageway, a security guard suddenly appeared with a bottle of water in his hand. He remained in the room. Despite the lack of physical restraints, the message was clear: They were being observed by others, and Tsadka was going nowhere in the immediate future.

Lavi went out of the room, followed by Malik, Abby, and Aaron. They took a few steps down the corridor and then circled close to one another.

"Tell us about The Builders," Malik said

"They are members of a secret society. We know very little about them."

"Are these guys Jews?" Aaron asked.

"Far from it. Before we latched on to Tsadka, all we could piece together was that they are bedrock fundamentalist Christians, and that they are obsessed with preparing for the Second Coming of Christ."

"Why would they approach Samaritans?" Abby asked.

"This you need to hear directly from Tsadka." Lavi held out his arm in the direction of the cellblock, indicating it was time to return.

Tsadka was beginning to look tired. Dark shadows became prominent beneath his eyes.

"When can I see a lawyer and call my family?"

"This session is not going to last too much longer. I hope you can be patient with us. We need to understand what is going on. We left off talking about your meeting with Carlson in the Old City," Lavi said.

Tsadka leaned back and closed his eyes.

"It was a beautiful and clear October Friday, toward the end of the month. I believe that the Jewish High Holy Days had just concluded. The Old City had returned to its normal quotient of tourists, which meant that restaurants in the Christian quarter were nearly empty. Carlson was seated with two men at a table on the western edge of the rooftop. I could see the empty narrow streets below. A couple of Christian gift shops were open. Just as I was sitting down, the bells from a nearby church clock tower began tolling the noon hour. At the same instant the loudspeakers in the Muslim Quarter began sounding the Friday call to prayer. You might say it was a very interfaith moment.

"Carlson introduced his guests to me."

"Describe them please," Lavi said.

"Reverend Jones, the one I figured was the head guy or leader was about sixty-five or seventy years of age. He was stocky. I would guess he was nearly two meters in height, but I could not be sure. He remained seated the whole time. He had piercing blue eyes and a thick head of very white wavy hair. His skin was sunburned red and very clean-shaven"

"Why do you say, 'Very clean-shaven'?"

"His face was as smooth as a baby's bottom. No shadow. He had very bushy white eyebrows that looked as if they had never been trimmed. He spoke with what you Americans call a Southern accent."

"Now how would you know that?" Aaron asked.

"As leader of the Samaritan community, it was my duty to study our history at Michigan State University. It was a very diverse campus. I heard all kinds of accents."

"Is that where you learned English?" Abby asked. "It is very good."

"I lived in East Lansing as a young boy and went to school there. My father was fulfilling his responsibilities as leader of our community."

"Could we get back to the meeting?" Malik said. "Describe the second man."

"I think he is the son of the older gentleman. He was introduced with a different last name. I think the names were false. Reverend Jones was the older guy and Reverend Smith was the younger."

"Please describe Reverend Smith."

"Smith had the same piercing blue eyes. That is why I thought they were related. He appeared to be a quarter meter taller. His skin was tanned, but it looked artificial. He was a *ring-nik*.

"A what?" Aaron asked.

"It is an Israeli term for American men who love to wear big rings on their hands." Lavi explained.

"Can you describe the rings?" Malik asked.

"The wedding ring was a wide band of gold with no decoration. On the last finger of the same hand was a small band with a large diamond. On his other hand was a bulky ring with a large blue stone. It had images of buildings on both sides of the band. Oh yes, the stone had a gold cross inlaid into the blue stone."

"Sounds like the class ring of a Christian college or seminary," Abby said. "There must be a zillion of them of the same design."

Aaron nodded. "It might help if we ever catch up with these guys."

"So now that we have described the place and the people, tell us about the content of your meeting," Lavi said.

"They started right off by trying to blackmail me."

"How so?"

"The older reverend threatened to expose our money smuggling operations on the West Bank. He showed me the business card of an Israeli Police Major. He said it would be simple for him to place one call and half of my community would be locked up."

"Then what did he say?"

"He warned me that I could reveal nothing of this meeting. They knew where I lived. I would be a dead man in less than twenty-four hours after I spoke with the police. And they call themselves Christians."

"Go on."

"As incredible as this sounds, they are actually planning to blow up the Dome of the Rock. They are convinced that God has come to them in a vision and instructed them to build the third Temple, after which Jesus will return and save the faithful. They claim to have allies in the Ultra-Orthodox Jewish communities. Their special role in the drama will be to start a civil war between Orthodox and secular Jews. At the same time, The Builders intend to hold the Church of the Holy Sepulcher as a hostage while the construction is taking place. If they are left alone, the church will survive. If not, they will blow it up."

"So what does this have to do with the Samaritans and their ancient temple? Abby asked.

"The Builders are of the impression that the Samaritan Temple was identical to the first version of the Second Temple. They wanted to carefully measure the ancient Samaritan Temple. They want to get the design just right. I guess Jesus won't return if the Third Temple is shoddy."

"Did you believe that they could carry out this scheme?"

"Not at first, but as they were talking, I became aware of their attention to detail, their meticulous planning. I thought to myself, they could actually carry this off."

"If they had the ability to kill or blackmail you, why did they pay you off instead?"

"They may have been just blowing smoke, but they said they needed our cooperation and talents for the success of their project. In their narrow Christian worldview, we Samaritans have many defects but we have great connections and the ability to move things back and forth freely between

Israel, the West Bank, Syria, and Lebanon. They cannot succeed without someone like us to act as facilitators. The Builders convinced me that they are amazing fundraisers. With their TV shows and stadium concerts they can raise billions from the gullible, the hopeless and the hopeful. I naively thought that we could use their wealth to our advantage without causing damage to our community."

"What did they want from you, then and there?" Lavi asked.

"They wanted to set up a materials distribution center within our community in Nablus. They were going to finance the building of immense underground warehouses out of solid rock for the storage of materials for building and explosives for demolition. Our under-employed Samaritan youth would be put to work at going rates. They wanted me to say yes to the plan and then sell it to the community elders as an economic development plan for our entire community."

"Did you say yes?" Malik asked

"I said I would have to think about it and get back to them. Selling it to the elders would not be easy. I asked for time."

"Did they give you time?"

"The thing that impressed me the most was their patience. As they described it, this was a long-term plan, maybe five to ten years from now to completion. They asked for my decision by April first. They were giving me six months to make it happen. I could not believe it.

"Then, a week ago, before the deadline, they called and told me that they had a problem that could cause the entire project to collapse. Their problem was Rabbi Stone, Sergeant Keller, and the scroll."

"Who, specifically were you talking to?"

"The reverends Smith and Jones were both on the line. They claimed that Professor Carlson had just examined an ancient scroll that could lead to the discovery of an original Torah scroll among the Samaritans, one older than the oldest biblical text known to be in existence. The reverends were fearful that such a text would undermine claims of divine authorship for the Torah. Since for most Christians, the truth of Jesus' divine nature is based on acceptance of the divine authorship of Torah, such a discovery would have a devastating effect on Christian fundamentalists. They asked me to arrange for a few accidents that would turn Keller and Stone away from their pursuit of the original Torah."

"A bomb is no accident," Abby said.

"Bombs go off all the time around here. It was supposed to be a weak bomb, meant to scare and not kill. The Palestinian men I hired saw this as an opportunity to do more than superficial damage.

"You did agree to carry out their request for accidents?" Malik asked.

"I did, but then I made a side deal with Carlson."

"What kind of side deal?" Aaron asked.

"As soon as the Reverends hung up, Carlson called. He wanted to give me information about the travel plans of the Rabbi and the Sergeant, so I could arrange the necessary accident. Then he mentioned that he had possession of the actual scroll. I made him an offer. Ten million Euros for the Ezra scroll. I was going to buy it on behalf of my community. It could lead to a discovery that would insure our very survival."

"You paid Carlson with half of the money you were getting from the Reverends?" Abby asked.

"Precisely. I just could not let them destroy such an essential piece of my people's heritage. "

"So now we know that the Builders are dead set against the discovery of that so-called original Torah," Lavi said. "We also know that, for the moment, they are unaware that the Ezra scroll is safely in our hands."

"There is just one more thing," Tsadka said.

"What might that be?" Abby asked.

"The very fear that stirred up the Reverends to commission accidents and violence to prevent the Ezra scroll from seeing the light of day, caused them to look at other very real threats to the foundation of their faith."

"Meaning what, exactly?" Aaron asked.

"Meaning that they also intend to blow up the Shrine of the Book at the Israel Museum."

When brothers live together and one of them dies and has no son, the wife of the deceased shall not be married outside the family to a strange man. Her husband's brother shall go in to her and take her to himself as wife and perform the duty of a husband's brother to her. It shall be that the firstborn whom she bears shall assume the name of his dead brother, so that his name will not be blotted out from Israel. But if the man does not desire to take his brother's wife, then his brother's wife shall go up to the gate to the elders and say, 'My husband's brother refuses to establish a name for his brother in Israel; he is not willing to perform the duty of a husband's brother to me.' Then the elders of his city shall summon him and speak to him. And if he persists and says, 'I do not desire to take her,' then his brother's wife shall come to him in the sight of the elders, and pull his sandal off his foot and spit in his face; and she shall declare, 'Thus it is done to the man who does not build up his brother's house.' In Israel his name shall be called, 'The house of him whose sandal is removed'. (Deuteronomy 25:5-9)

Chapter Thirty-Six

DATE: The Fourteenth Day of the Fourth Month, In the Sixty-Eighth Year Since the Destruction of Jerusalem

TIME: First Hour of the Second Watch

PLACE: Market Square, Pumbedita, Babylonia

The conversation could be put off no longer. It would have to be today or never. Hospitality beneath Hilkiah's roof had its limitations, even for family. It was time for Yeshai to make his way on his own. The local Judean population treated him with caution and suspicion. He arrived without a wife or family. He was still suspected of being a Persian, though his hair growth was finally covering his scalp. The older generation of Judeans were appalled that he was so matter-of-fact about abandoning his Nazirite vows. No one would sit near him at the assembly house.

The only acceptance he received was due to his scribal skills. As soon as the locals realized that he charged half the going rate for documents and contracts, they approached him openly at his makeshift table in market. It was Elimelech's idea that he position his table between the cucumber stand and the melon stand. The space was more expensive, but clients were more likely to approach him near the earthy smell of cucumbers and the sweet fragrance of melons, than next to the stench of fresh goat's meat and chicken feathers.

Yeshai was finding it difficult to master the art of writing quickly. His customers had no interest in beautiful letters. They wanted their documents to be fast and mostly accurate. His quill was picking up speed with each day. The more he wrote, the more money he made. It was, nonetheless, barely enough to keep him alive. How could he imagine that this would be sufficient for a wife, let alone a family?

And why Ruth? Did he have real feelings for her or was she a convenient solution to a current problem? In three months of living under the same roof, he could not say that he knew anything about her, her character, her personality. Was she in his thoughts because she was an outsider like him? Most Judean exiles in Bavel were assimilated into all aspects of the local culture. A part of that culture was a routine openness when it came to arranging marriages. Judeans in Bavel sought brides for their sons that would advance the family's economic interests. If such were a Judean, so be it. If the bride under consideration were the daughter of a Judean man and a Moabite woman, like Ruth, then that was acceptable as well. But Ruth as a widow was considered spoiled grain, unfit for a priest.

Yeshai knew only the most basic information about Ruth and her father. Elimelech was a moderately successful merchant. He bought grain from the farmers of the flood plain and sold it upriver. How Hilkiah actually came to be Elimelech's son-in-law was unknown to Yeshai. Asking personal questions about family relationships would have been grossly inappropriate. Nevertheless, he did glean some basic information. Hilkiah was an orphan before his fourth year. The Great River Flood had claimed his father, Shallum and his mother, Aviva. His grandmother Miryam provided some stability in his chaotic life. She mentored him in scribal skills and took him into her confidence by telling him the complete version of their family story, including the murder of his grandfather, Miryam's husband. Having been trained as a scribe since his third year of life, Hilkiah would have been considered a worthy son-in-law for any Judean family. But being an orphan meant he had no family wealth to bring to the bridal canopy. Elimelech took advantage of this situation to arrange a marriage for his daughter Ruth. Despite the openness of the exile community to all peoples and cultures in Bavel, a daughter of a Moabite woman was still considered less than an ideal match. Hilkiah's mother's brother Mechir acted as his deceased parents' agent and quickly concluded the marriage pact. He was anxious to arrange marriages for his own three sons. Hilkiah was an inconvenient responsibility. The sooner his marriage was contracted, the sooner Mechir could locate brides for each of them. Ruth and Hilkiah were only husband and wife for three short months before Hilkiah died of the same kind of fever that took his parents.

Each evening since his arrival, Ruth sat across from Yeshai. Physically present, she was mentally distant from the table and only mildly interested in the food before her. With only the sound of earthenware scraping against the wood table and the ordinary noises that accompanied eating, Yeshai's imagination was his constant dinner companion. Nightly, in his mind, he would fill in the female form that must have existed beneath the shapeless garments of Ruth's widowhood. Only her face was visible. Her face set his heart on fire.

Framed by shinning stands of straight black hair that escaped the shelter of a tightly wrapped headscarf, her face was neither round nor oval but a perfect combination of the two. Her skin color was a perfect match for the cream tone of the inside of an almond. Her eyes were a color brown so dark they were at the line which separates brown from black. The small flames of the simple oil lamps on the table were magnified in the center of those eyes. Her nose had been broken when she was a child at play. Yeshai was convinced of this. Perhaps it was this imperfection that endeared her to him from that first day. It interrupted the line from her eyes to her lips, but the overall effect in Yeshai's mind was stunning. Her lips were naturally dark and full. Her teeth were white and solid. Her voice was strong and pleasant. Perhaps this was due to her habit of speaking loudly for her father who was hard of hearing.

Ruth was Yeshai's for the asking. He knew this. The traditions of Judah affirmed this. Yet he could not bring the words to his lips and declare his intention to claim her as his wife under the laws of the *Levir*. How could he be so callous as to take advantage of Hilkiah's untimely death?

Death was a constant in life. Death could happen at any time, in any place, and under almost any circumstance. Death's power could not be defeated. But the human wreckage left in death's wake could be repaired. Deep wounds could be cleansed and bound up. The rules of family, clan, and tribe were structured to protect those rendered powerless by the death of a parent or spouse. At the same time, the rules insured the proper care in the afterlife for the deceased. Having at least one child who could be depended upon to care for the afterlife of parents was the purpose of procreation. Dying childless was what the tradition referred to as "being cut off from your kin," a sign of abandonment by God. It was the worst of all possible divine punishments. Dying was natural. Dying without hope for an afterlife was terrifying.

Levirate marriage was a tribal solution to one specific yet common situation, a married male dying before fathering a child. Judean tradition sanctioned polygamy. It was what made levirate marriage deceivingly simple in theory. The nearest male relative to the deceased was obligated to marry his widow. The first child produced was not the child of the honorable kinsman. Rather, it was forever considered the child of the deceased. That child would inherit whatever was coming to the deceased. That child was also obligated to care for his deceased father's afterlife, whether in special prayers or sacrificial offerings.

Yeshai knew he was Hilkiah's closest kinsman. Memukan said so in order to convince Yeshai to join him in Bavel. In practice, levirate marriage by the nearest eligible kinsman was often avoided. This was especially true if that kinsman already had a wife and children. Polygamy was expensive. Yeshai concluded he had nothing to lose by raising the subject at table. Tonight would be the night.

The arrival of a potential customer for his scribal services interrupted his thoughts of marriage. A young man dressed in expensive cloth stood before his table, casually tossing a small melon in the air and catching it. Yes, it was time for Yeshai to tend to his craft. A wife and family would be expensive under the best of circumstances. Tonight he would, at last, declare his intention to fulfill the obligation of the nearest kinsman.

Elimelech beat him to it.

Ruth brought the simple evening meal to the table. In silence she placed each bowl in the center: rice, chickpea paste, and diced cucumbers. A moment later she returned with a plate filled with flatbread still warm from the clay brick oven. After Yeshai offered a brief prayer of thanksgiving, they began to eat. With a mouth full of food, Elimelech started to speak. Ruth admonished him with mock severity.

"Father, we cannot understand a word that you are saying. Finish what's in your mouth, then speak."

"I think he said he has something important to say," Yeshai said.

"Don't encourage his crude manners," Ruth said.

Yeshai held his hands up as if to signal surrender. Elimelech cleared his throat. He was ready to continue.

"Yeshai, when are you going to uphold the rules of Judah and fulfill your role as Hilkiah's nearest kinsman?

Yeshai nearly sprayed the food he was chewing across the table. Instead he started to choke on it and began to cough. He saw Ruth's face turn red.

"Father, how could you be so cruel? My husband has been dead for three months. I'm still grieving. How could you be so unfeeling for my situation?"

Yeshai stood up and made ready to leave the table.

"Where are you going?" Elimelech said. "You need to stay put."

"This discussion is not one for the ears of a stranger. I shall return when the two of you have finished."

"This conversation concerns you and my daughter. Sit down and listen."

"At least Yeshai was making an effort to be polite. There is no call for you to be giving orders like a Persian," Ruth said. "We are not your servants." She stood and turned from the table; her father placed his hand on her arm and prevented her from leaving the room.

Yeshai's heart leapt at the sound of his name. This was the first time he heard it from her lips. In all the time he had been living under their roof, she had never referred to him by name. She certainly never spoke to him directly. Over the past few months, when she addressed her father about their houseguest she referred to Yeshai as "the Samaritan."

"Daughter, your aging father requests most humbly that you return to your seat and hear me out."

Ruth returned to her seat.

"Yes, it has been three months since your beloved Hilkiah's death. I have seen no signs that you are bearing his child."

"How could you be so crass?" Ruth asked. "This is not a conversation for the dinner table."

"Our traditions make clear that you may not remarry before a full year has passed from the day your husband died. This is true and I am not suggesting that you violate this tradition. But there are relatives of Hilkiah on his mother's side of the family who are making claims at the seat of judgment in the city gates."

"What kind of claims?" Yeshai asked.

"They want this house and the land it sits on. They intend to sell it and make a quick profit."

"They are not asking for Ruth?" Yeshai's question sounded like a fearful pleading. Ruth faced Yeshai and saw him in a new light.

"Of course not. They have no obligations in that regard."

Yeshai knew this but wanted to make sure that the tradition did not have some local variation unique to Bavel.

"My only thought is for your security. If Yeshai makes a public pronouncement now of his intention to fulfill his obligation to Hilkiah, the possibility of Hilkiah's property going to that side of the family is ended. We must not wait for a year to pass for Yeshai to declare himself. No wedding will take place before that time. That is all I am saying."

"Ruth, I make this declaration to you, here and now, that I will fulfill my obligation to my cousin Hilkiah and marry you when a full year has passed since the day of his death. I further acknowledge, that should the God of our ancestors bless us with children, the first child that is born will be Hilkiah's child in every respect. I promise that I will love you and provide for you as it is proper for a son of Judah to do for his bride."

"Well said! It sounds like wedding contracts have been your specialty at your table in the market. There is only one problem."

"What's that?" Yeshai and Ruth spoke in unison then looked at each other in confusion.

"Yeshai's declaration means nothing until it is uttered in the presence of the people of the land at the city gate."

"Of course, we knew that." Again they spoke in unison. Yeshai smiled, then laughed. Ruth smiled, then laughed. Elimelech's laughter could be heard out in the street. The room appeared brighter and warmer. Laughter had returned to the house of Hilkiah. In nine more months it would become the house of Ruth and Yeshai. But tomorrow, Yeshai would make his intentions known in the presence of witnesses.

Ten chairs sat atop a platform by the city gates. The Sabbath would arrive at sunset this day. Not all Judeans made an effort to observe the Sabbath, but those who did would be well away from the city gates by the time the sun was directly overhead. The chairs would be occupied by ten notables of the city, appointed by the Persian governor to act as a court of first resort. Routine legal disputes and contracts were handled by the People of the Land. This was the standard venue for making legal notices in the presence of witnesses. Yeshai would seek an opportunity to declare before the "People of the Land" his intent to marry Ruth under the venerable Judean rules of the *levir*.

A rather large crowd had gathered before the platform in anticipation of the airing of an ongoing dispute between a Persian carter and a Judean cloth merchant. This was the third and final time the People of the Land would hear the matter. If it achieved resolution, fine. If it did not, the dispute would be settled by the arbitrary ruling of the governor. Neither side wanted to take a chance on the whims of the governor. A murmur of voices passed like a wave through the sea. The members of the People of the Land were making their way to their seats.

Two hours later, after charge and countercharge, the matter between the Persian and the Judean was settled. Neither side won. But that was the whole point. The crowd, expecting violence and a show of tempers, drifted away from the gates and went about their ordinary business.

Exhausted from the tedium of the proceedings, a well-dressed looking Persian, the leader of the day's session, was about to declare the meeting of the People of the Land over, when Yeshai sprang to his feet and declared at the top of his voice:

"My lords, I have come today to declare before you my promise to marry Ruth, widow of the scribe Hilkiah, as soon as the days of her mourning are complete. In keeping with the traditions of our ancestors from Judah, I further declare that the firstborn of our union will be the son of Hilkiah in all matters of inheritance and family status. I freely undertake this obligation as the closest kin to Hilkiah, being the grandson of his grandfather's brother from Judah."

"Cannot this matter wait until our next session?" The Persian leader of the panel asked in frustration.

"With the greatest of respect, my lord, I must say it cannot."

"Why not?" asked a heavily bearded large Judean on the platform.

"Because I am trying to prevent this body from assigning the property of my cousin to his relatives on his mother's side of the family. If you receive this declaration, it will put an end to their designs on his property and protect his widow, as well as raise up Hilkiah's name by insuring he will have an heir."

"How do we know you are Hilkiah's real kinsman?"

"My lords, if I may speak?"

"Speak, Elimelech."

"I will vouch for his identity as Hilkiah's cousin."

"The man is touched by the matter. He cannot provide testimony," the bearded Judean said.

"Then I shall vouch for his identity." A sudden quiet and all heads turned in the direction of the new speaker. It was the governor, Memukan, dressed in his official silk robes.

"I brought this man, Yeshai, from Judah to Pumbedita. He is a scribe of the first order, guardian of the sacred scrolls of the Judeans, rescued from their Sacred House in Jerusalem. He is the grandson of Eliezer and great-grandson of Achituv, as was Hilkiah. He is well known in Samaria and Judah. Among the exiles of Judah living in Samaria, he was their lead priest. Hilkiah and his mother were well known to me. They have done the Emperor and me many services over the years. I brought Yeshai here as a favor to Hilkiah."

There was nothing more to be said, no more questions to be asked. Memukan had made all questions moot. Yeshai bowed his head towards Memukan in gratitude. Another Judean member of the People of the Land stood and spoke in a loud voice.

"We have heard the testimony of our governor. Therefore, in keeping with the traditions of our people, the exiles of Judah, we acknowledge the claim of Yeshai son of Gilad as the nearest relative of Hilkiah, son of Shallum. He has made his promise to fulfill the obligation of the nearest kinsman of his cousin and in so doing raise up his name in the household of Judah. Furthermore, Elimelech is appointed the guardian of Hilkiah's property until Yeshai shall marry Hilkiah's widow, when the days of her mourning are completed."

"Do the People of the Land agree in this decision?" They could not wait to answer and leave.

"We do!" they shouted in unison.

"This session is concluded!"

Yeshai approached Ruth and Elimelech, now standing at the back of the crowd. He reached out for Ruth's hand, gave it a gentle squeeze as he looked directly into her eyes. They were filled with tears. He did not know if they were tears of mourning or joy. He knew that the tears welling up in his own eyes were of joy. He intended to linger in that moment, but a heavy hand rested on his shoulder and directed him to turn away from Ruth.

"I must speak with you—now!" The order came from an elderly Judean. His robes were of fine quality, but had seen better days. His hands were stained black from the thick ink of scribes. His head was covered in the manner of the priests and Levites. His beard was full and completely silver in color.

"And you are?" Yeshai inquired.

"Meremot son of Uriah, the current guardian of the sacred scrolls of Judah in Exile."

Chapter Thirty-Seven

DATE: March 19, 2009

TIME: 11:30 A.M. Local Time

PLACE: Café Michal, 230 Dizengoff Street, Tel Aviv

"I'm as hungry and thirsty as the next person, so why are we sitting here sipping lattes and ordering salads when a couple of crazies are plotting the destruction of The Shrine of the Book? Is the security in your office so bad that you need to sit in a sidewalk café to avoid listening devices?" Aaron said.

"Sergeant, it's a beautiful spring day. The food is good here and I think better when I am not distracted by the operations of my office. Besides, we know when the Builders plan to do the deed. Our sources tell us we have two days before they make their attempt," Lavi said.

"Call the waiter over and let's order. It's been a long morning and as *S'gan Aluf* Lavi suggested, I am indeed hungry." Malik pronounced his verdict on the matter, as if he heard not one word of Lavi's startling revelation.

"Two days?" Aaron said. He looked to be the only one refusing to glance at a menu.

The others watched intently as food came out of the kitchen, then checked their menus to guess which item was which. It did not matter. When they were ready to order, the waiters seemed to have disappeared.

"How do they do that?"

"Do what?"

"Know exactly when to vanish into thin air."

"Can we, perhaps multi-task, like your generation is fond of doing?" Malik's eyes were focused on his menu but his mind was turning over the details of the Tsadka interrogation.

"First, what do you really know about Reverends Smith and Jones?"

Lavi withdrew a folder from his metal briefcase. It had a stiff blue cardstock cover with a plastic spiral binding on the side. He flipped a few pages over and then began reciting.

"Their real names are Ervin and Lemuel Rumsey. They are indeed father and son. Reverend Ervin is the son of an Alabama share cropper, whatever that is."

"It means he came from a family that was very poor," Aaron said.

"Anyway, Ervin's story is pretty typical. He quit school when he was in the seventh grade and helped his father grow pecans. When he was fifteen, his parents' house or shack or whatever you call it, caught fire in the middle of the night. Both parents died, but Ervin survived. The fire was suspicious but no charges were ever filed against anyone.

"Ervin the orphan was taken under the wing of his family pastor, Reverend Silas Mercer. Mercer put Ervin back in school and ultimately paid for his education at Bob Jones University in Greenville, South Carolina.

"Ervin was ordained a Southern Baptist minister in 1975. He actually had a gift for preaching and was in demand as a charismatic speaker at Baptist revivals and conventions. In 1985 he founded The Church of the Risen Christ, in Eldorado, Arkansas. The Church grew and eventually moved to Shreveport, Louisiana. There, Ervin met and married the seventeen-year old daughter of a church elder. They had one child, a son, Lemuel. The wife died trying to give birth to their second child, a stillborn daughter.

"The child, Lemuel, was a prodigy, at least when it came to Bible thumping."

"Where did you get this stuff?" Abby asked. "Bible thumping is an American expression."

"Sergeant Ramon put this together for me. She is very thorough."

"I wonder if she knows what Bible thumping is?"

"Indeed, she does. Her parents were *shlichim* at the JCC in Atlanta. She went to high school there. I am sure she knows what Bible thumping is. You can ask her yourself."

"I know what Bible thumping is. But what are *shlichim?*" Aaron asked.

"*Shlichim* are like ambassadors of Israeli culture sent by the State of Israel to Jewish communities around the world. It's supposed to connect diaspora Jews with Israel," Abby said.

Aaron nodded his thanks and Lavi then continued with the report.

"By 1990, The Church of the Risen Christ had a very slick TV show that led in the ratings for religious broadcasting six years in a row. The show brought in millions in donations."

"So Tsadka was not far from the truth. These guys do have the capacity to raise the money for such an operation," Aaron said.

"This is where the secrecy begins. For elite level donations, followers would be admitted into an exclusive club with regular access to the great preacher. He called this club The Builders. The membership of The Builders was a closely guarded secret. Rumors swirled but no facts were developed as to who The Builders actually were. Then, suddenly, in late September 2001, The Builders simply disappeared."

"What do you mean disappeared?" Malik asked.

"They vanished from all publications, broadcasts and internet materials produced by the Church of the Risen Christ. It was as if they had never existed."

"They must have been going underground," Aaron said.

"We do not know when, where, or how their ideology or mission changed. Carlson's contacts with the two reverends is the first time The Builders have surfaced since 2001." Lavi closed the notebook.

"Professor, do you buy all this stuff about rebuilding the Temple?" Abby asked.

"Given the number of crazies, both individuals and groups, who believe that God has called them to rebuild the Temple, I would not be surprised if one or another of them was actually taking steps to see such a plan to fruition. What I do not buy is Tsadka's theory about why The Builders want to destroy the Shrine of the Book." Malik closed his eyes and began stroking his chin.

"What's the problem?" Abby asked.

"The problem is most Christians view the Shrine of the Book as confirming by proxy the historicity of the New Testament. For them the Dead Sea Scrolls are witness to an incredibly long and faithful tradition for the Hebrew Scriptures. With the exception of one or two heresies that broke out in the early Church, most denominations acknowledge a deep spiritual connection to the Torah, the Prophets and the Writings of the Hebrew Scriptures. Even the most dedicated of Christian fundamentalists see the Hebrew Scriptures as the essential prophecies foretelling the arrival and mission of Jesus.

"Despite all of the fantasy and media hype, the Shrine's collection has not contradicted one sentence of the Hebrew Scriptures. To put it crassly, the Red Sea still parts and the Israelites still walk on dry land. With the glaring exception of the Book of Esther, they are all present and accounted for in the Dead Sea Scrolls. The Builders gain nothing by destroying the Shrine of the Book."

The waiter walked over. His face resembled pictures of the dark side of the moon with pocks and valleys. His once white food-stained apron looked like it was holding up his pants as well as protecting them. A three-day growth of Yassir Arafat-like beard completed the totally unappetizing package of customer service. But he had a huge smile on his face.

"Friends, may I take your orders?"

After the food arrived, everyone became lost in his own thoughts and food. Then Aaron threw out an answer to Malik's question of motive.

"Professor, what if the bombing is not religious but political?"

"Go on, tell me more."

"This may be off the wall, but suppose the purpose is to discredit Israel's stewardship of the Dead Sea Scrolls. Remember the accusations of anti-Semitism and favoritism leveled at the original Scroll scholars?"

"How do you know this stuff?" Abby asked.

Lavi looked up. "What stuff?"

"I know all about the controversy surrounding the Scrolls. Actually, there were multiple controversies connected with their ownership, discovery, meaning, and the right to read and publish scholarly articles."

"And you know this how?" Lavi challenged.

"I wrote a report on the Scrolls for my Bar Mitzvah project."

"You have got to be kidding." Abby laughed.

"I'm deadly serious. My rabbi said I did an excellent job. I'll have you know, it was because of that report I was able to recognize the Paleo-Hebrew script of the Ezra scroll.

"Anyway, if major artifacts and scrolls were destroyed in a terror attack it would start a groundswell of anti-Israel agitation and an international outcry."

"Resulting in what?" Malik asked.

"The removal of the scrolls from Israel's control altogether."

"That's not going to happen, not ever," Lavi said.

"What if The Builders are going for the original Torah?" Abby asked. "The Shrine is a diversion. They blow it up and then while everyone is collecting body parts and scroll fragments, they break into the museum and locate the bone box of Shoshana bat Talmon."

"They are going for the biggest scroll find of all!" Malik nodded in agreement with Abby's suggestion.

"But why do they want it? It can't mean anything to them," Aaron said.

"What if Israel drowns in the Red Sea in the original Torah?" Abby asked.

"You cannot mean that."

"You're right. I don't mean that exactly. But what if The Builders are afraid that the original is different from the Torah we have now, in some basic, fundamental and important way?"

"Very good," Malik said. "Please continue."

Abby nodded. "So, let's say that there is an essential idea in Christianity that is based on some concept in the Torah. Then, with the bone box scroll we discover that that crucial idea is downplayed or is nowhere to be found in the original Torah."

"Like what?" Lavi asked.

"Atonement through sacrifice." Abby folded her hands. "Did I ask you for sacrifices in the wilderness?" Abby continued.

"What is that supposed to mean?" Aaron asked.

"It's a passage from the prophet Jeremiah, Malik said. "He poses the question and implies that whatever the Israelites are doing in the Temple of Solomon, God did not command them to do so."

"That passage has always troubled me. Jeremiah, speaking on behalf of

God, is almost offhand about the comment, as if everyone knows it to be true but is unwilling to say so out loud. Sacrifices appear throughout the Torah, even in sections determined to be from non-priestly authors," Abby said. "I am never sure what Jeremiah's point, or rather God's point is."

"What do you mean, 'non-priestly' authors?" Aaron asked.

"Do you remember what I said about the so-called Documentary Hypothesis?" Malik asked.

"Yeah, so?"

"According to that hypothesis, the newest material in the Torah is from the time of Ezra in Babylonia, around the year 443 BCE. That material includes the entire book of Leviticus and major sections of Exodus. Even though there are passages throughout the rest of the Torah that have been identified as 'priestly,' it is very clear that Leviticus was written by the *Cohanim.* These are the priests. They place a heavy emphasis on the atoning value of sacrifice and the importance of achieving that atonement through a sacrificial cult operated exclusively by the Sons of Aaron. The older material in the Torah came from non-priestly sources."

"I get it. Leviticus is relatively new and adds the idea of killing dumb animals to atone for sin. But what has this got to do with Christians?"

"Try to keep up, Sergeant," Abby said.

"Just give me the short version."

"When the Romans destroyed the Temple in 70 CE, all of Judah was left in a serious quandary. With the Temple gone, what would they do to achieve atonement for their sins before God? By that time, they believed that the destruction of the Temple of Solomon in 586 BCE was an atoning act for the rampant idolatry of the Israelites. For all of the Jewish communities of that time, including the early followers of Jesus and the various Jewish sects in conflict, the Temple was still the single most important symbol of their spiritual life. It was the only thing that united them as a people. When the Romans destroyed Herod's upgraded version of the Second Temple in the year 70 CE, how could these communities find atonement? The Christian solution was to interpret Jesus' life and death in terms of an atoning sacrifice."

"Jesus died to atone for the sins of mankind."

"Now you got it! That was the innovation that transformed early Christianity. They saw in the sacrificial death of Jesus a substitute for the destroyed Temple."

"So, if the whole sacrificial atonement thing was not originally in the Torah, then the notion of killing something to atone for sin is not an integral part of ancient Judaism."

"Actually, all it means is that the idea of atonement sacrifice may have come from Babylon or Persia," Malik said.

"All of this scholarly chit chat is very nice, but it still does not rise to the level of a motive for destroying the Shrine of the Book and breaking into the museum in the hopes of stealing an original Torah, if there even is such a thing," Lavi said. "The Builders are fundamentalist Christians. They never cared about the Documentary Hypothesis, Darwin, the Big Bang Theory or anything else that challenged their belief that God Himself wrote every single word"

"*S'gan Aluf*, you just found your motive. Before the discovery of the Ezra scroll, all of this Graf-Wellhaausen documentary hypothesis stuff was just an elaborate theory that only Bible scholars and their grad students could follow."

"Thank you, Rabbi Stone, for the left-handed complement." Malik said.

"All I meant, Professor, was that the entire hypothesis is built on circumstantial evidence. The evidence is overwhelming but still circumstantial. As a cop, *S'gan Aluf* Lavi, you should appreciate the difference between circumstantial evidence and a smoking gun."

"I have been known to win a case or two on both kinds of evidence."

"I think that The Builders want to find and ultimately destroy that scroll in Shoshana bat Talmon's bone box. It is the smoking gun of Biblical history. If it exists, it would prove that Torah is a human invention. It could prove that the Documentary Hypothesis is now documentary fact. For me it's like having my own understanding vindicated."

"I would imagine there might be a quite a few religious communities who would be troubled by that," Aaron said.

"Religious wars have been started over much less," Lavi said.

"Now what?" Aaron asked.

"We pay a visit to the remains of Shoshana bat Talmon, tonight," Malik said. "That scroll is part of my family's heritage. I am not going to let some Bible thumpers destroy it."

"We're going to steal it?" Abby said.

"Shaa! Not so loud. Calm yourself." Malik looked around the café to make sure that no one was listening.

"Why can't we just call the museum authorities and explain what's going on?" Aaron asked. "They might even help us locate the box."

"Museum authorities, hah! I know those mamzers. They will spend three weeks convening meetings of the Museum Governing Board. Then they will conduct a hearing, at which we will be called to present our evidence that the bone box contains the original Torah scroll. The Ministry of Antiquities will immediately call the press. They cannot pass up an opportunity to campaign for more funding. Theirs is a simple formula. If you find something, if you find anything, ask for more funding. Representatives from the Ministry of Religion sit on that board. They will call their rabbis and leak to them the news of the potential find of an original Torah. After putting all of us in *Cherem*, a state similar to excommunication, and saying *Kaddish*, the rabbis will reach out to The Builders, inviting them to destroy the scroll. The Builders will happily oblige and then use their involvement to raise funds among their faithful."

"We need to take possession of the scroll and catch the Builders in the act of breaking into the museum," Lavi said, thinking out loud.

"You're a cop. You cannot condone this kind of talk," Abby said.

"I did not say steal it. I said take possession of it. A terrorist plot has come to my attention. As an officer of the law I am obligated to take steps to prevent the plot from succeeding. This will not be an easy operation." Lavi shook his head and looked across the street. "First, we need to make sure that the actual bone box is in the possession of the museum and second, we need to find a way to gain access to the collection without setting off any alarms."

"In that case, I need to chat up some of my old friends and call in some favors. We need to be prepared for anything."

Malik made it sound as if he was going to ask one of those friends for center orchestra seats at an Israel Philharmonic concert. For all Abby and Aaron knew, Zubin Mehta might be one of Malik's personal friends. Except that this request was not for concert tickets. It was for assistance in "taking unauthorized possession" of antiquities from the State of Israel. Under ordinary circumstances, theft of antiquities would be treated very harshly in a state that views antiquities as family heirlooms. Breaking into the "national attic," would never be forgiven, unless the attic and its precious contents were protected in the end.

"We shouldn't continue this discussion here. I think we should go back to *S'gan Aluf* Lavi's office now," Aaron said. "We need to do some tactical planning."

"The Sergeant is absolutely correct. It is time to get down to business. Lunch is on me, *Chevre*." Lavi stood up and drew out a wad of cash, pealing off a number of Israeli shekels and putting them on the table under a coffee cup. He then turned and started in the direction of his office. The others followed close behind.

Lavi brought them into a small conference room adjacent to his office. The south end of the room had a white board. Abby and Aaron were writing questions on the board in blue ink. If they had an answer, it was written in red. Malik had taken possession of the only landline phone in the room. His first call was his most difficult. He needed to ask a favor from his daughter-in-law, Professor Michal Levski. Actually, she was his ex-daughter-in-law: brilliant, beautiful, and Bulgarian. Her parents, both mathematicians, arrived in the 1980's from Bulgaria. She was born in Jerusalem and studied in Israel and Europe before taking up a position with the Israel Museum as a curator of Balkan Jewish History. She combined that post with a part-time lectureship at the Hebrew University. Her fall course: "Sephardic Jewry in the Ottoman Empire" was always over-enrolled. The university offered her a rare full-time teaching and research position. Michal declined. The air of academe was too rarified and boring for her. That was a major reason for her divorce from Malik's son, Yonatan.

Yoni expected Michal to take the Hebrew U job because the salary was significantly higher than her post at the museum. But the museum was her first love, even ahead of Yoni. Holding history in her hands—a diary, a photograph, a passport—almost sent a charge of electricity through her body. She felt a mystical connection with the subjects of her work. They were all, in a way, her aunts, uncles and cousins. Eighty percent of the artifacts she handled were directly connected to the Bulgarians who survived the Holocaust. She could not leave these precious effects to the care of strangers.

Michal had nothing to do with the Shrine of the Book, nor was she particularly involved in the warehousing of museum collections. All she had was security access to the entire museum collection. That was enough. Would her anger at Yoni prevent her from helping in the recovery of the single greatest artifact in Jewish history? It was time to find out.

Chapter Thirty-Eight

DATE: **The Fifteenth Day of the Fourth Month, In the Sixty-Eighth Year Since the Destruction of Jerusalem**

TIME: **Third Hour of the Second Watch**

PLACE: **Before the City Gates, Pumbedita, Bavel**

"Meremot son of Uriah, what is so important that it cannot wait until the end of the Sabbath?"

Yeshai had no interest in delaying his return to the house of Hilkiah. He knew that this evening the meal would resemble a true festival. He anticipated being able to gaze into Ruth's eyes as long as he wished, without shame or embarrassment. But Meremot would not be deterred.

"Your cousin assigned me a task and I must fulfill it. I have given my personal oath to him. It was most likely his last wish before he died. He instructed me to give you this letter." And so saying, Meremot placed in Yeshai's hand, a small scroll bound with thick and coarse twine.

"Now that you have fulfilled your oath, I wish you peace. Please step aside that I may continue to make necessary preparations for the Sabbath."

"My young friend, do not be in such a hurry. When you read this scroll, you will need one additional piece of information. The meeting will take place at sunset on the first day of the coming week at the house of Elias son of Yehochanan." Without waiting for Yeshai to respond or ask questions, Meremot turned away and seemed to disappear into the crowd.

Dumbfounded, Yeshai spoke to himself in a whisper: "What meeting?"

The irresistible aroma of roasted lamb with glorious herbs and spices filled the modest house of Hilkiah the scribe. Now Yeshai understood Elimelech's late arrival at the city gate. He was organizing and preparing the Sabbath feast. The meal was wonderful. The conversation at the table had a comfort level that was usually reserved for close friends and family. Eventually, the table had been cleared and Elimelech poured an extra cup of thick sweet wine for each of them.

"I am a happy man. My daughter is protected. My son-in-law is protected, and I shall also be the *chotein*, to a famous scribe of Samaria. With any luck at all before I die, children shall call me *Sabba*."

"Father, do not get ahead of time and events. It pleases me to know that Yeshai will one day be my husband. But that day is nine months from now. A great deal can happen in such a length of time."

"Listen to yourself. But a few days ago you were disconsolate about your future because you had none. Now everything is possible. This reminds me of a song."

"Father, don't you dare!"

"I only thought that since there was still nearly an hour of oil left in the lamps we might continue to enjoy each other's company a little while longer before we have to turn in."

"That reminds me," Yeshai said.

"I am pleased that you now feel yourself to be a part of this family. I thought you had already fallen asleep." Elimelech said.

"The strangest thing happened at the city gates. Just when the session was concluded, an old man approached me with this." Yeshai produced the scroll from the pocket of his robe and proceeded to describe the conversation with Meremot.

"Perhaps it is time to read Hilkiah's message," Yeshai offered.

"Then you should do so privately. My late husband went to a great deal of trouble to make sure you would receive this letter. Maybe it is not meant for my eyes or ears."

"Ruth may be right, you know."

"Please forgive my directness. I will not keep secrets from you nor your father. Secrets breed suspicion and unhappiness. We must learn to trust one another in all matters. We should begin to do so now, here."

"So be it."

Yeshai unrolled the small scroll. It was actually two sheets, one inside the other. The letter was written on a material pressed and formed from the stalks of reeds, found in abundance along the banks of every river in lower Bavel. The writing was flowing, as if without pause or hesitation. Yeshai was not surprised to see that the form of each letter followed the scribal traditions of Judah, as taught in the last days of the Sacred House before the exile. As he examined the message, he had the growing sense that the shape of the letters was a special bond that connected all members of his family.

Dear Cousin:

If you are Yeshai son of Gilad son of Eliezer son of Achituv from Gezer, and you are reading these words, then what I have feared most has come to pass. I am making my journey to Sheol, leaving my beautiful wife, Ruth as a widow. Only Ruth and her devoted father know the truth. I have been poisoned, slowly over time, but poisoned nonetheless…

"Is this true?" Yeshai said. "Did you know this? Why didn't you tell me?"

"Read the letter and then we will talk of poison. Know this, we are all in danger," Elimelech said.

Shaking his head, Yeshai continued to read aloud.

How I know this to be true is of little consequence now. What matters is the protection of the sacred scrolls of Judah. The path of your life and mine have never intersected but they have passed many of the same boundary stones. We are both the third generation descendants of Achituv of Gezer. We are both priests and scribes of the first order. We are both the sworn guardians of the sacred scrolls of our people, rescued from the flames that engulfed the Sacred House sixty-eight years ago.

Six months ago, during the course of a single week, every single hair on my body fell out. A year earlier, the slow and painful death of my father began in the exact same manner. I knew then that I did not have long to live. I had to prepare for my certain death. Without an heir, the safety and preservation of the Sacred scrolls would become the responsibility of the very people who were killing me. Fulfilling our task, upholding our oath, will be dangerous. My death will be proof that our exiled community is divided into factions. At least one of these groups is willing to kill those who oppose them.

My first step was to entreat Memukan, the Persian Pehcha, to locate you and bring you to Pumbedita. For many years he has been a true friend of the House of Judah, doing more than is necessary to sustain Judeans in exile, as well as the community of returnees now in Judah. Your captivity in Jerusalem was not an accident. The reach of the poisoners is long. It extends from Bavel to Judah. As you were the publicly acknowledged guardian of the Sacred scrolls preserved in Samaria, they had to find a way to take them from you. You had to be disgraced and murdered to enable their plans to succeed. And what is it they seek that they will commit murder to achieve? They seek to throw off the yoke of Persia, build an opulent Sacred House and place a descendant of David on the throne. As consecrated priests, they will build their own Judean empire on the free will offerings of the poor. They can do this because they possess the Mishkan scroll. Elimelech and Ruth will explain to you about the abomination known as the Mishkan. The scrolls you protect are the only proof that the Mishkan scroll is not the work of the God of Moses but rather the assembled lies of the false prophet, Ezekiel.

You must be present at the next gathering of the scribes of Judah in exile. If you are reading this letter it means that Meremot son of Uriah has informed you of the time and place of that gathering. You may trust him. Put your trust also in Ruth and her father, Elimelech. They will guide you. They know who is true to our tradition and who is false.

My final prayer is that you will fulfill the obligation of the levir, marry Ruth, and sire my son. Thus the house of Achituv will continue and my name will not be blotted out from under heaven. Please love her and care for her. She is as much a daughter of Judah as my mother and grandmother were.

May the peace of our God be upon us all.

Hilkiah son of Shallum- Hacohein v' hasofer.

The letter bore a puddle of red wax the size of a large thumb. The imprint of a cylinder-seal had been rolled across the wax when it was pliable. The impression was identical to a broken cylinder-seal Yesahi had noticed suspended from a leather thong around Ruth's neck. When Yeshai looked up from the scroll he saw large tears welling up in Ruth's eyes. She turned away from his gaze and wiped her eyes. Elimelech tried but failed to clear his throat. He too was overwhelmed. Yeshai wanted answers. He could not wait for these emotions to pass. He needed answers now.

"Who is poisoning us and how is he doing it?"

Elimelech's eyes narrowed. "Not 'he,' they. They are poisoning us!"

"All right, who are they?"

"They are members of the priestly clan of Ezekiel. You will not understand unless I tell you the whole story."

"Then begin at the beginning."

Elimelech cleared his throat. "The leader of the exiles of Judah at the time of their shame and humiliation was a priest and prophet named Ezekiel ben Buzzi. He is the one who divided the sacred scrolls and sent twelve of them with your grandfather Eliezer, into hiding in Samaria. The other twelve followed the exiles to Bavel. Hilkiah's grandfather Zadok was the guardian of the scrolls sent to Bavel. As our exile community settled into a life of sorts, in exile, this Ezekiel took for himself the title of High Priest and became like a father to Zadok."

Over the course of the next hour, with their worried faces reflected in the yellow glow of the Sabbath oil lamps, Elimelech and Ruth related the story of Zadok's discovery of the *Mishkan* scroll; the construction of the *Mishkan* in Bavel; Zadok's realization that the *Mishkan* scroll was actually written by Ezekiel; the murder of Zadok; the flood that destroyed the *Mishkan* and caused the death of Shallum and Aviva, Hilkiah's father and mother; the strength of Miryam in raising Hilkiah and preserving the scribal tradition; and finally the Persian conquest of Bavel and the apparent end of the exile.

"One day I must tell you of the Judean exiles in Samaria and our own efforts to preserve the sacred scrolls, but I am overwhelmed with questions from your story. I must begin with the most important question of all, how are you being poisoned?"

"We only know that it is from our food or water. Perhaps it is from everything we eat, drink or touch, " Ruth said.

"Then we must find a way to acquire food and water from families we trust who show no signs of sickness. At the same time, we must appear to be eating and drinking from our usual sources. We dare not risk forcing our enemies. Perhaps we begin by speaking with Meremot.

"My next question has to do with your service of the God of our ancestors. You have no Sacred House. Do you worship at all?"

"When the *Mishkan* was destroyed, for a brief time the exiles of Judah were united in viewing it as a sign from God that a great sin had been committed. But the flood occurred at virtually the same time as the Persian conquest of Bavel. When Cyrus proclaimed the end of the exile and encouraged the Judeans to return to Judah, Ezekiel's loyal followers, priests and Levites who were powerful in the days when the *Mishkan* stood, were desperate to maintain their power and status. Though Ezekiel had died before the *Mishkan* was destroyed, Ezekiel's followers continued to use the *Mishkan* scroll as a sign of priestly authority over the exiles. They managed this even without a place of worship. They continued to elect a High Priest and organized themselves into watches. They paraded around in priestly garb and extorted gifts from the poor on the promise that their sacrifices would be pleasing to God.

"They knew that the people would not tolerate another *Mishkan* in Bavel so they offered sacrifices in the courtyard of the home of the High Priest. It was a Sacred House in everything but opulence. The priests taught the people that as soon as the Sacred House was restored in Judah, they would end the sacrifices in Bavel. But the followers of Ezekiel only spoke of rebuilding the Sacred House. They prophesied and dreamt about its dimensions, its materials, its splendor. This is how they raised money in Bavel for the reconstruction in Judah. But the money never got there. For nearly twenty years after the exile had ended, no one was raising a beam or a wall for a new Sacred House. Ezekiel's clan grew rich in Bavel, all the while blaming the tribes of Edom, Ammon, Moab, and Samaria for preventing construction of the Sacred House. They insisted that God would decide when it was time to build. Perhaps God did decide, after all. Darius, Emperor of Persia ordered the priests of Judah to rebuild or return the gold, silver, and bronze artifacts that had been given them by Cyrus. Only then did the clan of Ezekiel undertake an actual rebuilding of the Sacred House."

"And where do you and the rest of the Judean exiles in Bavel worship?"

"We worship in our homes and sometimes in places of meeting."

"Do you offer sacrifices at these meetings?"

"Certainly not!" Ruth said.

"We only know for certain what takes place here in Pumbedita. Most of those who gather for these meetings are scribes and their families. We are fortunate to be in the town where the sacred scrolls are kept. The guardian of the scrolls will bring forth one or more of the scrolls and read them to the people. The people will praise God for the words on the scrolls and for keeping the people together, even in exile."

"How many Judeans are at these meetings and how often do they take place?"

"We do not take a count. That would be an affront to God. You will see for yourself at the gathering the day after tomorrow. We meet whenever we can be sure that the clan of Ezekiel is not watching. The first day of the week is a festival day for the Persians. Ezekiel's clan has been invited to the governor's palace to join in the celebration. Let's just say that we were able to arrange the invitation for them."

The last remaining oil in the last lamp still illuminated, sputtered out. There was darkness and there was silence.

"It's time we turned in. There's much to think about before the Sabbath ends," Yeshai said.

Sleep was a stranger to Yeshai that night. His mind raced as he tried to make sense of the complex story of the exiles in Bavel. One thing was certain, the guardians of the scrolls in Bavel might be just as anxious to end his life as the returned priests were in Jerusalem. Elimelech did not see things from the same perspective as Yeshai did. He was convinced that Yeshai's story and his leadership of the Judean exiles in Samaria would prove to be powerful arguments for the scribes of Bavel to elect Yeshai as the successor to Hilkiah's leadership. Who would be proven correct?

Questions tormented his sleep. How would the Bavel guardians react to the news that the Samaritan scrolls were turned to ashes, on purpose? Could a scribe who is an accomplice to the destruction of sacred texts be trusted to guard the remaining twelve scrolls? Did he dare show them the single scroll of Eliezer? Would they understand or would they condemn? For that matter, how would Ruth react?

As the first dull glow of dawn entered the house of Hilkiah, Yeshai resolved to tell Ruth and Elimelech the complete truth as he knew it. The

God who rescued him from the murderous clutches of the priests of Jerusalem and safely carried him on his journey to Bavel would not abandon him. In any event, he made sure to offer prayers that this would be the case. A vision of Ruth's beautiful face appeared to Yeshai on the wall opposite his bed. He took this pleasant vision as a sign that his prayer was being answered. With a great smile on his face, he drifted off into a deep and dreamless sleep. Sleeping until noon on the Sabbath was not a sin.

The guardians of the sacred scrolls had chosen the meeting location well. The house of Elias son of Yehochanan was outside of the walls of Pumbedita. It was ideal for a clandestine gathering, not because it was some distance outside of Pumbedita, but because the house was surrounded by an awful stench. Elias was a master tanner. The stench arose from the four enormous clay cauldrons set against the southern wall of Elias' courtyard. They were the next step in the making of leather. Their contents were a trade secret known only to the master tanners of Bavel. The fragrance given off by the tanning process was very effective at keeping the gathering private.

The attendees arrived singly or at most, two at a time. When the meeting began, there were seventeen men and eleven women present. Most of the men and women were in their late thirties, early forties. The oldest person in the room was Elimelech. From his demeanor it was clear that he was uncomfortable being there. He was more relaxed attending gatherings of the river traders. Meremot began the meeting. For the next hour it was worship and not the politics of religion that engaged them. The rhythmic droning voices of the participants, nearly put Yeshai into a trance. Suddenly, he realized that he was very familiar with the contents of their prayers. They were reciting lines and whole paragraphs from the Sacred Scrolls. No one had the scrolls before his eyes. They were reciting from memory.

Yeshai pondered the significance of the gathering of Judeans who did not speak in the Judean tongue, when everyone around him stood up and turned toward the western wall of the room. Meremot had walked to a wooden cabinet.

The droning changed to a more musical mode as Meremot opened the cabinet doors. The interior of the box was plain, without ornamentation of any kind. A jumble of parchment scrolls stood leaning against the rear wall of the box. Although Yeshai could not count the scrolls, he was sure that there were twelve of them. These were the twelve scrolls of the exile in Bavel. Were they copies or were they the originals?

Meremot removed one of the scrolls and closed the cabinet doors. He walked slowly to the center of the square and placed it gently on a table. He untied the string that was holding the scroll together and slowly unrolled the parchment. Two men arose and went to either side of Meremot and held the edges of the scroll down by placing the end of their sleeves on the scroll. Their hands did not make contact with the parchment.

Meremot read the text in a kind of chant. Yeshai found this strange. In Samaria it was the custom to chant from the sacred scrolls only those passages that were written in the form of songs. The rest of the text would be read and not chanted. Here everything was being chanted. The style was new to Yeshai's ears but he found it very pleasant. Meremot was skilled and had a fine singing voice. Yeshai was feeling guilty about his cold treatment of Meremot when they first met. He would have to offer his apology.

The passage Meremot chanted was the story of Joseph in an Egyptian prison. Yeshai knew it well. As soon as the story concluded, the person standing to Meremot's right began reciting the very same story in Aramaic. It did not sound like a word for word translation. In fact, the Aramaic storyteller was adding a few embellishments of his own. Yeshai's Aramaic skills were not perfect, so he had a difficult time understanding why there were so many outbursts of laughter. He did not think that Joseph's story was amusing, but he could be wrong. When the readings had concluded, the entire gathering stood as the scroll was returned to the cabinet.

"Scribes of Judah, let our decisions be guided by the God who stood with Joseph in an Egyptian prison." The speaker was the tanner, Elias son of Yehochanan. He stood at the reading table and made a sharp noise with a small clay lamp against the wooden tabletop. His garments were not those of a poor man. In fact, they were of the finest materials, none of which were leather.

"We are joined today by a brother scribe of Judah, more recently of Samaria. I speak of Yeshai son of Gilad son of Eliezer son of Achituv of Gezer. He is Hilkiah's cousin and the current guardian of the twelve scrolls of the Sacred House preserved among the Judean exiles in Samaria."

"With utmost respect, Elias son of Yehochanan, Please permit me to correct your statement. I <u>was</u> the guardian of the scrolls. That <u>was</u> true. But now those twelve scrolls of the Sacred House exist no more."

Whatever decorum existed in that gathering now dissolved into a deluge of angry questions coming from everyone in the room. Elias was banging the clay lamp so hard it shattered into sharp pieces and went flying throughout the room. The explosion of clay fragments caused a moment of silence. It was just enough time for Elias to shout everyone back down into his seat.

"Now would be a good time to let Yeshai, son of Gilad explain his statement. If you please…" He gestured to Yeshai to come forward.

For the next hour, Yeshai told the gathering the entire story of the twelve sacred scrolls that were protected by his grandfather and father before him, during their exile sojourn in the territory of Samaria. He concluded with a detailed description of the hidden scroll: his grandfather Eliezer's compilation of the twelve scrolls into one continuous text and the oath taken by Gilad and Yeshai to destroy the original twelve scrolls. He did not tell the gathering about leaving a copy of the hidden scroll in Shoshana's bone box. He trusted the members of the gathering completely, but he also did not want the clan of Ezekiel to be able to destroy every single copy of the hidden scroll.

"I still do not understand how anyone, let alone a priestly scribe and guardian of the sacred scrolls could deliberately destroy the last remaining connection to the Sacred House of Solomon. These scrolls are important reminders of who we are. Bringing all twelve of them together again in Jerusalem would have been a powerful moment in the restoration of the Sacred House and the people of Israel." The speaker was Bani son of Kadmiel, a rotund scribe who earned his daily bread by baking bread. Murmurs of agreement followed his question.

"My brothers and sisters, from the moment my eyes encountered the hidden scroll, I began a routine of reading from it every day. I committed its contents to memory. After six months of daily readings I came to understand my grandfather's purpose in assembling the hidden scroll. Each of you is very familiar with the contents of the twelve scrolls preserved here in Bavel. Tell me, which tribes are represented in the scrolls?"

"What do you mean 'represented' in the scrolls?" Bani asked.

"When you read the scrolls, what tribes are named?" Yeshai asked.

"The tribes of Judah and Benjamin, of course!" Elias answered.

"You say 'of course' like that is the way things are supposed to be. My grandfather saw a great danger in the constant mention of Judah and Benjamin in the sacred scrolls."

"The other tribes, those who parted from us after the death of Solomon, are cursed." Meremot said. "It is not for us to mention them or speak of them."

"Eliezer knew the tradition of scorn," Yeshai said. "He understood the hostility towards the vanished tribes of the Northern Kingdom of Israel. He understood that to pronounce their names would be like lifting a divine curse from their shameful exile. He also understood that for Judah to have any hope at redemption it would be necessary to bring the ten tribes of Israel back into the covenant with the God of Abraham, Isaac and Jacob."

"How can you bring back a people that has vanished from the earth? There are no Israelite exiles in Persia or anywhere else." Meremot asked.

"When my grandfather faithfully assembled the texts of the twelve scrolls into the one hidden scroll, he left nothing out from the twelve sacred scrolls. But as I read each column carefully and compared it to the original sacred text, I discovered that he did add some text. He added explanations for words or ideas that might not be understood today. If he is guilty of any sin against the God of our ancestors it might be his other additions. He did expand the story to include mentioning by name the tribes of the North. Those statements did nothing to change the story or any outcomes for good or for evil purposes. All his life he feared that, should the God of Abraham redeem Judah from exile, Judah redeemed could not stand alone, even with Benjamin at his side. He believed that just as not all Judeans were taken into exile in Bavel, so too, not all Israelites from the ten Northern tribes were captured by Asshur. Through the hidden scroll he was issuing a call to all Israelites, all descendants of Jacob, to rally to Jerusalem and the house of David and Solomon."

"This would even be in agreement with the visions of Ezekiel ben Buzzi. While alive, he always spoke of the whole nation of Israel coming from the four directions and being gathered together in Judah." Elimelech said.

"How do we know that Yeshai's grandfather was not inspired by the God of our ancestors? If it is true that Eliezer left nothing of the twelve scrolls out of the single hidden scroll, then I for one wish to examine this scroll for myself, before passing final judgement." Meremot said.

"I too wish to study the scroll of Eliezer." Bani stood, his gaze focusing on Yeshai.

A handful of others, including Ruth, stood and spoke of their desire to read the scroll.

"Well, then, the first thing we must do is make sure that there are enough faithful copies of the hidden scroll for all who wish to read it, Meremot said. "Yeshai, you had better be the one to make the first copy and keep it in your dwelling. When it is finished, bring the original hidden scroll to me. I shall make a copy of it and pass the original to Elias. From there, Elias will make a copy of the original and pass it on to Bani and so forth, until all who wish to read it have an opportunity to do so."

"What do we do about the clan of Ezekiel?" Yeshai asked.

"We tell them nothing and we show them nothing," Elias said

"You realize that we could all be charged with blasphemy, especially those who actively made copies?" Yeshai said. "Your lives might be at risk over what you decide to do."

"If the hidden scroll is faithful to the contents of the twelve sacred scrolls, what could be blasphemous about it?" Bani asked.

"It is not the twelve sacred scrolls I am worried about. You have another scroll presented to the people as if it were the thirteenth sacred scroll. The clan of Ezekiel might be upset when they find out that there is no mention of the *Mishkan* in the hidden scroll. My grandfather never saw the Mishkan scroll. He only knew that it was the reason for the death of his beloved twin brother. For Eliezer to even consider its inclusion in the hidden scroll would have been a real case of blasphemy."

"Could we stop referring to Eliezer's scroll as the hidden scroll?" Meremot asked.

"What would you call it?" Elias asked.

"Let's call it what it is, The Scroll of the Teaching of Moses-*sefer torat Moshe*." Elimelech knew that that was the way that Gilad father of Yeshai referred to the hidden scroll in his letters to Hilkiah. How appropriate.

"*Sefer Torat Moshe* it shall be.

Chapter Thirty-Nine

DATE: March 20, 2009

TIME: 3:45 P.M. Israel Time

PLACE: Police HQ, Tel Aviv

I f Michal could have transmitted an especially painful dose of rabies through cell phone transmission towers and microwaves, she would have done so with great satisfaction. She also would have preferred to receive a phone call from Muammar Khadafi than her ex-father-in-law. Malik felt the seething anger and decided to get to the point.

"I need your help on a matter of national security," he said.

"Since when does our country's security depend on *alte kocker* fugitives from Baghdad?" Michal was not moved.

"*Sgan-Aluf* Lavi, would you please speak with my daughter-in-law?"

Lavi was staring at the "list of things to consider" on the white board when Malik handed him the phone. Malik had a look of pleading in his eyes. With a return look that said "What do you expect me to do?" Lavi took the phone.

"Michal, it's Ronnie." Malik's eyes opened wide in surprise at the level of familiarity.

"I was her commander during her military service." Lavi explained in a whisper, covering the mouthpiece and shrugging his shoulders at the same time.

"Listen, time is very short and we need your help on a matter of national importance." He practically ordered her to join them at Police Headquarters.

"Ronnie, I am in Jerusalem and I am scheduled to lead a tour in an hour. I can't leave now."

"Cancel it. Cancel it now and get down here. I will expect you in my office at 4:00."

Michal knew that tone of voice. Something important was brewing. She agreed to join them. Now she was curious. What part of national security could require the presence of a curator of Southeastern European Jewish History?

"She's on her way," Lavi said.

Abby looked at Lavi closely and detected in the *Sgan-Aluf* more than a professional interest in Malik's ex-daughter-in-law.

Unaware of Abby's scrutiny, Lavi continued making phone calls to assemble the entry team. Only one call was actually necessary. The rest of the calls were made by members of the team in accord with a well-established phone tree. Lavi's next call was to Rafi and Omar. He wanted to make sure that the intelligence services were aware of what he was about to do. He was also trolling for information. Although unlikely, it might happen that the *Shin Bet* had some information on The Builders that might prove useful. Eventually, all of his phone calls reached their intended targets. Everyone agreed to meet at Police Headquarters at 4:00.

"What have you gotten me into, Sergeant?" Abby brushed up against Aaron who was doing his own note taking on an Israeli version of a legal pad.

"I seem to recall that you were the one who insisted we needed to get an expert's opinion from your college. Without our little road-trip, I would be back in Falujah training Iraqis to dodge IED's."

Abby looked around the room and made sure everyone but Aaron was looking the other way. Then she suddenly pulled Aaron toward her and kissed him firmly on the lips, let go just as suddenly, and whispered, "But look at what both of us would have missed out on, if you had not requested a consultation on your circumcision."

Their hearty laughter at the shared confidence seemed very inappropriate, given the place and the circumstances. They each retreated to their own place at the conference table and continued to make notes. For Abby, the notes were more questions than answers.

> » Where did the Builders come by their desire to rebuild the Temple?
>
> » Are the Builders acting alone?
>
> » Who else knows about the Ezra scroll?
>
> » Who else knows about the original Torah?

So many questions, so little time for answers. Abby was exhausted by the stress and the accompanying adrenaline rushes. She slowly put her head down on the table and closed her eyes.

Before she awoke from her catnap, Abby's last thought was: How will good-ole-boy, Marine Sergeant Aaron Keller go over with mom and dad? He is Jewish, even if he is from South Carolina. I cannot wait to introduce him to them. She raised her head with an enigmatic smile on her lips.

At a quarter to four in the afternoon, Michal arrived at the conference room in the Tel Aviv Police Headquarters complex with a flourish. Her tall frame was shrouded in a billowy floral print dress that surrounded her neck and descended to just above her ankles. With the right kind of cheap wig, she could slip unnoticed through the streets of Mea Shearim or Bnai Brak. But instead, her shiny, long flowing natural red hair declared that this was a modern woman of fashion. Beneath the billows there were hints of a figure some would call 'statuesque.' Others would find it difficult not to stare. Malik understood what his son had seen in her. He was seeing it for himself, yet again. And then there was her voice—gravel falling over a mountainside.

Michal was in a state of vehement disbelief. Her briefing with *Sgan Aluf* Lavi was not going well.

"Tell me what is really going on. If you continue to tell me *bubbe meises,* I will not lift a finger to help you. Can you give me a one hundred percent kosher guarantee that I won't lose my job over this? You found the original

Torah, yeah right. Really! I have a tunnel I want to sell you that goes from Saudi Arabia to Eilat. We can use it to suck all the oil from the Arabian Peninsula and King Fahd will never know. What is this about, really?" Her machine pistol rant had finally concluded.

"Michal, I realize you and I do not have a great many bonds of trust between us," Malik said.

"Oh, you do, do you? Why should I listen to you, of all people?"

"I have never lied to you about anything and I am not lying now. In your museum warehouse is the discovery of the ages. It will make the Dead Sea Scrolls seem ordinary by comparison. Here, finally, is the answer to all those attempts to delegitimize our nation by denying our very history. We believe we have discovered the one document that makes the Documentary Hypothesis fact and not theory. Without you we will lose this scroll. Without you the crazy Builders may even succeed in blowing up the Shrine of the Book. We must get there before them. And we do not have much time."

"How do you even know the ossuary is there?"

"We don't," Abby said. "All we know is that the excavation of a site in Samaria uncovered nearly two hundred ossuaries. According to museum records, all of them were brought to Jerusalem and stored in the museum warehouse. It has to be there."

"But you don't know that. You are hoping and guessing, but you don't know anything for sure." Michal countered.

"Enough!" Rafi swept the room and immediately took charge. Omar was right behind him.

"So nice of you to join our party," Aaron said.

"It is nice to know that the *Shin Bet* can be of assistance to the United States Marines," Rafi replied. He walked to the front of the room and loaded a flash drive into the wall-mounted computer. He pulled down the keyboard and started typing. With a few keystrokes here and a password there, Rafi had loaded a Power Point program and dimmed the lights over the screen on the presentation board.

The screen illuminated the entire room with the bright light given off by a schematic drawing. The label in the lower left-hand corner revealed in Hebrew and English that this was page one of the architectural drawings for the Israel Museum Antiquities Warehouse. The drawing was dated July 1971.

"Lavi briefed me on the entire situation," Omar said. "I think we can be more than helpful. Here is the target building.

"Perimeter security is provided by concealed cameras covering the entire exterior on all sides. The cameras are monitored by the museum guards seated at the main entrance to the Museum. It's not the best system. The guards are constantly being distracted by Museum visitors during business hours and lazy about checking their screens after the museum has closed. I think you will find it interesting that our people have detected an electronic intrusion into the closed circuit system."

"And this means what, precisely?" Michal asked.

"It means, Professor Levski, that someone has already hacked the security cameras and will probably upload a pre-recorded view of peace and tranquility," Lavi said. "Whoever breached the security system will make their entrance unseen by the guards."

"Nu—what will be our response?" Malik asked.

"We are not going to prevent them from entering, Rafi said. "We are going to be inside waiting for them."

"And you need me for what, exactly?" Michal asked.

"Getting inside is the easy part. We need your security pass and codes to access the controlled atmosphere storage room. That is where the ossuaries are being kept."

"Says who?"

"The museum director," Lavi said.

"You spoke with Avichai?" Michal gave Lavi a hard look.

"No, I spoke to him this afternoon," Malik said.

"I did not lie to him. I simply asked if I, as a scholar, would be able to take my grad students to the museum to view the Samaritan ossuaries on a private tour. He explained that they were not presently on display, that they were in storage and protected from light and air because they had some wonderful examples of Samaritan decoration on them. The colors, he wanted me to know, were still vivid, even after 2,500 years. The curators concluded that this was due to the lack of exposure to the elements. They decided not to take chances with the storage of the boxes."

"And he was not the least bit suspicious of your motives?"

"He made an appointment for two weeks from now and promised to show me the collection himself."

"This is like a watchdog leading the criminal to the family Jewels," Aaron said.

Malik smiled. "I resent that comparison, Sergeant."

"Will you get us in, Michal?" Lavi asked.

"Only if you promise to support me in my old age. I'm sure to lose my pension and benefits over this."

"Do you want Ronnie's hand in marriage?" Malik teased.

"Actually, I do! Only kidding. I know I'm going to regret this, but I will get you in."

"Our sources tell us that The Builders are planning to detonate the explosives at the Shrine of the Book at 01:30 hours this morning. We need to be inside the warehouse by 1900 hours tonight," Omar said.

"Why so early?" Abby asked.

"Just in case The Builders have already placed the museum complex under surveillance. We will enter one at a time, starting at 1700 and not draw any undue attention to ourselves."

"How many of us will there be inside?" Aaron asked.

"Sixteen including everyone here, Rafi said. "That should be more than enough. We will have the advantage of surprise."

"I don't know about you guys, but whenever I think I'm operating with the advantage of surprise, the surprise rises up to bite me in the ass," Aaron said.

"We need to go downstairs and select our gear for this evening's entertainment," Lavi said.

"Rabbi, you know how to shoot one of these?" Omar asked, as he handed Abby a Beretta nine millimeter automatic with a tactical fiber holster.

"Can I test it out on your right foot?" As she said this she expertly jacked the action open and shut, confirming that there were no bullets in the chamber. Then she slid a fifteen shot magazine into the handle receiver. She walked over to a loading barrel in the corner and once again jacked the chamber, inserting a round.

"Now I've seen everything," Omar said. "Even a pistol packing rabbi."

"What's the point of entering one at a time, if we are all wearing such obvious combat gear?" Abby gave voice to Aaron's own question about the tactic.

The team members were wearing black, from black Kevlar helmets on their heads to the black Israeli-made boots on their feet. Once Aaron was convinced that he had selected the right sizes, he put on his gear with the effortlessness of one who has done this many times. As he adjusted his tactical vest he mused on the differences between the police in Fallujah and the Israeli team. All of the Israelis were more or less trained for this. Even Michal had suited up and was sporting a side arm. Malik actually looked fierce in his combat get-up, especially with his chinstrap cinched firmly in place.

Aaron's mind drifted to recalling a book he had read about Jewish gangsters in New York. The book was titled, *Tough Jews*. Tough Jews my ass! They were pussies. The people in this room are the tough Jews. All except Omar, he is one tough Druse.

Chapter Forty

DATE: In the Twentieth Year of King Artaxerxes of Persia, Corresponding to the One Hundred Forty-First Year Since the Destruction of Jerusalem, In the Month of Nisan, The First Month, On the Twentieth Day of the Month

TIME: Second Hour of the First Watch

PLACE: The Fortress of Shushan, Persia

"My lord counselor, your brother, Hanani has just arrived. He seeks an immediate audience with you. He says his business with you is urgent. I must also inform you that with him are several men from Judah. Shall I show them in?"

"Yes of course by all means, Teresh, show them in!" Nehemiah ordered.

Nehemiah ben Hacaliah was a fourth-generation descendant of the exiles of Judah. Today, and for the last six years he was Fourth Counselor to the Emperor of Persia, and Manager of the Imperial Household. He was a large man. His personal servants told stories of reinforcing and redesigning furniture to accommodate his weight and girth.

The moment Nehemiah's brother's arrival was announced, he quickly stood and started to pace nervously in the Fourth Counselor's office. His pacing accelerated. The room could not contain his anxiety. Nehemiah knew that things were bad in Judah. He needed to know for sure just how bad they were. During the past year, merchants and travelers from the Province Beyond The Rivers related tales of constant warfare and destruction throughout the region. The lawlessness and brigandage had begun more than a generation before. In those days, the Persian Empire was dangerously weakened by its fierce and constant wars with the Greeks. Every trained soldier in the Empire, including Judean Levites assigned to provide security for the Sacred House, was pressed into service.

Dissident tribes used the absence of Persian authority to target Judah and Jerusalem and especially the rebuilt Sacred House itself for plunder. It did not matter whether it was the Samaritans, the Edomites, the Moabites, the Ammonites, or the Phoenicians; each tribe grabbed all the wealth it could from the treasury of the Sacred House, and then, for good measure, took Judeans captive for ransom. The remaining Judeans paid any price to redeem their brothers and sisters and put an end to outright murder. They did so to make the captives more valuable alive than dead.

In addition to amassing wealth and spoil, the Samaritans mounted endless attacks on Judah for another reason—revenge. For more than ninety-four years, since the time of the return of the Judeans from exile under Cyrus, the Samaritans resented the support given by Persia to the Judeans. The Samaritans believed that the God of Israel had chosen them to rule in the Land of Israel. They routinely accused Judeans of disloyalty and treachery. In most cases, their lies fell on deaf Persian ears.

"Hanani son of Hacaliah and a delegation from Judah," Teresh, the Persian servant announced with an important air. Six men entered the chamber. Only one was dressed in the manner of Persia. The rest wore Judean garments worn thin from use and still covered in dust and dirt from their journey.

"My lord Counselor, permit me to introduce five representatives of the people of the land of Jerusalem, judges at the gates of the city herself." Upon making their entrance, Hanani gave a formal bow before his brother. Nehemiah, a mountain in motion, rushed to greet Hanani and embrace him with a smothering hug.

"Teresh, please leave us and close the door behind you!"

"As you command, lord Counselor."

"Let me look at you, brother. You have survived a difficult journey. I am grateful for your service and the Emperor himself shall know of your heroism."

"Nehemiah, please do not go on with this talk of heroism. How heroic could I be with a detachment of Imperial soldiers to protect me?"

Hanani was six years younger than Nehemiah. He favored his mother. Always thin, he now looked almost gaunt from his journey. He was slightly shorter than his brother.

"Please introduce your guests."

"I have the honor to present members of the People of the Land, the chosen leadership of Jerusalem: Zacur, son of Imri, Uriah son of Hakoz, Meshullam son of Berachiah, Zadok, son of Baana, and Yoiada, son of Paseach."

"Brothers, I thank you for making this dangerous journey. I thank you for leaving your possessions and family behind to fulfill this important mission. Take your time and tell me everything. We are alone. You may speak freely."

"As you wish, brother, but our news may not be to your liking," Hanani said. "Our brothers and sisters in Judah are on the edge of total defeat. Jerusalem's walls are full of breaches and every one of the city's gates has been destroyed by fire. Perhaps the only good news in all of this is that a large number of captives taken by the Samaritans over the past few years, has returned home. These former captives are impoverished and feeling disgraced at having survived their captivity while other family members have not. Some of them may be able to stand guard, but most are weakened with starvation and disease. Winter rains and snows have sent the bands of Samaritans, Ammonites, and Moabites back to their lands, but there is no doubt that with the end of the spring rains, the coming of summer will see their return to finish the destruction of Judah and Jerusalem."

"May I add something to the conversation, my lord?" Zacur son of Imri said.

"I need as much information as you have to tell me. Please continue, but you will have to speak louder. I can barely hear you."

"Over the past two months we have been betrayed and lied to by our own Judean brethren," Zacur said. "It is difficult to trust that what we say in this chamber will not be on the streets of Shushan before the day is over."

"Speak plainly, son of Imri," Hanani said.

"Very well. As you wish." Zacur faced Nehemiah directly.

"Your brother's report is accurate. The conditions in Judah are as he has recounted. What he left out of the report, and what made our journey so dangerous, was the fact that some of our brothers and sisters in Judah are urging the people to join with the Samaritans and put an end to Persian rule in the Province Beyond The Rivers."

"Zacur is telling the truth," Zadok, son of Baana said. "We are all victims of Samaritan and Judean lies. The Samaritans and their Judean traitors tried to prevent the departure of our delegation for Persia. Each one of us was accused of being in league with the enemies of Persia to seek its overthrow. They are describing the Samaritans as our brothers, joined together by the protection of the God of Israel.

"Merchants loyal to the God of Abraham and His Sacred House have reported in detail of their visits to Samaria. These travelers witnessed descendants of Judean priests living in Samaria since the time of the exile, leading Judeans in daily worship in the abomination the Samaritans call the Sacred House on Mt. Gerizim."

The oldest member of the delegation from Judah, Meshullam son of Berachiah took up the tale in a voice weakened by age and the difficulties of travel.

"My Lord Counselor, may I have some water? My throat is as dry as the wilderness that separates Judah from Bavel."

Nehemiah walked to a small table in the far corner of the room and poured a cup of water from a clay jug with unusual geometric designs and flowers.

"Please continue when you are ready," Nehemiah said.

"Since I am the one who instigated the act, I must be the one to inform Your Excellency that we removed the sacred utensils from the ruins of the Sacred House and have brought them with us to Persia." Meshullam turned his face toward the floor.

"What!" Nehemiah shouted loudly.

"But why would you do such a thing? The Emperor will be very angry. His great grandfather saw to it that the sacred objects of the House in Jerusalem were returned along with the exiles. You had no right to steal them!"

"Calm yourself, brother." Hanani placed his hand lightly on Nehemiah's shoulder. "There was a serious and worthy reason for us to bring the sacred objects to Persia. The gold and silver, the lavers and basins and all the rest, including the lamp stand, were about to be plundered by the Samaritans and placed in their Temple on Mt. Gerizim. These worthies of Judah are true heroes, not thieves. The objects they brought from the Sacred House of Solomon shall not become the tools of Samaritan blasphemy. We brought these sacred items to Persia, because only here are they safe, until such time as we are able to return them to a reborn Jerusalem."

"There is more news, my lord Counselor," Zacur said.

"Continue, then."

"The Samaritans have a scroll. They describe it as the Scroll of the teaching of Moses."

"There are many such scrolls with that name among the scribes. So what does this particular scroll contain?"

"Mostly the well known stories of our tradition and those of the Kingdom of Israel before they were exiled."

"I have heard that our Judean scribes in Pumbedita also have such a scroll. What of it? Is there a problem with this?"

"The Judean scribes have a scroll, but not like the Samaritans. The Samaritan scroll establishes Mt. Gerizim, not Jerusalem, as God's chosen location for the Sacred House. The people are being duped into believing that the presence of God will dwell in the Samaritan Sacred House on Mt. Gerizim, for all time. The Samaritans are referring to the Sacred House in Jerusalem as an abomination abhorred by God. They are vowing to plow it under by this coming summer and use it to pasture their goats and sheep."

"Where did this Samaritan scroll come from?"

"Many ordinary people believe that this scroll is the actual written work of Moses son of Amram himself. In truth, no one really knows."

"Have any of you actually seen it?"

"I have, my lord."

"And you are...?"

"I am Yoiada, son of Paseach."

"Brother, Yoiada is a scribe from a priestly order." Hanani said.

"Tell me what you saw."

"When the Samaritans invaded Judah forty years ago, they assembled every scribe they could lay their hands on. One of them was my father. They forced the scribes to make copies of the scroll they called the Scroll of the teaching of Moses. To prevent mistakes, each scribe was given three months to prepare a scroll, using the closely guarded original as the source. I was only a young boy, but I remember the armed guards standing in my father's workroom as he transcribed from the Moses text day and night, resting only on the Sabbath. When he finished, the guards removed the original and my father's copy.

"The Samaritan Scroll of Moses that I saw was written on very old parchment. The text was in the language of Abraham and King David."

"Since that time," Yoiada said. "The scroll and the copies are brought before the people in Samaria on every festival and public occasion. Passages are publicly read and translated into Aramaic so that all will understand. They read it so frequently that it has become a beloved tradition among the Samaritans. Groups of Judeans in Judah are using this scroll to turn our people away from the Sacred House on Mt. Moriah and toward the abomination on Mt. Gerizim."

As he listened to the report of the delegation from Judah, Nehemiah was already making plans to thwart the Samaritans.

"I have heard enough! Men of Judah, I thank you once again for your bravery and your service."

"Teresh!" Nehemiah shouted. The Persian servant was very close. He was inside the room in an instant.

"Please provide my guests with lodging and food, as well as appropriate clothing for the Royal court. Let them refresh themselves and guide them around our city. Perhaps you could show them the areas where our fellow Judeans reside. Bring them back to the fortress at the end of the second watch. I intend to present them to the Emperor."

"As you command, my Lord."

"Hanani, stay here a moment. I wish to speak with you further about this matter."

"Of course, brother."

When they were alone, Nehemiah took a pair of ornately carved armchairs from against the wall and placed them at his worktable. He indicated for Hanani to seat himself. Nehemiah sat down slowly, squeezing his girth carefully between the graceful curved arms of the chair. He looked directly into Hanani's eyes. For an instant, he was stunned into silence. It was as if he were gazing into the face of their beloved mother.

"I know what I must do and I must be quick about it. I shall speak with the Emperor this afternoon. I only hope he listens to what I have to say. There is no time to waste. I shall return to Jerusalem with you immediately.

"As much as I am distressed by the conditions of Judah and Jerusalem, I am also very concerned about the so-called Scroll of Moses possessed by the Samaritans. Great rulers know that sacred traditions are powerful tools. They can motivate whole armies faster than the promise of spoil. I know I have to do something about it, but I need more information. Prepare yourself for our return to Judah. We shall leave as soon as I secure permission from the Emperor. In two weeks' time we should be in Pumbedita in Bavel."

"That is a bit out of the way if we are trying to return to Judah as soon as possible. Are we going to Pumbedita because a prosperous community of Judeans lives there? Are we going to seek donations from them?" Hanani asked.

"We don't need their donations. I want you to meet a very bright friend of mine."

"What is his name? Do I know him?"

"I don't think so. I first met him five years ago on a grain purchasing mission to Bavel. You had already settled in Jerusalem. His name is Ezra, son of Seriah, son of Azariah, son of Hilkiah, the scribe."

It took nearly two hours for couriers to shuttle notes back and forth to and from the palace for Nehemiah to receive the required permission to enter the palace and attend the afternoon audience with the Emperor.

Since the initial successes of Cyrus almost a century earlier, the Empire had accumulated vast riches across an enormous territory. It appeared to Nehemiah as if all of those riches were on display in the Palace of the Emperor in his reception hall. No matter how many times he presented himself to his ruler, he could not overcome his childish sense of wonder at it all. Precious stones, coins, metals, sculptures, carpets, wild animal skins, and fabrics of exotic origin were all in abundance. Each visit revealed something different. The sheer quantity of the spoils of empire available meant that the room was in a constant state of change.

Nehemiah was taking a small chance that he would not be admitted to speak with the Emperor. He had not been summoned and the Viceroy was displeased that he made his request for permission to attend at the last instant. He still might not get an opportunity to speak at the audience. If the Emperor was in a decent mood, he would be heard. If not, he would have to wait a few days and try again. Nehemiah knew he did not have the time to wait upon the whims of the Emperor. He had to be heard today.

"Grant Your servant success today, and dispose that man to be compassionate toward him," Nehemiah whispered.

"What did you say, you fat Judean pig?" The First Counselor, Haman the son of Hamadetha the Agagite, hated all Judeans, and especially Nehemiah.

"I was offering a prayer to my God."

"In this room, it would be wise to confine your praying to the gods of Persia. From what I hear, your god is not very successful in protecting your people or your land."

There was no question in Nehemiah's mind that his so-called loyal servant Teresh had already informed Haman of all the details of his morning meeting with the Judean delegation. Haman was in charge of making all sub-counselor appointments in the Fortress. Nehemiah just assumed that Teresh was Haman's spy. He often used that fact to his advantage, planting false information that could be turned against Haman. In this particular instance, great subterfuge was not necessary. The Emperor was already severely paranoid. He would be pre-disposed to believing that the Samaritans were plotting against him. They had been doing so from the day when Persia took control of the Province Beyond the Rivers. The real question was what could Haman do to prevent Nehemiah from getting his way with the Emperor?

As was the custom, whenever Nehemiah appeared before the Emperor, he carried a small pottery wine jug and silver wine goblet. The jug was sealed with a thick blob of bee's wax and along with the impression of Nehemiah's personal cylinder seal. This was to insure that if the Emperor died of poisoning, the blame would fall immediately and directly upon Nehemiah. With his face cast toward the ground, Nehemiah offered the jug and goblet to Haman. Haman inspected the seal and the goblet then handed them back to Nehemiah, who now had permission to open the jug and pour wine for the Emperor. As he poured, taking care no to spill a single drop, he noticed that the Emperor was not dressed in his formal court attire. Instead, he wore a simple white linen tunic over a long sleeved white linen robe. Both were trimmed in gold thread.

Artaxerxes was of ordinary height but exuded power and strength. His muscles were clearly defined on his exposed limbs. Battle scars were visible on his forearms. There were even a few cuts still in the process of healing. His head was cleanly shaven. Persian women would certainly describe him as handsome.

Nehemiah had a reputation at court for being a boisterous and gregarious fellow, trading stories and making hilarious comments about this or that member of the government. He was always careful never to embarrass the subject of his wit. In fact, many of his targets felt that, if Nehemiah had chosen them for comment, their status at court was enhanced. There was no sparkle to his eyes, no smile on his lips, as he offered the goblet to the Emperor.

"Nehemiah, look at me!" Artaxerxes said. "Look into my eyes."

"As you command, my Lord Emperor." He lifted his head slightly and looked directly into the eyes of the most powerful man in the world. His gaze was broken when the Emperor raised the goblet and drank from it.

"Excellent wine! Must be from the Lebanon, no? What troubles you, my friend? I miss your laughter and your stories. I could use some laughter today. Haman has just finished depressing me with the taxation reports from the eastern edges of the realm."

"With your permission, Majesty, may I speak freely?"

"Your majesty!" Haman said. "May I respectfully suggest that we do not have time for one of Nehemiah's stories. We have much business of state to conduct."

"Of course you may speak, my friend." The Emperor replied to Nehemiah while staring menacingly at Haman. The First Counselor shrank into the background behind the throne.

"May the Emperor live forever! Why should my face not look sad when Jerusalem, the city where my ancestors are buried, lies in ruins and its gates have been destroyed by fire?"

"Haman has informed me of the most recent events in the Province Beyond the Rivers. In what way could I lift the sadness from your shoulders?"

"If it pleases his majesty and if your servant has found favor in his sight, let him send me to Jerusalem in Judah so that I may rebuild it."

"Your Majesty, these Judeans are a drain on the royal treasury as it is! We have no resources to fund a reconstruction of Jerusalem. On the orders of your fathers, they pay less in taxes than all of your other subject peoples," Haman said.

"Emperor of all Persia," Nehemiah said. "A weakened and defenseless Judah is an invitation to Egypt and Samaria. Let me strengthen Judah as a bulwark against them both. This is what your fathers intended when they sent my people back to their homes in Judah."

"Your Majesty," Haman said. "Might I point out that the Judeans have had almost one hundred years to become a bulwark against Egypt and Samaria. They spent all of your assistance and that of your fathers on building a temple to their god and not on the supply and training of troops. What makes you believe that they will do now what they have failed to do before?"

"The First Counselor makes a valid point, Nehemiah. How can you succeed where others have failed?"

Nehemiah had prepared for this question by trying out answers with Hanani an hour earlier.

"Your Highness, there are two reasons we will not fail. First, our people in Judah know that your fathers were delivered victories over their enemies by the God of my ancestors. In return, your fathers released my people from their exile in Bavel and returned them to their homes in Judah. I know in my heart that the people of Judah will rally to me and to you, their emperor. They know that this is their last chance at redemption from their sins.

"The second reason is that we have a common enemy, the Samaritans. Since the day my ancestors were taken into exile, the Samaritans have not ceased to plot the removal of Persian rule in the Province Beyond the Rivers. They know that only Judah and its people stand in the way of their alliances with Ammon and Moab, Edom and Tyre, and of course, Egypt. The end of your battles with the Greeks has meant that the soldiers of my people have returned to Judah. Once they see the destruction the Samarians have done to Judah while they were off fighting against the Greeks, they will assist me without hesitation. They will be fighting for their own homes and lands."

"Haman, clear the hall and close the doors behind you. I wish to speak with Nehemiah, in private."

Two weeks later, Nehemiah's armed military caravan arrived in Pumbedita. The Emperor insisted that Nehemiah travel as if he were the Emperor himself on a formal state visit. Spring was almost in total bloom in the river town. Wondrous colors appeared from even the smallest patches of dirt on the poorest of lanes. At the entrance to the city, flower petals were strewn before Nehemiah, the Judeans, and the military escort. The city elders welcomed the important visitors from the capital. The great hall of the city was put at their disposal for the length of their visit.

Mixed feelings greeted Nehemiah's announcement that they would be staying only long enough to resupply and hire riverboats for the next leg of the journey to Jerusalem. On the one hand, their visit brought money and commerce. That was good for Pumbedita. On the other hand, Nehemiah was a trusted agent of the Emperor. What evil reports would he convey back to the capital? The elders prayed that the people would behave themselves until the entourage departed.

"Hanani, how much time do we have before we must continue our journey?"

"I believe I shall be able to hire the necessary riverboats by early this afternoon. We will start to fill them with supplies and may have them loaded and ready to go shortly after dawn tomorrow."

"We are not going to set out tomorrow. Have you lost all track of time? Shabbat begins at sunset tonight."

"I knew that; I only thought that our mission was of such importance that you would tolerate no delays."

"Let's call this a strategic delay. Give the order for our company to refresh themselves with food and rest. We shall depart by noon on the day after Shabbat. This could be the last opportunity for rest between here and Judah. We will need our strength and wits about us. Samaria stands between here and Judah. Even with our Persian escort, we will be a tempting target for the enemies of the Empire."

Before Hanani had turned to leave, a local messenger was admitted to the meeting hall by one of the Persian sentries. Bowing low, with his forehead touching the ground, the messenger extended his right hand upwards toward Nehemiah. A parchment scroll tied with a blue chord was extended towards the Emperor's Fourth Counselor.

"I have been instructed by my master to await your reply," the messenger said."

Nehemiah untied the chord and unrolled the scroll. He had received two previous letters from the hand of Ezra the scribe. There was no question as to the identity of its author. The writing was bold and without hesitation. At the same time, it was also beautiful. Nehemiah read quickly, re-rolled the scroll and instructed the messenger.

"Tell your master that my brother and I are honored to accept his gracious invitation to join him and his family for the Sabbath."

"His home is not far from here. I will return one hour before sunset and guide you to it."

"Then so be it. Thank you."

By the standards of Pumbedita, the home of Ezra the priest/scribe was rather large. The elevation of the house afforded a nearly unobstructed view of the riverfront from the main gate. It was a mud-brick and plaster walled compound more than eighty cubits square. The living spaces were bounded by the south and western walls of the compound and occupied a full quarter of the total space within the walls. The rest of the space was a carefully watered and tended garden. The bulk of the plantings in the garden were intended for the kitchen. Still, there was ample room for a raised bed of decorative flowers and plants. The overall effect was to create a sense of tranquility, despite the four young children, two boys and two girls, shouting and squealing as they played some sort of game that involved hiding between the rows of cucumber vines and getting very dirty.

"Children! It's time to come in and get cleaned up for Shabbat—now!" The order came from a solidly built woman dressed in a roughly woven blackish brown garment that covered her from her neck to her sandaled feet. A simple cotton white headscarf kept her hair well hidden.

"I win!" announced the oldest girl.

"We didn't finish, so no one is the winner!" objected the oldest boy.

"Oh my goodness, you are here so early, my Lord Counselor. We are preparing a proper welcome for you and your brother, but it is not ready yet."

"Do you wish us to leave and return in an hour?" Hanani asked.

"Now that would be stupid, my Lord. Oh dear! I did not mean that like it sounded. Please forgive me. I am so mixed up. I have forgotten my manners. I am Yocheved, wife of Ezra and mother of Ari, Ben-ami, Galia, and Dinah. You are most welcome in our home. Please come this way, there is a washstand where you may freshen up before we gather for Shabbat. Ezra is on his way home from the Assembly House and will be here any moment."

"Dear woman, please call me Nehemiah and my brother is called Hanani. May the coming Shabbat find you and your household at peace."

"After two dusty weeks on the road, this meal was like a taste of what the Persians call paradise, a garden of tasty delights. Everything was delicious!"

Nehemiah felt like he was enduring starvation on the journey. This was a welcome change. His ample stomach was full. When the last morsel was consumed and the last prayer of thanksgiving for the wonderful meal was recited, Ezra stood and spoke with a bit of urgency in his voice.

"My Lords, I have something I must show you. Please follow me."

Ezra led his guests up a flight of mud brick stairs to his workroom. The room was six cubits square with wide windows on three sides. A doorway on the fourth side opened onto a flat rooftop covered with straw mats. This night the distinguished guests from Shushan would sleep here in the cool outdoor air, under a brilliant blanket of stars.

"You honor our house with your visit. I am so pleased that we could enjoy Shabbat in your presence." Ezra was plumping up enormous pillows for the long couch that went nearly the entire length of the eastern wall of the room. Then he began filling wine cups with a thick sweet wine to make sure that his two guests were comfortable. The room was a sanctuary of quiet.

With cup in hand, Nehemiah sipped and slowly walked the perimeter of the workroom. Three large tables formed a three-sided square with the fourth side open. Nine high stools with basket-weave tops were scattered around the tables. A basket sat in the center of each table, filled with potsherds, presumably to hold down rolls of parchment. Clay inkpots were stored on wooden shelves in between the windows, along with the ingredients and tools for making ink, quills, and parchment.

"Please be seated," Ezra said.

Walking to the center of the room, Ezra knealt on the floor and lifted the bright red wool rug. He inserted the tip of a scribe's knife into a notch that was all but invisible in the centermost board. Carefully he pried it upward. Beneath the board was a long, finely stitched leather drawstring bag. Ezra loosened the drawstring and withdrew a scroll that was a full cubit in length and two handbreadths thick.

"Is all this secrecy and caution necessary?" Hanani asked.

"The spies from Judah are everywhere. We have worked too long and too hard on this scroll to have it taken from us now. This scroll will bring all of Judah, all of the Household of Israel together"

Ezra untied a blue chord around the scroll and unrolled it on the table. He then secured it with several of the potsherds. Nehemiah leaned in with a small clay oil lamp in his right hand, careful not to drip olive oil onto the parchment.

"It is so beautiful. Is it the work of one scribe?" Nehemiah asked.

"Yes."

"Are you that scribe?" Hanani asked.

"I am the scribe but I am not the sole author or editor."

"What is that supposed to mean?"

"It means, my Lord, that a group of us known to each other as the *Shomronim,* the Guardians, are responsible for the end result of this effort." Ezra smiled.

"Very amusing!"

"What is, my brother?" Hanani asked.

"The exiles prepare a scroll to empower Judah in its battle against the Samaritans, and they call themselves Shomronim, the very name of the Samaritans in Hebrew. Very clever."

"My Lord, do you know the source of the deep and bitter enmity that exists now between the Judeans and the Samaritans?" Ezra asked.

"Probably nothing more than the endless squabbles of empire, I would imagine. Children need to be reassured, from time to time, that their father, in this case, Artaxerxes, prefers them over all others."

Nehemiah took another sip of wine.

"You can be so Persian sometimes, my brother," Hanani chided.

"Now what does that mean?"

"It means that when you have the power of the empire in your hands and at your disposal, you tend to see things only from the heights of majesty. You need to take a moment and come down to ground level where the simple people live. It will give you and your Emperor some much needed perspective."

"Excuse me, my Lords, but I have much to discuss with you and given the brevity of your sojourn among us, so little time. Perhaps I can also give you that ground level perspective you seek.

"This scroll spread out before you is the reason for the hatred."

"You must be joking!" Nehemiah said.

Ezra raised an eyebrow. "I am being deadly serious."

"This scroll is the centerpiece of a battle of wits between Judah and Samariah for the soul of our people. That battle began with a different and at the same time common enemy, nearly a century ago.

"On the very day that the walls of the Sacred House in Jerusalem were breached by the Bavliim, twenty-four sacred scrolls were rescued from the flames of Jerusalem. Imagine if you will, a precious library containing the sacred history and literature of our people about to go up in flames. Two young boys, apprentice scribes, were charged by their master with the task of rescuing the library. The apprentices are twin brothers: Eliezer and Zadok, sons of Achituv of Gezer.

"At a time of disaster, when the future of the Household of Israel was unknown, the boys divided the scrolls into two parcels, with twelve scrolls in each. Eliezer took twelve of the scrolls and went into exile among the priests who had established themselves in Samaria. Zadok joined the long march of exiles to Bavel."

"Both of the brothers establish themselves as successful scribes in their own right, raise families, and teach the scribal arts to hundreds of students. Those students were privileged to be the only non-priests to have any contact with the scrolls, the last surviving remnants of the Sacred House of Solomon. As time passes in the exile communities of Samaria and Bavel, the scrolls become precious treasures reserved exclusively for study by members of the priesthood. They never see the light of day. Non-priests know they exist and that is all they know. Some of the priests actually read and teach lessons from them, but precisely because they are so sacred and untouchable, there is no true connection between the people and the scrolls."

"Hanani, you reported that the Samaritans were in possession of a sacred scroll they called the Scroll of the Teaching of Moses. You yourself said that they parade it about and teach from it. You said that scroll declares

Mount Gerizim in Samaria as the God protected site for the Sacred House, not Jerusalem," Nehemiah said. "If the sacred scrolls were so hidden and forgotten, where did the Samaritans come by this scroll?"

"I believe I can answer that vexing question, my Lord," Ezra said."

"The scroll the Samaritans now possess is actually the result of a very noble idea that went horribly wrong. You might say that it is all the fault of my great-great-grandfather, Eliezer son of Achituv."

"Explain yourself."

"As the number of exile years in Samaria and Bavel passed forty, my great-great-grandfather Eliezer became concerned about the future of Judah and the Judeans. He personally saw the community of Judeans in Samaria drifting away or melting into the clans of the Samaritans. He imagined that the same was happening to the descendants of his brother in Bavel. He felt in his heart that somehow the scrolls would be the key to redemption from exile. But he also believed that the twelve scrolls needed a single identity, needed to be a single narrative with a wondrous beginning, a dramatic middle, and a hopeful ending. But what would make the document compelling enough to serve as the rallying banner to be raised among the nations and redeem an exiled people?

"His inspiration came from the first sentence of one of the original twelve sacred scrolls. 'These are the words that Moses addressed to all Israel on the other side of the Jordan.' The 'Words' scroll, as it was then known by the few privileged souls who had studied it, contained Moses' admonition to the tribes of Israel as they were about to cross the Jordan and as he was about to die. And so Eliezer presented the entire combined scroll as the *torat Moshe,* the teaching of Moses."

"What is the connection between this scroll and Eliezer's scroll?" Nehemiah pointed to the parchment on the table before them.

"Before you answer, tell me this: how could Eliezer believe that Judean priests would accept his single large scroll as entirely the words of Moses?" Hanani asked.

"They didn't. In fact, the Judean priests living in Samaria never knew that the collective scroll Eliezer named "*Sefer Torat Moshe*" ever existed. Eliezer thought he had kept it well hidden. He was a fervent believer in the idea that Judah and Jerusalem would ultimately be redeemed by the God of Abraham. He instructed his son, Gilad to destroy the twelve sacred scrolls and then to publicly reveal the *Sefer Torat Moshe* when it was certain that the redemption would take place. The twelve sacred scrolls were destroyed by Gilad, and his son, Yeshai. Gilad died suddenly and it appeared that Yeshai was destined by God to be the one to reveal the *Sefer Torat Moshe*, when he made his own triumphant return to Judah."

"I never heard of this Yeshai before. Nor have I heard of any triumphant display of any *Sefer Torat Moshe* in Jerusalem. What happened to him?" Hanani asked.

"The hidden scroll, it turns out, was not so hidden. The Samaritans must have kept Yeshai under careful watch. They stole Eliezer's *Sefer Torat Moshe*, and then copied it and wrote their own Mount Gerizim version. It is the only possible explanation for how the Samaritans were able to parade their own scroll before the downcast faces of the returned Judean priests and declare their reconstruction work in Jerusalem to be an outrage against God. The work on the Sacred House was delayed for six months because the support of the people of Judah for a Sacred House in Jerusalem was exceedingly weak.

"The Judean Priests in Judah were so angry and shamed by the Samaritan scroll they made plans to capture and punish anyone even remotely connected with it. Since Yeshai was the Chief Priest in Samaria at that time, they were determined to seize Yeshai and burn him for blasphemy. Judean spies in Samaria told the Jerusalem priests that Yeshai was carrying the *Sefer Torat Moshe* with him as he marched south with the other returning exiles from Samaria. The Judean priests in Jerusalem thought he was carrying the very scroll the Samaritans had. Only the intervention of the Persian Governor, Memukan, prevented Yeshai from being executed."

"Was he carrying Eliezer's scroll?" Nehemiah asked.

"Not when he was captured by the Judeans. Yeshai had no scroll on his person. According to the story recounted by Yeshai's children, before he finished his journey to Jerusalem, he placed Eliezer's scroll in the hands of the priests of the village of Anatoth in Judah. They were kinsmen of the prophet Jeremiah. They promised to keep the scroll safe."

"I'm confused." Hanani said.

"I am truly sorry for this complicated tale, but there is one additional thing you need to know. The scroll left in Anatoth was not the original. The original, as far as I know, is still hidden in a burial cave in Samaria."

"Which one?" Nehemiah said hopefully.

"I believe that Eliezer placed that information in some sort of code," Ezra said.

"As I said, Yeshai was taken captive, but was rescued by the Persians and brought to Pumbedita. During that harrowing escape, Yeshai convinced the Persians to help him return to Anatoth for the copy of the Eliezer scroll. That is the scroll that ended up in Pumbedita."

"So, I say again, what is the connection between this scroll and the copy of Eliezer's scroll?" Nehemiah asked.

"This scroll lying before you is based largely upon that copy of Eliezer's scroll. But there have been additions."

"What additions?" Hanani asked.

"For this part of the story, our vision must turn to Zadok, brother of Eliezer, who lived and died an exile of Judah in Pumbedita."

Ezra proceeded to recount the story of Zadok and the priest Ezekiel and Ezekiel's *Mishkan* scroll and Zadok's death on orders from Ezekiel.

"When the *Mishkan* in Bavel was destroyed in the great flood, the priestly sons of Ezekiel ben Buzzi claimed that the only sacred scroll to survive was the *Mishkan* scroll. Then they put forth the idea that the copies of the sacred scrolls were riddled with errors. They rounded up every copy they could find and burned them. Eventually, only the *Mishkan* scroll and copies of that scroll survived in Bavel. When the great Cyrus permitted the Judeans to return to Judah and Jerusalem, it was only the *Mishkan* scroll that was brought directly to Judah. The priests tried to make good use of it. The text served to bolster the first efforts to rebuild the sacred house. The going was slow. It took twenty years for the returning priests to begin the work. Some said at the time, that it was due to the destructive power of the Samaritan scroll of Moses.

"In part, the delay was caused by a powerful military challenge to the authority of the returning exiled priests."

"The Egyptians were envious of the returning Judeans," Hanani said.

"Envy is the right word to describe the popular rage at the shower of special privileges washing over Judah. But it was the Samaritans and not the Egyptians who were angry enough to take steps to dislodge Judah from royal favor. The *Mishkan* scroll by itself could not bring the people of Judah together in common cause. It was written by and for priests. The people needed more to earn their respect and loyalty.

"The scroll you see before you is Eliezer's scroll combined with the Mishkan scroll. We agonized over whether to include it in the scroll of Moses or not. Caution prevailed. We must still have the support of the priests. They are more likely to proclaim the authority of this version of the scroll of Moses if the *Mishkan* scroll is included.

"My people, my fellow scribes, my *shomronim*, my Guardians believe that this scroll is the banner that will bring Judah together. I present it to you and the people of Judah. Guard it well. May it keep you safe on your long journey." Ezra bowed his head and held the rolled scroll across his outstretched hands toward Nehemiah.

"We dare not take it with us," Nehemiah said. "Too many people are interested in the failure of our mission to Jerusalem. There will come a time when the presentation of this scroll to the people will make all the difference, but not now. First we shall make Judah and Jerusalem secure. Then we shall send for you. You shall return to Judah with this scroll. We shall make a public presentation of it, when the time is right."

"I shall do as you ask, My Lord. May I make one special request?"

"Of course!" Nehemiah said.

Ezra removed a small scroll from his tunic and held it out to Nehemiah.

"This is the actual letter written by Eliezer son of Achituv, explaining his purpose in making the *Sefer Torat Moshe* and destroying the twelve sacred scrolls. It has been in my family's possession for several generations. I humbly request that you return this letter to the place where the original *Sefer Torat Moshe* is hidden."

"Why would you want me to do that?" Nehemiah was puzzled.

"So that the scroll and its scribe are united once again. I know it will be difficult, but if accomplished it would mean that the God of Abraham has returned His people to their land, all of it, even Samaria."

"But I do not know where it is hidden. You said something about a secret code?"

"The outer parchment that surrounds Ezekiel's letter is a psalm of the exiles of Judah. I believe it contains a code that if solved, will reveal the location of Eliezer's scroll."

"Have you been able to reveal the hidden contents of the psalm?" Hanni asked.

"We have tried many times and failed. Ezekiel hid his secret well. We believe that God will guide your heart and mind and reveal it to you when the time is right."

"Aren't you worried that I may expose the *Sefer Torat Moshe* as having been written by persons other than Moses?"

"I do not believe that you would destroy the faith of the people in the one thing that can bring Judah together and make Jerusalem strong once again."

Solemnly, Nehemiah nodded his head in agreement and took the letter scroll and placed it in the leather pouch tied around his waist.

The last of the oil lamps sparked and guttered. In near total darkness and complete silence, the three men made their way to the roof top door and walked out onto the sleeping space. All three looked up at the stars in the sky at nearly the same time. It was then that Nehemiah recalled an oft-told tale about the grandfather of Israel. As he remembered the exact words of God's promise to Abraham, a smile crossed his lips.

"I will make your offspring as numerous as the stars in the sky."

When Ezra was assured that his guests were comfortable, he made his way to his own bedchamber. His wife had a question for him.

"Did you give to Nehemiah Eliezer's letter and the psalm?" Yocheved asked.

"I did."

"What if they are stolen or destroyed?"

"I have made an exact copy of the letter and the psalm."

"How will you keep them safe?"

"They will be hidden among the other discarded sacred scrolls in the store room of the house of assembly. Only the Gaurdians will know they are there."

"Do you think that is wise?"

"I couldn't think of anywhere else to hide them."

Chapter Forty-One

DATE: March 20-21, 2009

TIME: 19:30 P.M.—2:30 A.M. Local Time

PLACE: Israel Museum Warehouse, Jerusalem

By 19:30 hours, the operational team consisting of sixteen people, including Stone, Keller, and Malik and Michal, were inside the warehouse. Rafi divided the sixteen into three teams. The first two teams, four members each, were made up of the police and *Shin Bet* personnel respectively. The six police counter-terrorist squad officers took up positions closest to the two entry points in the warehouse. The six *Shin Bet* agents had hidden themselves among the steel roof trusses in the center of the warehouse. Lavi would lead the police team at the doors. Rafi and Omar joined the *Shin Bet* team in the rafters. Malik, Abby, Aaron, and Michal, were ordered to stay out of the way and wait until the intruders were neutralized. They placed themselves behind packing crates along the Southern wall. Everyone inside did a final equipment check before settling in to wait for The Builders, including a radio check of their ear-pieces and helmet mounted microphones, making sure they were all on the same encoded frequency.

"*Chevre*, our honored guests have arrived." The information sounding in their earpieces was being provided by one of Lavi's counter-terrorism

343

specialists. He was positioned on the museum entrance roof, directly opposite the taxi stand. He spoke Hebrew but Abby was providing a running translation for Aaron.

"They are leaving their vehicle, a tan Chevy Suburban, at the taxi stand by the museum main entrance, there are four people in all. Each one looks fit and experienced. Running close to the ground. No visible weapons, but two are carrying black canvas bags. They are wearing night vision goggles. We have already disabled the Chevy. They will be at your location in two minutes."

Rafi keyed his mike twice resulting in two audible clicks, the agreed upon acknowledgement signal. Scratching sounds at the Western door of the warehouse alerted the inside take-down teams that the "guests" were working the locks to gain entrance. But nothing happened. The would-be intruders did not open the door. One minute passed, then two then three.

"What are they waiting for?" Abby asked.

"They are waiting for an explosion at the Shrine of the Book. The diversion, remember?" Malik said.

"Oh, right."

Just then the steel walls of the warehouse shook as in a sustained earthquake. A low rumble-like distant thunder accompanied the vibrations in the building. Car alarms both nearby and at a distance shrieked and wailed. Sirens from fire trucks and ambulances took up the chorus a few moments later. At what was later judged to be the peak of noise from the explosion, the door opened and four figures in black combat gear entered the warehouse. They scanned the enormous dark-as-night space from side to side with their night vision gear. The *Shin Bet*/Police take-down teams held their cover positions and remained invisible. Suddenly, the bright warehouse lights went on all at once, blinding the four intruders. Although Rafi had issued the same kind of optical gear to his team members, he instructed them not to put them on. He counted on the intruders wearing theirs and decided to use it to the team's advantage.

As the intruders struggled to remove their goggles and adjust to the light, the team members hidden in the rafters repelled down silently on nylon ropes. They landed directly on top of the intruders. Omar and Rafi, slid down the ropes and stood with weapons at the ready covering the intruders while restraints were being applied. In less than two minutes the intruders were being marched out of the warehouse and into a marked police prisoner conveyance van that had pulled up to the warehouse entrance.

"Shouldn't these guys be questioned, now?"

"It will wait, Rabbi. They are thugs for hire, no doubt. We need to keep moving." Omar said.

"Remind me why we have to do this like criminals," Aaron said.

"The Ministry of Antiquities demanded complete plausible deniability. If something goes wrong, this is not a government operation. It also has the advantage of keeping the Ministry of Religion and the Chief Rabbinate out of our way, should we actually find what we are looking for."

"I don't think using marked police vans and uniformed officers provides much deniability."

"When this gets to the press, and it will because we will make sure it does, the four we just arrested and anyone else rounded up for the Shrine of the Book explosion will be blamed for the break-in and the theft of any artifacts that are missing," Lavi said.

"Does anybody know how much damage the Builders did to the Shrine of the Book?" Abby asked.

"None." Rafi responded. He continued to explain.

"Our plan included rounding up the bombers before they were able to plant the devices. The delay was our fault. The demolition team had to move the devices far enough away from the Shrine so as to cause little or no damage. We had to detonate them in order to catch The Builders in the act. As a precaution, earlier this evening we instructed the curators to pull all the exhibits currently on display and put them in the security vault."

"*M'tsuyan*, well done," Abby said.

Abby, Aaron, Malik, Rafi, Omar, Lavi, and Michal, removed their helmets and protective gear. Lavi collected the side arms from Abby and Aaron.

"You won't need these now and I won't need to answer uncomfortable questions later, should you wind up on *Facebook* loaded for lion.

"Michal, it's your time to shine." Malik said.

The group followed Michal to the back of the warehouse.

The lights revealed a stand-alone structure inside the warehouse. Close to the corner of the structure was a double door nearly four meters wide. To the right of the door was a numeric keypad and small screen glowing green.

Michal approached the door, entered her personal code and placed her palm on the screen. A loud click signaled that the lock had opened. Pulling the door open, everyone craned for a look inside.

"What a *chazer-stahl*!" Rafi exclaimed.

"Pigsty," Abby translated for Aaron.

"I <u>know</u> what a *chazer* is. Thank you very much."

The comment was on target. The sealed room was a jumble of archeological stuff, piled haphazardly on steel shelves. Each item had a tag attached, but that was about the only sign of organization visible.

"Is there a key to locating stuff?" Aaron asked Michal.

"The staff is working on it." She said.

"Over here, everyone," Malik yelled.

"Look, up on top."

A row of clay containers, standing side by side like cereal boxes in a supermarket, occupied the top two shelves and covered a distance almost ten meters long. Each box was approximately fifty centimeters long and 25 centimeters wide.

"There must be two hundred of them," Abby said. "This is going to take some time."

"Rabbi, you and Professor Malik need to use this." Omar was referring to a rolling steel stairway he was moving close to the shelf unit that contained the ossuaries. The top of the stairway formed a square platform big enough for two people to stand on.

"Where did you get this contraption, the local Home Depot?" Aaron stationed himself at the base of the stairway, holding it steady, as first Malik and then Abby ascended. When they reached the upper platform they put on grey cotton gloves to prevent their body oils from damaging the boxes as they handled them. Omar passed up a light stand with two bright yellow-framed industrial flood lamps. They could be aligned to almost any angle. Malik turned the lamps on and adjusted each one for maximum coverage.

"Rabbi, there is no rush. We have until the museum office opens at 8:00 a.m. We need to get this right. Let's start by you pulling the first box out of line and then rotating it around so I can check for inscriptions. We will alternate holding the boxes so we maintain our strength."

Abby nodded. "Sounds like a plan, Professor."

The search was tedious and at the same time, fascinating. Most of the ossuaries were simple clay boxes. A few had very crude drawings of plants and animals fired directly into the clay. And then there were the boxes that could only be described as works of art. Centuries buried under rubble had faded most of the decoration, but once in a while a section or side revealed vibrant colors and talented artists. While some of the boxes were completely clean of any markings whatsoever, most had names inscribed in simple Paleo-Hebrew letters, each a few centimeters in height. Most of the lettering was in faded black ink. A few had the letters carved into them with some kind of sharp instrument.

At two hours and thirty-eight minutes into the search, Malik smiled and held out a lavishly decorated ossuary for Abby's inspection. *Shoshana bat Talmon, eshet Eliezer ben Achituv hacohein v'hasofer*- Shoshana, daughter of Talmon, wife of Eliezer, son of Achituv the priest and scribe.

The clean-up of the warehouse took nearly an hour. All who participated in the take-down and the discovery of Shoshana's box pitched in, wiping the place down and making sure that they left no trace of their presence. Abby placed a call to the Dean of Hebrew Union College's Jerusalem campus. After apologizing for waking him up in the middle of the night, she passed her phone to Rafi.

Rafi walked to a distant corner of the warehouse and continued the conversation with the Dean. After a long ten minutes, he returned to the group in the center of the warehouse. "The Dean has agreed to allow us to use the workroom at the college."

"And that's what that whole conversation was about?" Abby asked.

"He was cautious, at first. Then I hinted that the Prime Minister would look favorably upon the College's petition for additional land for expansion, as gratitude for the College's help. After he got over his shock that I was so well informed about the needs of the College, he told us to meet him in twenty minutes at the back entrance near Beit Shmuel."

The Dean escorted the team to the workroom and then departed. Michal, her task fulfilled, returned to her home in Tel Aviv with the thanks of the team and a passionate kiss and promise from Lavi to call her. The six who remained, Omar, Rafi, Lavi, Malik, Abby and Aaron were fidgeting with nervous anticipation. They chose not to open the box in the warehouse.

It would have left more trace evidence and more questions and more opportunities for government interference.

The flood lamps over the worktable put the box in a very dramatic circle of intense white light. In silence the team members slowly walked around the table and simply stared at it. The only sound in the room came from the climate control and air filtration system.

"Excuse me for asking, but are we going to open this up now, or what?"

"Sergeant, we must take our time and try to figure out how to open this box with the least amount of damage. It has been intact for two thousand five hundred years. I do not want to be the one who shatters it in one misapplied chisel blow."

"Professor, it is not necessary to hit it with a chisel. I may be a Jewboy from South Carolina, but I am very handy with a Dremel tool."

"A what?" Malik asked. Instead of explaining, Aaron turned to the shelf behind him and lifted a fist-sized device with what looked like a small drill bit with a disk on top. The disk was a sanding tool, very sharp at its edge.

"My advice is you take this tool and cut the bottom of the box all around. Then you simply lift the box, revealing its contents. Since the bottom is free of decoration you will not lose anything of historical value."

Malik's considerable eyebrows raised as he evaluated Aaron's advice.

"Not a bad idea. Does anyone have any objections?"

"We just have to make sure that nothing breaks when the box is lifted." Abby turned to Aaron, "You make the cut. Professor, you will lift the box when the cut is complete. The rest of us will take a side and stand at the ready to prevent anything from falling out and smashing to pieces."

Aaron located a pair of safety goggles on the shelf above the power tools and put them on. The Dremel tool was noisy and produced an enormous amount of dust. Abby anticipated the dust and provided the team members with surgical masks. Beneath the intense lighting the dust appeared like a terra cotta fog. Abby went to the doorway and flipped a fan switch. The high-powered exhaust fan removed the visible suspended dust in less than twenty seconds.

Malik, wearing cotton gloves, grasped the box from the two narrow ends and started to lift. As he lifted, the contents began to fall out onto the table. An assortment of sepia colored bones slowly cascaded from all sides.

Omar, Rafi, Abby and Aaron, made sure that nothing rolled off the table. Malik continued to lift the box from its base.

Disappointment hung in the air.

"With all due respect to Shashana bat Talmon, is that all there is?" Omar asked.

"Something is not right." Malik announced.

Abby crossed her arms. "No kidding."

"That is not what I meant. The box is heavier on one side than the other." Malik proceeded to invert the box and set it down on a clear part of the table, but still under the lights. The reason for the uneven weight distribution in the box became immediately apparent. There was a sealed rectangular clay box within the ossuary that ran from one end to the other and was half as wide as the width of the box.

"Sergeant, you are pretty handy with that Dremel thing. Do you think you can make precise cuts along the top so we can see what is in the box? I don't want to put any unnecessary pressure on you but this cut needs to be very carefully done. First because we do not want to ruin the ossuary itself, and second, because we do not want to damage the contents of this compartment."

"I can handle it," Aaron said. He lowered the safety goggles resting on his forehead, studied the compartment from a number of different angles and started the cut from the unattached corner and continued down the long side. He moved the tool very slowly. In less than ten minutes the top was free.

Malik reached in and carefully picked up the clay piece with both hands and lifted it out of the box. An object wrapped in leather filled the compartment. Everyone drew a breath. Malik gently lifted the leather package out and lowered it slowly to the table. There was no thong or rope binder. The leather was exceedingly dry and brittle.

"Stand back," Abby said. With a small spray bottle she sprayed a mist over the entire length of the leather object.

"What are you doing? You will ruin it," Omar said.

"Relax! This is a weak mixture of water and mineral oil. It will moisten the leather just enough to allow us to open it up. I am not spraying anything beneath the outer layer."

Gently, Abby started to loosen the leather wrapping. There was some flaking of the dry leather but most of it was intact. The leather surrounded the object it was protecting three times. With the leather now flat on the worktable, an ancient scroll was revealed.

"Professor, it's your turn." Abby said with a smile.

"I can't believe that I am so nervous. My hands are shaking!"

"You can do this, Professor," Omar said.

"Here goes." Malik inspected the parchment with a large self-illuminated magnifying glass. With a featherweight amount of pressure he touched the scroll with his gloved hand.

"It does not appear to be brittle. We can thank the atmospheric controls at the museum for its state of preservation. In fact, it is probable that the condition of the parchment improved since the time when the ossuary was brought to Jerusalem for storage. The moisture content of the parchment would have been gradually increased. That would have been the best way."

"Could you please get on with it and save the 'Ask Mr. Science' lecture for later?" Aaron asked.

"Sergeant, I am surprised at your impatience. This scroll has been waiting for this moment for 2,500 years. We should take our time and use great care."

"Please accept my sincerest apologies."

Malik took a flat narrow spatula-like instrument and slid it under the edge of the parchment roll. He was making sure that there was nothing causing the outer edge to stick to the layer beneath.

"So far, so good," Malik said.

After thirty minutes of very careful prying, the first columns of the text were revealed. The writing was very small, Paleo-Hebrew. There were no spaces between the words.

"B'reshit bara elohim et hashamayim v'et haaretz." Malik was holding a wooden stick. It was a stylus actually. He moved it along as he attempted to read the words. His eyes were moist with tears of sheer joy.

"In beginning, God created the heavens and the earth…" Abby could not help herself. Her translation came as an almost involuntary reflex to hearing the Hebrew as Malik continued to read.

Chapter Forty-Two

DATE: March 21, 22, 2009

TIME: 4:00 A.M.—12:30 A.M. Local Time

PLACE: Hebrew Union College School of Biblical Archeology 13
                 King David Street, Jerusalem

D awn came and went. The unrolling and reading continued. Students
sought to enter the workroom for their morning classes and were
blocked by two police officers in combat fatigues. Meals were brought in.
Trash was removed. Abby started to alternate with Malik in the reading of
the text itself. Along the way they noted variations in the text from that of the
Masoretic Hebrew text, established as the standard since the ninth century.
At 2:30 in the afternoon they realized that the Book of Exodus was missing
any and all references to a *Mishkan*-Tabernacle.

"This is an astonishing development. Just as some scholars had imagined
over the years, this is clear evidence that the Biblical Israelites had no tradition
of a tabernacle in the wilderness. No wonder The Builders wanted this scroll
destroyed. Temples were not a part of ancient Israelite religious tradition."
Malik shook his head.

With pauses only for personal necessity and cold cardboard pizza, the
reading and unrolling finally concluded at 9:30 p.m. As the last curled

section of parchment was unrolled, there would be yet one more surprise. Perhaps this would be the greatest find of them all.

Several small sheets of thin parchment were tightly rolled and placed in the center of the main scroll. Even an amateur could see that the lettering on the sheets was by the same hand as the entire main scroll. Both Malik and Abby had trouble separating the letters into words and sentences. For the main scroll there was a Biblical context to guide them. For these additional sheets there was no frame of reference. After thirty-five minutes the task became more straightforward. The smaller parchment sheets formed a letter from Eliezer ben Achituv. It told his story and that of his twin brother. Malik read the text of the letter out loud. He was especially moved by Eliezer's account of his reasons for destroying the sacred scrolls and composing a single *sefer torat moshe*. When Malik finished deciphering the letter, no one uttered a comment or even a sound. The only exceptions to absolute silence were the soft rhythmic clicks of a clock on the wall.

"Extraordinary!" Abby finally broke the tension.

"We are entering our second day without sleep. Now what do we do, *chevre?*" Rafi was seated on a bench behind the table. He head was resting against the wall. His eyes were closed.

"Well, I will tell you one thing we are not going to do," Malik said, finding strength from some reservoir reserved only for eighty-year-old *Shin Bet* agents.

"What's that?" Abby asked.

"We are not going to ship this off to some lazy-ass philologists who will parse this discovery into a million bits of disconnected information and publish two lines a year in a journal so obscure not even Google can find it."

"Gee, professor, tell us how you really feel." Aaron smiled.

"I am as serious as I have ever been in this matter. We are going to publish our find, tonight!"

"Oh please, you cannot mean that. We have not slept for two days. We cannot even see straight. I don't even know what journal to submit the publication to," Abby said.

"We are not using a journal. We are not going to print our findings. That is precisely the point. We are going to use CNN, SKYNEWS, *Al Jazeera*—OK, maybe not *Al Jazeera*."

"*Sgan Aluf* Lavi, call your public information officer and tell him or her we have an amazing discovery to announce and we are doing it now, tonight!"

"Should I describe the nature of the discovery?"

"Tell the officer anything that will get all the networks here in two hours."

"Why two hours? It will be midnight." Abby asked.

"Because each of us is going to grab a shower back at Beit Shmuel, but only one of us will do so at a time. We are not leaving this discovery out of our sight, even for an instant. By having the cameras and reporters here, we will reduce the urgency for some fanatic or other to steal or destroy the artifact."

It seemed to everyone in the workroom that Malik's plan was beginning to make sense.

The networks were more cooperative than Abby and Aaron would have expected. When everyone realized that the time difference would make the Evening News in the States, or at the very least a prime time news flash, they found their own second wind. The showers worked their temporary magic and each team member returned to the workroom refreshed. At least that is what they told themselves to keep upright on their feet.

The networks started showing up after 11:00 p.m. King David Street was bumper to bumper with satellite transmission trucks from Mammillah street to just past the King David Hotel. Under klieg lights, a gaggle of reporters were doing stand-up introductions in front of the main gate to the Hebrew Union College. They were describing the information they had been given so far and then filled time with fact-less speculation.

Abby and Aaron stood at the top floor window and gazed out at the chaotic scene.

"Now what happens to us?"

"Well, ma'am, do I go back to saluting you and you save my ass from a court marshall?"

"That is not what I meant, and you know it!"

"How's about I file a petition with my CO for permission to marry a superior officer?"

Abby caught her breath. Aaron continued to ramble on.

"I am truly having a problem with one aspect of our relationship."

"OK, here it comes."

"I do not know which is going to give our married life more problems: the fact that you outrank me or the fact that you are and always will be my rabbi."

Aaron pulled Abby away from the window and surrounded her with a loving and firm embrace. They kissed for an eternity, or at least until Rafi and Omar cleared their collective *Shin Bet* throats.

"Please excuse us, but the Dean has just opened the gates and the press is descending upon us." Rafi said.

It took several elevator trips for the assembled members of the press to reach the workroom. There wasn't a spare centimeter of space left. The Dean insisted that, as the CEO of the Jerusalem campus, it was his duty to welcome the press and introduce Professor Malik. The Ezra Scroll Team, as they started to style themselves, agreed that Professor Malik should introduce the team members, describe their individual contribution to the discovery, and make an opening statement detailing what was found.

At the insistence of Lavi, Rafi, and Omar, Malik left out the juicy parts about trucks ramming cars on the Jerusalem highway, bombs destroying tea shops, and the involvment of the Samaritan community in general.

Malik helped the press to connect the Ezra Scroll discovery to the break-in at the Shrine of the Book and the Israel Museum warehouse. That morning the press had already been given information that characterized The Builders as a Christian Fundamentalist terror organization bent on the destruction of the Dead Sea Scrolls and anything else that challenged their devout understanding of Scripture. The media were even given the video to prove it.

"How do you know that this scroll is not just some well orchestrated hoax? We have had these sensational announcements before, you know." A very attractive female reporter from SKYNEWS, with more than eight years experience covering Israel, posed the first question with plenty of attitude.

"Christine, the scroll will have to be subjected to the usual testing and analysis to confirm the date of the materials used, but the discovery of the scroll came as a result of an ancient coded message discovered two weeks ago, hundreds of miles away."

"Where, Professor?"

"Where what?" Malik asked.

"Where was the coded message discovered?"

"I am not at liberty to tell you that, right now. To do so would jeopardize even more unprecedented discoveries. I am hopeful that there will soon come a time when we can reveal the reasons for our lack of candor on this matter.

"Next question. You." Malik was pointing at the chief of NBC's Middle East Bureau.

"You were vague about the role of the rabbi and Mr. Berg in this matter. Are you hiding something?"

The team agreed that revealing the true identity of Abby and Aaron would allow a connection to be made quickly to Aaron's posting in Fallujah. The two of them were wearing simple yet effective disguises—a blonde streaked wig for Stone, a shaggy layered wig and bushy mustache for Aaron.

"They were instrumental in bringing the coded message to my attention."

"And that's it?"

"That's it. You in the second row, what is your question?" Malik indicated a reporter for the Israel daily newspaper, Haaretz. He was also a stringer for the New York Times.

"In your professional scholarly opinion, what is the significance of this discovery?"

"Since the days of Spinoza, scholars have theorized about the probability of multiple authors of the Torah. We call this the Documentary Hypothesis. A central element of that hypothesis is the assumption that some individual or group was responsible for arranging and editing a number of distinct texts into the document we refer to as the Torah. Until today we did not know the actual Who or the How. Now we know."

"Aren't you concerned that this will do great damage to people's faith in the divine nature of the scriptures?"

"Look, since the nineteenth century millions of followers of non-orthodox religious traditions have taught and still teach that the Hebrew Scriptures represent a human document describing how ordinary humans related to God in a particular place and at a particular time in history. Our discovery helps us move from theory to fact. One commentator described

355

the Hebrew Scriptures as a library. I look at the matter in this way. Today we have been able to reveal the identity of the librarian and his descendants. The literature is still magnificent, compelling, passionate, and insightful. That will never change."

The midnight news conference concluded at 1:30 on the morning of March 22. There were no unexpected questions. The reporters probed for the true identities of Abby and Aaron, but got nowhere. Rafi was skeptical as to how long it would be before their real names were revealed. Omar drove them to a *Shin Bet* safe house in a convoy of ten identical black Chevy Suburbans. Like a moving deck of cards, the SUV's were shuffled multiple times. Anyone attempting to follow them to their ultimate destination would fail. All the maneuvers made the trip to Tel Aviv longer by an hour and a half.

The safe house was a run down hotel two blocks from the Promenade. Only the lobby and exterior of the hotel were run down. Agents from the security service played every role in the hotel, from front desk operations to service staff in the coffee shop. No one was going to get past them for any reason. Above the ground floor, everything was first rate, modern and clean. Keller and Stone were given the keys to the penthouse suite, courtesy of Rafi.

There were almost twenty days left on their thirty-day pass before they had to return to their respective military postings. They decided to stay under the covers except for meals. On the best weather days they went down to the beach for a swim, thirty minutes before sunset. As the sky glowed with an amazing array of pastel reds and oranges, they sat holding hands and gazed to the west.

The international news cycle treated the Ezra Scroll story with the same respect reserved for all monumental and earth shattering events. In three days it faded completely from view.

Late in the morning of their last day in Israel, an agency car had been sent to take them back to Haifa. Aaron and Abby stood in a close embrace in their suite, trying to make the moment last forever. The night before, the entire team reassembled for a going-away dinner party. Malik was treating Abby and Aaron as his own children, alternating hugs with unsolicited marital advice. Both had mild hangovers, so the embrace had the effect of keeping them steady, at least for the moment.

"It's time," Aaron said without conviction

"Yeah, it's time." Abby pulled him to her for one last kiss.

Abby's cell phone rang with the University of Michigan fight song blaring away.

"Did you have to put that on the max?"

"There is no ID on this call."

"It might be Omar or Rafi. It is unlikely that their calls would be identified. Go ahead and answer it.

"Good morning Abby. How are you and Sergeant Keller doing? I have been following with great interest and delight your adventures in Jerusalem."

Abby placed her hand over the phone and feverishly pantomimed to Keller that the caller was none other than Professor Carlson. Aaron motioned for her to continue the conversation while he went to the room phone and alerted the agents of the *Shin Bet* in the hotel.

"Professor Carlson? Where are you?"

"It does not matter where I am. What matters is where I shall be."

"And where is that?" Abby placed the call on speakerphone so Aaron could hear.

"I am working on transportation to a *genizah* site known well to Sergeant Keller. Have a nice life." Carlson disconnected.

Abby and Aaron looked at each other, shook their heads, and said in unison: "He's going to Fallujah."

Author's Note

The Ezra Scroll is a work of fiction. The discovery, in Iraq, of an ancient text older than the Dead Sea Scrolls never happened. But the scholarly consensus that the original text of the Torah, the first five books of the Hebrew Scriptures, is a human invention, is very real. Over the last four hundred years, prominent Bible scholars and religious skeptics alike have been convinced that the Hebrew Scriptures, including the Torah, represent a very human library of religious history and theology. The library contains the literary traditions of ordinary people from a particular place and a particular time. *The Ezra Scroll* seeks to provide answers to two questions raised by the existence of the Hebrew Scriptures. How did that unique library actually come to be? Why?

As might be expected, scholarly arguments and well-meaning efforts to precisely date the events leading to the invention of the Torah would not make for exciting reading. Nevertheless, there are times when the story needs grounding in facts. It is for this reason that I have created the classroom chapters. The discussion among the grad students at Tel Aviv University reflects the main lines of current scholarly thought on the subject.

Eliezer and Zadok are fictional characters. But they, like many others in the ancient parts of the story, are derived from persons who do appear in the text of the Hebrew Scriptures. Anything which does not comport with the characterizations in those scriptures are creations of the author's imagination.

Motivations, thoughts, and emotions are rare in Biblical narratives. The exegetical process known as *midrash*, "...the eliciting from biblical verses of meanings beyond the literal" (Robert M. Seltzer, *Jewish People, Jewish Thought* p.267) is the inspiration for the story of Eliezer and Zadok and their descendants.

There is no Biblical evidence that the prophet Ezekiel murdered anyone. That is total invention. There is evidence that he was indeed the leader of the Judeans in Babylonian exile. At least one scholar has suggested that Ezekiel was very much concerned with the impurity of the Judeans who remained behind at the time of the exile.

The documentary hypothesis of Biblical authorship proposed by Julius Graf-Welhausen transformed our understanding of the Biblical text and the societies that produced it. The *Mishkan* Scroll is fiction. It was intended to answer a number of challenging questions. The prophet Jeremiah, speaking the words God implanted within him, denounces the sins of the Judeans. He asks: "Did I ask for sacrifices in the wilderness?" Anyone who reads Exodus, Numbers and Deuteronomy is aware of the great attention given to sacrifices in the wilderness, symbolized by the construction and operation of the Tabernacle /*Mishkan*. How can a prophet claim that God never demanded sacrifices in the wilderness, if the Israelites had constructed a sanctuary, a *mishkan*, for just such a purpose? Since the days of Graf-Welhausen, biblical scholars have commented on the flow of the Exodus text that is apparently interrupted by the building of the Tabernacle. If the Tabernacle narrative is removed, the story of Israel in the wilderness still makes sense, albeit a very different sense than the editors of the Hebrew Scriptures intended.

The Mishkan scroll fiction in this story addresses another conundrum. How did the Judeans worship in exile? Conventional wisdom says they created the synagogue in their exile. Yet, even according to the Biblical text itself, when Ezra and his party return to Judah, among them are musicians, gatekeepers and other functionaries unique to a temple that had ceased to exist for ninety years at most, and fifty years at the very least. This story provides a possible answer.

The ancient Samaritans were indeed peoples from the east who were uprooted in 721 BCE from their native land by the Assyrians and settled in the hill country that previously was home to the Kingdom of Israel. These transplanted peoples adopted the worship of the local god, known to the Israelites as YHWH. Since everything we know about them in the Biblical period comes to us through the filter of the Judean returnees from Babylonia, caution is advised when relying on Biblical descriptions of their hostility toward Judeans. In some ways, the existence of an exiled Judean community in Samaria would provide answers to vexing historical problems.

The modern Samaritans are a very real community, but they are neither murderers nor terrorists. That is fiction. Today, they do live in both Israel and on the West Bank. Their status in Israel and in the Palestinian Territories is ambiguous. They are very much caught in the middle of a political conflict not of their making or choosing.

The storage of religious documents in a *genizah* is a real custom of some Jewish congregations. The *genizah* in the al Jolan district of Fallujah is fiction. The ancient name of Fallujah, Pumbedita, is fact, as well as Pumbedita being identified as a center of Jewish life and culture in ancient Mesopotamia.

The *Taggim*—decorative crowns on letters in Hebrew texts became customary by the ninth century CE. Little is known for sure about their origins.

Over the course of thirty-plus years of teaching the Hebrew Scriptures, my students persisted in asking tough questions over and over again. *The Ezra Scroll* began as an effort to answer some those questions. Thanks to them, it became a labor of love. The creation of the Torah did not have to take place as I have imagined, but it could have.

Mark Leslie Shook
St. Louis, Missouri

Acknowledgments

Mere words cannot express my gratitude to the Saturday Morning Bible Class of Congregation Temple Israel in St. Louis, Missouri. Each week, for twenty-five years, they have asked great questions. Their love for the Biblical text and its history has inspired and energized me. I list them all: **Evelyn Bernstein, Neil Bernstein, Marcia Bernstein, Gordon Bloomberg, Terry Bloomberg, Marchall Brockman, Burt Bromberg, Fred Cohen, Vera Cohen, Pamela Dern, Stephen Edison, Michael Freiman, Sarah Jane Frieman, Marshall Friedman, Mary Friedman, Barbra Horn, David Kreipke, Martha Kreipke, Jane Langsam, David Levine, Cheryl Perlstein, Laurence Perlstein, Robert Schnurman, Barbara Sandmel, Marcee Silverstein, Merle Silverstein, Ruth Steele, Marcia Thompson, Peter Weiss, Jeffery Wilson, Carol Winston, Peter Winston.**

For the past twenty years, the nearly 800 students who have endured my teaching of Philosophy 348/349 at Saint Louis University helped to broaden my perspective. I thank them for their patience and diligence. Their questions helped me to hone my answers.

Father Ted Vitali, chair of the Department of Philosophy at Saint Louis University has provided great support and encouragement. His sense of humor is his secret spiritual weapon. He is a healing metaphysician. He taught me that laughter is non-denominational.

When I began *The Ezra Scroll* project, I had the broad outlines of the story clear in my head. I did not have control over the little details that add realism to fiction. I engaged a smart and tech savvy student, **Jerry Thomeczek** and sent him forth to locate the enriching details. He did a marvelous job and made the single discovery that opened up all sorts of possibilities. He made the historical connection between ancient Pumbedita and modern Fallujah. The mistakes in the details are all on me. Thank you, Jerry.

Everyone needs someone who looks beyond. This is the person who sees the finished diamond beyond the rough uncut stone. On an impulse, I sent **Rabbi Donald Gerber** some early versions of *The Ezra Scroll*. His unbridled enthusiasm, his conviction that this was a book with great potential, kept me going forward. Our editorial conferences on the deck of a swimming pool in Palm Desert, California, gave me the sounding board I needed when plot dilemmas emerged. That made all the difference. Thank you, Don.

My colleague and friend, **Rabbi Jeffrey Stiffman** actually has distant family members in the Samaritan community. He was kind enough to assist me in gathering materials on the Samaritans now living in Israel. Their part of the story is totally fiction. I thank him for his insights and stories.

Imagination is one thing, reality is another. I may have had a clear image of the Ezra Scroll in my mind, but it still had to be given reality by a talented scribe. **Tsila Schwartz** is that talented scribe. She listened to my vision and brought it to life. Thank you, Tsila for your artistry, enthusiasm, and patience.

There is a select group of people who read early versions of *The Ezra Scroll* and provided valuable feedback. I deeply appreciate their comments and advice. **Lynn DeTurk, Rabbi Amy Feder, Rabbi Michael Alper, Gary Follman, Joyce Follman, Gale Hilberg, Ralph Kalish, Jr., Sydney Masin, Deborah Morosohk, Burton Newman, Carol Shook, Tom Shook, Merle Silverstein, Marcee Silverstein, David Weinstein, Liz Weinstein.**

Karen Venable is my editor. She is also my teacher. She helped me to discover the power of compelling dialogue and to avoid the most obvious errors. There may have been times when I chose not to listen to her advice, but that is all on me.

Barbara Sandmel was kind and courageous enough to undertake the proof-reading of the final version of the story. Her attention to the details of grammatical usage was invaluable. If mistakes in grammar and punctuation remain, they are all mine.

And last but certainly not least, I thank **Mark Biernacki** who was always enthusiastic about the project and put the idea of self publishing into my head.

MLS

Sources

My teacher, **Rabbi Chanan Brichto** (may his memory be for a blessing), taught me to see the text of the Torah as a masterpiece of editing and story telling. I hear his voice while I am teaching, asking profound questions about the authors of Torah. There are other sources that provided inspiration and material for The Ezra Scroll as well. I list them here:

Akenson, Donald Harmon, *Surpassing Wonder: The Invention of the Bible and the Talmuds*, Harcourt Brace and Co. 1998.

Anderson, Robert T and Giles, *The Keepers: An Introduction to the History and Culture of the Samaritans*, Hendrickson Publishers Inc., Massachusetts, 2002.

Demsky, Aaron, "Who Came First, Ezra or Nehemiah? The Synchronistic Approach," Hebrew Union College Annual, Vol. XLV 1994.

Mantel, Hugo, "The Dichotomy of Judaism During the Second Temple," HUC Annual, Vol. XLIV 1973.

Morgenstern, Julian, "Jerusalem 485 BCE," HUC Annual, Vol. XXVII, 1956.

Rom-Shiloni, Dalit, "Ezekiel and the Voice of the Exiles and Constructor of Exilic Ideology, HUC Annual Vol.

Rom-Shiloni, Dalit, *Exclusive Inclusivity: Identity Conflicts Between The Exiles and the Ones Who Remained*, Continuum 2012.